IN AT THE KILL

About the Author

Gerald Seymour spent fifteen years as an international television news reporter with ITN, covering Vietnam and the Middle East, and specialising in the subject of terrorism across the world. Seymour was on the streets of Londonderry on the afternoon of Bloody Sunday, and was a witness to the massacre of Israeli athletes at the Munich Olympics. Gerald Seymour exploded onto the literary scene with the massive bestseller *Harry's Game*, that has since been picked by the *Sunday Times* as one of the 100 best thrillers written since 1945. He has been a full-time writer since 1978, and six of his novels have been filmed for television in the UK and US. *In At The Kill* is his thirty-ninth novel.

Also by Gerald Seymour

Harry's Game
The Glory Boys
Kingfisher
Red Fox
The Contract
Archangel
In Honour Bound
Field of Blood
A Song in the Morning
At Close Quarters
Home Run
Condition Black
The Journeyman Tailor
The Fighting Man
The Heart of Danger
Killing Ground
The Waiting Time
A Line in the Sand
Holding the Zero

The Untouchable
Traitor's Kiss
The Unknown Soldier
Rat Run
The Walking Dead
Timebomb
The Collaborator
The Dealer and the Dead
A Deniable Death
The Outsiders
The Corporal's Wife
Vagabond
No Mortal Thing
Jericho's War
A Damned Serious Business
Battle Sight Zero
Beyond Recall
The Crocodile Hunter
The Foot Soldiers

IN
AT
THE
KILL

Gerald Seymour

HODDER &
STOUGHTON

First published in Great Britain in 2023 by Hodder & Stoughton
An Hachette UK company

1

Copyright © Gerald Seymour 2023

A CIP catalogue record for this title is available from the British Library

Hardback ISBN 978 1 529 34045 7
Trade Paperback ISBN 978 1 529 34046 4
eBook ISBN 978 1 529 34047 1

Typeset in Plantin Light by Hewer Text UK Ltd, Edinburgh
Printed and bound in Great Britain by Clays Ltd, Elcograf S.p.A.

Hodder & Stoughton policy is to use papers that are natural, renewable
and recyclable products and made from wood grown in sustainable forests.
The logging and manufacturing processes are expected to conform
to the environmental regulations of the country of origin.

Hodder & Stoughton Ltd
Carmelite House
50 Victoria Embankment
London EC4Y 0DZ

www.hodder.co.uk

For Gillian

PROLOGUE

He edged forward and with each step his breath came faster.

Every time Pablo moved closer he increased the risk that their dogs would see him, hear him, smell him.

But he had to go closer because Nikko had demanded detail. The questions he must answer were specific. He could not even see the building yet but was aware of the drone of machinery and of the arrival of more vehicles.

He was there because of his kid brother. Pablo was middle-aged, near to his 45th birthday. He was married – happily, he thought – and was the father of three children, two boys and a girl. Neither his wife nor children knew where he was at that moment in the dwindling afternoon light, nor would they benefit in any way from what he was doing. This was all about his kid brother who would be locked in the crowded cages of the prisoners awaiting trial or investigation in the La Modelo gaol in Bogotá. Each time Pablo thought of his kid brother, 22 years old, an afterthought or accident by his parents, and the reputation of violence and bestiality in the prison of 11,000 inmates, his resolve was strengthened. He edged forward, pushing away undergrowth. Thorns cut his face and hands, and sometimes he scuffed dead leaves and foliage. He was careful to avoid fallen branches where the sap had long gone – they would be brittle, would crack easily, noisily.

His home was four rooms, a bath behind a curtain off the kitchen, and a living area where the TV was. He and his wife shared one bedroom and his children slept in the other, which was an increasing area of difficulty as they grew older and more sensitive about their own sex. At the back was a brick shed for the toilet with a drop under the seat, and beside the shed was a lock-up garage. Pablo parked his vehicle at the front of his one-storey home, built of concrete blocks with a roof of corrugated iron. In the garage, protected by a padlock, he stored the tins of paint that he tried to sell six days a week at his stall in the town's market. The ability to feed and clothe his family depended on the amount of paint that he sold. He could have made a better living if it had not been necessary to pay a sum each month to the enforcers of a "prominent person" in the town, and also to contribute to the wages of the local municipal office, and sometimes to the police.

Now, his pick-up – 16 years old and with 110,000 klicks on the clock after at least two modifications of the gauge – was parked on the verge of a main road, four kilometres out of the town of Leticia. Pablo had walked, and then crawled, and his trousers were filthy from the mud and his fingers bled, and insects swarmed around him, searching for the softness of his ears and his eyelids and his nose, but he did not swat them away or clap them between the palms of his hands.

The river was a meld of reds and browns, and was constantly changing in texture. It was raining. When the rain came down from low leaden clouds, the river rose quickly, and the mosquitoes multiplied: he had been brought up to exercise self-control and had been lectured at home, in school, in church, that it was wrong to blaspheme. The mosquitoes were feeding off him now, and when he hissed at them some took advantage and flew into his mouth and found his tonsils and went behind his yellowed teeth and he had to stop himself spluttering.

It was the dogs he feared most. The engineers had brought them and the older, fiercer ones were kept hungry and were tied to running wires, but there were also the family dogs and puppies that some of the men were fond of. Pablo knew about the dogs from the many times he had edged close to where the work was taking place on this bank of the upper reaches of the Amazon river. The only times in his life that he had been close to messing his trousers had been when he was close to the big shelter that had been built and where a generator throbbed and where the dogs barked, sometimes in a frenzy and sometimes out of boredom. Men patrolled the perimeter of the site, where the cleared ground met the wall of the jungle. They carried automatic weapons and he presumed them to be veterans from the war with the guerrillas: they had faces as hard as those of their guard dogs. Pablo had not been in the military, had never owned a firearm. Here, away from the town, a shot would not be heard, and a body could be quickly lost: a shallow pit would suffice or a splash in the river and a brief feeding opportunity for catfish and piranha.

He had seen the strange craft grow over the period of seven weeks that he had been coming to this place and each time he came he was more terrified. After pillars had been sunk and the steel frame erected, a roof had been built to cover the first stages of the craft's construction. Day after day, and usually long into the night, the generator moaned and cried, and the welders had fastened the fierce lights, and hammers had belted at the joints, and twice a week Pablo had taken up his position and had observed.

It was a huge project, building the craft – would have cost more money than he could imagine – here in the dense jungle beside the river, and with skills that he could barely comprehend. He did not know where it would sail to, how far, and through what dangers if it were not assembled with every rivet, nut, bolt and sealant secured, and an engine inside that must not fail, and the risk – so great – of the men in it drowning . . . But he did know what its cargo would be, the white powder that ruled with such violence, and brought such rewards. Pablo had felt quite safe at the start but it was different now as the long length of the hull had become recognisable and more men had come to the site by the slipway that a bulldozer had fashioned. More armed men and more dogs and all of them hungrier. Last week a portable crane had lifted the diesel engine into place. The fuel tanks were already there and the previous evening they had been filled and Pablo had estimated that the tanks had each been capable of carrying 20,000 litres. A small, squat tower sat on top of the craft and he had seen two men who disappeared into the hatch more often than the others – and he assumed they would sail with it when it was launched and went down the river towards the open ocean. It frightened Pablo, now that it had taken the shape of a boat that could travel underwater, just to look at it, and he tried to imagine how far away was its destination. When they had tested the engine at the back it had raced, chucking out fumes, acrid and black.

Pick-ups arrived in convoy, came along the track to the building inside which the craft had been built. Pablo thought the cargo was stored here because those who held the guns had become more menacing and the dogs took a cue from them. There was a bedlam of noise. Pablo needed to be closer, needed to see better. And fear became almost terror. He knew, as would anyone who lived in that town on the Colombian frontier where the state's boundary was marked by the winding path of the Amazon river, what fate would be handed out to him if he went too close. But he moved forward, . . . and the mosquitoes attacked his face in waves, and the thorn bushes were dense and caught at his clothing and he had to unpick himself each time and not let the material rip. He had to get closer if he were to assess the quantity of the cargo, its weight and its packaging. And he was there because of his kid brother.

The boy was an idiot. He had none of the disciplines taught to Pablo by his parents. He had been spoiled, protected from the reality of humble life, and had repaid his parents with shame and anguish. The last few years of the family's life had been made a misery by the choices of the little bastard. It was not good enough for him to make a living through hard graft. He wanted affluence, and fast. He started work as a junior in the lower ranks of a cartel that functioned in the capital. The kid had been a courier and had ridden his scooter into a chicane set up by the paramilitary police. Had been arrested, and been relieved of ten kilos of pure uncut cocaine powder. Had gone into the communal cell at La Modelo, and Pablo winced at the thought of what might happen there to his kid brother. He had been spotted by an agent of what they called the Administration who would have been trawling through new prisoners to identify some who might be useful. He had gabbled out to the agent where his parents eked out their last years: irrelevant . . . Had spoken of an elder brother who lived in that useless backwater of a town, Leticia: a chord struck, interest piqued. A military helicopter had flown the agent from Bogotá and had landed him in the compound of the community hospital. He had sat astride the pillion of a Honda bike and been driven away into the night to a lock-up garage at the back of Pablo's bungalow. Not a negotiation, not a matter of haggling as it would have been over the price of paint.

"Quite simple, my friend. Easy for you to understand what I have to offer," Pablo had been told. A cigarette had hung from the side of the man's mouth. He spoke with a calm American drawl and seemed unconcerned at the matters he spoke of. "Your little brother is in a bad place, my friend, and I would not like to contemplate his future until he has aged, lost his looks, and the passage between his cheeks is no longer tight. Luckily, for him and for you, I happened across him. It is possible that – for very specific information – I might find the time to intervene on his behalf and see to it that he gets a gentle ride, and is soon at liberty. That's one side of the coin. The reverse of the coin is that I do not have the information that is important to me and I do not have the time to get the kid a better outcome. You are with me? Not too difficult to understand?"

"What do I have to do? What information?"

The smoke from Nikko's cigarette kept the insects at bay. Pablo had had to strain to hear him, he spoke so quietly. "The information I need is exact and particular. I don't want shit. Fuck with me, Pablo, and the kid has a hard time of it. Cooperate with me, it is possible that he might one day see the light of day. I don't do charity, Pablo. I do deals, and I rely on honesty in return. Your kid brother would wish you to comprehend the terms of what I offer. You are following me?"

"What must I bring you?"

He had been told. He had been given contact codes. He had been handed a mobile phone that was programmed to transmit only text messages and with only one number loaded. A last drag on his cigarette. He had been shown a photograph of what he was told was a similar craft to the one about to be built on the river bank downstream from the town. The cigarette was thrown away, then stamped on. "You do not deliver, I do not deliver. Understand, I could intervene in mid-build, any day I want, and could catch a crowd of little guys, but I'm hankering after bigger cats. They're not here, they're way down river, far from here. So . . . This is good, my friend, because I want to know when the big splash happens in the river and you want your kid brother to get clear of that gaol. My word is my bond . . . Keep thinking of the boy and where he is. Been a pleasure to meet you."

A quarter of an hour later Pablo had heard a helicopter go low over the town, almost above his home, and veer away into the night. He had been told the next morning that a woman in the San Rafael hospital was enduring a difficult birth and had been airlifted to a larger medical unit, and people seemed satisfied with that reason for an army Huey flight coming in during darkness. He had looked outside his garage before setting up his stall in the market and had found the crushed cigarette, half smoked, a Marlboro Light. A week later he had started his regular vigils on the river bank and reported on the phone given him . . . and each time he was there, and the fear began to merge with terror, he would try to imagine what his kid brother, the idiot, might be going through.

The rain was torrential and the cloud ceiling seemed barely above the caps of the trees. In front of him, mostly masked, the work had intensified. More noise, more clamour, more shouting. He thought it must have been a tractor that had dragged the shape out from under the protection of the roof. Next came a torrent of men carrying packages the size of the sacks used for cement, but he could not see clearly, not enough to satisfy him that he had fulfilled his obligation to the American who called himself Nikko. Had to perform the duty or the kid would remain in the cage at La Modelo, where old men would want to penetrate him. He went even closer. It was about family blood and family responsibility, and he moved closer still. He crawled on his stomach, prising creepers and low branches aside, and tried not to curse the insects hovering around his face, or the thorns snatching at his clothes.

He saw the tankers' pipes had been detached, the fuelling finished, and the trucks reversing away. All done as a military operation. Ladders against the hull and men on different rungs, taking the packages and dropping them down through the hatch: he saw the way that the men buckled under their weight and realised that several tonnes of cargo were being loaded. He recognised faces. One from the bank where he lodged money every week, precious little of it. One from the police, traffic section – a joke in Leticia because there were so few vehicles – who had gained a good discount from him for paint, avocado colour, to decorate his home. And another stallholder who had ordered three tins of magnolia for freshening the interior of a parochial hall. He needed to go closer because the mosquitoes had bitten around his eyes and they were swollen and his vision was poorer. It had rained each day of the last nine, and each night, and was worse than he could remember.

A small branch snapped under the weight of his right hand as he pressed down to lever himself closer. He had almost reached the line where the foliage finished and the cleared space started.

He had not noticed the branch until his weight rested on it. It made a sharp crack. Would have been a half-centimetre in diameter ... he might have eased from his path, just that evening, a hundred branches of that size. This one had broken. He froze, and thought he was rewarded with luck. The knots in his shoulders loosened. The loading continued, the armed men strutted in front of him, laughing and smoking, and the tractor had been driven off to the far side and he saw two men in dark boilersuits being hugged and kissed: he assumed them to be the crew and knew it was very near the time that the beast, all gleaming metal, went down into the water. He would see it engulfed by a wave of mud-brown water, would watch it go out into the river, would send his message to the man, from the Administration, would turn around and head back the way he had come.

He heard a little high-pitched squeal and a snort of breath. He decided he would say that he had drunk too much beer – the Costeña label – and had fallen asleep on his porch and the

mosquitoes had found him. That's what he would say to the other
stallholders in the morning to explain the state of his face. The
squealing was in his ears, and warm breath was panting on his
face. He thought it was a rat. Only the black caimans of the crocodile family could keep the number of rats along the river bank
under some sort of control. He lashed out at the creature. It
screamed, and he felt teeth fasten on his hand, needle sharp, and
he could not free them. A moment of agony coursed through him,
and the craft was moving down towards the waterline and torches
were following its progress . . . He had struck a puppy. Its mother
came fast. The bitch was snarling, and heading for Pablo, and the
dogs on the wires took up the frenzy, and the men with guns
turned away from watching the hull, moving on tree trunk rollers,
towards the dark expanse of the water.

The bitch found him and only then did the puppy loosen its
teeth from his hand, and more dogs came, and torches. The craft
went into the water and a rippling wave surged across the width of
the river. He had the phone out, and tried to read the screen and
to hit the right keys. Just needed the one word. *Launched.* Should
try to add something about his brother, and the validity of the deal
struck, but the bitch had a hold of his shoulder and was dragging
him towards the cleared ground. He thought he had pressed Send,
did not know if he had, and lost his grip on the phone. A torch
shone in his face and alongside the beam he would see the short
barrel of a rifle, and more men came running. The bitch was
pulled off him and kicks began to land on his head and
shoulders.

A voice called out, "That you, Pablo? What the fuck are you
here for?"

Another voice. "A spy. What else? A fucking spy."

He was lifted, sagged, then stood. He was punched and then
clubbed across his head with a rifle. More men came. Perhaps
they were distracted, perhaps the major moment was behind
them, the launch into the river; perhaps it was surprise at finding
him there – Pablo, the poor cretin who sold cheap paint off a stall
in the market each day. Perhaps it was confusion based on his

sodden appearance and his puffed and damaged face. Perhaps . . . There would not be another moment, that he knew. He turned in a quick swivel movement, stamped his feet and lifted his knees, and tried to charge away back into the undergrowth. The dogs came with him. He thought they did not shoot because of the dogs. He was stumbling, slipping; they were jumping clear of the branches and the vines, and birds scattered above them. The torches from behind showed him the way towards the river and the ground dropped. It was a game for the dogs. The shouting of the men dinned in his ears. If they had hold of him they would interrogate him, torture him. After they had tortured him, and gained the name of Nikko from the Administration, they would kill him. After they had killed him they would go to his home, the bungalow where his wife and children were, and they would burn it and then set light to the garage where he stored his paint. He heard a blundering pursuit, had only a few more metres to fight through before he came to the sodden bank and could slither into the water.

There was much that Pablo did not know.

That a minimum sum of one million American dollars had been budgeted for the building of the craft.

That the total weight of the cargo was four tonnes.

That the street value of the cargo, pure cocaine powder, would be in excess of 300 million euros, a currency he had never seen nor heard of.

That the craft was starting its journey to the mouth of the Amazon river that was 2980 kilometres away, and then would attempt to cross an ocean and sail another 6000 kilometres.

Knew only of the deal done with Nikko and the presence of a stamped-out cigarette to prove they had met. He loathed the drugs, detested the agony they made in his life, hated them for where they had put his kid brother.

He slid into the water. The dogs gathered on the bank and their barking was raucous behind him. Away to his right he could see the outline of the craft, a shadow on the deep brown murkiness of the water, and could hear the engine engage and smell the foul belch of the diesel fumes. And he went under. He kicked and struggled and panicked and floundered, and imagined the circling piranha and catfish, and thought a black caiman would soon find him and they could grow to five metres in length and had wicked jaws. The rain spattered on the water around him. He could barely see, and for the last time – and with a prayer in his mind – he went under.

The craft passed, and the river swirled hard against him and he saw the name of Maria Bernarda painted on the hull. Then Pablo's consciousness failed and the last sensation he was aware of was the churn of a propeller driven by a modern 350 horsepower diesel engine. He sank, gulping river water into his lungs, and no longer had the prayer in his mind or the image of his brother.

I

The wind was in his face. There were not many mornings, as Jonas Merrick maintained his schedule and crossed the bridge over the Thames, that the damn wind was not blowing. One more morning when his raincoat was plastered against his back and he needed to have a firm hold on his trilby.

He was shovelled along by the gusts and felt uncertain on his feet. Out on the mid-way spans of Lambeth Bridge the memories came hard and bad. Truth to tell, an expression that his wife, Vera, liked to use, his recall of the matter of the bridge and his fall into the water, his near-death experience and his ultimate rescue, was never to be erased from his consciousness. Jonas had been "loaned" by his employer, the Security Service, to its rival and senior organisation, the Secret Intelligence Service – as welcome as a cuckoo in a songbird's nest – to root out a traitor in their building, a leaker to the hostile Russian agencies. He had succeeded, had identified the miscreant, and in a foolish moment of vanity had dispelled his image of boring naivety, and had handcuffed the guilty party to his own wrist as they approached a discreet welcoming party of detectives from the Branch. Totally unexpectedly, she had seemed to face a death wish who had plunged over the bridge balustrade, and taken him too, throwing him down into the cold, dark, strong and hideous current. All more than a year ago and still as fresh as the previous hour.

It was his habit to walk from Waterloo station along the embankment beside the wall of the Archbishop's Palace and then turn sharp right and, using the bridge pavement, face his destination. The bleak, grey stonework of Thames House was where he would end up each weekday morning, and in the late afternoon, punctually enough to set a wristwatch by, he would reverse the trek and stride out for the station and the crowded commuter link to his home. He did not have to walk. He could have taken a bus over Westminster Bridge and walked past the House of Commons, or he could have taken a taxi each way. He walked because he always had done and prayed God that he always would. Protection was now offered only on random days. If that Friday had been chosen, by now the first part of his escort would have peeled off. Sometimes they were in uniform, sometimes obviously armed, sometimes drifting along behind him in "civvie" dress. He approached the high point of the bridge, and always quickened his stride to reach it. Could not really help himself, same every morning and afternoon, every crossing. He would look away from the pavement, from the traffic lanes and from the safety of the parapet and balustrade, and would peer down at the water. Often he would lose sight of oncoming pedestrians and bump into them or get in their way. Sometimes he was cursed, sometimes snarled at: he never apologised. Jonas Merrick never apologised for anything or to anyone.

He gazed down at the water. The wind buffeted him. He held tight to the handle of his faded and water-damaged briefcase that was linked by a fine chain to a handcuff bracelet on his right wrist. He wore the same coat that he had worn that weekend morning and the same brogues, and the lifeboat team had fished out the same hat which had lost a little of its shape, and he had on the same jacket and the same trousers. Vera would turn up her nose at them, complain they still stank, but had not binned them. On his right wrist, close to the bracelet, was the white scar where the police-issue handcuff fastening him to that woman – called herself Frank, had a lowly rank, but total access – had dragged away a ring of skin when they had gone down together into the river. Then must have had a second thought about dying in the cause of a faraway motherland. Might have reckoned, with icy water swamping her, that Czar Vladdy's regime was only worth living for, not dying for. Had changed her mind, and had heaved him up, fastened him to a rope dangling from a moored barge, and had made her farewells. Always saw her face, quite calm, and to hear her voice – "I had a good run, enjoyed it, walked all over them. Goodbye, Mr Merrick." Had rather liked her, had rather admired her, and all his own fault anyway for wanting the vanity bit of planting cuffs on her wrists and leading her towards the cage.

It never seemed good, the water flowing beneath the arches of the bridge. Cruel, mysterious. That morning a little tug boat was pulling a line of barges weighed down low by a load of gravel. He shivered, had cause to, and kept going.

He saw Kev and Leroy coming towards him. Nobody barged into them. Nobody swore at them, was sarcastic, complained if they got in the way. Both had H&Ks in their hands and Glocks in holsters bouncing on their thighs, and gas and flash-bang grenades hooked to their belts, and both were huge in vests that were supposed to be proof against low-velocity bullets. Always, if they were on shift, they came a little across the bridge to meet him and then walk behind him as he completed his journey. There would be light conversation: the weather usually did the business. Some 2000 men and women, from a kaleidoscope of races and ethnic origins, worked in Thames House, and none was brought by escort to the bridge's median point and then handed over to the care of other guns . . . only Jonas Merrick.

He had been parked in a backwater. Little was expected from him, and he would be out of harm's way.

Her body had never been found upriver or down towards the estuary. Not all bodies were recovered but the Thames gave up, in time, most of those who had gone in and drowned in the foul water. It was possible that she, "Frank something", had survived. Possible, but not probable. But a difficulty *if* she had made it out of the river. Quite a big difficulty. A difficulty that would have put Jonas Merrick's life in the cross hairs. Two men from Czar Vladdy's "elite" GRU assassination team, on a mission into Denmark to take down a defector had, with Jonas the puppetmaster pulling the strings, been killed by British "irregulars". He always let a sneer play at the sides of his mouth when the word "elite" was used, thought it exaggerated and seldom an adequate description of incompetence . . . but dead, they were. That pretty young woman with the gold hair and the starched blouses would have known that he, old Jonas and past his retirement age, had done the necessary, been the facilitator.

Pack the job in? A flat refusal.

Move house, go into hiding? Not considered.

Close protection? For a few days, then withdrawn. But he was seen off the train some mornings and into work, and back again in time for the 17.39. That, with a poor grace, he accepted.

Kev and Leroy watched him carefully. Both had seen him go into the water, both had thought him lost. Both would have blamed themselves without having cause to.

"Morning, Mr Merrick."

No familiarity. A curt response. Jonas seldom showed warmth. "Morning."

Kev suggested there could be a shower before midday, and Leroy believed it would get brighter in the west, and the wind was expected to drop.

"Have a good day, Mr Merrick."

"Will try . . ."

Actually, he rather enjoyed the backwater into which he had been dunked. He went for his coffee and pastry in the café by the side door of Thames House. The backwater into which he had been put was crime. Jonas was off counter-terror, withdrawn from counter-espionage, and concerned himself now with OCGs. The *Organised Crime Groups* had swallowed his interest. That morning he wolfed down his Danish, gulped his coffee, and hurried to his desk because a tasty little business was coming to a completion. Enjoyable, most certainly.

Jonas took a lift to the third floor, walked along the south-facing corridor, went into Room 12. The surveillance people had the room and he was left with a cubicle in a corner, a locked door and frosted glass to screen him. Facing him were a rogues' gallery and a large-scale map that showed land masses at the extreme west and extreme east and otherwise was ocean, but he ignored those. On the wall in front of his work surface, above his computer screens, was a soft-focus blow-up that showed a youngish man – slept-in jeans with worn knees, a crumpled T-shirt, a light-weight windcheater, a gaunt and pale face with a week's growth of beard and tousled hair – who leaned against the door jamb of a corner shop. Seemed to be a busted wreck of a young man, all ambition gone, and maybe waiting for his next dose of brown, or some smack. Jonas took off his raincoat and hung it on the hook below the one holding his trilby, detached his briefcase from his wrist, and took out his lunch box and a Thermos for later. He switched on his computer and sat while it ground through its wake-up.

Jonas looked up, smiled as if to a friend, said softly, "Morning, Kenny, hope you slept well, had a good night."

Low sunshine blistered on to his face.

He blinked to clear his eyes and coughed to free up his throat, then sharply shook his head as if to rid himself of his mind's confusion.

Where was he? Why was he there? Most important, who was he?

It was a ritual that needed doing every morning, and was better performed alone. He could hear her in the kitchen, bare feet slithering, and a kettle starting to scream. Started to find answers – and who was she? More blinking and more coughing and more shaking his head and the answers came and the boxes were ticked. He arched his back, yawned. He heard cupboards opening and closing, then the clatter of mugs being set down. Did he want milk? She had a prim voice, tutored with the help of a language school but her idioms were flawless and she owned that confident – arrogant – gait of the Dutch, and he was long down the road from merely liking her. Yes, milk but no sugar.

Where? Easy. In a renovated cottage, once part of a cattle barn, on the outskirts of a village on the Atlantic shore. Rented it – one bedroom, a good living space with a kitchen at the back, a bathroom, and a patio with views across the harbour and then the expanse of the sea. The place was Camariñas and the outlook was over the *Costa da Morte*, and he hoped that the cottage brought him only to within touching distance of death, but no closer.

She carried two mugs from the kitchen.

Why? Always important in his circumstances to wake and get those damned questions answered, not to slip head over heels before he was alert. He was there because of his work. The work was in the main city of the region, Corunna ... Never did count the tourist trap of Santiago as the principal place with its hotels that fleeced visitors who had come on pilgrimage or to gawp at old churches. Corunna was almost 50 miles away and he did the round trip three or four times a week. He was an investment advisor. A grand title. Here, he was called an *asesor de inversiones registrado* – important to be "registered" which gave a ring of honesty to what he did. In uncertain times, where pitfalls were littered to trip up the ignorant, he took savings and placed them where they were safe and could be relied upon. Had been there just over three years and had put together a respectable portfolio of clients, mostly with small sums, some who had believed in him sufficiently to place larger amounts that they needed to safeguard from the scandalous greed of the tax authorities, and a very few who needed the full washing machine treatment.

He pushed himself up and his shoulders were high against the bedhead. She wore nothing. None of her own clothing, nor any of his, not even a towel. She walked towards him and held the mugs firmly and did not slop any of the coffee, and did not have to step over or around any discarded underwear thrown off in a hurry. Not that sort of an occasion. All rather orderly. Everything folded neatly. His were in a stack on a hardback chair by the window, his shoes placed together on the floor. Hers were on the lower chair and lying on the cushions. Done slowly. She had started to strip off in that way, carefully, no shyness, and he had followed her example. There would have been in Corunna or Santiago plenty of celibate monks who knew what it was to have purposefully tied a knot in it: this was the first time since he had come to live in the Galicia region that he had shared the bed, old and with ferociously noisy springs, with a girl, with a woman, with a friend or with a lover, and both of them stone sober. "They", his crowd, were advised against "relationships". They were warned of complications. Top of that list would be speaking, half awake, of a dream or a nightmare and then having to offer an explanation, or of the pillow talk when queries were dripped in an ear while fingers played on the lower stomach. "Better not to," the psychologists urged, "better to just go and take a cold shower, alone." No regrets and he thought her brilliant. Brilliant and important. He took the coffee mug. She sat beside him, made no effort to cover herself with the rumpled sheet.

Who? The time of maximum danger was on waking. The "where" and the "why" could be fudged, not the "who". Had to have in place who he was that day . . . bad times ahead if the legends became knotted, twisted. Seriously bad times if he were living the identity that he had cast off before travelling on the slow ferry across the Biscay and docking at Santander, or the one he had perfected before that, and worse than bad times if he slipped back into the times when he knew his own name and so did everyone else who knew him, at school and at work, and his parents – and his wife, and his son and daughter. Had to scrub them out. She was looking hard at him. He felt the coffee slurping over the mug's rim and was sprinkling across his stomach, and more of it glistening on the pendant that hung on a chain around his neck. He was 29 – which was a constant in all of the legends – and was unmarried and not tied down, and she'd said that she was two years older and had no ties, no complications . . . Not a one-night stand, not an occasion on which lifestyle journalists laid down behavioural rules. He thought there was a possibility that it was a relationship with legs – needed one, and thought he deserved one – and that it could go places when the matter was closed down, curtained off, and he had moved on. When he had ditched the legends and the deceits, had handed in his card, had cut the links. Big stuff for him to think of and the coffee had scalded his stomach. His work would likely be done by the end of the coming week, and then it would be time for a fast exit. He pulled a face, grimaced.

"You all right? I have that effect on you, that you tremble?"

A limp smile. "I'm good. Fine. You know, waking, getting bearings. And another dull day lining itself up . . . The coffee, thanks."

He was beyond allotted time anyway, and should have been withdrawn months earlier, had been almost ready to leave with all the attendant complications left hanging. A quiet voice had come through on his phone, with a tinniness that meant it played through the scrambler connection, so quiet that he had to strain to listen with the mobile clamped to his ear. He thought it an old man's voice, and he had been told that he was staying in place, not a request – just told. And work had started to fidget for his attention and only for a few more minutes could its demands be delayed, which was a bastard. Reasonable to assume his long-time control officer had been bypassed and was now outside the inner loop of the new regime handling him. He grimaced, like that was a nervous tick when he lied. And the week, he predicted, would come fast, always did at the end, would stampede, be hard to keep abreast of: with the lies came danger.

"Promise?"

"Very good – and thinking you very special."

She laughed, more of a chuckle, and used her hand to wipe the coffee off his stomach. Then kissed him lightly. "And I am happy that you said it, Kenny."

Like a well manufactured cobweb, fine lines stretched out across an ocean, across a continent and half the length of a country. At the heart of the web, in the cubicle inside a work area designated as 3/S/12, devouring information and coordinating action, an elderly man played the part of a spider.

"Right, Mrs Govier, I'll get that done."

That evening's reservations were to be cancelled. No explanation, nor one expected. New ones to be made, same destination but different routes. No apology, as most of her customers would have given. But this was a prized customer, the most important.

Whenever she took a booking from Doloures Govier, Nansie's

cheeks flushed and her voice took on a slight stutter. Her name was Nanette, but to "Jimbo" Rawe she was "Nansie". That morning, early and in a pleasant enough shopping arcade off a tree-lined avenue in one of Liverpool's more expensive housing areas, Nansie was – again – between the bloody rock and the bloody hard place. When Doloures Govier, or one of her family or associates, came to arrange a flight booking and accommodation, Nansie would see to their business inside her personal office at the back of the shop. She'd leave the door open, so she still had a view of the girls at their desks and their punters, and could see the posters of Mediterranean and Caribbean beach resorts displayed in the windows, and out into the street. It was a pretty ordinary vehicle for what she assumed the Govier clan was worth, a VW Passat, and her son was at the wheel and had a window open and dropped fag ends on the pavement. And wouldn't care, why would he?

The rock was the Govier family. The hard place was "Jimbo" Rawe.

The reservations were in the name of Smythe. The passports to be used matched that name. The travel agency's facilities were required so that neither a paper nor an electronic trail was left behind. Phones usually used would be left at home: those carried would be switched off before the journey to the airport, away across country in the north-east of Britain, and in the air, and during the transit in Prague, and another in Milan, and before the final onward leg. Cumbersome procedures but relatively foolproof . . . It was Friday, and Doloures Govier and her younger son, Patrick, would be flying out of the UK on the following Tuesday. The eyes of the woman across the desk from Nansie were hard and powerful, seemed to penetrate her inner thoughts – which were about fear – which was why her cheeks had coloured and her speech had become a stammer and she made several errors on the screen in front of her and needed to correct them. The Goviers had money invested in the little business that Nansie ran: it had seemed a good idea at the start-up when capital was required, now was a millstone. They were the rock. Their authority, Nansie was sure of it, survived on a diet of violence. Out on the street, visible between the posters and at the wheel of the VW Passat, with a fag always in his mouth, was Xavier – who was mental, who was violent, who would disfigure her, who would display not a pinch of mercy if she were thought to have betrayed them.

And the hard place was "Jimbo" Rawe. Two years, he had been on her back and leaching information from her. Would have had the tip-off from HMRC that she might be "useful", could be "helpful". No one in Nansie's family had ever had a business of their own, climbed up that ladder, and might even, one day, have enough to start a second branch of the agency. Had been free and easy and a bit casual with the Value Added Tax payments in the early days and that had become a habit and the records were covered up, and there were shortfalls on the National Insurance, and "Jimbo" Rawe had wandered in and the girls out front were leaving and he'd hung the CLOSED sign in the window and had smiled expansively, and had gone through to the back and sat himself down. He'd said, matter of fact and making out that it was not a "big deal", that the VAT business added up to fraud and that the National Insurance was a criminal discrepancy. The penalties for VAT fraud and NI abuse would certainly lead to a business closure with an insolvency order, or maybe a few months for meditation in HMP Styal; he sounded relaxed and fished in his pocket for his pipe. Had told her what he wanted of her. She'd blurted, "They'd fucking kill me." He'd grinned, but icy cold. "Try us, we might top that." He was a detective inspector, semi-retired but not quite, had been around since Noah beached the Ark. She'd had no doubt that he would have turned her over for a full Revenue investigation had she refused him. Harder at first than now, but she gave details to him of any business coming her way through the Govier clan.

She did the printout, handed the sheet to Doloures Govier.

The woman across the table felt in her handbag and a purse emerged, bulging with the load of cash, big bank notes, that it contained. The cost of the flights was checked and the necessary money counted out. It was always cash. Confirmed that the return was open and via Rome and Vienna. She did not get a handshake, nor thanks, knew the power of the customer. Had thought that if she, Nansie, had those assets then she would have dressed like it was party-time every morning and come to work in a sports car, open top, and flashing jewellery. Opposite her, the chair was scraped back and the Matriarch, what one of her girls had called her once and giggled and been rewarded with a kick on her ankle from Nansie, was on her way. A miserable cow of a woman, and the boy behind the wheel was pure evil and everybody said that, and . . . She'd have a coffee, a strong one, then find an excuse, make a call, and arrange a meeting. "Jimbo" Rawe liked to meet in an underpass where there was graffiti, and broken light fittings and a powerful smell of piss, and maybe a few needles on the ground.

A rock and a hard place and when they were smacked together, they caused proper pain. Nansie was trapped and had no idea how to shift herself clear, not an idea in hell. She made an excuse to the girls, and was gone. There had been more customers in the waiting area, leafing through brochures and expecting her to welcome them and have their business. But she was between that piece of granite and that heavy anvil and had bigger priorities – and might go to prison for fraud and might end up in A&E with her face sliced open.

The spider figure crouched in his chair in front of his desk. The strands of the cobweb all led to him and were kept as separate as he could manage. Some days there was pandemonium in the room beyond his door, when the surveillance crowd were rushing to an emergency stake-out, and sometimes they were raucous in their reaction to a "good" lift. Jonas Merrick ignored diversions. News came to him from many quarters and he stored and fed from it, and plotted its further use.

The cloud down low and the rain coming in at an acute angle.

No stability inside what they called the cockpit. And certain suicide, to be out of the safety the cockpit offered and trying to get forward on the narrow decking, more than 15 metres long, and to the hatch sealing off the cargo compartment and work it loose. Impossible. The vessel shook and rolled, cannoned into walls of wave. The stink inside was constant, the chance of sleep was small, and tempers were frayed. There had been a good mood and morale had been high at the start, and the weather had been kind at the extreme west of the Atlantic when they had left the Amazon delta. Not any longer. Now the craft was less responsive to the wheel adjustments and navigation was harder, and the food had become more repetitive and disgusting.

The captain, the man paid to make the decisions, was Diego. He did not wear a uniform and there were no bars of rank on his shoulders. His position of authority was marked instead by the reward he would be given for sailing the semi-submersible from the Amazon to a rendezvous on the eastern side of the Atlantic, close to the archipelago of the Azores. He had banked $75,000 already, had assumed command two days sailing downstream. His crew were Emiliano and Matias, and they had received only $25,000 each as their first payment. On completion, Diego would be paid an additional $175,000, Emiliano would receive a further $50,000 and Matias $100,000 because he was the engineer and *important*: without him four tonnes of pure cocaine was not going to cross the Atlantic. They thought it a fair deal. They were Colombian nationals and from a shit town higher up the Amazon basin, from Leticia where the beast had been built, but Diego was a European and from the town of Cambados on the Galician coast. None of them would have risked that eventual payday by emerging from the cockpit, which was a metre above the waterline when they rose and a metre below it when down in a trough. Communication was by shortwave radio, low power and low range, and unlikely to be monitored.

It was the second day that they had attempted to make a transfer, and the second day they had failed.

In the low light and with the spray rinsing the heavy-duty Perspex of the cockpit hatch, Diego could just see the final wave from the two pilots. He knew them both. Once, long ago, Diego had been a star speedboat driver.

The fast craft came out from the inlets on the Costa da Morte and powered far into the Atlantic and did a meeting off navigation co-ordinates, and took on board a cargo – worth tens of millions of American dollars when cut and beefed and wrapped and made ready for sale on a street corner anywhere in Spain or Germany or the Netherlands or France, and most especially on any street in the United Kingdom which was the milch-cow of the trade.

Except that he had once been an amateur boxer too, which was a good pedigree for pulling the girls but the wear and tear had done him down and his headaches had become more frequent and he had, in a state of almost blackout, written off a speedboat valued at 750,000 euros, Italian built and the best, on a reef off the coast from Pontevedra – it could do 60 knots before he'd wrecked it. His craft now, this monster, was capable, if the diesel engine prospered, of managing eight knots, nine maximum.

Diego had not been happy at the two speedboats circling him so close to his hull. He had shouted on the radio that they were too close and had sworn at them. Crazy bastards, like all speedboat pilots. The craziest, the lunatic and the best – Diego's accolade – was Laureano Munoz. Had seen him wave one last time, turn his craft, and gun it. It had seemed to rise up in the water, thrust by five outboards and generating close to 2000 horsepower. Laureano would be home for a late dinner with his family with time enough to report confirmation of the decision taken the previous evening to abort, but to make one last try in daylight.

The weather had not changed. The sea was whipped by a Force Nine. The weather, for those inside the semi-submersible, had been hideous, and they had rocked and swayed and been catapulted against the walls, been lifted and dropped. An awful experience, the worst he had known. For those in the speedboats, open to the weather and with waves breaking over them, it would have been worse than a watery hell, Diego was sure of it. Each time that he had seen Laureano's face as he circled, it had been wreathed in a smile that was manic . . .

There was a fallback plan. Natural, when the cargo weighed in at four tonnes, when the street value was in excess of $300 million.

They lost sight of the speedboats. Diego made the calculations, and checked his compass reckoning. They needed the money, Diego needed the money. They had chugged away from the sparse landmass of the Azores, and had now been crushed in the cockpit cabin with the rolling bunks and the microwave cooker and the hard porn movies and the crap bucket for three weeks. He expected, very soon, there would be an explosion of temper, was ready for it. He dreamed of the money, always the best sedative for stress. He was confident that their progress was not monitored, that they were too low in the water for satellite recognition. They were over and past the mid-Atlantic Ridge. Between the Vema Fracture Zone and the Kane Fracture Zone they had heard an aircraft but he did not believe it had altered course. The water beat incessantly at the cockpit window and the engine coughed rhythmically, and the fumes coated the insides of their throats . . . All of them needed the money. The engine was well maintained by Matias who was a motor mechanic in his home town. They went forward and the swell cut around them.

"We do another week. We have a landfall there in a week. That is Thursday evening. But I believe it travels with us, the fucking storm."

The information came up on his screen.

Jonas, ignorant of most areas of science, mathematics, and engineering, read and absorbed and finally made sense of the map and the jagged line marking a route taken and the line of numbers, longitude and latitude. He moved his mouse, clicked relevantly, was shown a digest of the weather to the east of the Azores archipelago, pulled a face, pushed out his lower lip and acknowledged that it would be "inclement" in the confines of the craft.

He acknowledged the signal. *Thank you, Nikko.*

You're a lucky sonofabitch, Jono, know that. All going to fall well for you if you don't fuck up. Will drop in your lap. In the meantime, won't exactly be a chauffeur ride for them. Have a nice day.

There was a routine in the recent days of Jonas's life in the backwater. Marginally, he thought himself blessed that his professional life no longer revolved around matters of espionage, and the business of terror and its consequences. The backwater, crime, had put a spring in his step when he came to work. He had developed almost a fondness for Nikko, welcomed the informa- tion fed to him on the progress of a semi-submersible that traversed the Atlantic, from west to east, and was now marooned in hideous weather. It would be tossed like a crisp packet dropped on a pavement on a gusty day, and would have abandoned hopes of a successful rendezvous off the Azores islands, and seemed to be headed now for a transfer of cargo off the shores of the European mainland.

Not that he had met Nikko, not that he had a photograph of the American, not that he had ever spoken with Nikko, not that Jonas had ever before worked hand in glove with an agent of the Drug Enforcement Administration. Their relationship had been based these last weeks on crisp exchanges of information via encrypted messaging on their computers.

Jonas typed. *All rather outside my experience. When might they be expected to land?*

A week, give or take a day. Weather dependent. Around a week.

He could wait a week. Had it all finished that evening or into that night, it would have been a rushed operation. Not all the bricks in place. He could use the week, do better coordination, tie tighter knots in the loose strings. There were big fish to be netted in the backwater – bigger and heavier and with sharper teeth than Winston Gunn, unwillingly wearing a primed suicide vest – or Cameron Jilkes, who had overdosed on pain and hatred – or Frank, or a colonel without a name who had run foot soldiers who killed in order to pay their meagre living expenses. The trouble, Jonas reflected, with the species of fish in the backwater, was that they tended to bite, had unpleasant rows of teeth in their mouths. The fish had names. Were a family. Had a mother, a father, two sons and a daughter. Jonas leaned back in his chair and it creaked under the strain, and the team in the work area outside his cubicle was gathering, laughing, dumping heavy gear, joshing, and ignored his shadow shape through the frosted glass of the cubicle.

The fish were a target. He could picture them, all of them, mostly in monochrome and from surveillance or police station photographs. All of the fish would add to a good catch but he thought the elder son would be the superior specimen to net. He had the most recent stolen surveillance shot of him in the file locked in his drawer: Bengal.

He dropped off his mother.

Watched her climb awkwardly out of the car. Would have been flashing her thighs, maybe even her knickers, as she made it on to the pavement. Bengal did not help her. He thought his mother cared too much about his brother Patrick, about his sister Theresa, not enough about him. His father was Mikey, Two Bellies, who had been away for nine years and would be gone for at least four more – so the sentencing judge had said . . . and in HMP Walton. Bengal reckoned he alone had saved the prestige of the family, had carried them.

He gunned the engine, had business on his mind.

Doloures stared down at him from the pavement. Smoothed her clothes, straightened her hair, clung to her bag. The look was sour . . . His mother had not needed to spend the journey from the travel agent to their home talking only about fucking Patrick and fucking Theresa, like he did not exist, like he needed to know how clever his young sister was and how essential to the family was the brain of his kid brother while Dad was on his arse in his cell. He yearned for her praise and seldom received it. She went through the gate, left him like he was her bloody driver and not the guy who held the family and its future together. His opinion: her opinion was that she possessed ambition, that Patrick had a view of where they should be heading as a family, that Theresa had an understanding of money . . . him, he was just their driver, their enforcer. His opinion: they short-changed him and there was too much talk of international links, of going abroad where they were strangers, where they had no reputation. They sneered at him, looked down on him, increasingly cut him out of the planning. He lit a fag, heaved the nicotine into his guts, coughed, spat at the floor between his feet.

On Bengal's mind was, in his opinion, important business.

That area of "important business", she left to him. Business that important would have led, Bengal reckoned, to precious Patrick toppling over on his face in a faint. Would have led to Theresa, had she watched from the sidelines, chucking up her breakfast in a corner and against the wall of plastic sheeting.

He was Bengal . . . his birth certificate said Xavier which was a priest's name, the one who had married his ma and his dad, and himself making it bloody hard for her to fit into the wedding dress without a quick alteration at the back. The name he was known by at home, amongst their people and to the police at Merseyside and the National Crime Agency – Bengal – had been given him by a screw at Newton-le-Willows, in the Redbank secure unit for young offenders. The screw was an east Londoner, liked the slang and liked to use his fists which was why he could dish out names and was only rarely – and painfully – corrected. He had called the prisoner, doing time after conviction for Bodily Harm, Grievous, a "bit of a chancer". "Chancer" went with "Lancer" . . . *The Lives of a Bengal Lancer* was a movie made bloody years ago, the main part played by a Yank called Gary Cooper; the screw had never heard of the film or the star, but it had stuck. Used by other kids in the block, by the staff, told to his ma and his dad on a visit, used by crime teams when he was pulled in. It had stuck.

As he steered away from the kerb he reckoned there might have been a glint of light in the low wall opposite, just saw it for a moment, then lost it. Just a flicker . . . and he was thinking of the business to be done that day. A light in brickwork which made no sense, on the opposite side of the road from the family home, where Ma was, and saw her slam the door shut, had given it a kick with her heel without a backward glance at him – no bloody thanks – and he accelerated.

He drove north, used the back doubles and narrow avenues splitting terraced housing and the rat runs, and was far enough from the territory covered by traffic cameras and by the vehicle recognition kit up on poles. Bengal – how he thought of himself now – had put behind him irritated thoughts of his ma. Also behind him were the images of the tart that Ma insisted on using, Nanette, who always looked at him half frightened and half like he was dogshit on her shoe. Would give her . . . Forgot about what he would have given her.

Bengal would drive to within a mile of the location, a terrace of lock-up garages. A taxi would pick him up, a trusted driver who would take him on a loop around the garage block so he could see for himself that there were no police wagons and no unmarked cars loitering close by. A scarf around his head and a flat cap low on his forehead, Bengal would walk the last quarter of a mile to the garage.

The interior would have been screened off with plastic sheeting covering the walls and the concrete floor. Other men, equally trusted, would have carried out the preparatory work. An iron chair would have been screwed to the floor. Restraints were on the chair, would hold a man securely. At the side of the garage, but in full view of the chair, was a shelf and on it was a lump hammer. It would have cost £20 if bought singly but Bengal had done a good deal with a hardware business up in the west suburbs of the city and had bought ten and had been charged, because he had insisted on paying something, £100 for the lot. Other men would now either have been at the point of picking up the man with whom Bengal wished to have a conversation or had already done so and were now ferrying him through the back streets to the garage. There others would wait and watch the streets and would have pay-for-use mobile phones and would warn of any potential police interference. Many men were involved that morning in Bengal's bit of business and all were trusted. All were dependent on his patronage, and all would have believed in the length of his arm and the certainty of his retribution. All would know this was to be lump hammer business and that Bengal himself would use it. And they would all know that, before the bars and restaurants opened for lunchtime service, a man who had broken the trust would be screaming, the sound distorted by a gag around his mouth, for the mercy of death. All would have rock-solid alibis, men prepared to swear on any bible, on the health of their mother, on the heartbeat of their kids, that each of the guys involved in the preparation for a punishment session had been innocent of any connection with violence: they would have been at home, they could have been out of the city with witnesses . . . It was all about trust. Also, about the certainty that Bengal would come after any of them who betrayed the family. They waxed fat on the monthly wage he paid them.

A top target for both Merseyside police and the National Crime Agency, Bengal had good knowledge of the men and women who were paid to investigate him, track him, bring him to court, lock him up. With the cash, wads of it, that always bulged in the hip pocket of his old jeans, he could buy that information as easily as going any morning of the week into the Asian-owned convenience store to collect a couple of packets of fags . . . He knew them, thought them shit. Knew of their commanders, rated them as piss, not one of them capable of nailing him.

He drove comfortably. Did not break the speed limit, nor cross double lines, violated none of the traffic laws, but twice did a double circuit of a roundabout, and used his mirrors with care. His breathing was even. He had the radio on quietly, and listened to Liverpool Live. Felt good, relaxed, had forgotten his mother, his brother and sister . . . Always felt good, relaxed, when a lump hammer was laid out ready for him, this one would be the fourth of the ten he had bought. Using a lump hammer was part of Bengal's business. The hammer ensured trust and the certainty of fear . . . For fuck's sake, the family did not survive without trust and without the aching cringe that fear created. Bengal was always the one who used the hammer.

He turned into an empty street. People at work if they had jobs, or shopping if they had money, kids at school. On the left was a line of semi-detached houses. The fourth one down was lived in by a man who was trusted and the forecourt was empty, as he had known it would be. He parked there, went to find his taxi. He was calm and his life was organised to suit him. Walking past the last house in the street he noted a chocolate bar wrapper on the edge of the pavement, lodged behind the weeds and pressed against the brickwork of a low wall . . . And remembered a similar wall, and a

similar house, and similar bricks, but not a flash of light, and for a
moment he was puzzled . . . but kept walking. Fear was important,
trust was important; respect and loyalty were important. Trust
had been broken and fear had not kept a man in line. Respect was
in a trash can and loyalty had been ditched. What the man had
done was not in itself a great crime against the family but it had
broken discipline. Drunk in a pub in the Anfield district and with
an unpaid debt against him of only £3000, and with the bravado
of alcohol and not caring about anything said "by that ugly bitch,
Doloures Govier, fat cow who needs a good shagging which she's
not getting", and also mouthing about him that he was "a big
fucking pansy, all fucking piss and wind, that Bengal, as he likes to
be called". Just alcohol talk because the man would have known
better. But it was public and needed answering, which elevated
the morning's work to lump hammer business . . . There was a bit
of ground in an allotment up towards Southport ready for the
man who had once had too big a mouth and he'd be found in the
morning, and not pretty. The plastic sheeting would be burned in
an oil drum, laced with paraffin. And the hammer? The hammer
was destined for the dark and mud-stained waters between the
city and Birkenhead, would be lost from a crossing ferry.

The taxi was waiting for him.

The A Section surveillance watchers were gone from 3/S/12.
Quiet ruled, as Jonas liked it. When he had been in counter-terror
or ranging what he regarded as his limited talents against espionage, subversion, that bag of tricks, he would have been able to
throw a net wide and trawl deep. Different in the backwater. Had
to make choices, had to follow that rather bulbous nose from
which a small mole grew and on which his spectacles sat. It had
been put to him bluntly: "Jonas, you keep half a dozen rats hungry.
They are desperate for a meal. You put a paint splodge on the
shoulders of each of them, different colour. You make a judgement. You put your money on a colour – vermilion, violet, alabaster,
amber, cardinal – only one chance and that is the rat you are
backing as the winner. You could put them all in a sack and let

them fight it out and then when the kerfuffle is over you could open the sack and see if you picked a winner. But, no point, because by then it's too late and has only been useful in detecting the value of your judgement." One rat chosen from the families in Liverpool where the rats were of good pedigree.

But for a deal, and a criminal trail, and an investigation that would humour him, Jonas Merrick had needed another vermin family and had studied his maps, had learned, and with the help of Nikko, had come up with the territory of the Spanish "autonomous community" of Galicia, with four provinces, had found that a Level One was based there and had made a choice as to which rat would be the best to have his shirt on, a tattersall with a prominent check. Had bet on a family there, and Nikko had not disagreed. Another file and another stack of photographs were locked away in a drawer. It was a gamble – should he have chosen poorly the lagoons of the backwater would ripple with activity and a shipment would likely be landed. Did anyone care if £300 million, street price and cut, reached the market for consumption? Not too many, but Jonas Merrick would care: not because of the collateral of human misery but because he detested being wrong, loathed being responsible for error. In a trade-off there would be two families. He poured himself a coffee, already laced with milk, that Vera had prepared for his Thermos.

His mother had gone to her hairdresser in Pontevedra.

Sergio did the bookkeeping. From an admired university in the Italian city of Milan, he had gained a respectable degree in Business Studies. There would have been many on the same three-year course who had been awarded more notable marks from the examiners, and who had been more widely praised for the diligence displayed during lectures and for the quality of their essays. He worked on the family accounts, the movement in and out of money owed them and owed by them. He had a mind, where assets were concerned, that was exact, and he savoured the detail of what he did in areas of profit and loss. While supposedly studying, he had gained favours from female students because of his appearance and his morals. With the former he was blessed, on the latter he was destitute. He had come home to Galicia seven years ago and his looks had lasted and his reliance on those few moral principles had further diminished. Good-looking, dark hair carefully cut, and mahogany-coloured eyes, a nose that was a major feature of his face and seemed to show strength, and always well dressed but not flamboyant ... His mother would have snarled her displeasure if he had flaunted the wealth of the family. He had turned his back on Milan, retained only that part of his education that was relevant – had left behind his best and truest friends who were both Italian and from the far south: a girl had come from an *'Ndrangheta* clan based in the Calabrian mountains – specialising in cocaine importation – and had been under occasional surveillance by, she said dismissively, the *carabinieri*. The boy he had spent time with was confined to a wheelchair; he had spinal damage and his body retained frag-ments of bullets too closely lodged among bone and tissue for the surgeons to remove. His father had been a moderate level *capo* in a *cosa nostra* family in Palermo, not in the highest reaches but well placed, and they dealt primarily in laundering and heroin importation. He had survived an assassination attempt but his son had been too close to him to escape injury. Once every month he would have a tail of *guardia de finanza* people which was hard for him to throw off because of his wheelchair. The Italian girl and the Italian boy were the only close friend-ships Sergio had made in three years and he had learned from both of them and had watched closely the care with which they countered the watchers assigned them. He had known many girls in Milan, good for sleeping with but none had lasted more than a couple of weeks before he had moved on. So many students had out-performed Sergio in the examination halls. Probably a few now lived reasonably well and were on the short-term contracts used by the major finance houses and the international banks, and might even have thought themselves successful – but not by the standards enjoyed by the family of Sergio Munoz.

He enjoyed sleeping with women, but preferred the book-keeping which confirmed the wealth of his mother, Isabella, of himself, and of his brother, Laureano.

Isabella's husband, Sergio's father, was Tomas. The old man rarely figured in her thoughts, his or those of his brother. Tomas lived an almost monastic life in a converted apartment in Pontevedra. He had been a big man, an importer of quality product, had done time in all the high-security Spanish gaols and had earned the greatest respect. Tomas had been on a beach where a cargo was to be landed, had slipped on seaweed, had cracked open his pelvis on unforgiving rock, and surgical intervention had failed to restore him. He spent his days in his apartment, sat in a chair, watching TV, or playing *juego de damas* with old friends, and telling stories, and the games of checkers were now the limits of his interests in winning or losing. He was no longer consulted. Isabella would visit him after she had been to the hairdresser, Laureano might go once a month, Sergio no longer wished to listen to those old stories.

The lecturers in Milan would have had little comprehension of business dealings where the profits could be so immediate, and the losses so devastating. No written contracts existed, no document was witnessed by a notary. A word of agreement was exchanged, hands might touch, there were understandings.

There were good days and not such good days.

Sergio dealt with men who lived in remote farms – in unusual luxury – 8000 kilometres away in the depths of the Colombian mountains and forests. He traded with men of exceptional brutality.

In the one column for his day's work was a figure received via courier from a new and as yet untested client, a payment in advance and more to follow later in the week – a shipment was delayed. The cash was to be moved in secure circumstances that afternoon, marked for investment. The other column caused his forehead to knit. Two nights before, the news bulletin on the *Los Una* station had carried reports, unconfirmed by the authorities, of the interception of a freighter off the Cape Verde islands, 3000 kilometres to the south. It was claimed that a tonne of cocaine had been seized in an operation involving Portuguese and Spanish agencies. The information, according to the broadcast, had been suppressed for a week. The shipment was intended for Sergio's family. A problem, one that he must always be prepared to deal with, lay with the Colombians accepting the honesty of such a report. It was always a problem convincing Colombians that they had not been tricked, cheated. Would be bad for *el rehén*, for the hostage, sent to Latin America as proof of good faith. The Colombians were never slow to take action if they believed they were victims of deceit, that their partners were lying.

And Laureano's speedboats were hammering home in poor weather and had not taken off the cargo from the submarine, another matter of concern.

The mist had not lifted and was close around her and the cliff edge in front was hard to see clearly. They called the siren on the lighthouse, the *Vaca de Fisterra* – the Cow of Finisterre. It sounded an appropriate dull bleat of a warning cry that could be heard as far as 20 miles out to sea. She was at the end of the earth, the promontory given that name by Roman traders two millennia earlier, a place feared by the most intrepid of Phoenician sailors, and now on a heavily used trading route. She could hear the muted sound of the siren and the murmuring crash of the waves against the rocks 300 feet below.

She did not regret the night.

Had Anna Jensen been asked if she was pleased with having accepted the invitation to Kenny Blake's cottage, she would have shrugged, not committed herself.

Had she been quizzed if the experience in bed had been pleasurable or an anti-climax, she would also have shrugged . . .

She had been in Galicia for nearly four years, had gone almost native. Spoke the national language with fluency and had a decent handle on the local dialect. She was 31 years old. Anna supposed herself the sort of woman who was prepared to let herself be seen in a state of perpetual mess. She never worried about the quality of her clothes or the absence of make-up on her face, and her hair was a tangle of gold and yellow, sometimes hooked up or knotted or sometimes tied back. She thought she turned men's heads, and that would have been a good enough reason for her to have made few friends, during those years on the Atlantic coast. She made no effort to look attractive, which probably was reason enough to piss off most of the local women of her age – they probably thought she was a rich girl who must be living off a parental allowance, and frittered away her time painting on the precarious cliff paths.

She was squatting on a collapsible three-legged stool. She wore a faded fleece and a pair of old dungarees with a tear at the right knee clumsily repaired. On her lap was an open box of artist's crayons. In front of her, needing to be gripped each time a gust came in off the Atlantic, was an easel. She might have worked from memory, or might have been finishing off an effort she had started earlier, before the mist, or fog, had settled over the seascape.

She created an image but now would have seen only the heather by her feet, and she heard only the siren cry of the cow built into the loudspeakers of the lighthouse, the rhythm of the waves imploding on the base of the cliffs, and the shriek of the sea birds. Had she been a romantic she might have marvelled at how they were able to fly so steadily in the wind, and sometimes as if in curiosity, they seemed to materialise out of the blank white wall of mist around her. They flew over her, squawked at her and checked whether she had dropped food around her stool.

She thought only the gulls watched her, that she was alone . . . Later, would she go back to the cottage where he lived? Repeat the action of the previous night? Cook for him? Leave her dungarees folded on the chair? Might, might not. Depended on how long she could endure the solitude of the cliffs, and the noise of the siren and the breaking waves and the gulls. Rain was forecast for later, and the cold cut through to her body.

One slow smile, spreading wide and highlighting the freckles on her cheeks and the sparkle in her eyes . . . He would have warmed to her, had uses. The mist and the gathering chill seemed to her to make Kenny Blake a degree, or several, more attractive . . . The weather showed no sign of lifting, and she worked with her crayons at the view displayed on her easel. It was where she had met him. She had met him on the cliff paths above the bays and inlets, often in the dusk, and in all conditions – sunshine, gales, sheeting rain, blistering heat. Something else they shared, obviously, a love of those wild spaces where a continental landmass met the vast spread of an ocean.

A wild place and known for catastrophe and killing, and justifying the name of Coast of Death, a harsh place . . . and thought herself alone.

In the café the atmosphere could have been cut with a blunt knife.

Kenny ordered his coffee, an *Americano*, what he always had. Had allowed his own thoughts and concerns to stifle his awareness – which was stupid and insensitive, and dangerous. It was a small café, a single line of tables, all taken, and the standing room at the counter was busy. Fredo seemed not to hear him, did not catch his eye, did not acknowledge him. Kenny was late getting into Corunna, had not yet been to his office. The drive up from the coast had been slow, and on a lane where he could usually get up a good speed he had been held up by a ponderous herd of cattle and then a broken-down tractor. These were not places where a foreigner would throw around his weight, not places where a stranger would shout for a road to be cleared.

He always came here for his *Americano* and then went to work. He was being ignored, and it was a moment before he read the mood.

The café was in a narrow street that ran parallel to the big, historic buildings that fronted the esplanade and the harbour area. It was next door to the office space that Kenny rented. Fredo had been one of Kenny's first customers, and Fredo had organised the signwriter who had fashioned the business name for him, done it on dark wood – *La Lata de Galletas*. Fredo had brought in his extended family as additional clients, and Fredo had a boy, Gabriel, who was "away", and Fredo had a cousin by marriage and the cousin also had a boy who was ... A taxi pulled up, blocking the street. Kenny stood at the bar.

The atmosphere was that of a wake, a gathering to offer sympathy for the living and respect for the dead.

He was distracted. The Dutch girl, the wandering artist, was the first girl he had slept with since the break-up of his marriage, which was back in the fog of time and not supposed to have been inside the lines of his memory.

Usually he was greeted as a favoured friend and the talk would have been about football, the weather, fish catches, and the cousin by marriage might have been there.

Instructors on Level One courses told them to keep it zipped in their pants and if that was difficult then go take a cold shower, and alone. Sleeping with women, out of loneliness, dulled caution and exacerbated risk.

"Away" was the far side of the Atlantic. "Away" was an offering to demonstrate good faith. Fredo's boy, Gabriel, was a cheeky kid who loved to slouch in new trainers on the harbour front, and who had gone "away" to ensure honest enterprise on a shipment that Kenny had heard was delayed. The cousin's boy was another layabout with a fucked-up education who did gofer work around the Munoz clan, and had been put on the big bird that had flown west over the sea five weeks earlier and was too dumb to have acknowledged that he was sitting in an aeroplane as the assurance for a shipment coming by slow freighter which the TV channel had said was intercepted, no confirmation . . .

Traffic built behind the taxi. A delivery van, two cars, a pick-up with scaffolding poles, another car. No one hooted and no one shouted.

Fredo took his cousin in his arms and hugged him close. Nothing was said. No weeping, no kissing, no talking. That was not the way of the Galician people, as Kenny had learned. The cousin picked up an overnight bag from the floor and went out into the street. Some time in the night he would have been telegraphed, by the Spanish embassy or a consulate in Colombia, informing him that his son had been killed, then dumped awaiting collection.

The taxi pulled away. The traffic surged. The bar emptied. Fredo busied himself clearing tables and wiping the counter.

"An *Americano*, Kenny?"

"Please, yes . . . Fredo, I am very sorry."

No response. Attention on the coffee machines, and a cup and saucer clattering on to the counter, and a little sweet dry biscuit. It would have been, in Colombia, a bad death. Fredo remarked on the possible transfer of a central defender from a Madrid team to the Celta team, down the coast in Vigo. The local side, Deportivo from Corunna, was now in freefall and those keen to follow the game had switched allegiance to the Royal Club Celta de Vigo which was a sort of heresy but accepted . . . Marks of torture on the body would be visible; the message to signal that the cartels would not be messed with, not cheated. It was easy conversation and Kenny had learned to make anodyne responses, not take sides in matters of football. Nor have opinions on issues outside his brief: which was to make money for investors who came to this back street, always in shadow because of the towering buildings either side, and climbed the stairs to the office that Kenny called the Biscuit Tin . . . A terrifying death and probably inflicted with knives and done slowly, and a part of the process could have been laid at his door.

His coffee was poured.

It was dirty work, foul and filthy, and he should have been out of it months before but a quiet voice over a secure telephone had told him – not asked him, *told* him – to stay on. It became fouler, filthier, more dirty, and there was another week to go, more dangerous by each hour. Behind the bar was a framed photograph of Fredo with his wife and son, all wearing the scarves of the *Os Celestes*, smiling and happy, outside the stadium in Vigo . . . He drank his coffee.

They were good sandwiches. Because it was Friday, Vera had put a little extra mayonnaise into the tuna and cucumber filling. She seemed to think that the end of the working week was something to be celebrated. He would not have agreed with her, rather resented not being at his desk; facing two full days in front of him when he would have to have searched hard for a good enough excuse to come back into London. Between mouthfuls of his sandwich and swills from his Thermos, he gathered together the biographies of his new acquaintances.

Jonas Merrick would not have referred to the individuals whose lives he pried into as either "friends" or "enemies". They were Subjects of Interest and what they had in common was association with the backwater. They were what crime threw up.

It concerned families. Where were they? Principally in the city of Liverpool. Old-world docks and old-world manufacturing industries, and now a bit of a reinvention in culture and night life, and a rising reputation for the marketing of the Class A drug, cocaine. More families there than Manchester or Glasgow, more of note than in London. He had worked through the biographies of the relevant families. His old friend, a long-retired detective sergeant from a crime squad in Belfast, now confined, with acute arthritis, to his conservatory in rural County Antrim, had told him: *Forget the terror stuff and the espionage crap. Serious crime rings the bells, and the units that are important are all families. Through blood and marriage deals they have security and they resist outsiders. It's the strength of the families that they cannot be broken into ... The one weakness: they cannot do it all themselves.*

A woman he had never met, never would, who did not even know Jonas's name, ran an addicts' drop-in and, speaking from a west Midlands town he had never visited, had lectured him: *Find the hungriest. The ones who are falling back are those who are complacent. The hungriest and the greediest.* A Catholic priest in a deprived West Yorkshire parish had said: *They cannot stand still and survive. They have to be bigger, or they are swallowed. It is the law of the jungle, or worse. And cruelty seems to cement power.* A retired judge with a reputation for his severity of sentencing: *I'm taking a hell of a chance speaking to you, whoever you are, whatever corner of Box you come from, but my niece is there and she'd bollock me – her word – if I didn't speak to you. Greedy and hungry, yes. Family, yes. But, they have to have accountants, lawyers, drivers, couriers. Can't do it all themselves but they have a sanction on the hired help. Keep Need to Know as a creed, and that help is held in line by the certainty of retribution if lines are crossed. Ambition, yes ... and I'll give you something else to chew on. We had an Italian judge over here a couple of years back and I'm borrowing this from him ...* The old beggar's voice had dropped, as if he were an old-fashioned Shakespearean ham on a repertory theatre tour. The words had dripped into Jonas's ear: *Try for a matriarch. Got that? A matriarch. Go for her but go carefully, Mr Box, because she'll scratch your eyes out if you nail her and if she knows you nailed her. A matriarch.*

All done a year ago ... Had the right city, the right trade, and thought he had the right family. Had been through the McGoverns and the Kanes and the Wilkins and the Sanders and the Moriartys. Jonas had pored over police records and newspaper cuttings and court transcripts. He had been like one of those wannabe householders on the afternoon TV who wanted to buy a house in the country and had a shopping list of requirements; rejecting and discarding until he had learned of the Govier clan.

He had their photographs on his desk. Patrick and Theresa, and Xavier, and Mikey – who was detained and out of the game – and had a decent image of Doloures. She was in fluffy slippers and a pink bathrobe loosely tied at the waist, and her hair was in a towel and she was filling a green bin at the front gate. Just so ordinary, but Jonas had wagered on her as his matriarch – and would be annoyed if she proved him wrong. All beginning to happen, he believed, and the pace quickening, and his sandwich tasted good.

2

What galls me, he's just a bloody clerk.

The phone line was open, the link was to Merseyside Police. Jonas had been in the middle of a call to them. Had put the receiver down on his desk, had activated the speaker while he crouched at the wall safe beside his desk and rummaged for a file. Another voice responded.

I heard on the rumour mill what they call him. He's the Eternal Flame – his arse glued to a chair.

Easy enough to imagine. He had been talking with a detective inspector based in Liverpool. The officer was Fergal Rawe, seemed to want to be everyone's chum and introduced himself as "Jimbo" – so Jonas, with his trademark stubbornness, called him Mister Rawe. A senior man would have come into the work area and the time was ripe for a whinge. Jonas reckoned himself a frequent cause for whinges and whines, and rather enjoyed that element of relationships.

Treats me on a goddamn Need to Know basis.

But, more's the pity, he has authority.

God knows where that was cobbled from. I reckon he's one of those odious little feckers that sits in a room and hoards the stuff that's fed him ... One of those bloody pensioners that dies alone at home and then is found to have accumulated a dozen years of newspapers and food wrappings, needs bloody fumigation ... Just a clerk, and laying down the law.

Jonas had the volume turned too high. Had taken him a moment to realise that the outer area of 3/S/12 had gone quiet as if all the conversations beyond the walls of frosted glass that blocked off his cubicle had ceased so that the exchange could be better heard.

The word that had captured them was "clerk", and the repeat of it had caused a cascade of laughter amongst the surveillance people from A Section who would have been preparing for the next stake-out. Laughter that was cold and without generosity.

He had no friends at work: perhaps the grudging respect of Aggie Burns who headed that team. Jonas Merrick had worked in Thames House, known in their trade as "Box", for more than three decades and did not have a friend there. Had not wanted one, had not sought one. Had joined no club that Fivers could belong to and enjoy their facilities: gyms, wine tasting, sports teams, sailing and dancing, bridge and knitting, whatever – did not attend any of the socials arranged by the MI5 Caravan Club. Had there been an internal society for the worship of Norwegian forest cats he would not have joined. He did not use the subsidised canteen nor the in-house bar. There was a fair turnover in the A Section and he would have remained an enigma to most of them, veterans and new intake, unloved and uncared for. Most times his greetings when he came in to work, or packed up and left at the same time each afternoon, were cursory to the point of rudeness.

Except that when our Big Bosswoman took it up with Box, and had the clout of Assistant Chief Constable and was talking to their Deputy Director, she had her dainty little knuckles rapped like she was an impertinent schoolgirl. Pretty much told to stop moaning and fall into line.

I pass stuff on and I'm only allowed to share it with him. Where's it all going, what's the end game? I've never been treated like this, ever.

And no one's even met him, and . . .

The laughter had cooled to a snigger. He had found his file, nudged the safe door closed again, picked up his phone.

"Thank you so much for holding, Mister Rawe. I'll just repeat the data of the flight times and that'll be all. And – not a request but an instruction – the detail of what you have told me does not get shared in your building, amongst your colleagues. Anything further, I'd like it straight and direct."

He rang off. He had never believed that popularity was necessary for his work. Very few enjoyed his company, but he supposed that the two fine policemen who did shifts of guard duty on the building, Kev and Leroy, were as close as any – and a lady who presided at Reception and another in the Archive, not more . . . Certainly no effort would be made to heal the irritation of an aggrieved Merseyside inspector. He imagined it would have been a commander in that force who had wandered into Rawe's territory. The one important individual in Thames House for Jonas Merrick was his protector. The Assistant Deputy Director General, AssDepDG, who watched his back and made certain that his authority could not be challenged.

He studied the flight timetables.

He thought them very close now to calling down the heavy fist on the operation, getting the arrest teams into place. Not that Jonas saw as much of AssDepDG now that he swam in the backwater. Anti-terror and counter-espionage attracted attention and resources, and crime was a poor relation, had to fight to get at the teats of the cash cow. He would have accepted, brooked no argument, that his target family, and their trade, were a worthwhile opponent.

The sandwiches that Vera had made him had been good. He always enjoyed the Friday offering, tuna and cucumber, and his coffee stayed warm enough in the Thermos. Often on a Friday, he would have enjoyed a half hour's doze before waking fully, stretching, going for a corridor walk, and then tidying up those inevitable loose ends before leaving for the weekend. And Vera usually did a chop on a Friday night which was a favourite.

It was her knicker drawer that burdened him. Most of the contents – which used to come only from Marks & Spencer, but were now augmented from catalogues – affected him not at all. The weight on his shoulders was bred from what she hid at the back of the drawer, behind and beneath underwear that seldom saw the light of day. Among the lacy bits, and some of the racier items, were the medals. She had secreted there the Queen's

Gallantry Medal awarded to him after his disarming of the suicide vest worn by Winston Gunn, and there was a Bar to the QGM which recognised his work in tracking, locating and then capturing Cameron Jilkes before an intended attack on an RAF station from which the drones were flown in lethal combat against ISIS activists. Nothing had been pushed to the back of the knicker drawer to mark his work in stripping the cover from a deep-burrowing mole in the heart of the 'sister service', the Sixers' place across the river, and it was unlikely he would ever feature on their Christmas card list. The medal and the bar, and the fulsome congratulation of a Director General – particularly for the embarrassment and discomfort of the Sixers – had raised the bar high. Too high, Jonas reckoned. The Liverpool people were probably spot on in their evaluation: an over-promoted *clerk*. A collector of information, yes, but he was asked to act on it. A high bar, and he could reflect that he carried a crushing weight on his shoulders when he attempted to get over the bar. The weight was "responsibility". By acting on it, moving person- alities across a board, he endangered them. Stood to reason. Risk went with the game.

He was a facilitator, a coordinator.

Jonas used his phone. Went through the security procedures. It was answered.

He gave the flight times. Reported what he knew of a semi- submersible's progress. Heard distant traffic noise in his ear and a siren, and inevitably the cry of gulls. Told him, staccato sentences, what he had. Should have wished him well, but didn't. Thought he spoke to the front line of one of those dreary, endless wars. Rang off.

Needed to breathe deeply, tried to find calm. It was where responsibility weighed most heavily and where risk was greatest. The picture on the wall showed a skeleton-thin guy, poorly dressed, haggard and unshaven, jeans and T-shirt and hands deep in a wind-cheater's pockets; the only photo Jonas had of him, of Kenny Blake.

★   ★   ★

"Right, Boss, we'll be on our way."

Kenny thought there was a reluctance on Hugo's part to be gone.

"Yes, if we're to keep to the schedule, Boss, have to be moving." And an equal reluctance from Wilf to be leaving him.

He gave each of them a cuff on the shoulder and grinned and might have seemed sheepish. Hugo and Wilf were the muscle that Kenny Blake had on tap . . . except that the barrel was damn near empty and most hours of the day and night the delivery was too far away to do the necessary business. Put more simply, which Kenny Blake did not like to do, they were supposed to be his protection, the quick response backup, but they lived on a smallholding way up the coast road going east, and then a turning south and into the Cantabrian mountains. They were former marines, inseparable, had been together in 45 Commando, and the relationship had been the source of too much tittle and excess tattle and they'd gone their own way and had found a sort of haven where they bred goats, kept hens, made cheese and had hives for honey. And also had Makharov pistols and AK assault rifles, from Syrian military stores – abandoned weaponry. Along with protection they were tasked with work as couriers. Hugo was tall and heavily built and had arms draped in tattoos, a shaven head and an earring in the right lobe, and a squeaky voice. His friend was of the opposite physique, slight and thin, with a scalp of greying hair and no punctures in his ears and no doodles on his forearms. Both, aged 18, had fought in the night battle for the capture of the Two Sisters strongpoint overlooking Stanley on the Falkland Isles. Neither cared to discuss that experience . . . instead they talked about milk to be collected each day from their goats, and the animals' lifespan, possible ailments and breeding cycle.

Wilf lifted the suitcase off the bench.

Hugo lit a last fag and there was already a dusting of ash and littered stubs by his feet and they had stayed longer than was either sensible or usual.

"We'll be hitting the road then, Boss."

"Just shout, Boss, any time, day or night."

"Be back next week – but if we're needed earlier . . ."

"Just call, do that, Boss."

A wreath of smoke, and the barely used cigarette was dropped on the paving stone, and they were off. Kenny always met them in the San Carlos Garden. The flowerbeds had known better days and were usually freshly planted in the summer months when the tourists came, but it was still off-season and the corporation workmen's jobs were scaled back. What stayed constant was the view from the Garden on to Corunna's old harbour below . . . the site of a Peninsular war battle – January 1809 – between the English, helping to defend Spain, and the invading French. A British general had died, Sir John Moore, Moore of Corunna, who had been buried in the Garden. The old grave, augmented with a tomb and engraved with a poem, was the usual rendezvous for Kenny Blake and the "muscle" who gave him some comfort when the stress counters went off the dial.

A year back, they had received a phone call, no warning. A quiet voice. A security procedure put in place. A second call, both of them dressed for milking, no question raised of convenience. Nor did they ask this man, an elderly one by his voice, how he had found them, what trail they had left. A proposition put. Nothing about Queen and Country. Duty not mentioned. *We would like you to do this, it would be helpful.* A one-time phone number had been given to them. It was made clear that the instruction came from an Assistant Deputy Director General of the Security Service. A local DHL vehicle had pitched up a week later, the driver full of complaint about the state of the track. Inside the plastic wrapping was a grey Samsonite suitcase. They had unpacked it on the kitchen table. A pair of Makharovs in oil paper wrapping, and another as a spare, and ammunition and magazines; a pair of Kalashnikov rifles in one package, folded back, and again another as a spare, and more ammunition and more magazines, and some flash-and-bang canisters, and ones filled with gas. Simple, like it was every day . . . Wilf had said he'd a cousin whose dog food was delivered by DHL in Devon, and Hugo had told him that an old aunt, in Sheffield, had a monthly wine delivery done by DHL, always reliable. And the rifles and the pistols were reliable and had been tested on a foul night with a thunderstorm in the clouds so the noise was contained and anyway, the neighbours were not close. Kenny Blake took a degree of heart from this story.

He watched them go. The suitcase tilted Wilf over. Kenny supposed that a test had been carried out to discover what size case was needed to carry a million in high denomination sterling notes. They would each be worth £50. He picked up his own suitcase – it had been hard work lugging it from his narrow street and having to cross a couple of main drags and into the Garden. This one was empty. It was a basic precaution . . . they brought the empty case and he brought the full one, and they swapped.

He paused by the tomb. Kenny knew little poetry but this verse was seared in his mind, knew it by heart, six verses, had been told to learn it. *Not a drum was heard, not a funeral note,* was the message he'd send to the goat keepers to tell them to prepare to take away a shipment. *As his corse to the rampart we hurried* told them to come the next day, late afternoon as the light faded. Two more lines mattered for Kenny. *Slowly and sadly we laid him down* indicated that his anxieties were spilling over and *From the field of his fame fresh and gory* was the emergency signal, immediate . . . but they were three hours' drive away. It was what he had, where he was, all that he had been given.

He carried the empty Samsonite out of the garden. Imagined it filled with notes, a family doing it, all hands to the job. Pressing the bundles down so that more could be packed inside. Cursing in their own dialect that Kenny had never been able to imitate – could do Yorkshire and Geordie and the west Middlesex whine, but not the Scouser talk. Seemed to see them because their photos had been sent to him, had been committed to memory, had been burned and the ashes scattered in a bin across the street.

He crossed the two main roads, walked back up the narrow street. The café owned by Fredo had closed and was darkened. The cousin would by now be ready to board the long flight from Madrid to Bogotá. Fredo would be at home with his wife and they would be praying, together but in silence, that a submersible craft made it safely across the Atlantic and that their boy would survive as a hostage in the hands of a Colombian cartel. He bit at his lip, swallowed hard, unlocked his door, and squeezed his eyes shut for a moment – fuck all else he could do. And wondered where she was, whether she would come for him, whether he should go to her, and dumped the empty case and shuddered.

Remembered what Wilf had asked, "You good, Boss?"

And his answer, "Just fine."

From Hugo, "Not looking great, Boss."

A spat answer: "Just fine. Why wouldn't I be?"

Kenny sat in his desk chair. The Biscuit Tin had a week to run. It was a business based on trust – also on extreme greed – and the clients had rated him as honest. They handed over their money to him. When he did his runner they would lose all of their investments, swallowed up in the bureaucracy of the fiscal dead hand of Spain. Whether they could afford to have their nest eggs denied them or not, all of those clients would hate him with a vengeance, would want to sharpen knives and slice bits off him. If he was suspected in these last hours then his fate would be bad, seriously bad. He felt more fear now, as time drifted towards the conclusion. Fredo had been one of the first. The very first had been an old woman, two sticks and having trouble with the stairs, and 100 euros taken from her purse and passed to him, and him replying, "Money that the tax man does not need to know about. Always good to have a tin box and hide it under the bed, and keep it safe – for a rainy day. Except that I can do a bit better for you than just leaving it there. Safe as a well-built house, your investment, *Señora.*" He'd be gone in a week, telephone unplugged, a note left on the door, a queue on the stairs and others gathering in Fredo's bar, and cursing the day he was born . . . It was what Kenny Blake did.

★   ★   ★

"Where's that bloody hammer?"

"Bengal took it."

"Why?"

"You know why."

"What are we supposed to do?"

"Fall arse over tit down the hole – how do I know?"

"What's Ma doing?" Patrick's voice was rising.

"We're going to do it, with or without Bengal's hammer," Theresa snarled back at her brother.

They stood either side of the rolled-back carpet. The hole gaped in front of them. Behind, and dumped against the TV set, 59-inch home cinema, were three floorboards.

"Why isn't Ma here?"

"Ma's not here because she's out. Out is where she goes to meet lawyers, accountants, contacts, or perhaps she's gone to the fucking supermarket. Ma is out and Bengal is out. Bengal has taken his hammer with him. We are left – Ma said it – to put the boards back. Can you do that, Patrick, without Bengal's hammer, or do I ring Ma and tell her you aren't capable of putting three planks back? Do I?"

"Can't you do it?"

"I've just done my nails. No, I can't."

Bengal had brought Ma home. Bengal had rolled back the carpet. Heavy-duty Axminster, had cost a fortune. And Bengal had loosened the floorboards, done it so they could be lifted clear. He had left with his hammer, the one with the extra weight in the head. Ma knew what he would do with it, and Theresa did, and Patrick would have been simpler than she rated him if he'd not known. Patrick stayed close to Ma like that was the way he would be safe from where his dad was. Had seen him there when Ma dragged him through to the Visitor Section of HMP Walton. Patrick, Theresa thought, had nightmares about that place and was always moaning when Ma left him. And Theresa? She had gone down into the hole, dark till she switched on the torch, and crawling with spiders, big bastards, and she had lifted out the sacks of money. Nowhere else to keep the bloody stuff. The floorboards of the living room and the dining room and the hall all had a nice soft sound to them which was not the quality of the carpeting, but because of the plastic bags stashed between them which deadened any footsteps. How much money was down there? God alone knew, and Theresa didn't, not to the nearest hundred thousand, maybe not to the nearest quarter of a million. There was a drainage pipe down there that must have leaked and some of the bags they'd retrieved stank of damp. Theresa's solution had been to get a deodorant spray from the bathroom and had squirted it around them, over them. She had done her nails while leaving Patrick to count out the next million, repeat what they had done a week before ... Trouble was, a week before, Bengal had not removed the hammer that he kept in a tool box on a shelf in the garage. In the last year they had kept more money under the floorboards because Ma was increasingly nervous at the capacity they had for laundering their earnings, anxious about the footprints their assets left. Could only be short-term because the space under the downstairs floorboards was almost filled.

She thought Patrick panicked. Patrick was always frantic if he reckoned he was going to fall short in Ma's eyes. Theresa did not know where Bengal kept his other hammers . . . all the family knew why Bengal had taken a hammer out with him that day, and that by now, at the end of the afternoon, the hammer had been used and was ready for disposal. Theresa was not helping get the floorboards fastened back in place now the money for the second shipment had been lifted out, counted and bundled, not after she'd done her nails: salmon pink, she thought, suited her. But she went outside and into the garage and she carefully felt on the shelves until she found a heavy-duty spanner. Might have been what her dad had used back in the old days. Her dad had been in one of the last groups that had gone after Securicor and Security Express vans carrying Friday wages. Her dad had only started out on 'phets and brown and smack when the money vans stopped. The spanner might have been something he'd used when dinosaurs walked the Liverpool shoreline. She tossed it at Patrick and scooped up the bundles and took them into the kitchen.

She heard her brother start to manoeuvre the first plank into place, then begin to hammer it down. He'd be belting the protruding nails. There was a yelp and he swore, and would have hit a finger . . . he was useless, a tosser. She was counting. And some truths ran in her mind . . . It was her ma's aim that Patrick would eventually be the brains in the family and preside over the future fortunes of the family empire. Patrick often accompanied Ma to clandestine meetings with their favoured accountant and favoured lawyer, and favoured politician in the local scene. Herself? She believed she was the family equivalent of the turkey hen fattened up for the Christmas feast, kept well presented and well looked after and would eventually be shipped out. She would be married off in the interests of a liaison: probably a kid with the intelligence of Bengal and be slapped around and shagged rotten and the work on her back would help towards the next dynasty – and likely Ma with the same aim, would find a girl for Patrick? The idea that she would pick her own guy, branch out on her own, was crap – no chance. There were times when boys looked at her: on a dance floor, at Aintree races or in the foyer of a charity gala concert. Boys would stare blatantly at her flat chest and her wide hips, like they stripped her, and would whisper of "giving her one" but only whisper and giggle if Bengal were not there, not minding her. She knew that without Bengal the family was doomed because he alone created the fear that was their authority. Without him, they would be brushed aside, and Ma seemed not to want to recognise it. The power of a lump hammer . . . Bengal had talked it through one Sunday lunch that Ma had cooked. A fulsome description of the process of beating, savaging and hearing the screaming through the gag or the hood, then killing. Ma had listened, showed no reaction. Patrick had put his head in his hands, had eaten nothing and Theresa had risen from the table and had stumbled to a downstairs toilet and had knelt on the mat and had vomited what she had eaten of her lunch and her breakfast, had retched until her throat was raw.

She thought she had counted a million in sterling.

A laundry bag, strong plastic, was used. She tipped it in. The hammering had finished. She heard the car pulling up outside . . . Like they were all on a treadmill and no opportunity to jump clear, and the speed ratcheting. Patrick called for her to help him flatten the carpet.

Her mother came through the front door, looked into the living room, gave her a smile, pecked Patrick's cheek.

They had seen the car pull into the driveway. Seen the Govier woman climb out of her four- or five-year-old BMW 3-series saloon, had seen her unlock the front door and then it was shut and a bird flew across the front garden.

Where the Potters sat, not in their best chairs and overlooking the road, but at the back where they had a kitchen diner. They had opened the glass doors that gave them a view across their own – now rarely used – principal living room and then out through a bay window and across their shallow front garden and above a low brick wall. The bird, a thrush, landed in the flowerbed on the Potters' side of that front wall. They were David and Jenny. They had managed a synchronised retirement two years back – him from his job as a water board engineer and she as a deputy head librarian – and their children were up and gone. Neither would have said that retirement was what they hoped. They lived in a state of anxiety, and their nerves had further deteriorated a full year back. The bird pecked in the bed, searching for a worm, and both could see clearly the marginally different colour of the mortar used to bind the bricks there, which was the cause of the further sinking of their morale.

A year back, cold, with a fleck of ice in the air, a woman had been walking her dog, a tugging Jack Russell, and it had pulled its collar over its ears, freed itself, and had darted out into the middle of the road. A car, coming in the opposite direction at speed, had swerved, skidded, mounted the pavement and had come to rest against the Potters' wall, and in the process had levelled a clear yard of it. An insurance job, of course. David had assured the driver that there was no pain attached, no grief, but the police should be informed for protocol's sake, and Jenny had made a pot of tea to calm the dog owner. The family opposite had trooped out, had absorbed the scene, had said nothing constructive or polite, had gone back inside . . . That evening, after dark, a van had arrived with a ladder on the roof, displaying a logo about General Building Work and something about Nothing too Small and Free Quotations and . . . a harassed middle-aged woman, their judgement of her, had come from the passenger side and the driver had followed her to the Potters' door.

The Potters had met DCI Fanny Thomas.

First real involvement they had ever had with the police and a detective chief inspector from a Serious Crime Unit. Had exchanged messages, increasingly desperate, with an anti-social-behaviour team who fielded their complaints about the people across the road but that was years back, when the feral kids there were young. They knew about the Govier family – the family featured in carefully written references in the *Liverpool Echo*, and they had seen the dawn police raid almost ten years back when Mikey Govier had been led out handcuffed. They had thought that evening that Fanny Thomas looked half-dead on her feet from exhaustion, and . . . she had not hung about. "I don't plead and I don't gild it. You would be taking a risk and I am not going to minimise the scale of such a risk. I'd rather you did not quote me to your extended family or other neighbours because this is something between you and me, and on my side would have very, very limited circulation. I'm sitting at my desk and anything involving this road, because of your neighbours across it, comes up on my screen. I know when you have your bin collections, I know when you have pothole problems, when those very fetching trees out there need pruning, and there's a minor RTA – sorry, Road Traffic Accident. I see where it is and this evening I've noted its exact position and the amount of work required to reinstate the wall. I would appreciate your permission to carry out that work . . . not me personally, but a firm we use . . . and while doing the work we will insert a camera with a lens that focuses on that front garden and that front door. It will be a hidden camera, and we will set up a battery replacement procedure and it will give us coverage of their movements in and out and who visits and what they bring with them. You are perfectly entitled to refuse. I would like to confide that my work, day and too long into the night, involves this family that you live cheek by jowl with. For the team I lead they are our principal targets. I am asking for help, not on a bent knee but *asking*. The family are millionaires several times over and are successful importers of cocaine. Do you want to think about it? My husband's a useless cook, my kids are worse than useless. They'll be around a table and griping and waiting and I'll get a pizza in from the Co-op and feed them, which is why I'm not hanging about and doing the persuasive stuff, and not very good at it, actually. So, decline, think or . . . What do you say?"

They had both spoken together. Would not refuse, did not need to think. The same van had come back a couple of days later and the wall had been rebuilt – and from that day they had had neither sight nor sound of Fanny Thomas.

They were the type of people, David and Jenny Potter, who felt rather blessed at having the chance to help bring down what they had read was termed as an Organised Crime Group, especially one right across from their own front door. Felt almost proud to have been chosen, and days had gone by, and weeks and then months, and the talk of *risk* had steadily diminished in their minds. They knew nothing of the current investigations in their own city, nor those in other countries, nor of a bucking, rocking craft ploughing through a swell in the eastern Atlantic, nor of anyone whose life was in extreme danger . . .

By the wall, where the mortar was a different shade, the thrush found a worm that wriggled in its beak before it was swallowed.

There was an outer gate, guarded. It was opened smartly and the Range Rover drove through and then braked hard and the head-lights speared into the room and lit Sergio and his mother. He saw them as he swung the wheel, a tight turn that scattered gravel, and a few of the stones would have rattled the glass. Laureano was home.

He was tired near to exhaustion. His arms ached from the effort of hanging on to the steering of his craft, and his ears rang with the howl, in spite of defenders, from the array of outboard engines, and his body shook like an old man's from the motion – and for nothing.

They had started their meal without him. Perhaps his mother had business to attend to. Perhaps his brother had a woman waiting for him . . . Perhaps they didn't have the patience to wait and hear how it had been to do the round trip far out to the Cape Verde islands and then come back with no cargo to show for it. The hallway oozed what he thought was class but not marked up so that it shouted expense. Would have been if Laureano had been consulted. His mother always said that style dictated taste . . . Not consulted but he was responsible for the choice: spend big and obvious, spend big and understated, he did the work that gained the family wealth – but not that day.

They were eating pig. He could smell it. He was ravenously hungry. His throat was dry, parched, and he needed a bottle of Estrella Galicia and the contents would not touch the sides of his throat. He stood in the centre of the hall and now their knives and forks had been set down and they watched him through the open door. He peeled off his heavy duty anorak and then the lighter one underneath, then the heavy knit sweater and a T-shirt and a vest, let the clothes fall. He bent and loosened the laces of his boots, supposedly waterproof, comfortable and old, then kicked them off, and some of the water of the big wide Atlantic spilled on to the marble floor. Then his socks, dripping, leaving more water flowing in little rivers across the marble. Waterproof trousers, thermal under-trousers, underpants, all were dropped on the floor. He stood naked, scratched an armpit, then ran his fingers through the tangle of his hair. He went into the dining room, leaving the stench of the sea and fuel behind him. His place was laid. He sat, his hair dripping steadily on to his shoulders.

There was silence around him until the kitchen door swept open: Concepcion, who was the cook and housekeeper, and who had once been the nanny responsible for rearing first Laureano and then Sergio while their mother and father worked at the family business. She came with his beer and had taken off the cap, and showed no reaction at the sight of his bare body and the hair flattened on it, and would scurry away and dish up his plate for him. His mother had a pocket calculator in front of her, had pushed her plate to the side. His mother usually brought her calculator to the table.

His brother stabbed the question at Laureano, "So, you could not bring it back?"

More moisture oozed from his hair and his breath came in sharp pants . . . one thing to steer the speedboats out into the ocean and bring them home, but then they needed to be guided back up the inlets north of their home at Cambados, then lifted by crane from the quayside, loaded on to lorries and covered with tarpaulins, then driven to the hidden store sheds where they were kept. A million euros for a boat, a million euros for the outboards powering it, and the boats and their engines were prime targets for the GRECO police . . . Not like some fucking hotel in Madrid where his mother or Sergio might go and toss the keys of a Mercedes to a doorman and have him drive it away to a garage. They were the integral necessities of the family business.

"No."

His food came. He began to eat. Concepcion's hand, warm from the plate, brushed the skin of his shoulder, would have seen him naked since he was a baby. She was the widow of a crewman from a trawler used by the family decades before to go out and meet the freighters bringing cocaine from Colombia. He had been washed overboard, and she would have employment till the day she died.

"A poor outcome."

"Do you have ears on your fucking head?"

"I have ears. I heard myself say it was a poor outcome."

"Can you hear anything through your fucking ears?"

"Only your eating, and I . . ."

"Can you not hear the wind?"

"Only your eating, which is disgusting."

"The wind. I tell you what, dear brother, would be disgusting, is for you to be at sea in that wind, and chucking up your guts. That would be disgusting. Remind me to invite you out next time the wind blows – come with me."

"So, the wind is difficult and . . ."

"You know nothing."

"I know that a cargo is still at sea. The forecast continues to be poor, I know that. I know a submersible is heading here and may have to beach. That is catastrophic for us. Beach and unload four tonnes weight. How long does that take? Not at sea, not far out, but on a beach where GRECO swarm. Could you not have worked harder?"

"You know nothing."

"I tell you what I do know . . . We lost a shipment off Cape Verde. Now we have a shipment by submersible that is at risk. What if we lose that, and we have money up front from Colombia, paid and banked? Then, we cannot deliver what they have paid for. How do we respond? Do we shrug? Tell them we did our best and . . .? What I do know, and know because I have seen it. The Colombians are not good people to make angry . . . We have this British woman who has bought into the shipment and she I do not worry about – I am not interested if she loses her stake. What can she do to us? What I do know is the Colombians can do much to us. I have to hope, dear brother, that we get the cargo ashore as we have been paid to do and that the Colombians do not have cause for anger."

Laureano could not argue. He ate, and he drank another bottle that Concepcion brought him, and her face was without expression when she took a folded napkin from the side plate before him, shook it out and dropped it casually, and expertly, so that his groin was covered. He had cleared his plate and drank from the neck of the second bottle.

The waves had been ferocious, brutal. He was the finest pilot on the coast, he was a hero to the kids. He was an enforcer. He was inside a family of growing prestige. The weather had beaten him.

His mother stayed outside the inquest, her fingers flickering across the keys of her calculator. Laureano had experience of the Colombians: on his one trip to their country, outside Medellín, and as a favoured guest, he had watched as the skin was flayed from the body of a man described as an informer for the DEA, and Laureano could still hear his screams. When his mother and Sergio had travelled there a year later they had been shown the execution of another informer, like it was a cabaret event after dinner, a killing rather than the performance of a celebrity singer ... Not that Laureano had sympathy for an informer, a worm wriggling into the intestine of the family.

Out of the lift, into the atrium, and Jonas was spotted by the AssDepDG who turned away from the woman he had been talking with, and came towards Jonas, who barely slowed: had a train to catch.

A dropped voice. "How does it go, Jonas?"

"It goes. Sufficient?"

"Do not forget, Jonas, those obligations."

"Not forgotten. It goes on at pace. Does that satisfy?"

"Just to remind you that – while counter-terror and counter-espionage are scratching each other's eyes out for resources – you are busy spending money like Christmas is next week. The undercover, the banking system, the protection set-up, are all drinking money ... and – as my wife likes to tell me – 'and another thing', I continue to get irate calls from the police hierarchy, from the National Crime Agency, and they all ask me the same question – who the fuck is Jonas Merrick? The latest is the Sixer mob demanding to know why you, *you*, are dealing directly with DEA in Colombia and sidelining them. You have made a web for yourself and I seem tangled in it."

"Probably coming to a conclusion."

"And ... and ... and apparently we are demanding that agencies and forces cease to share what they have but instead direct their material only to you. That is a total contradiction of everything preached in law enforcement, a step back to the bad old days when every agency regarded a neighbour as an enemy. The complaint is that we seem to regard all these forces as institutionally corrupt. Even by your standards, Jonas, that is a weighty accusation."

"It minimises chatter. Justified."

"That the best I am getting from you?"

"It is a good 'best'. Hope it doesn't spoil the weekend mood, but lives are on the line. Some of the individuals I know of and some I do not, but I calculate the risks are high. A few bruised conceits come cheap, lives and welfare are pricier. Please, excuse me."

"Jonas, just hear me. We called crime a backwater. A way of sweetening the pill. Actually as far as this building is concerned it is a dead-end cul-de-sac. Nobody gives a flying fuck for crime and . . . It was somewhere to put you after the Sixer business and your splash in the river. Put you out of sight, out of mind, beyond an ability to make mischief."

"Good night."

He went out into the dusk.

He saw Kev and Leroy on their guard duty, weapons hanging on their vests and their belts loaded. They nodded. He responded. One of them went out into the traffic and halted the flow. He crossed the road and did not look back and did not thank them, and was on the pavement of the bridge and kept walking, set himself a cracking pace because the AssDepDG had delayed him. The wind was up and buffeted his trilby, and he was glad that his Harris tweed jacket and his raincoat were proof against the cold, and his brogues were firm on his feet.

One morning, soon after he had returned to work, he had paused at the exit from Waterloo station and had asked the flower-seller for a spray of autumn gold chrysanthemums, just a fiver's worth. Rather sheepishly, he had carried them to the centre of the bridge and had dropped them, had watched them fall, then be swept into the tide race. Had stayed long enough to see them disappear under the wash of a tug pulling a line of barges. They had never found her. He had not expected they would. He was thinking now of those he knew and those he did not know. He was safe, anonymous in the investigation where he gathered in the strands – the only danger stalking him was the weight of responsibility.

Money well spent? Not for him to say, he was only a clerk. Just a dull little man. He chuckled, beside the high wall of the Lambeth Palace grounds, recited the words exchanged in a message two months before with Nikko. It was soon after he had first heard of the construction of a semi-submersible craft in a jungle beside an Amazon tributary, been warned and then had claimed the information as for his eyes only.

My name, Jonas, is from my Greek extraction. Where my family are from. A dainty little island, Karpathos. Some tourism, not much. But mountains and forests, gangsters and smugglers – exotic.

Sounds blissful.

Anything in your life that is exotic, Jonas?

Oh, yes – where I live is very exotic. A definition of exotic is Raynes Park.

Rare for Jonas Merrick to laugh out loud, but he often remembered that exchange when thinking of the craft battering its way towards the Spanish coast, and what its progress meant for so many. But then the grin would freeze on his face because they had moved on from "exotic" to the news of the day, and the words that had skipped up on his screen. *We had this guy who was what you call a Confidential Human Intelligence Source. We had him to report on progress on the submarine thing they were building. Had a business selling paint in the market at Leticia. He missed a call which meant he was blown. We managed to get a drone up some days later but that took a hell of a risk. He was in the water, and fish were nibbling at him. The camera showed his face and the fish had not yet started there. We missed the launch and didn't catch up with it until it was almost into the ocean. Win some and lose some, my creed. Pity about that, about the guy.*

Jonas reckoned that Nikko might carry the responsibilities better than he, Jonas Merrick, was able to. They burdened him more each hour of each day, responsibilities for manipulations of the lives of some he knew and some he did not. He hurried, and reckoned he would catch his train. It would be bad for those on the semi-submersible, his reading of the forecasts west of Biscay.

As the light dipped, Matias took the watch.

It was darker when they plunged into the gullies between the swell, and darker still when the waves closed over the windows set flush in the cockpit, and each time that happened Emiliano would let out a little squeal, and Diego would offer up an obscenity ... When Matias was taking the watch, clinging to the stanchions, he was silent, holding his breath and counting, feeling the roll and hearing the creaking strain on the superstructure and wondering if it would ever right itself, flatten out and he would see sunlight or even clouds. He could not swim. Matias had believed he needed the money so greatly that the cash would remove any chance of him refusing the offer. He was the engineer, responsible for keeping the engine in working order. He was the one-eyed in a place of the blind. Diego, the captain and the navigator, would not have known one end of the engine from another. Emiliano had a pregnant girlfriend and was likely to have his throat slit by the girl's family if he was not there to marry her in the Catedral de Nuestra Señora de la Paz on his return – Matias thought it a fine church and liked to be in the tower of an evening, away from his workshop, and see the parrots and the swallows return to their nests and roost there, and ... if the engine failed Emiliano could not repair it. It depended on Matias and they were lost if he were swept away. One faint light threw a wavering beam behind him and from that he had to read the compass bearings. He had almost lost count of the days since they had left the river delta, three weeks perhaps, and one more week to go and it was Matias's belief that the weather would further deteriorate as they rolled and plunged, seemed to tip almost to the point of capsizing, and rose again. There were moments when the nose went down and the *Maria Bernarda* assumed such an angle that the propellers were out of the water and thrashed at the air and screamed. If the engine failed and he could not fix it, he would drown, and the others with him.

He said some prayers, but quietly, and sang some hymns, but to himself. Diego had said they would reach land in a week and he did not know if he could last that long with his nerves shredded and his bowels emptied and his body battered. And they went down again, nose first, and the darkness came again and the sky was lost and he clung to a bar for support and did not dare count how long since he had lost sight of the crests of the waves . . .

She had to hold tight to the easel's legs.

If she held the easel with one hand then it was hard for her to use the crayon gripped in her right fist. She thought he would come, expected him to. He would lock up his business, hang out the sign to say he would be open again in the morning. If it were waved in front of them, what she had to offer, they usually came.

The wind seemed to have shifted. It came more from the north and less from the west. She heard the siren on the lighthouse and the gulls' screams and the hammering of the waves against the base of the cliffs below her, but she heard no engines. Had listened but her efforts were rewarded only by the birds and the waves and the siren cry and sometimes by a sound like singing that came when the single low tree nearest to her was caught by a gust of wind.

She did not think she would complain when he did come. In her life, Anna Jensen was low on the number of men with whom she might share a little of her time. Not much of her life, because most of it was masked, but some. There had been no man since she had come from Rotterdam, the last workplace in her own country, and had seemed to drift with her art for company to Galicia. The last man who had sought to own Anna had been a professor at Hague University, anthropology or something like that, who wanted to own her, and pompous after first being amusing: she had ditched him, binned like a pair of old knickers. She quite liked Kenny – which made it more of a problem.

★   ★   ★

He had found her car, which had been enough to guide him to her.

Kenny Blake could not for the life of him imagine why she stayed out on a headland near to the Cape Finisterre lighthouse, which was only identifiable by the muffled shout of its siren and by the dulled rotating flash of its light.

He would not have said she had any particular talent as an artist whether she were using crayon or oil paint or watercolour. He assumed that with the harshness of the coastline, cliffs and gullies and inlets that led to beaches or to narrow fast-flowing rivers, oil and crayon would be the best for her. He had asked her way back, when they had first met up on the cliffs where she had lugged her easel and her materials box and the tripod stool, whether she sold much. Rude, if he thought about it, to ask her such a question. She said, self-deprecating, that she did best in the summer, when the tourists were on hand and they might have taken out their purses because they felt sorry for her, or because she was a good-looking girl and therefore some pleasure came from seeing her smile.

He looked over her shoulder at what she had created that day.

She grimaced, then muttered something about needing to stock up on work during the off-season months. She'd be behind a collapsible table in Corunna or at Pontevedra when the Germans came, or her fellow Dutch. The answer to Kenny was clear enough. A bit of a spoiled brat, and indulged, and she'd have had a decent stipend and was allowed to mess with life as a working artist, and find a place on the headlands.

He looked into a wall of mist. There was a powerful wind but it failed to shift the density of it. There had been enough ships over the centuries to have capsized here and the lighthouse lamp and the siren were more than justified. There was no threat in her picture. A view over heather that was coming into flower and then on to a rock face above which gulls wheeled, and then white caps, and a promontory where the lighthouse had been built . . . Chief among the casualties Kenny knew of was the British ship, HMS *Captain*, that had gone down off here in 1870, within sight of

these masked rocks and reefs, biggest loss of life from any wrecked
vessel on the Costa de Morte, 482 drowned and only 27 survivors
when she finally rolled over. Or HMS *Serpent*, the most modern
warship in Britain's fleet, that had impaled itself on the rocks in
1890 in another of those fearful storms and broken up in an hour:
172 crew lost and three had lived. Anna's work that day showed
none of the ferocious turns that gales and heavy fog could lead
to ... which he supposed was the reason for the strength of the
sea-navigating heritage that the people had here – which in turn
made them such hellishly good importers. And today's trade was
in cocaine, and was the reason why Kenny Blake lived here.

"Very good," he said.

"Do you lie?"

"Never been known to. Honest as the day I was born."

"And you came to find me? Finished your work and came to
look for me? Why?"

"Pretty obvious. Does it need spelling out? Had a hard day,
need a drink, then need something to eat ... Would like to do the
drinking and eating with you, and . . ."

"And?"

"And whatever blows in over the horizon."

He liked the shrug she did, as if it were not a matter of the
greatest importance. And another lift of her shoulders, and a little
wry smile. The paper she was working with went into her bag with
the crayon box and the stool, and the easel legs were kicked
together then hitched up on her shoulder. He offered to help but
she declined, as if making it plain that she did not need him. But
she put her hand into his bent elbow and they started out back
along the path. The wind jolted them forward. The day it was due
to end, the Friday of the following week, was the day before Kenny
Blake's birthday, would be his 30th. She had a firm hold on him,
as if it were useful to enjoy that support on the uneven path and
especially when they were close to the cliff's edge, and her hair
flew wide and tickled his face.

Eleven years before, on his 19th birthday, he had joined the
police, gone in as the rookie recruit. Had left his home in the

Berkshire town of Newbury, had been waved off by his mum and dad, had gone on his motorcycle to the training camp used by the Thames Valley force. Had been at a comprehensive, moderate marks, no love of learning, and had thought himself blessed as the wind careered around him. Not long after that birthday he had found that disappointment was cruel. Was bored, and unimpressed with the men and women who controlled the uniformed units in the city of Reading. Of course there were interesting squads, but he did not get to work with them. Did a few "domestics", did plenty of "anti-social", handed out crime prevention leaflets – and manipulated the system after a year and had himself "borrowed" by CID and volunteered to let his hair grow and stop shaving and rub flour into his face so that the colour left him, and was given a run on the Oxford Road. Had an advance of cash, signed for in triplicate, and could buy. Was not supposed to hear it, but two members of a drugs team had been talking of him: "A bucketload of self-belief, an arrogance and independence, and another bucketload but that's charm." Went off the Oxford Road and into the Whitley estates on the west side of the town, and was making progress and small fry were being sent down by the Crown Court, and he had his sights on some of the bigger fish, wanted more time, demanded more financial support for buying, and had the row. Found himself on the periphery of the force's narcotics unit, out of Reading and attached to Headquarters. Had the row. Less of the charm and more of the arrogance. The big man in that year's drug squad wanted better statistics for the Thames Valley area. Good arrest rates came from pulling in small fish – big fish, kings in the pond, came slowly and came pricey. A bit of a serious row . . . he was now attached to CID full time but was not much distant from being a probationer and was never going to win the equivalent of a bare-knuckle fight with a superintendent. And . . . and was newly married to Hannah, and Eddie was on the way. And . . . whatever his name was then, he did not step aside and let seniority have its way. Did some more time, welcomed little Eddie, began to see the bump grow on Hannah's belly that would eventually be Joanne, and turned his back on the local force and joined the Metropolitan up in London. Did a bit of uniform, like it was necessary to have his feet under the table, and applied to join SC&O10 who he thought were the cream of all policing. He was just 23, which was ridiculous when he was called in by Specialist Crime and Operations 10 for an interview, and still looked young and the job had not yet aged him. What had aged was the marriage.

They came together off the coast path and went down a slight hill and there was a small parking area and only their cars, and the mist showed no sign of thinning or lifting and he could still hear the siren call . . . Just a week to go, but he thought he had fallen on his feet, and was lucky as hell to have met her, a piss-poor artist but a quite lovely girl. Just a week to the exit call and perhaps time to let a thought of the future germinate a bit. They said, the men and women who taught the Level Ones, that distraction was dangerous, should be avoided, and romance was about top of the list of negatives – but it would be over in a week, all of it.

He said where they could eat. She agreed. Did she need to go home first? She did not. Had fallen well on his feet, and maybe he was owed that.

Supper eaten and cleared away, Vera with the crossword, and Jonas with his briefcase beside him, a couple of files already taken out and laid on a coffee table, and Olaf, contented, on his lap.

When Jonas was due to return to work, ready to step out with his hat and coat on and his lunch loaded in the same old briefcase, with the Thermos chained to his wrist from habit, Vera had demanded, "You'll not do anything stupid? Not again?"

He had answered her, "I have no intention of acting stupidly, rashly, recklessly. No intention."

Quite a bold statement for Jonas Merrick to make, even in the safety of the snug off the kitchen of their semi-detached 1930s home in this London suburb. He had left the house and had not looked back. He would not have been allowed beyond the front door had it not been for his assurance. He had put her through several degrees of hell since being carted home, half drowned, and with a prime target missing . . . Some had called it fortunate that the target was not available to be put through the courts in a grandstand display of spook failure and treachery: others wanted her locked away, the key thrown to the winds . . . And then the possibility had arisen that she was safe and well, in the control of her Russian handlers and babbling names and secrets which would have put Jonas in their cross hairs. If he had had to appear in court then chance was Vera would also have been a potential casualty.

He read and stroked Olaf's head and the big beast rumbled with pleasure.

Police had come to live with them. Two nights it had lasted. A team had examined the house. Had checked the windows and shaken their heads at the glass-fronted cabinet where ornaments were displayed, and talked about the dangers of flying glass if a hand grenade had exploded there, had shown their disapproval of the thin curtains in the front bay and had suggested that thicker lining was needed, were dissatisfied with the locks. And had wanted to come outside when Olaf was put out last thing. They had taken over the snug, piled their kit – and guns and ammunition – on the central rug, and had talked about the tumbler wires that would have to go round the rear garden and the cameras that would be installed. The next morning, Jonas had come down to make tea for himself and Vera, and both the guards had been asleep and the room stank from their broken wind . . . Worst of all were their contemptuous glances at the little items in the cabinet, which were important to Jonas and Vera.

That night matters had come to a head, the ground floor already reeking from their use of the microwave to heat up curries – "Jeez, Pam, you'd expect this to be in a museum" – and Olaf had defiantly taken his place in his usual chair. Pam's partner was Charlie. Charlie reckoned it was his right to sit in an easy chair, but it was already occupied by the cat. Jonas was on the boil. Vera would never complain but wore a knitted frown and they were in the front room and the inadequate curtains were drawn tight, and a scream had rent the house. A scream of shock and of pain. Charlie, heavy in his bulletproof vest and with his holstered Glock bouncing on his thigh and his H&K hanging over his vest, had reached out to push the cat from the chair and Olaf's fangs had fastened on his hand and had bitten down hard. He had drawn blood, then had raked Charlie's wrist with the claws on his front paws, then rolled on his side and had ripped his hand with the claws on his back feet. Only when Jonas appeared did the cat retract his claws and drop the bloodied hand.

Jonas had said, "You were lucky. Last red meat he had was a full grown mouse, all eaten bar the tail. Very fortunate."

They had picked up their kit and decamped to their vehicle parked in front of the house. That level of protection was withdrawn. It was reported to them that the police officer had spent some hours at the local hospital awaiting treatment. Vera, normally a kindly person, had given Olaf extra food that night. Help, they were told, would be close at hand, and a phone number was given to them.

Jonas gutted the files, learning the lives of the families.

He kept in his mind the image of the gaunt young man leaning against a shop's doorway and who lived a permanent lie and whose safety remained on the edge . . .

. . . and thought of a woman who betrayed trust and ran a small travel agency . . . and thought of a couple who had allowed their home to be used as a vantage point . . . He moved his hand from the cat's neck and fiddled with his phone's keypad and learned the latest positioning from the satellite of the semi-submersible's progress . . . and saw the weather forecast for the Atlantic, gales coming in from the south-west . . . And he had been sent an image of the damaged corpse recovered from the Amazon . . . and another of Nikko in full US-style combat gear, holding an M16 rifle and with the DEA initials on a forage cap . . . He sat in his chair, his cardigan buttoned and wearing his slippers . . . and opposite him, Vera had permitted herself a slight chuckle of pleasure and was busy filling in a solved clue.

He said, "Of course, it's only a backwater where the present kerfuffle is but they've put a clerk in charge of sorting it out. That's me, what they think of me, a clerk."

"They can call you what they want, Jonas, but I retain your promise that you will do nothing stupid."

"Nothing further from my intentions than stupidity."

3

"Just going to walk down to the station for a paper."

Jonas stood at the bottom of the stairs and waited for an acknowledgement. The vacuum cleaner was switched off.

A reply, tart, from Vera. "Why?"

"To collect a paper I ordered."

"Is it the caravan one?"

"No, it is not."

A pause. He had his mackintosh on and belted, his tweed jacket underneath and his brogues on his feet, and his trilby low on his head. Just as he appeared on the five days in the week that he went to work, except that he had no briefcase, nor the bracelet chain fastening it to his wrist. He had never before gone to buy a newspaper from the railway station on a Saturday morning.

"Well, just off then – won't be long."

Rather plaintive from the landing, but laced with suspicion. "You're not up to anything stupid, Jonas? You promised me . . ."

"Just getting a paper – nothing stupid."

Which was a denial that he ever contemplated stupidity, though Jonas would not have admitted that the disarming of Winston Gunn and the capture of Cameron Jilkes – both gaining him Queen's Gallantry Medal recognition – and the attempted arrest of the Sixer girl and the resulting dunking in the Thames, *were stupid*. The vacuum cleaner was switched back on. Was he believed? Perhaps, perhaps not . . . He smiled at the cat, his comrade in arms, went out through the front door, shut it quietly, walked past the parked caravan – with its new and expensive rewiring – and set off along the pavement.

His neighbour, Derbyshire, was running a leather over his car, a Honda, his pride and joy. Derbyshire worked for a company selling soundproofed glass for conservatories. They had little contact other than polite greetings outside. The same that morning. To Derbyshire and his wife, Jonas would have been "the original miserable old prat", and Vera "a saint, has to be to put up with him". Might have gone through Derbyshire's mind to wonder where Jonas Merrick was going that Saturday morning, but he would get no explanation. Nor had he been offered one when Jonas had warranted armed police presence in his home, and heavy bags were being ferried inside. Jonas had shrugged, said nothing, Vera had only offered that it was "something of nothing, only a bit of this and that". After that first week the operation seemed to have been abandoned. Perhaps Derbyshire's wife had suggested "Could be that he's actually very special, secret, spooky," and perhaps Derbyshire had retorted, "If Merrick's a definition of a Secret Service officer then God alone help us."

News of him would have been passed over garden fences on both sides of the street and he would have been a source of bewilderment and amusement. They were all honourable and decent people, as far as he knew, and he was charged to protect them. He was an officer, or a *clerk*, in the Security Service, motto *Regnum Defende*. He was paid to keep them safe – safe from bombs, safe from hostile espionage, safe from the ravages of cocaine addiction – but it was rare for him to allow his work to insinuate into his weekend . . . Normally he would be tinkering on the caravan.

He reached the station, and explained to the woman behind the counter that he had ordered the Saturday edition of the *Liverpool Echo*.

It was searched for and found. He paid for it and it was handed over. He started to scan it . . . could, of course, have taken all he wanted off the digital edition but Jonas Merrick preferred paper, was unlikely to change the habit.

The woman quizzed him. "Staying in touch? You from there? I've an aunt who . . ."

Jonas was averse to chatter. He lied. "No, it's for my wife."

He started to retrace his walk. Saturday, he had been told, was always good for "crime" stories, and he was not disappointed. Drugs cash had been seized – "bad" heroin was being peddled in the city – armed police had arrested two pensioners and retrieved a hand gun – more drugs than usual were circulating in local gaols – a man had had his arms slashed as his £55,000 Rolex was snatched. He read as he walked home. Had never been to Liverpool, no reason to. Thought the paper, a tabloid, gave him a whiff of its scent. No requirement for him to have lied, but he had. And no requirement for him to have scratched at Vera's anxiety. "Nothing stupid." Would he change the world with his work? Hardly . . . Just a job and he was paid to perform it – paid reasonably well for his low civil service grade and they lived almost frugally, and a useful pension awaited him. When he reached home, Derbyshire's car was a picture of polished splendour. He dropped the paper, mostly unread, into his wheelie bin.

He told Vera, who had the vacuum downstairs and was doing the snug, that he was making coffee. The cat scowled at him, at her. He said he was going to the caravan, carried Olaf out, and his mug, and unlocked its door. After what Jonas had had to pay after mouse damage to the cabling, the cat was given the run of the caravan once a week to do "search and destroy". He shut the door after him, let the cat begin roaming and sniffing, and took out his phone.

He dialled, heard the ring tone, then the connection was made. Had a blast of music in his ear. Heard a woman's voice.

"For God's sake. Turn it down . . . yes, down. No, correction, turn that fucking music off . . . Yes, Fanny Thomas here. Right, this is my work phone and it is Saturday morning and . . . Switch it off, off . . . So, who is calling me?"

"Jonas Merrick."

His idea of a biscuit tin was like those that his mother bought for aunts or older cousins, who were only seen once a year so a gift was in order. The tin's contents, shortbread or chocolate biscuits, would be finished within a week or so and then the tin would take on greater value. Items of value could be kept there, hidden away. Part of Kenny Blake's sales pitch involved the concept of the biscuit tin – *La Lata de Galletas* – and it had been enjoyed by the early clients.

A small wooden sign beside the street door advertised the services of a financial investor, and his name and impressive initials that could be backed up with documentation, and flyers were on the counter in the café and some portrayed a biscuit tin with a display of roses in bloom and others of a picture postcard view of an English village.

They said in the courses run for Level One officers in SC&O10 that the most effective route into an Organised Crime Group – into the closed world of the clan or the family – was through the money trail. Off season, remote rural hotels were taken over, their staff reduced to a minimum, and the Level Ones would come and those who taught them; and the route taken by the money was highlighted as the one area where the family might have to open its doors, share secrets, call in outside help, because the expertise was beyond them. *Never forget the greed factor. Quite naked greed. Always wanting the best rate and return on an investment, but don't have the skill to do that for themselves. Stay with their own people and they'll likely be ripped off or buy bad. They are practised at negotiating deals and shipments, and rates for the distributors, and can do their enforcement – handing out the heavy punishment, all in the interest of maintaining fear, discipline, authority – but handling the money is the weak point, likely to be the unprotected heel.* At their expense, Kenny – then his name, and working on the legend to support it – had gone off to a north-east business college to learn the handling of money, and its movement, then had gone for six intense weeks to an investment management company, in the financial heart of London. Other students had partied and then crammed as exams approached, and other newcomers to the company had drifted away to the wine bars in the late afternoons but he had kept sober, had stayed at his desk until mid-evening. If the rest of them flunked exams they'd have their knuckles rapped and have to sit them again; if Kenny failed to pass the tests he would likely have his throat cut, after his fingernails had been taken off with pliers. At home he had become a stranger.

Kenny did not talk about his new life, or discuss with Hannah what his work involved. He was barely there to share the parenting of Eddie, and soon to be Joanne. Most weekends he went home, a two-bedroom flat in Newbury and close to his mum and dad, dead-drop tired and slept on the sofa . . . If a door slammed he reacted fast and rolled into a protective posture, eyes wide; once a car had backfired when he was pushing Eddie in a buggy and he had been down on his knees, his body draped over the child. Conversations with Hannah seemed to get interrupted because neither knew how to conduct them and both would give up. Silences ever longer. Laughter ever rarer. When he left to go back to work, with the clothes that fitted the job in a holdall – ready to change into them at the toilets at the station – and the growth on his cheeks, it shamed him that the adrenaline rush was surging. Or going to a Level One course in the Hampshire training centre, or to the airbnb in Pimlico where he was put for the company stint, then he reckoned he walked tall and with purpose. Would have helped if he could have told Hannah but that was a capital offence as far as his instructors were concerned. "Very unwise. To be avoided," from the unit psychologist. The marriage was a casualty. None of the handlers seemed to think that a big deal. A marriage flushed down the pan . . . most of them were.

His dad had said to him, "Can't tell you how to live your life, son, but . . . but . . . it's powerful grief you're making."

His mum had said, "I don't know what you do or where you go. Just hope you think it worthwhile."

He accepted he made the grief, told himself it was worthwhile.

On that Saturday morning, in Corunna, he was at work. Difficult to accept was that the next Saturday morning he'd be in a cabin on the ferry out of Santander, midway across the Biscay, and a few more hours before docking at Plymouth – and an end to the Level One life lived in the name of Kenny Blake. Worth being at work on a Saturday because usually clients came in off the street and up the stairs, no appointment, and some had money in a plastic supermarket bag and some had it in their purses and some had it in wads in their hip pockets. Some came boldly, some furtively. Some had hardly enough cash to cover the bottom of a biscuit tin and some, a very few, brought it in by the sackload.

He was not himself that Saturday morning, but it was not every Friday night that he entertained. He had drunk a bit, not too much, and gone to bed early, but had hardly slept. Had held her and had sweated with her, and had been fearful that he would lose her – which meant that it was a time of maximum danger. He was with his third client of the morning, and needed to maintain the calm sales pitch, to drip honesty. This was a fisherman, a man who did long lines off a rowing boat beyond a harbour wall on the approach to the Nueva Dársena, and did well enough out of mackerel and black bream and squid to think it worth putting aside some of the rewards, and would have heard that this young man – with good enough Spanish and understanding the dialect – was to be trusted, had integrity. Would have been fatal to Kenny's survival if he had seemed uninterested, and a client had left in annoyance and passed the word around that the investment manager seemed to have a different agenda. The fisherman brought a thousand euros.

Kenny was finding it hard to concentrate. He was thinking too much of the Dutch girl, and jumbled in those thoughts were the sounds of the arguments he had had with Hannah and the crying of the little boy when their voices were raised.

A piece of paper was passed between them. A standard photo-copied form. The client's name and contact details – not advised to write in Mickey Mouse, but pretty much anything was accept-able – and the sum to be invested, and their signatures: his was fast and not more than a scribble, and the fisherman's was laboured. The cash would go into the safe. The instructors preached that the time of maximum danger was when an arrest was imminent, when the shipment was close, when suspicion was rife . . . He could not remember another day when he had so much wanted to make a future with a girl, and had a fear that she'd not share it.

He thanked the fisherman. Kenny would be well clear when he realised his biscuit tin offering was included in the paperwork submitted to the Agencia Estatal de Administración Tributaria. Thanked him and escorted him to the door, and had another client waiting. In the doorway, the fisherman hugged him momentarily, a gesture of total trust, and went off down the stairs.

Kenny would have said it was not in his make-up to concern himself with the deceit bred in his job. He was just a policeman going about his daily work. Would have said that . . . and lied.

Fanny Thomas never had, at home, the respect that was given her in the Serious Crime Unit because of her rank of Detective Chief Inspector. Was she going on holiday with them, or was she not? Going with her husband and her three kids, or not? A guesthouse in the Lakes, going to be there or not? How the fuck did she know . . . and breakfast not cleared away and all of the family glowering at her. She had fielded a call from Jonas Merrick – and her phone was pinging message alerts – and the house not cleaned, and . . . she rang a true friend. Just in case she started to chuck the crockery round the kitchen.

"Jimbo? Thank God you picked up. Jimbo, I have to speak to you. I just had that little bugger on the phone. The Box man. Called himself by a code. Thought he was Jonas something. Said this morning, Saturday bloody morning, that he was 3/S/12. What does that mean? Three Ess Twelve. Not a request but a fucking statement. Whatever I learn of the Govier crowd I am not to pursue, not to share, except with him. Fuck's sake, the Govier crowd are my chief target. My team is dedicated to bringing them down. Except he says that I am to do nothing until I am told, given my instructions, only then I am permitted to react. He rings off. I mean, what is Box doing pissing about over a lowlife Scouser family? When did Box give a toss about cocaine importation? Are the Russians bringing in Class A? Are ISIS doing it? No explanation offered. I rang the Boss. Out on the bloody golf course. Gave him an earful . . . Reckon half the green heard it. He says I am to do as I'm told, instructed, demanded – can call it *requested* if that soothes my ego.

"You know me, Jimbo, I do not have an ego. Not one of my faults. Jimbo, we've been working on the Goviers for two years. You know and I know, they are pure evil, twenty-five-carat bad, and I'm told to back off, do nothing, sit on my hands, and . . . There's allotments out on the Southport side and there's a stiff turned up there. Hard to recognise because of what was done to him. I don't have the pathology yet, but the word is that his hands and feet and face had some rearranging done. There was a CHIS gave us stuff last week. But vague and hadn't heard it himself. What he said, apparently, there was a dealer mouthing off in a bar, and was full of unwise insults directed at the mother. That's Doloures and she is seriously horrid . . . You know that, Jimbo, course you do . . . I don't have confirmation but I'll bet my next pair of clean undies that it'll be the dealer who ended up with the leeks and the spuds. Except I can't do anything. You had the same business? Your CHIS, in the travel shop, didn't you get a block on sharing? Jimbo, what is going on?

"I cannot track an OCG on a five days a week shift, with built-in office hours, and we're supposed to be on holiday at the end of the week.

"Is it, Jimbo, that you don't know or aren't saying? And your CHIS, Jimbo? Are you going to tell me what she is spouting, or not? I just might go down to London, dig the little bastard out and fucking strangle him . . . I would take it bad if I failed to nail that family, if I was obstructed. Who are these people at Box? What is the picture they're seeing which is too God Almighty important for me to know about?"

They were doing casts and photographing the newest tyre prints in the allotment car park and the recent rain was a bonus. Fanny Thomas arrived after a careering rush round the supermarket. She parked. Her car was a 3-series BMW, and she'd fitted top-range audio stuff. A bit of defiance. Had bought it in the weeks after an OCG trial and a good result for the team, though she had missed a school prize-giving and a soccer cup final. The car, leather seats, gave her the bottle feel, the balls, to keep going in the dark times. Some clever joker had once said, *Things are going to get a lot worse before they get worse,* and she'd not argue it. She loved that car.

No popularity polls for the forensic people because the gardening folk were not permitted entry, and Saturday morning was the most popular time for the diggers and rakers.

"How long will you be?" they asked.

"As long as I need," was the sergeant's answer.

Fanny Thomas was taken to see the body. She walked briskly between the plots, some a shambles of weeds, and some kept proudly and might be producing prize-winning entries. She was told a wheelbarrow had been used to ferry him from the car park to where he was tipped out.

"He's not pretty, ma'am."

"Neither am I, and expect we've seen worse."

"Maybe, ma'am, but not often ... It's the work of a right animal."

She did the dressing up, boots and gloves and a wraparound apron. They approached the tent and stepped on to a path of plastic duckboards. The full team was there, and a flashlight illuminated the interior and a camera was clicking.

"I'm not in a hurry to shift him," she said. "We'll get it right, not be in a rush. Won't bore you with the politics that are going on around me – and you're just so damn lucky, Joe, that it's above your head – but I am not permitted, because of other investigations that outrank me, to grab a warrant and go haul in who I would like to. So, we do it by the book . . . not forgetting the camera feed in their street, possible gold dust, possible rubbish."

She saw the congealed blood, the bruised and closed eyes, saw the finger stumps, saw a leg angle away to the right and the bone splintered and sharp enough to have punctured the trouser leg. The smell was bad, urine and faeces, but no one was going to complain that the poor blighter's bowels and bladder had given out on him . . .

She had history with this family. Had put Mikey Govier away, when she'd been given the lead in the interrogation suite, had him nailed on a conspiracy to murder that ranked top of a useful list, and the judge had liked her and had done a tariff that was about as good as she'd hoped. Mikey Govier had looked round at her, and she was a detective sergeant then, just before he was taken down. There had been a smirk on his face. Seemed to say, "I know where you live, darling, know the street and know the number." Might have done, might not. She had bolts and extra locks put on the doors and windows, but her husband and the kids thought them tiresome. Her own assessment – Mikey Govier was over-rated. Top of the tree was his wife. Two kids who would not make the grade on any Most Wanted list, and then there was Xavier, who they called Bengal.

Bengal stood back from the window, against the far wall, no light on. He shouted for his sister to come.

A grey morning, with a wind that scattered the dead leaves on the street and pushed them up from the kerb and over the pavement and left them to rest against the low wall. She called back that she was helping their Ma.

His home was in a new block in the city centre, near the Town Hall, what the property people called "prestigious". A two-bedroom place with a concierge and underground garage, but crawling with cameras. He was there most nights, sometimes with company and sometimes on his own, but came back to the family place with a plastic bag full of his laundry, and to raid the freezer for microwave meals. He told her, snarled it, to get off her arse and come to him.

As well as where he had been and what he had done the previous afternoon, was the matter of the trip his Ma planned. They were a divided family . . . Ma and Patrick were for it, Theresa he rated as too dumb to understand where it led, himself and his Dad were against it. And there was the business of what he saw from where he stood against the back wall of the living room – and the carpet had not been relaid well but would have to do and the floorboards creaked and he could have sworn the space underneath made an echo effect even with the pile – and looked out, and it needed a car to pass, going left to right. She came. Usually did when he had that whip in his tone.

He told her what they were looking for. They waited for a car. He unwrapped a stick of gum, peppermint flavour, and gave it her and told her to start chewing. He thought she read him well enough to do it, not argue . . . Ma called and wanted Theresa back. He told her. Theresa was coming back when he'd finished with her. Both of them quiet, both waiting for a car or a delivery van, any vehicle that came down their road with its headlights on because it was a dull and dreary day, and not about to brighten up. The couple emerged from the house opposite. None of the family ever spoke to them. No cause to. They had been gawping from behind the curtains when his dad was taken away, armed police and all that shit, and a photographer from the *Echo* brought along for the ride. The couple went out every Saturday, usually for three or four hours, a routine. A car came . . . an old car. Came slowly. Good that it was not speeding, and the headlights lit the road surface. And the light spread. He had told her what to look for, and where to look for it, and he heard the gum squelching in her mouth.

A flash of light. Looked like a raindrop had somehow attached to the wall and had positioned itself in the mortar.

"Saw it?"

"Got it."

"How many bricks up? How many bricks along from the gate?"

Convenient that a weed grew close to the point they'd identi-fied, would act as a marker, was the only weed that the man opposite had missed, now had a use. She took the gum out of her mouth, slipped it into the hip pocket of her jeans.

Jak Peters heard a growling voice which had something of Liverpool and something of the Republic. Recognised it.

"Mister Peters?"

"I am."

"And I am . . ."

"I know who you are."

"I am looking for help."

"If that is within my remit."

"Do not, Mister Peters, I beg of you, play feckin' pedantic bollocks with me."

"I don't play games. Nor am I usually able to be helpful. Try me."

"There was that auction. My force bid for a Level One. We wanted finance. Had three or four families that were kind of flexing and looking to go higher into the markets and the Galicia coast seemed a decent bet."

"Don't find nostalgia helps me through my day. What do you want?"

"We, that is the Merseyside force, put our shirt on getting a financial man into the Galicia territory. We wanted eyes on the ground and ears. We reckoned that finance offered us a flight path. I'm not pissing about. This guy is my man. I feel good about him, except that where he went was violent and dangerous. You had responsibility for his safety and you'll back my assessment. He does a couple of years. He should have come out. I recommended that he was brought home."

"Getting tedious, Mr Rawe, and repetitive."

"What I heard . . . he was all lined up to leave, close his business down, return to civilisation, and from where he had been it was the least he deserved. Except that he was persuaded otherwise. Pressure was put on him. Finance was reckoned as the families' weak place, am I right? He had done his time and would have been getting vulnerable: his work was useful in the prosecution of the Coveneys and the Symonds groups. Box stepped in. Those feckers have no morality, and less mercy and no charity. Box leaned on him and he accepted an open-ended extension. My opinion, sincerely held, Mister Peters, is that you should have stamped your foot, safeguarded your man. You were his control, you were SC&O10, you were running him – should have told Box to feck off. The pressures on him would have been intolerable, and pressures lead to mistakes."

"I am not a bloody social worker."

"Mister Peters, you have responsibilities and should not shirk them."

"If he doesn't like it he can always transfer to Traffic, do the M25. How about that?"

"Are you shut out as well?"

"I am not sure that I can . . ."

"Outside that loop are you? Not allowed in the bubble? Are you?"

"I was in the loop. Not now. I no longer get intelligence that comes from him. I'm blanked."

Jak Peters was 38 years old. Married to Sophie. He wore a tie and a suit to work each day and was a regular in the control team of SC&O10. His wife earned, in a bad year, five times what he was paid. His children were Benjamin and Augustus and he and his wife managed to be home for their tea and helped with homework and after the boys were in bed, the couple would work on their laptops at the kitchen table. His wife lived for work, and he did too . . . A small matter but the move of Box to isolate him from Kenny Blake was the first – so far, only – major setback he had experienced. He saw the expenses claims, and saw the subsistence payments, but was no longer on a reading list for the reports sent in by the Level One officer. Jak Peters understood that he was a favoured outsider as far as Box's operation went.

He had been granted an audience: only once. He had been met at the south side of Lambeth Bridge, had crossed the river with an old guy dressed in charity shop finest, had had to take his arm to steady him as they crossed the bridge in pouring rain and a gale blowing. Had broken his normal rules of reticence and had talked against the bloody gulls and the bloody wind and the bloody traffic noise and the bloody chimes of Big Ben, had spilled what he knew and received nothing in return, had been "let go" at the bridge's far side. Thanked with bare courtesy and dumped.

"I am not in the loop. On Need to Know."

"You were trampled on."

"I put one scenario to him, something vague about imminent arrests – can't even remember clearly what it was. But I can remember the answer, 'Can neither confirm your assessment nor deny it.' Treated me like a temporary skivvy called in to help with scullery duties. But he seemed a rather humble little guy and I couldn't make out his status."

"He has status, pocketfuls of it. We tested it at Assistant Chief Constable level and were slapped down."

"What do you want of me?"

"What I want, Mr Peters, is . . ."

He was told. "And no more feckin' about, mind you."

The cat had completed its rodent check, had shouted at the closed door, had been let out and had returned to the house. Jonas Merrick sat alone on the bench seat, and contemplated. A scenario played out in his mind and he found it comforting that a plan was forming.

It was warm inside the caravan but he kept his jacket on, his shirt collar buttoned and his tie knotted. The plan was dismissed, too early by a few days to be acted on immediately, but he was glad he had one. He marvelled at the qualities of the people into whose lives and activities he now sought to intrude – might get there with the swing of a pick axe or might use a scalpel. He would get inside them, deep enough to fracture and bludgeon and slice their lives and their organisations.

The source of marvel was their ability to run their empires. He had been more than three decades in the Security Service. Had seen it grow in terms of employment opportunities – not thinking of Aggie Burns's crowd stalking the *jihadis* and tracking the Russian diplomats and not thinking of the teams entering buildings for the "deep rummage" of files and leaving without a sign of their entry. Not thinking of the sophistication of bugging equipment and the abilities to hack computers; thinking instead of the bureaucracy required to keep the sharp-end Fivers on the road. Human Resources, Accounting, Requisitioning – from paper clips to bread rolls to laptops and carpets for the DG's suite ... Crowds of personnel trudged into work each morning, followed by an army of lycra-clad cyclists and joggers, and all there to keep the damn place merely ticking over.

How did they do it, the families? There were no Presidents, or Chief Executives or Financial Directors. But there would have been OCGs that, if legitimate, their business portfolios would have required medium-sized office towers of worker ants – investing, and planning the future deals, and paying pensions to former workers, and maintenance to the spouses of those who had died or were banged away in gaols. They could not have electronic trails nor bulging cardboard files – held everything in their heads . . . Remarkable, incredible.

Jonas gave one of his infrequent chuckles, and let it ripple. They would not have had him. Jonas Merrick, QGM and Bar, *clerk*, and resident of 3/S/12, relied on paper, would have been shown the door . . . Enough of the dreaming.

He could note that money had arrived in Corunna, sent by courier from Liverpool and had been moved on. Could note also that monies had been passed to the Biscuit Tin by the Munoz crowd. Very satisfactory. He had started with a blank sheet of paper. Had begun to scribble names, had filled a sheet. Had worked a contact list and been passed on and had learned. *They used to have great families on the Galician scene who dominated the smuggling trade, went from the necessities like penicillin, then into cigarettes, then into hashish, and finally fastened onto cocaine. They had a pedigree of either out smarting or buying up the state's investigators. They lived high on the hog in mansions – the Minanco or Oubina or Charlin clans – and became too big, too complacent, started filling the gaols. Look for the new people.*

Talked with the DEA and with FBI and with a Czech official at Europol, and the Vienna people at the UN Office of Drugs and Crime. *The modern people – the ones who concern us – are not into gold taps, fifteen-bedroom villas with a dozen bathrooms, and whores on tap and champagne at five grand a bottle. The ones who matter live quite humbly . . . Look for the new business elite, those who have trawlers and warehouses and a canning operation for quality seafood . . . who are good at staying beneath the radar. Except that their real assets are way, way above what they can legally declare.*

Had the conversations, interrupted by the hacking cough of a drugs liaison officer from Customs, and on long-term sick leave. *They will seem pretty ordinary. Won't flaunt it. Have the money but cannot use it for personal fripperies, because that would run the flag up the pole. Don't want to draw attention. Their bug is trading, cheating the system, and having power – addicted to power.*

An old Sixer, put out to grass after an expenses claim for educating his daughters at private school was declared as fraud, and him too sensitive to be banged up in a cell block and airing his grievances: *At the heart of it, power comes via the creation of fear. Fear is the currency of extreme violence. Up there, in Galicia, they cannot operate without the exercise of terror, the certainty of brutality ... A few newcomers are appearing, rising to the top of the pile. They are secretive, cautious, suspicious of anyone outside their immediate circle. Most times government agencies turn a man on the periphery of a clan, then the vengeance is swift and sweet: he dies, his family dies, the witness stand stays empty on the magic day ... I tell you, I would prefer to walk on hot cobblestones than go undercover and betray that lot. You wanted a name, I can give you three.*

And there was the man in an anti-narcotics unit, the Special Operations Command in Colombia's capital city, a soft voice over a secure phone, and telling the same story as Nikko had. *Go for the Munoz clan. The father is a vegetable and out of the game. The mother is the big shot, brains and looks and authority, and one boy who took the right grades at business school, and one who is the wild kid. Got that name? Munoz.* Had noted it, and the message had come through almost a year ago Kenny Blake was providing services for the family . . . and another message had reached Jonas that money from the Govier tribe had been delivered to the Biscuit Tin by the Munoz family. All knitting nicely, except for . . . "collateral, casualties, consequences" – a price to be paid.

Said it out loud: "Stay careful, Kenny, and stay safe."

Kenny Blake knew a part of the system, but only a small part.

He showed the client out of his office. Went down the stairs with her because she was elderly, needed a stick, and saw her on to the street. Little traffic that Saturday at midday and few people about, and no waiting customers. The café was closed, darkened ... and Fredo's cousin would about now be touching down at the airport for Bogotá. Like he was suffocated, like the world closed around him, like he was an agent of pain and a master at inflicting it. When the old lady was at the end of the street she smiled and gave him a wave, discreet because they shared a confidence, and he smiled back and nodded confirmation of it, and went back inside.

Her money – she had said there were 4750 euros in old bank notes, sizeable in her budget – would go into his safe. By the end of the week he would be ready for another shipment and, with the other deposits, it would be taken from the safe and loaded into the Samsonite case. Then a trip, after the line of verse had been texted to the Garden above the harbour where the elm trees were considered a feature and gave good cover, and the meeting with Hugo and Wilf. Another conversation about his security and indications of their growing anxieties, and the cases would be swapped and they'd slip away. The case would be taken by road towards Oviedo, and before Avilés was the Aerodromo La Margal which took light aircraft, and waiting would be a twin-engine Cessna, ostensibly there to cater for the few who could afford bespoke wildlife tours in the Picos de Europa. The distance between Avilés and the destination was some 400 miles, a direct course across the Biscay and a landfall on the island of Guernsey. British territory, and the benefit of useful tax regulations and banking from a back street in St Peter Port at premises which respected confidentiality.

The monies were handled by a team ... he knew no more. He did not deal with them. Kenny could presume only that the finances of his operation were supervised by the man with the quiet voice; sometimes he was Jonas, sometimes he was 3/S/12, sometimes he was just the voice, and always there seemed a concern for him that Kenny thought genuine, which was unsettling. The movement of his investors' finances, big and small, huge or miserly, indicated to this Level One the stakes of the game being played.

He rated Isabella Munoz as his most significant client. He went to get himself a roll and some cheese, would then drive back to Camariñas and kill the hours till darkness, until the girl could no longer paint on the cliffs. Reckoned Isabella Munoz would fight like a cornered rat if trapped, rated her reaction to betrayal would be ferocious.

All who knew of her regarded Isabella Munoz as formidable, not to be trifled with. And all who had learned of her – national politicians, local leaders, senior detectives, rivals in the cocaine trade, and men she dealt with who lived far away on the other side of the Atlantic – would describe her status as that of *matriarca*. She was a leader in her field.

Isabella was always well dressed. She wore clothes that showed off her body – well tended and showing no sign of the birth of two children – but were neither ostentatious nor vulgar. She had purchased her jewellery for herself, usually on visits to Madrid. Anyone who knew the finer detail of diamonds would recognise that she carried thousands of euros from her ears, around her neck, on her right wrist, on her ring finger. She wore the same style of clothes whether she was in the company of a politician, a businessman in the canning trade when she was bent over papers at house in conference with Sergio, if she were meeting in a darkened car park or in a Léon hotel room – with a power broker from Colombia, and when she was on a beach at dead of night among the flickering lights, and watching the shadows carrying the sacks from her son's speedboats.

Isabella Munoz, on that Saturday morning, was in her usual boutique in Pontevedra and being handed a simple but tasteful black dress. At 54 years old, she was nine years younger than her husband, the pathetic vegetable. Her father had been a trawler skipper who had netted more cocaine than fish, and he had taught Tomas Munoz the ways of the sea and its dangers and how its exploitation could bring rich rewards. Her father used to say, "Fuck the fish that come out of the sea in a net, fucking waste of time, get the white stuff up on board when the freighter drops it off. Fuck anything else". In her teenage years she had been the most sought after girl in Pontevedra, and some would claim also in Noia and Padrón and Cambados, and all the way down the coast to Vigo. Tomas Munoz had been chosen for her, thought by her father to be the future for the importation to Galicia of South American cocaine.

Only the owner of the boutique was with her; all the staff had been sent outside for an hour, to the coffee shops in the shadow of the Basilica de Santa Maria la Mayor. She liked the boutique, the owner understood her needs. She looked at herself in the mirror . . . the owner stayed silent. Other than by her sons, Isabella was never interrupted, no wise soul would seek to influence her, liberties were not taken. She tugged, pecked at the material with her fingers, gestured for the back zip to be lifted . . . Years back, it was said, the star entrepreneur of a Santiago business family had let his hand rest on the left cheek of her arse, and it was said that it was Laureano, then sixteen years old, who had called on the man at his home, taken a knife to his face, cut lines across his left cheek, disfiguring him for the rest of his days. A nod, she would take the dress, and she pulled it up and over her head and smoothed her hair. Many men, knowing of the collapse of Tomas, might have harboured ideas . . . many knew of that scarred face in Santiago – but they admired from a distance.

She came regularly to Pontevedra, for her hair that was dark and cut short, following the contours of her skull, and for the boutique. If a frown appeared on her face it was because of three other locations in the town, and the people who worked there. There was the gaol, La Parda, where her husband had been held twice before being shipped off to maximum security in the south. She had visited him, had found the experience humiliating. There was the Palacio de Justicia, a building of drab, tired stone on the Rua Rosália de Castro, bars on all the upper windows and little slits at pavement level to let minimal light into the cells. And there was the unremarkable office on Rua Joaquin Costa, a Spanish flag hanging limp over the main door, where GRECO people worked. Each time her husband had been arrested, convicted, sent away, it was by them. Tomas had been able to shrug his way through the process of investigation, sentencing, and locking up, as if it were a necessary evil of the trade – not Isabella Munoz. She knew she was a High Value Target to investigators, the tax police and to any of the ambitious prosecutors in the capital seeking to enhance their reputations: if a cell door clanged shut on her, all of them would celebrate.

She wanted two new dresses to augment her wardrobe. She had clients coming the next week from England, should have been here now except for the weather off the islands of the Azores. She expected them to be peasants.

Again the nod and a second dress was chosen. A gust of wind brought rain that hammered on the outside of the door. The blind was down but the sound was sudden, violent. A small TV screen on the counter showed the boutique entrance and the pedestrian precinct and figures running, rain bouncing off their knees.

She giggled and the boutique owner turned, startled, as if offence had been caused, or a mistake made . . . But Isabella was thinking about the Biscuit Tin. What was "put aside for a rainy day, because you never know when the Heavens will open". Felt confident in that boy, Kenny. She had, through him, a large biscuit tin, money stacked, far removed from the Panama investments, where she had taken a hit two years before, and the Caymans and the City of London, where the handling fees were robbery, and the armies of advisors were capable of ripping her trust into pieces. If all else failed her then she would have a biscuit tin for solace . . . a simple boy and not worthy of Laureano's hostility. She paid for her dresses. The rain slashed down as the blind on the door was raised.

Isabella picked up her bag of purchases, expanded a small umbrella. Did she want to be escorted to the car park? She did not. Felt anxiety because one shipment had gone down, and a hostage taken, and another shipment was delayed and those were times of danger.

★   ★   ★

Emiliano was at the wheel.

Behind him on the two bunks were Diego, their captain, and Matias, on whom their lives depended. More than the navigation, it was engine failure that would sink them.

Sometimes he was able to see the blue of the sky between the softening of the clouds but then it seemed the white caps covered the slit windows and he could not see again until the water sluiced down and the craft rose again from a trough.

He looked behind him. On the two bunks both men slept with their backs to him and he thought them exhausted, as he was. He was uncertain whether to wake them.

It could have been a gull, could have been a piece of debris thrown up by a spit of wind as a wave broke. Could have been an aeroplane that had found a hole in the cloud ceiling and had spotted them.

He did not see it again but thought he heard the engines but they were fainter and then lost, and he did not wake either Diego or Matias. He had little comprehension of the scale of the operation he was a minor part of – and of the numbers of people on both sides of the ocean who would benefit from its successful conclusion . . . And he did not understand the complexity and technology of the forces arrayed against any "successful conclusion" of the *Maria Bernarda*'s voyage.

The vessel rolled and ducked and climbed, and they pressed on.

His phone pinged with a message.

A satellite feed malfunction. The track of an almost submerged target had been lost. A search plane had been sent up.

Jonas Merrick believed himself blessed with the resources given him. He cringed. All out of his league. The Drug Enforcement Administration had the space on the satellite download booked and had lost the contact. He had done an electronic shrug, muttered about "better luck next time" and the state of the weather. A message sent in the DEA's name from Springfield, Virginia, reported the failure, reported also that a USAF search plane had taken off from the Air Force base at Lajes Field on Terceira, an island in the Azores archipelago, that it had flown in severe to adverse weather conditions and had briefly been rewarded with a cloud break, an opportunity to go lower, and had caught a fleeting glimpse of a craft that was half-submerged and half out of the water on a wave crest. A message accompanied a grainy monochrome photograph: *Not a good place to be in that type of transport. They will be enduring an uncomfortable ride. Still on schedule for a landfall on north-west Galicia coast night of Thursday/Friday next. Glad to be of help.* Coordinates were included, and it was signed off by a duty officer and copied on from DEA Operations.

He studied the image. It looked like a beast that had surfaced from the depths, the lens quality highlighting barnacles and rust and discolouration on the hull. He thought he identified a faint light shining from the back of the cockpit, whatever they called it. The photograph was evidence to Jonas that the scenario given him was true, all of it. Because of this sea creature, one man was already dead. He felt a sense of shame at the level of excitement it aroused in him.

He stood, patted down the cushions he had sat on. His plotting seemed reasonable.

He went into the house. Vera was repairing a tear in his pyjama jacket. She had suggested binning it and buying a new pair but he had urged her to have a last try. Beside his own chair was the book-case where the maps and atlases were kept. The road atlas he chose was a well-worn one, his favourite. He could not sit in his chair because the cat had taken his place, and was asleep.

Jonas said quietly, "I think we might be able to get away next week, with the caravan."

"I'm not owed leave this month." Vera worked in a small art gallery, more for love than for money.

"They're always very obliging," Jonas said, as if that fact was insufficient reason to ditch the prospect.

"Suppose I might manage a few days. When from?"

"The middle of the week. New territory for us. The north Wales coast. Go up across country and have a bit of time on a pleasant site."

"What's up there to interest you?"

"There are Roman bits and pieces and Iron Age settlements. Past Rhyl and Llandudno, beyond Conwy. I think we'd both like that."

"You're sure?"

"Be a welcome break . . ."

She stopped her sewing and stared at him. If she had asked him directly whether he planned stupidity, he would have followed his own mantra of *neither* confirming *nor* denying but he had puzzled her. Jonas started to delve into his archive of maps. He supposed he owed it to himself to be there at the kill, certainly owed it to all those now enmeshed in the web he wove.

Felt the duty call, as any clerk would have.

4

He had never seen a million pounds in cash. Found it hard to imagine in terms of its bulk. It would have been moved in a Samsonite case, about the size that people going away for a ten-day business trip might use. He wondered if Kenny had needed to sit on the case in order to close it. All a mystery to Jonas . . . At present rates, and he had recently been awarded a slight pay increase, it would take him two decades to make that kind of money. He corrected himself: more than two decades because both his tax and his pension contributions would have been deducted, and there was a further £1450 for his season ticket . . . He had little comprehension as to the life-changing effect such a sum would have on his life, and Vera's.

He had enjoyed his supper. Had made an excuse, a hollow one, and had again retreated to the caravan, ostensibly to check the toilet pan sealant. Vera seemed not to notice him go and was buried in maps and atlases, surveying what he had offered: sites of Roman civilisation were apparently to be found, and her interest was keen. In the caravan he could use his phone.

Jonas Merrick loathed weekends, except for those in the caravan. Preferred to spend his days in his cubicle, hidden behind the frosted glass walls of 3/S/12, within earshot of the conversations and laughter, sometimes raucous, of the surveillance people. Alone there, undisturbed, except by the occasional warbling summons of the telephone, he wove the webs or pulled strings tighter, or tied the netting that would trap opponents. A very satisfactory life for a man who would need more than 20 years to cobble together a similar sum of money as that in the suitcase that had been ferried from an airstrip in north-west Spain to the

Channel Islands. The power he now owned was intimidating . . . and the monies sloshing between the Organised Crime Groups was awesome.

Drug trafficking rewards, their sheer scale, dictated much of his planning. Some reckoned him parsimonious, others who had never seen him fork out cash thought him mean. Money made him nervous. He thought it could so easily, too easily, corrupt a person and the pursuit of it was, his opinion, distasteful. Not much money circulating in the *jihadi* world, no one getting rich on the back of it, and in espionage the Russians and the Chinese preferred "compromise" as a trigger for suborning a target rather than greed. Everything connected with crime was about money and the sums were too great for Jonas to find them real.

If the Goviers had sold up, released their assets, he assumed they would be able to fill many Samsonites. Assumed also that the clan in Galicia, on the raw Atlantic coast, could have doubled, trebled, or multiplied by ten that number of suitcases. And both families needed protection from law enforcement, and needed information on and obstruction of investigations and could pay for it, pay well. He hated that word, *corrupt,* about betrayal and deceit. This way of combating corruption was to maintain his own levels of secrecy, not to share, to let those prepared to deceive starve through lack of information. At this end he had cut out Fanny Thomas and Fergal Rawe and Jak Peters – and the Customs teams in Spain and the GRECO unit and the Finance Police. He had heard too often of raids failing, of seizures drawing a blank on finding a warehouse stripped and empty, of evidence going missing from secure offices. He had no trust . . . Would anyone ever offer Jonas Merrick a million in used notes? Would he take it? He scrubbed the question from his mind because thinking of it unsettled him.

He, of course, would not be the casualty from corruption, nor would Vera be. The casualty would be Kenny Blake. Had to be Kenny Blake if a worm wriggled in the heart of the Crime Agency or the Merseyside lot, or in the Spanish police buildings in Corunna or Pontevedra.

Vera would have imagined, that Saturday evening, that Jonas was in the caravan to clear the electrical wiring, to check the gas cylinder that powered the oven and the hot water, and see that the TV aerial was secure after the winter storms. She had given him the clean bedding to make up the foldaway bed, and he needed to make certain that spiders had not nested among the crockery and that the cutlery was not tarnished. He had done none of those important jobs, but had sat and had conjured up the face of his man, of Kenny Blake, and had felt waves of guilt. The man had been coming home. Had done two useful years but had achieved nothing outstanding. Would have been ticking off the days, would have been planning in his head for the 20-page report he would write of his key conclusions from doing Level One in Corunna. Would have had his bags, maybe even a Samsonite, pretty much packed. Would have been ready to switch off the lights, lock the door and go down the stairs, walk past his car and go to the bus station and buy a ticket for the Santander ferry and drop the office and car keys in any convenient bin. Would have been looking forward to the sleep of the nearly good on a bunk in a ferry cabin. And Jonas had rung him.

What Jonas had heard, when he had researched the role of a Level One, was that their psychologists regarded it as "criminal pressure" to persuade an undercover to cancel his exit and drift on without an end date in sight. Supposed that his soft voice, putting the "request" to hang on in there, would have sounded cold, merciless – quiet and persuasive, but brutal. Jonas had no pride and the weight of what he had done crushed him.

He sat in the caravan, his head resting on the pile of bedding. Only had a night light on ... They would not do "pomp and circumstance" funerals for an undercover who had hung around too long, been beaten by applied pressure, and had made a mistake – only needed one. Only the one mistake ... Light flooded on to him. His head jerked up.

"What are you doing, Jonas?"

"Not very much, Vera. I'm just brooding a bit."

"In the dark, Jonas – what's it about?"

"Nothing in particular, probably a bit jaded," Jonas said, sheepishly. "I'll be in pretty soon. Just a couple of calls to make, things I ought to have wrapped up. I'm looking forward to our trip, should be an experience."

The door closed on him. He was alerted and took his phone from his jacket pocket. A suitcase had arrived safely in the premises of an investment company in the Guernsey main town, St Peter Port. It was an efficient and adequately oiled machine, worked well . . . It would be good to be in at the kill, an experience and a powerful one.

Kenny Blake sat in his car, parked off the road opposite her cottage, almost out of sight of the headlights of passing vehicles – not many on that winding road where the trees pressed close to each other and leaves were dripping rain – and listened to a local radio station, and watched for her.

He felt like a teenage boy, leaning on his bike and waiting for the star girl of Year Eight to come out of the library and walk down to the bus stop. Had not specifically been invited and no time given, but told that his dinner would be cooked; he had brought a bottle. As a Level One he was a paid-up member of the most secretive club in the UK's police forces. She would be a lunatic if she stayed out much longer on the open cliff paths in the weather that now bitched over the Galicia coast . . . he thought something of that lunacy attracted him, had dug deep hooks in him.

There was a man who loved Kenny Blake. Loved him by that name, and his previous name and the one before, but had never used the name under which his birth certificate had been issued. The man was obese, had a round, cherubic face and spluttered when he laughed. He was a psychologist. Used to say that Kenny, and all those who had gone before, were star patients, the best. Used to congratulate him. *What fascinates me about you, Kenny – which will do for today – is that you need arrogance, and conceit in your own ability to survive, but you don't wear it like a chip on your shoulder. I don't think you are a crusader, with a message pinned on your sleeve, but I believe you are a 'winner'. Need to win. My advice, please don't quote me, is to refuse to wear a wire. They bite us on the arse, in my opinion, and it's too dangerous because there will always be one wretched fellow who challenges and it's a piping hot day and you've a jacket on to hide the gear. Don't wear one. I admire your ability, on the hoof, to make what we call 'dynamic risk assessments'. To make them without stacking the odds too high, but then to go forward to bad places. Sorry to hear about the marriage collapse, usually messy in your trade, relationships. You'll meet nice people, already have and plenty more in line, and you'll enjoy their company when you're peddling their stuff and learning to be their friend and getting their trust . . . But you're going to do the dirty on them, Kenny, do it big time. You have to compartmentalise your feelings, Kenny, store them all away in separate boxes. What I'm saying, Kenny, is that I will so enjoy sitting down with you when this one is over and hearing how it was. Off you go, Kenny, back to the trenches, and stay safe and spare me some time . . . only thing to add, don't, not ever, let down your guard.*

Kenny had always found the psychologist to be amusing company. It was said that he split his time between Level Ones and Special Forces. He had seen Kenny before he had gone to Galicia, and on a leave 15 months ago, and then Kenny had travelled back to Spain and it was intended that he should wrap matters up after the help he'd given in gaoling two families from the north-west. But a call had come, from a soft-voiced man who didn't seem to brook alternatives. Before he'd travelled the first time, and set up the Biscuit Tin business, he had done one political infiltration, right-wing, and getting towards the stage of buying their first shooter when he'd pulled the plug on them, and then been able to grow his hair again from the skinhead scalp . . . Had done time with a druggie crowd in Sheffield and they'd all liked him because he was the failed accountant who took short cuts, risks, and kept them in good investment portfolios. When they were taken out, cuffed, they would have seen, fleetingly, that he was being ushered away by the Armed Response team and into their car and his back slapped and they would have been mental with fury – and had many years more to let the anger burn while they did their stretch in Belmarsh or Long Lartin.

It never went on for long. Guys either went native and started long relationships, and kids turned up. The alternative seemed to be PTSD, and nightmares and knowing the punishments that the gangs dished out and hearing chainsaws and cordless drills. Not a career with a future. A job for an idiot, one that didn't fit in any peg hole, one who wanted to be shacked up with a lunatic.

Doloures Govier accepted that she was not a handsome woman.

She went to a hairdresser up the road, but only for a cut. Her eyes were deep and dark, and few could read warmth in them, and her skin was pale and the first tracks were appearing at the sides of her mouth, and at her eyes, and some wrinkles were materialising at her throat. If she were concerned that the aging process had begun to catch her, she gave no sign of it. She had always dressed older than her years and that was because her family had taught her the value of charity shops; she had been frugal all her life and would be until the day she dropped – now she bought her clothes from chainstores in the city centre. She wore a smear of lipstick and pearl stud earrings and her only ring was a simple one on her wedding finger. She looked like any other hard-working housewife, bent under the weight of work, child rearing, money concerns, and with little in her life to cherish as a good memory or to look forward to. But Doloures Govier wanted no sympathy. She regarded the huge majority of those who passed her in the street as pathetic, without value. If police passed by her, either in uniform or in an unmarked car, she'd have identified them without hesitation, and mentally spat on the pavement.

Only the most astute observer would have recognised her as an icon of success in her chosen trading field, and the talent spotting had come early. Two years out of school, just had her eighteenth birthday and a bit of a disco in the backyard, a few from school roped in and some kids of the families who worked alongside her parents' stalls in a local street market – and a gatecrasher had turned up. Her dad had not thrown him out. He was Mikey Govier. Had already done Young Offenders, was what the papers called a "tearaway", and had a broken nose that had been badly set and came from a family with a reputation. Why was he there? Doloures had learned soon enough that Mikey Govier had pitched up at her party because she had already laid down markers that were recognised. One, she was a "cold bitch". Two, she was a "hard cow". His parents reckoned she was what Mikey needed, a good match and someone who would help his career advancement. And she was plain which would have been regarded as an additional bonus. And she had known how their early marriage years were considered by Mikey's circle. *Back in Walton, isn't he? Best place for him, and clear of her. Imagine waking up and that's the first thing you see. Must be pissed out of his mind, each time he shags her.* Doloures was not concerned with what others might say about her looks and about the romance in her life, or absence of it. She had been married 32 years and to show for it was Xavier who was 28, Theresa who was 23, and Patrick 21. There had been no chance of any more as Mikey Govier had been "away", and after Patrick she had been spare with her favours before he'd been carted off, handcuffed, for another, longer spell in the local cell blocks. When Mikey was banged up she had not entertained the thought of having another man in her bed, had not given it a moment's thought.

Nor did she have a confidante to whom she bled the details of her emotional life, what there was of it. No inclination to share any part of her life. There was a dog, a Jack Russell terrier cross. Brown and white, smooth haired, a snout mouth, decent teeth and a vice-like jaw, an occasional screeched bark, and usually close to her. The dog was at her mother's place, Doloures had planned to have been in northern Spain and taking delivery of a cargo for which she had paid an advance that was steep, through the bloody roof, in fact, and with more to come. She would not have trusted any of her children to care for the dog while she was away and she would not have contradicted a view that she loved the foul-tempered dog more than any of her children, more than her absent husband.

No friends, but certainly a few people whom she detested. Top of that list was a police officer, Fanny Thomas, whom she'd come across when the woman was a detective sergeant. Now she knew she had been promoted from inspector to detective chief inspector. There was also a man in National Crime, Harry Williams, who was showing an interest in her, but not to the extent of Fanny Thomas. That woman had built a life around harassing the Govier family. Had shafted Mikey, had pulled Xavier in every year and held him for 24 or 36 hours and done trawling exercises until the family's solicitors had freed him. She had authorised the tails put every few months on Theresa and Patrick. Doloures Govier had watched Fanny Thomas give evidence against her husband, had memorised her face and her voice, her build, her clothes. Had done homework on Fanny Thomas and the contacts had reported back that the woman was unlikely to allow a little envelope to slip into her handbag: was said to be incorruptible, was said to be devoted to her work, was said to have a file on her desk computer on all of the family, always up to date. Fanny Thomas was her *enemy*. Not a word that Doloures used lightly. There were trading rivals, who would trick, deceive, fuck up her business deals if that were to their advantage, but she would do the same. Only Fanny Thomas was an enemy. Doloures knew that Fanny Thomas's aim was to put her behind bars, and send down Theresa with her, and Patrick, and Xavier. She knew where Fanny Thomas lived, and where her husband worked and where her kids went to school and knew the registration number of her BMW. She could have had the husband slashed and the kids beaten and the car wrecked – except that her lawyers advised that "interfering" with Fanny Thomas might just be the grand design "mistake" of her life.

The force driving Doloures – that morning, every morning, tomorrow morning – was power. Power was money. Accumulating wealth – not displaying it, not flashing it – was the inner excitement that thrilled her. A never-ending pursuit of it . . . could not stand still. Had to expand to maintain the power. Had a villa down at Estepona, on the Costa del Sol, but never thought of packing up the family home, selling off the furniture, going down there to lounge away the weeks beside a pool. Within a month the power would have started to slide away and within a year her markets would have been snaffled by the next family in the queue. Not while she had breath in her body.

She assumed, when she was in Galicia, that she would receive the respect due to her, be treated as she deserved to be. Looked forward to it.

She and Patrick worked at the kitchen table, and did the accounts, and the scrap paper they used would go into a shredder and the remains would then be burned. Doloures was paranoid about mistakes, about surveillance, and about all of the clever tricks that Fanny Thomas's crowd – and the Crime Agency – could play against them. Had the radio on the local station, loud enough to kill their voices. Monday mornings was when the guy came in who swept the house for bugs. She heard Xavier leave the house and he shouted from the door to Theresa.

"Well go on, get on with it. Won't fucking bite you."

Bengal had business to do. He had to meet the family's dealers, keep the supply chain secure.

He had driven from the family home in his old VW. He could compromise on the style of car he drove, and the clothes he wore, and did not have to hang a gold chain round his neck. But he could not slacken on the meting out of violence to those who danced in his face, fucked about with him, and could not show any sign of weakness to those on the big payroll, or they would be gone.

A hell of a payroll. Lorry drivers, van drivers, and bikers to move the white stuff around in Liverpool and into Manchester, where he had made inroads, and up north as far as Lancaster and south to Stafford. More and more men that had to be sub-contracted into the wage structure – gave him a bloody headache. He would be touring that afternoon and into the evening and the men he met would want to see him looking cheerful, positive, no doubt on his face, showing authority: and expecting him to be paying them enough to ensure their loyalty . . . until they had a better offer. He often wondered why he couldn't just cool off on a lounger now and then and watch: no chance.

Bengal had to assume that his sister was capable of doing the job asked of her. He could not have told Patrick to do it because he would have complained to Ma. Patrick fed off him, but as soon as he was asked to carry out a job then he'd run to Ma and moan – useless piece of shit . . . and there was business to do on behalf of his Pa.

Bengal did not often visit his Pa. Pa had nothing to contribute, could not help with the load, and his ideas were way past their shelf life, but he liked him and missed him. Not enough to waste an afternoon standing in a line of zombies with kids bawling and then get searched and scanned, and then have precious nothing to talk about and have to listen to a monologue on prison conditions and prison food and prison sex and prison . . . but he had once been good company. Pa's authority was failing. He had been insulted, called a "nobody" by a smart arse kid on his landing. After nine years inside his Pa was unable to answer the insult for himself, had asked Xavier to handle it. The kid had a brother, and the brother was due a session with the lump hammer. It had taken time for Bengal to slot it into his schedule. Most Saturday nights the brother went to a snooker club. It would be crawling with cameras, but others who had "loyalties" to Bengal would call him outside and there was an area of the car park down the side of the building where Bengal would be waiting and where it was known the cameras did not reach. The brother would be well enough in a week or so, from his bed in the orthopaedic trauma section of the Royal Liverpool, to send a message to the smart arse. Bengal had a busy evening ahead and he had to hope that a simple but valuable piece of work would be carried out by his sister.

The Surveillance Camera Commissioner would not permit a camera with a wide-angle, fisheye lens that covered the street and the pavements on both sides: deemed it intrusive and unjustified. And the camera could certainly not record the movements of the target's neighbours. The camera would only have been allowed to focus on the front gate of the Govier house, and up the short path to the front door. The angle covered was perhaps 15 degrees wide not 180 degrees which was important in the instructions given her by Bengal. Theresa had discussed this with her mother who had nodded. Her mother, and this was also locked in her memory, had given Bengal big grief five or six years earlier when he had come home and recounted a confrontation with a surveillance man, police, outside Tesco where he had been buying some fags and some cans. Had caught the surveillance man peering into the parked car, trying the handle, then backing off, then being dumb enough to produce his warrant card. A bit of a waste, but Bengal had used the cans, in a plastic bag, to fracture his windscreen, frost it so that the bastard had needed to put his elbow through it before he could see to scarper, then had run his keys down the side as it had pulled away. Had described the guy's white face and staring eyes, hyperventilating like he thought he was dead meat. Ma had said it was "not clever", but had smiled.

From her hip pocket Theresa took the piece of chewing gum, slotted it in her mouth, and went out the front door. Turned sharp right, walked to the next street and right again, and kept going. After about a hundred yards she retraced her steps until she was back on their own road. The street lights were dull in the growing dusk. She reached the Potters' little gate. Their house was dark except for a light in the hallway. She counted the bricks along and the bricks up and Bengal had told her, cross his heart, that she'd not have been registered. She took the gum out of her mouth, knelt and peered and saw the bloody thing with her own eyes half the size of her little fingernail. The mortar around it was dark, stained, but the glass had a touch of lustre.

She put the gum over it, pressed firmly.

The Potters had had a pleasant day out, but it had gone on longer than either would have wished. He liked a small Scotch before bed, and she liked a session with her crossword book and a cup of camomile tea. The car headlights lit their wall as they swung into the parking space and then fastened on the front windows of their home and David braked in front of the garage doors. Because of the spit of rain in the air and the wind he wouldn't bother to put the car away. He hurried to unlock the front door and then dived inside to deactivate the alarm system. Jenny followed.

She needed the toilet and didn't look back.

He did. Before closing the front door, David Potter paused and stared across the street to the front door opposite and noticed lights inside. Not that he would have admitted it to his wife, but his life for months had been one of regret. Easy enough, confronted by that policewoman, to have agreed with her; hard enough to have said to her face that he wanted nothing to do with her pursuit of his neighbours. Everyone in the street knew that they lived within kicking distance of a prominent Merseyside crime family, and everyone knew of the family's reputation for violence, but everyone pretended they knew nothing. Would nod to the family leader – while her husband was "away" – when she took her dog out and would get no response. Would smile briefly if they met the younger kids, eye contact unavoidable, and be looked through as if they did not exist. Would grunt an apology of a greeting if Xavier was visiting, aware of the power rippling in his tattooed arms and the gleam of his shaved skull and see malevolence in his gaze.

David Potter had been an engineer, quite a senior position in the water company, and a bit of an expert on the grading of concrete mixtures – but by a peculiar contrariness his grammar school had insisted on Latin being taught to all pupils. *Alea iacta est.* The words of Julius Caesar leading his army across the Rubicon river. *The die is cast.* A point of no return. He had agreed, justifying it with self-complimentary thoughts about "fulfilling civic duty". Had not then, nor since, been able to summon the courage to ring Fanny Thomas, and tell her that he no longer wished to harbour her camera. Looked at the house across the road, and realised the family were an obsession . . . he was terrified of them.

Jonas was back out in the caravan, had pleaded the requirement for one or two more calls. Had sweetened it with the suggestion that he had to run to clear his workload before setting off for Wales. Jonas and Vera had already started to read about the possible locations of interest that they would find there, and they'd studied the advance weather forecast.

He rang Aggie Burns. Aggie was in charge of the surveillance team in the main space of 3/S/12. He would not have described her as a friend but thought he had her respect, which was enough. Aggie Burns despised crime, thought it policemen's work. Crime was beneath the skills of her people.

"Hello, Jonas. Still chasing burglars? What do you want?"

Would pitch it simple. Demand the moon and he'd get slapped down. The rain had come on heavy and beat on the caravan roof. The best thing about Aggie Burns was that she would not ask, "What do you want that for?" The wind funnelled up the street and buffeted the caravan. He said what he wanted. If the weather did not lift in the following week then the coastline he and Vera were planning to visit would be miserable. He told her where it would be used and she didn't pass comment.

"Be ready Monday. And you'll need some paint, usually blue paint. Don't you get bored with not doing anything that matters?"

He rang off. Jonas could see from the caravan window, a distorted view because of the rain, that an upstairs light was on. Vera would have given up on him. His principal anxiety was still eating at him. He dialled the international number. The connection was made. Not often that Jonas was able to bury his worries for Kenny Blake.

Hugo put down the phone.

"Want to know?"

"I'd like to know," Wilf answered. He had a kid on his lap, fed it milk from a baby's bottle. Both cared equally for the survival of the tiny, shivering animal, born prematurely, and its mother hovered close and the floor was covered with mud, and straw and now with droppings.

"He asked about our boy, about how he's doing."

"I heard what you said."

"You know what it tells me?" Hugo sat at the kitchen table. Both had stiffened when the phone rang: might have been the call that they dreaded, the one that meant a long drive, weapons by their feet, and the reciting of a verse from the grave of the old general buried in the San Carlos Garden in Corunna. "Tells me that our man in London is not an officer."

"You've never seen him, let alone met him. Not an officer. Meaning?"

"An officer says, when his boy's under pressure 'If you don't like it then you shouldn't have joined. If you don't like it then go drive a refuse truck.' An officer wouldn't give a toss. So he's made up from the ranks and the level of the responsibility is outside his culture."

"No comfort area." Wilf held the kid close, like it was his own.

"Nothing about the shipment, but that's not important to him. Wanted to know only about Kenny."

"And you told him."

"You heard me. That he seemed usual. He is trained under-cover. Not going to have the shakes, be hyperventilating. Doesn't do big smiles and back slaps, and doesn't make useless cracks. Says what needs saying and drifts away. Same as us, you and me." Hugo sipped a fruit juice, homemade. A mark of the times, but neither drank alcohol now. Would not do so until they had seen Kenny Blake safe on to the ferry, might even sail with him, stand watch outside his cabin door and be there until the moment their charge had taken his first steps on to the quayside at Plymouth.

"But he is suffering."

"Because it is 'black dog time'. The end of a mission, last days and last hours . . . and the old one in London, same thing. Frightened for our boy . . . He's fearful that he's going to be found out, his limitations shown."

And the pistols and the gas grenades and the flash-and-bangs, and the assault rifles, cleaned of the Syrian shit and sand and mud, and their loaded magazines, were all within reach. Hugo watched Wilf with the kid and both would weep if they lost it.

Wilf said, "Going to be a long night . . . heh, but I think this little 'un will be all right. It's 'events' we've got to watch out for.

Out of a clear blue sky. They pinch your belly when you haven't seen them coming."

They lapsed into silence. The rain fell hard and the guttering overflowed and the gusts came strong, and the kid slept. And both of the veteran marines would roll the word in their minds "events". And both would see an unbroken sky, not even a puff of cloud, azure blue.

Jonas knew about events: something unpredictable, without warning given, and liable to trip him up.

And he knew about a clear blue sky: nothing good ever dropped from it.

Anna cooked. A mess of sea creatures probably ripped from their territory that morning, or netted. Gutted and cleaned, and dumped in oil, and Albariño wine poured on them. A salad tossed.

For an hour, Kenny Blake had sat in his car in front of the doorway of the dark building, had tried her phone but she had not answered. Now he sat in the living area and she was on the far side of a bead curtain, her back to him. The rain was incessant and the wind made a choir sing from the electric cable linked to the satellite dish on the roof. He had been in her cottage enough times before. This was nothing different from the first invitation except that he was likely to spend the night there which had not been on offer before. She had music playing, popular jazz, and she was swaying as she stirred the fish round the pan.

Anonymous music pretty much suited her place which revealed nothing of her. Supposed it different now that he slept with her, quite changed now because Kenny Blake had set his cap on taking her out of here – end of the week – or asking her to come and join him wherever he had pitched up. He had started to think about how he could best persuade her to accept his offer of something permanent. Not much of an offer because what he would have to give on his side of any bargain was sparse. Needed to know more about her. Had been here often enough to have prodded and poked about for the evidence of what she stood for, what baggage she carried but, then, it had not seemed necessary. He had a beer in his hand, drank from the neck, and realised the scale of that feeling of anonymity.

No pictures on the walls, nothing that showed her parents or any brothers or sisters, family holiday snaps, nothing of her childhood. No little ornaments, no line of books in Dutch that might have been precious volumes brought with her in a tea chest, favourites from school, or textbooks from university that had never been returned to the library. Her own work was on the walls and he knew she used a framer in Corunna and she'd told him that he gave her a good rate. Quite often, Kenny had sat in silence up on the cliffs beside her while she had painted or crayoned and there her art seemed to have something unsophisticated, bold, to distinguish it. An individual talent appeared on the canvas or paper when fastened to the easel frame, with the wind coming off the sea and often enough a spit of rain, and he'd been with her, drenched, while she had a plastic sack draped over the work, her hands moving underneath: there was one special crayon drawing of the Cemitério dos Ingleses in grim weather, where most of the drowned sailors of the Royal Navy's HMS *Serpent* had lain. He thought her work looked poor on the walls, which reinforced his opinion that she was wealthy, indulged by parents or a trust fund. Needed to know more of her if the big offer were to be made, and he'd likely blurt out his intentions as the coming week wound down.

Kenny thought it possible that even a deep rummage team would have drawn a blank if they had been given a whole day to strip the cottage down . . . and Kenny thought it just as likely that the same deep rummage team would come to his own place, his own rented cottage on the hillside above Camariñas, and fail. No photographs of his parents, nor of his former wife, nor of his children, and nothing on his own shelves to show for his past life, and . . . He was kissed on the cheek. Given another bottle, and the dead one taken from him.

He thought her a great girl, not a great artist. Laughed to himself, thought himself blessed. Thought he was lucky to have this distraction as the hours passed, as a semi-submersible edged closer, as the end came nearer – managing the last hours and then the bolt, the flight to get clear, and a sackful of consequences left behind for someone else to clear, and shivering at the thought of them. He tried to kiss her back but caught only her neck and she laughed. Perhaps it was the mischief that he liked most in her – or loved most – and the secrecy it guarded.

Sergio Munoz was in a bar. Had received a cryptic message on his phone and followed its instructions. He sat in a back area where the lights were always dimmed and there were discreet alcoves. He was obsessed with security, acted cautiously. Would not have come – at that time, in that weather – but for the code word that signified to him the sender and the location. The *mesonero* offered him a drink – of course, on the house – as any bar owner would have, but he declined. Too many had become complacent in power, had slackened their sense of suspicion. Expected that the contact would have been outside, low down in his seat in the parked car, and would have seen him enter.

He lit a cigarette and waited. In the bar music played and kids danced and the regular drinkers hogged the counter stools.

The submersible, limping through a storm on the last leg of an Atlantic voyage, carried a cargo worth more to Sergio's family than 300 million euros. A man had flown from Europe to Colombia the previous day to collect the body of his son, who had been lodged as a hostage. And people were travelling from Britain to meet them, unknown, but their advance payment had been validated.

A shadowy figure drifted into the back area, moved cautiously toward him. He had no respect for informants but had a need of them. Sergio paid him, 2500 euros each month. They had not met for 27 months but the retainer was paid without question, delivered by courier. His voice was low, and Sergio had to lean forward to hear him.

"I have to tell you that an individual has attracted the attention of both the police and customs. She is a female, a Dutch national and she plays the part of an artist, except that her work is worth-less. Her position in our society is unclear but she spends many hours alone, positioned above entry points for speedboats and ribs into bays and rivers, apparently painting. You should know about her, perhaps you need to know more. Myself, I cannot spec-ulate. I wish you well, and my most sincere regards to your mother. This is the address at which the woman has a residence permit. I did not consider this too trifling a matter to concern you with . . ."

A slip of paper was passed from the pocket of the dark coat worn by the off-duty member of the Finance Police, and under the name *Anna Jensen* was the address where she lived.

He assumed the cat read him, understood the sombreness of his mood.

Olaf sat with Vera, impeded her needlework, but was comfort-able. Most evenings before bed-time, the cat came to him. Jonas recognised his own sourness and the strain in his shoulders, and Vera left him to himself. Tomorrow they would work out a schedule for north Wales, she had said, where to go and what to see, and consider what clothing to take, but not make any decisions tonight.

Jonas had the young man's face in his mind. Knew his age and knew his assumed name, knew the detail of the legend he had created for his own safety. Knew also that the bogus National Insurance records for Kenny Blake had been examined, and his driving licence, and the proof of his accountancy training, and the record of dismissal, even a retired schoolmaster's query about a particular pupil, and a primed former maths teacher had satisfied the trawl. All done eight months before and the thoroughness and expense involved had told Jonas – and a one-time handler from the Metropolitan Police, now surplus to requirements – that large fish, worthy prey, circled *Una Lata de Galletas*.

The legend of Kenny Blake should by now have been binned. The young man ought by now to have "depressurised" from the Galicia assignment, thrown off that particular life of deception, and walked away from the police, or started out again with a new identity, or gone back to whatever police work that suited. Except that Jonas had demanded more time from him, which was a heavy weight.

Jonas and Vera had no children. They had the cat, Olaf, now in mid-life for the Norwegian Forest breed. Had "tried" for children. Vera had been for advice but Jonas had not accompanied her. She had been moderately enthusiastic, himself less so. It had not happened, and he had buried himself in his work in Thames House, and she had done longer hours in the art gallery. They had seen the Derbyshire children next door grow up, and plenty of others in their street. Had seen the development of rude children and polite children ... but there was much he had not known, experienced. Had *never* kicked a football to a toddler, or made a sandcastle, never taken a youngster to their first day at a new school, never waited for the envelope telling of exam results, never wondered where a boy or a girl was going to land their first job – had never felt pride or shame for the actions of a son or a daughter ... Had not actually thought much about the absence in his life of children and it was a matter not talked about at home and he really did not know what Vera thought.

... Until Kenny Blake turned up in a soft-focus photograph and Jonas had assumed a sort of responsibility for the young man. Each week, that responsibility seemed a greater burden, and what he asked of the boy became more dangerous. In extreme and late at night thoughts, Jonas believed he tipped the boy further towards growing risk. The money trail, so far so good, had stayed strong.

Behind the esplanade overlooking the harbour at St Peter Port, were narrow back streets. Their buildings had been renovated and the outer walls were festooned with well-maintained hanging baskets of bright flowers. Clever young people gathered behind windows of tinted glass and toiled at computer screens and moved money and oversaw money – large amounts of it. A small, well polished brass plate gave the name of a blue chip company in the third street back. There were five of them in the team that dealt with the cash coming in from the Biscuit Tin enterprise. They were well paid, top of the range, and would last a limited period in

114   Gerald Seymour
```

such a pressured environment and then would explode in different directions.

None had ever met Jonas and he had communicated with them initially through a probationer at Thames House, one thought to have a future. Jonas had briefed that young woman, given specific instructions: she was Hettie, now in counter-terror. To the letter, Jonas's demands were followed. The investment team were led on a sightseeing walk, and had ended up on the north side of the Thames, looking towards the channels running underneath Blackfriars Bridge. They were told, in Hettie's strong, clear voice, of the Vatican Bank in Rome, of colossal losses and of a man known as God's Banker: Roberto Calvi, disgraced for financial manipulation leading to the bank's collapse and defaulting on its investors – and his problem was not the papal money disappearing but the large sums of *mafia* cash. Calvi fled to London, imagined himself safe. Underestimated the length of an arm reaching out for vengeance. Hettie showed the team where scaffolding had been erected. On a June morning, 40 years before, a body had been spotted slowly turning in the breeze, hanged by the neck from the scaffold construction. Hettie would have told it well, chilled them. Then she would have handed each of them a mobile phone and Jonas had described to them the fate of anyone who trifled with *mafia* money. They had gone to Guernsey where they handled the investments given them – most often in bank notes still live with the traces of cocaine powder – off the light aircraft from the northern Spanish coast.

Hettie had apparently finished by dragging out of her bag foolscap pictures of Calvi's body when it had been retrieved from the scaffolding and the artist's impression of him suspended, used at the inquest – then had said, *You have to protect a good man, a brave man, and you don't short change him by sloppy, complacent work. If you are responsible for blowing his cover then – sure as night follows day – he will be killed, but probably more slowly and painfully than what was done to Calvi. Don't fuck up on him, just don't.* If he met Hettie in a lift, going up to the third floor, she would not have acknowledged Jonas. She had done as she was told to do: there was no requirement for social pleasantries.
```

Sometimes he breathed heavily and sometimes he seemed to shake his head as if to wipe away a nagging thought. Was in no hurry to go to bed because even there he would not lose the image of the boy who seemed to fill a space in his life . . . Went to make their cocoa . . . and the matter had a week to run. A long week beckoning him . . . brought back the cocoa.

"You all right, Jonas?"

"Fine, thank you."

"Just looking a bit peaky."

"Never felt better."

"And this trip – I'm so pleased."

"It'll be very pleasant," Jonas said.

5

On any Sunday morning, their street hummed with activity.

Except at the home of Jonas and Vera Merrick. In other front gardens there would be the grinding scrape of rakes on driveways and the removal of the last of the winter's leaves. Power blasters would be removing stains from the slabs and brickwork of the paths. Some cars would be returning from the first drive to the garden centre in Lower Morden loaded with trays of pansies and pelargonium plants. Hoses would be reeled off creaking storage frames and the washing of cars would start. Made little difference to the road's regular routine whether the weather was good, foul or predictably grey.

He had nothing to do with the front garden. His only point of interest there was the caravan parked on a concrete shoulder. In a month or two, Vera would come out with a yard brush and sweep the season's debris into the gutter and later Derbyshire, from next door, would come out and bag it up and offer a remark to anyone who would listen on the lines of, *He's not only a miserable old sod, but lazy with it.*

Jonas was inside, out of the rain, and the sounds of activity chorused from the front and were ignored.

Others would be out in their back gardens. Mowers being used for a first or second cut. Hedges clipped and shrubs getting a gentle pruning and work might have been started on a self-assembly garden shed or a kids' sandpit. Jonas left mowing to Vera, and rather liked the grass long enough to come over his brogues as that gave better cover to the rodent population that seemed alive and well in spite of Olaf and the shrubs were allowed to grow and give them added cover – and also make more of a jungle in which Olaf could play king emperor.

The road atlas was out on the kitchen table. They pored over details of the Dinas Dinlle Hill fort and the Segontium Roman Fort and the Church of St Tudclud, and Tomen y Mur where the Romans had built a staging camp in the mountain wilderness south of the Snowdonia National Park, and Vera enthused and Jonas seemed to be both excited and interested.

Also in their street that Sunday morning, and every Sunday – regardless of the weather – were those in athletics kit, setting out for a run, or bringing out their bikes for long-distance cycling, and parents who were taking their kids to sport and would be bawling abuse or encouragement. Jonas took no physical exercise other than the walk to the station five times a week, then from Waterloo to Thames House via Lambeth Bridge, reversing the route in the afternoon, catching the 5.39 back to Raynes Park. He thought himself overweight but not excessively. Vera chided him for the spread of his stomach but still did him white bread sand- wiches for his lunch, often with cheese, and sometimes a modest chocolate bar was popped in the box.

They might get across the Menai Strait, traverse it on Telford's original bridge, and get to see the outlines of the Neolithic round houses of Ty Mawr and maybe visit the buried chamber at Bryn Celli Ddu. Jonas made measurements on the atlas and calculated distances: how long it would take to get from Raynes Park up to the camping and caravan site in the Conwy Valley. Then he noted the mileages to the various sites that seemed of interest . . . there was an extra distance to be noted, going east and along the coastal dual carriageway: 60 miles, but a fast run and it would take him, he estimated, only an hour and a quarter. Time and distance were registered but he gave no indication of it. He had already booked the site, at the edge of the field, where there would probably be a hedgerow that Olaf might wish to visit.

Did she believe a word he said? Or merely humour him?

Though they were never spoken of, he assumed she had a pocket handkerchief of pride in those items secreted in her knicker drawer, the Queen's Gallantry Medal, and the Bar from a subsequent discreet investiture. *God, you again – ever considered taking things a bit more easily?* He had never relayed that remark back to her when he'd returned to the kitchen in Raynes Park. Had not mentioned it because he dreaded "taking things a bit more easily", clocking out with his ID card, then seeing it destroyed electronically and going home on the last day that his season ticket was valid, and making sure the alarm beside the bed was switched off. He smiled, hopefully with warmth.

Jonas said, "I think we'll get away either late on Tuesday or at dawn on Wednesday. Should be nice, should make a pleasant change."

"And you'll steal time from work? Will they miss you, can they spare you?"

She was laughing. But he didn't register, saw a young man – felt the responsibility.

He grimaced. "I expect they'll manage."

"Been meaning to say it, but isn't this a bit tacky? Why do you wear . . .?"

"Just leave it, please."

Her fingers had hooked on to the St Christopher that he wore on a fine chain around his neck. Sunday morning and he supposed that he was lonely and isolated and that she was bored, both of them still in bed, and the rain still persistent and the wind in the cables. Kenny Blake's medallion was made of pewter the size of a 10 pence piece, and it would have come off a Chinese factory production line and been cheap as dirt.

"It is ordinary. It has no value. You should not have . . .?"

"Please, just leave it."

Her fingers clung to it. In all the months he had known Anna Jensen, the artist without talent, the girl whom he had come to rely on for company and comfort, he had worn the St Christopher around his neck. Of course, in the cold, when they walked together on the coast paths that linked the lighthouse towers, he would have been wrapped up and it would have been easy to miss, but not in the warm months, not when they had first started to take coffees, eaten together, then when they had finally gone to bed. Plenty of chances then, an accumulation of them, for her to remark on it. Not that Kenny had dosed himself with religion but he had not been separated from the saint's image since it had been given to him, and would not be now.

"But it is rubbish, from a souvenir shop. It cannot be important to you to . . ."

"I am asking you – Anna – please, to leave it."

He lay on his back. He gave no explanation as to why he would not tolerate her sneering at it. Could not think of one . . . always told never to bluster into false explanations which might then be picked apart. A draught from an open window played on his body and she was resting her weight on one elbow, her other arm stretched across his chest, the fingers holding the medallion. He knew it was tacky, rubbish, from a souvenir shop. Kenny would like to have been exploring with her some of his ideas on where, "one day", they might end up – probably not in her country and not in his – and her painting and crayoning and him making ends meet with labouring and house maintenance and whatever pitched up, and joking and him giving no clue as to what he was leaving behind and her letting him break down the reticence of her past and her present. Her fingers had started to tug at the St Christopher and the chain had tightened and cut at the back of his neck. He had bought the chain when he had worked in the north, on his first Level One posting, had paid cash, probably twenty times more for the chain than the medallion had cost. Her eyes were close to his, a leg was hooked over his hip, she was touching him with her other hand. Important to see her eyes because they showed him what he had always thought, since first meeting her: the amusement and sense of fun that he had started to chase after. But now they were obstinate, bored, provoking.

"A man like you, Kenny, with your position should only have an ornament that represents your education, your status, your taste – not a trinket."

"Leave it." The first hint of hardness in his voice, but controlled . . . she also wore a pendant. A stone he did not recognise, a gold chain that was heavier than his. The medallion was important to Kenny Blake, because it had been given when he had a real name on a genuine birth certificate. His father and mother had been on a coach trip to Canterbury, a cathedral tour, and had stopped at the gift shop on the way out. What they had bought for themselves had gone in their kitchen, but the St Christopher had been for him, and it had been handed to him a couple of days before he had gone off on his first undercover assignment. Not that his father and mother had known where he'd been going nor any detail of his new work. Tacky, probably. Trinket, fair description . . . A mark of his parents' love for him, and he was to test it, and to hurt them. Hurt anyone else who ventured close to him.

"I think you should dump it."

"I think you should let it go."

"I think tomorrow I will shop for you in Corunna and buy you something that is suitable, and . . ."

She pulled. The chain went rigid. The line cut deeper in his neck. Did it matter? His hand caught hers, held it in a grip that was strong enough to prevent her snatching at the medallion and breaking the chain and stripping it from him. He saw the anger flash in her eyes. It was controlled, and then subsided. The chain fell free . . . she wiped the mood off her face. Kenny could do that. He never showed temper, had been trained. Like it had never happened, she straddled him, and they kissed, and the anger and the boredom and the goading were all binned.

Kenny hated disputes. When the fights with his wife had pitched over into real breakdown material she would scream at him and sometimes punch at his arms, and he would be standing in the kitchen or the living room, his hair grown down to his shoulders and a bag of filthy clothes by his feet, and the kids upstairs and sobbing, and what pissed her off most was that he never reacted and she could not draw him into retaliation. He would go back to work, and she would not know when he would next be home, and he'd be a stranger to his kids. His control, Peters at SC&O10,

would say, *Of course the relationship is screwed. Weren't you told that? You were . . . she doesn't know who she's married to, occasionally living with. Don't bleat to me about it. Goes with the job. You're either up for it or you are not – your decision.* He would go back to work, flog some more weed, deal in wraps of smack and brown, get closer to the big cats where the risks went higher – come home again and live out the same teary scenes and find his optimism once more kicked in the testicles. What he had close to him was the St Christopher.

The business with the medallion seemed erased from Anna's mind.

Kenny Blake would not have been a Level One had he not been able to act out enthusiasm. Would not have been able to run the Biscuit Tin business if he were not able to play a part. She was over him, holding him, and he was thinking of his dad, and of his mum, and of the grief he had given them, and what a St Christopher was supposed to mean and the gift put in his hand with just a gruff reminder that some still loved him . . . and all of it coming to an end and less than a week left to run.

Bengal had drunk champagne afterwards. Not from a glass, from the neck. Two empty bottles were beside his bed on the thick rug.

The brother of the smart arse had been brought out from the snooker hall and led into the shadowed recess in the car park. Might have reckoned that he had a chance of blagging himself clear of the "difficulty". Would, perhaps, have believed the chance existed until he had seen the short, squat shape of Bengal. He would already have realised that the men who called him out worked for Bengal, but would have hoped that the "difficulty", his brother's big fucking mouth, could be smoothed. Might have been, a pickaxe handle or a baseball club that was dangled close to Bengal's leg.

Himself, had it been him, Bengal – he would have fought. If any of the other crowds had lifted him, from the north of the city, or those who had a hold in Anfield, or across the water in Birkenhead. He would have fought fit to bust. Fists, boots, teeth, headbutt, fingers in the eyes, would have to have slotted him to have shut him down. Not this beggar.

Meek as a bloody lamb. Not even pleading when he recognised Bengal. Just sort of gave up which took most of the pleasure out of it, and the guys who had taken him from the snooker hall didn't need to hold him. Had belted him a few times. All straightforward and out of range of the CCTV, but no struggle meant no pleasure.

He was awake but drowsy after the two bottles of fizz. Light pitched in and the rain fell hard. He was still dressed and his boots had left mud on the bed cover. What to look forward to? Not a bagful, and likely another row with his mother, because of the trip she was making and because of the reach it made into the family assets. He would have pissed in the bed if he hadn't rolled off and started to stagger to the bathroom ... and could assume that by now the guy from the snooker hall was safely tucked up in a bay at A&E and waiting for the X-rays that would tell them what bones needed pinning ... and he didn't get to the bathroom in time.

"What am I going to wear?"

"How the hell do I know?"

"If you were coming, what would you wear?"

"Which is just bloody stupid because I am not coming."

Theresa and Patrick were alone in the house. Ma had gone to see her own mother and to check the dog hadn't starved, was being exercised, had its blankets in the bed, and its toys and its cushion, and ... and Xavier, bloody Bengal, was at his own place in the city. They bickered, usually did.

From Patrick, "What sort of people are they?"

From Theresa, "How the hell should I know?"

"Are they smart people, or are they peasants?"

"Probably the same as us."

"Then they're peasants – but Spanish."

"Think of when we're in Spain. Think who we meet."

"Just the people who do the pool and the bar at the club and the *tapas* place, clean the beach, drive the taxis – that's all the Spanish people we meet," said Patrick.

"You're asking me if they're big players, bigger than us . . . I don't know. How can I fucking know? We've sent them a million up front, and we're committed to another million. Is that petty cash or a life changer? I don't know," said Theresa.

A dropped voice, from Patrick. "That submarine isn't petty cash."

"Just wear what you want to wear, and don't take any shit from them."

"It's all done with a handshake. There are no guarantees, it's all taken in faith."

"It's where we are, kid, where Ma's taking us – what Ma calls 'the big time' and 'where we ought to be', you know," and Theresa's effort at mimicking her mother's accent would not have been dared in her hearing. "My advice, don't dress up – don't look like it's your first day at a new school – just go comfortable. I reckon they'll be peasants."

Theresa could see the low wall opposite – where the Potters lived – and the blob of gum was visible against the yellowing mortar. She went three days a week to business school. She had a portfolio of property investments and soon would start to be mentored by Jean-Luc, Doloures's number cruncher. She thought herself uninvolved with gangland, but thought also she'd not have the courage to walk away from the family . . . Her knowledge of Spain was based on holidays at the family villa in Estepona on the Costa del Sol, flowers blooming and a pool, and a high wall around the property that cut off all views except for the mountain top of Gibraltar down the coast. One holiday had been good, five years ago; the rest of them had been miserable, confined and watched by her mother and Xavier. The good one? Ma in bed, moaning from supposed food poisoning, and her meeting up with a German boy, an engineering student with halting English. Dancing, laughing, and him knowing nothing of her – and kissing. Going out with Patrick, gawky and spotty and 16, and taking a taxi into Marbella and telling him to "fuck off somewhere, anywhere" and coming back to the villa late, wide-eyed with excitement. It had never been repeated . . . one of the Darcy boys, from Knowsley, had once turned up when she and Xavier and Patrick were at a fun fair at Calderstones Park, had manoeuvred her into a shadowed corner, had put his hand up her skirt, high up. She'd squealed, slapped him, and squealed some more, and Xavier had come running. Didn't mess about, her big brother. Yanked the Darcy boy to a patch of concrete, stamped first on the kid's right hand and then the left, breaking every finger. Left him screaming and walked away . . . took Theresa and Patrick for a ride on the dodgem cars. Xavier still had the role of minding her, given it him by their mother . . . and Theresa did not know how to walk away, was uncertain if she even wished to.

"Yes, they'll be peasants – and Ma will piss all over them," Theresa said.

"When things start to go wrong for you, you'll probably be the last person to know it."

"I'll not argue with you."

"Just wanted to check on you, that it's still going ahead. Tell me – going wrong as best you know or a clear run to the finish?"

"Me, Nikko, I'm fine. My boy at the front concerns me – the danger time. He might recognise it, might not."

"Never get too fond of them, Jonas."

The call had come through from Bogotá. A man appeared on the screen, dressed in camouflage combat gear and wearing a flak jacket and a tin helmet, and with dark smears on his unshaven face. Nikko of the Drug Enforcement Administration announcing himself. The first time Jonas had seen him. Had been up-country, had gone into the Miraflores municipality of the Guaviare department, mountain and jungle, and had knocked out a laboratory, and they had taken "incoming" as the choppers had put down, and had "wasted" a few gooks, and had made a good bonfire of what they'd found. Perhaps, Jonas thought, the DEA agent had stood too close to the fire as the coke was cooking, sounded high, had even let go a few shots himself, "half a clip", but was uncertain whether he had "scored". Did Jonas ever go on this scale of operation? He did not. Was he ever allowed to get off his butt and go look for action? Not really. Did he wish he was riding on a gunship, doing the contours of a valley, bending treetops and scraping rock outcrops? Jonas had paused, had thought, had hesitated – had remembered how it had been when the cuff had gone on to Cameron Jilkes' wrist and how it had been when Frank, the Sixer, had realised she was being taken into custody by a ridiculous little man in his fancy dress of Harris tweed jacket and leather brogues and flannel trousers . . . Jonas said that the opportunity was unlikely to arise.

Jonas was in the garden, sitting by the fence beside the dripping fir tree, planted eleven years before, and now too tall and good only as a climbing frame for Olaf. He had brought a mug of coffee with him, and the wet canvas seat had already soaked his trousers.

He spoke slowly, carefully, was economical with his words. "We still have the track on the semi-submersible and your aerial sighting is backed with good satellite cover. We anticipate that landfall is at the end of this coming week. That information has not been shared with our own agencies or with the Spanish authorities. Two members of the Govier family are due to fly to Spain on Tuesday morning. Local police are instructed to monitor them until they leave, but have been told not to share any information with any other departments in their own force, or with sister organisations. We expect this family will be present as the cargo is brought ashore and we plan to give the Spanish agencies a late, very late, indication of the unloading beach. These people are major targets for us, that's the reason I am involved and our intention is to imprison them for many years. That's the message I wish to send. The Organised Crime Group at the Galicia end is, frankly, unimportant to me. I am cauterising each vein of information, cutting off the flow of any juices and by doing so, I hope to minimise the prospect of corruption and the leakage of information. The sums of cash that wallow in these circles daunt me, Nikko. I doubt I could say that I, *myself*, do not have a price. I hope I do not – but if an 'indecent proposal' were put to me then I cannot say I would never accept it."

He was told that his confidences were appreciated. Nikko was sitting beside a hangar where technicians were working on helicopter maintenance, he held a can of beer and was smoking a cheroot. Nikko said he felt good. How was Jonas?

Jonas felt a quaver in his voice. "It is the ration of consequences that hurts me. So many consequences and so many very decent people, and some know what they are into and some we keep in ignorance of what they might face. And now we are near the end."

"Everybody's end, and where the stress gets raw. Jonas, that is a diet I live off. Your boy with the abacus. If it has started to go wrong for him, then the chances are he won't even know it. Has he close protection?"

"He does not, at least not near to him."

"Gotten too fond of him? Wrong way to go, Jonas. My way of thinking, they're volunteers, it's their lifestyle. We lost a guy in the Amazon, where they built the big fish. I wasn't fond of him and I kicked his ass for him to get closer, and afterwards I signed off a cash grant to his family, and that's my limit. You being fond of him, your boy, where he sits and what he does, that won't help . . . Why do you do this work, Jonas?"

"No idea. It's a lunacy, Nikko. You?"

"Not do this? Not ride on a Huey bird, not go bust a laboratory, not get to blast half a magazine? Then I might have to go get a job, Jonas, and nothing would be half as much fun. Keep in touch."

"I'm going to take a liberty, send you a photograph, a picture of myself."

"Thank you, it'll go on my operations room wall."

Jonas rifled through his phone's memory, found the picture. Taken eleven months before and downloaded from the Thames House CCTV, a little souvenir from the AssDepDG. It showed a close-up view of the back of Jonas Merrick alone on Lambeth Bridge in the dusk, lit by a street lamp. His trilby was locked down on his scalp and his briefcase was tight in his hand. He highlighted it, then typed *Me in my combat gear, carrying my main armament, along with empty lunch box and thermos flask, another day in the trenches completed,* and sent it. Perhaps by now agent Nikko of the

Administration had pulled open another can and had lit another cheroot, and Jonas thought him a good man, which by his standards was an accolade. His coffee had gone cold.

But remembered, "When things start to go wrong for you, you'll probably be the last person to know it."

Sergio challenged his mother. "We don't need them."

Isabella Munoz answered him, "We have to trade."

"You don't know them."

"I know enough, they are a family with a reputation for moderate success, and they have ambition."

"But they are strangers."

"I trade in Colombia. I hardly go there. I do not walk the slums of Bogotá or Medellín. I do not drink their champagne or visit their ranches. I do not sit in a comfortable chair and watch their sport of killing those who have crossed them. But I trade with them."

"The people who are coming, they bring you nothing."

"Do not, please, interrupt your mother."

"They are not tested, have no pedigree."

"And when your father collapsed, became a husk of his old self, when I started to manage the family's affairs, I was not 'tested'. I was without 'pedigree'. You accept that?"

He did. He reached forward to his mother, and she frowned momentarily and then chuckled, and allowed him to take her head in his hands. A Sunday morning and she had already been to celebrate Mass, and had taken Concepcion with her, and had been shown to her usual place in the midst of the congregation – diminishing year on year because Galicians had less respect for the church, for its teachings and for the respectability it gave, *respetabilidad*, so precious. She allowed him to hold her head, his long fingers on her cheeks. Beautiful fingers. Not like those of his brother Laureano, who piloted the speedboats far out into the ocean and who could flex muscle and heave bales of pure cocaine from a deck to a jetty, and if one fell overboard would go into the sea and retrieve it, and bring it back. Laureano's fingers were short, calloused and blistered. Sergio's were like a pianist's. She believed neither son would survive without her. He shrugged, and told her that he was due to take his family to lunch at Vilagarcia at a fish restaurant they owned . . . So much that they owned, and so much money secreted in businesses and in properties. They must stay strong and protect what they owned, and show caution. She did not argue.

He believed his mother regarded him as little more than a useful "stud". That area of Galicia was well known as cattle country. Good beef came from here, and high-quality milk from which cheese was made. The herds required constant regeneration. Pride of place alongside the herds of milking cows were the revered bulls. Sergio presumed that he owned the reputation of a good stud, no less and no more. The use of a "stud" bull, even a champion, lasted until he failed to perform and then he would be supplanted, sent to the slaughter house. It would not be the first time that she had suggested this course of action for him . . . He would do it, always did as his mother demanded of him. It was necessary for him to prove his value, by way of competition with Laureano who took the speed-boats out towards the Cape Verde islands, even the Azores. And he mentioned the other nagging matter in his mind.

A Dutch woman. Always on the cliffs. Told his mother the source of the information. Told her what surveillance he had in place.

She said quietly, "They can be dangerous places, the cliffs. Sheer rock faces and insecure paths. Dangerous to a stranger."

Sergio said, "She has no contact with us that has emerged . . ."

"None?"

"None that is evident – but we exercise caution, until the tin can washes up, and while your visitors are with us . . . I have to go for my lunch."

He was allowed to kiss her cheek. He detested her, was afraid of her, was happy to be away from her.

Many who worked for the Munoz clan would have been at Mass. Two men were missing from their usual positions alongside their

wives and children. The men were foot soldiers in the pay of
Isabella Munoz. Paid handsomely, trusted, and had been given
that morning sights to witness that had caused them to grin, then
chuckle, then to let out low obscenities, then both had half-choked
on their fags and had spluttered till scarlet faced.

She, the target for their surveillance, had stood by the window
of the room at the north end of her cottage and had lifted the
blind. Then she had walked past the floor-to-ceiling glass window
of the living area, and into the kitchen and had stood at the sink
and had filled a kettle . . . had made coffee, two mugs and then had
gone back. So, first they had viewed her breasts and her front.
Now, they were treated to her spine, her bottom and the backs of
her thighs. Back in the bedroom a man was standing, revealing
little of himself, padding off with a towel around his middle, then
returning and starting to dress.

The two men frequented a brothel in Santiago, the better
brothels were in that religious city with its pilgrims and visiting
clergy, and the girls were usually Romanian and Bulgarian and, on
the money that the Munoz family paid them, they could choose
the best. This morning they were given a show, and appreciated it,
but good things ended and she too dressed.

They had found a fine place to park, up the hill from the short
length of track that came off the lane and towards the cottage. The
branches of the trees kept most of the rain off the windscreen and
the driver's window. They could not use the windscreen wipers nor
open the doors and activate the interior lighting. They had a good
view, good enough to create serious and pleasurable excitement.

They were not told why they watched the woman's cottage, had
not been given a reason by Sergio for his interest, and both men
were envious of Adriano who had the big lens on his camera.

Adriano had the Nikon viewfinder up to his eye, adjusted focus.

Two cars were parked outside the door. A small hatchback was
untidily filled with the supports of an easel and the crazy angles of
a three-legged stool, and he could see the top of the paint box and
a pile of heavy coats.

The second car had arrived later. A Seat saloon, a mass-produced vehicle that was anonymous in its ordinariness.

Adriano had in the last half hour already taken more than 60 images. He would not show them to Isabella Munoz, nor to Sergio Munoz, but he believed that Laureano – the wild boy and the speedboat pilot – would appreciate them. He might, he hoped, have Laureano's permission to sell, discreetly, the high-quality views of the Dutch woman. A cascade of definitive freckles and hair that was molten gold, except for the lower area, and . . .

Clothed, she was less attractive. In his studio he produced images – with the help of aspiring girls wishing for a career in modelling, all *young* – but they had a sanitised pose compared with what he had photographed through the rain and in the gloom from the scudding clouds. She held the front door open. He took more pictures and his camera shutter clattered.

Then a man. Adriano had been instructed to give particular attention to any visitor received by the Dutch woman . . . Checked focus, had the viewfinder hard against his eye, was breathing fast, steadied, grinned. Let the shutter loose.

They kissed.

Lucky bastard. Adriano worked for the Munoz family at surveillance, and had twice in the last 17 months produced photographs of police officers who met mistresses in hotels or in car parks. The pictures had been given to Sergio Munoz and new avenues of information valuable to the clan would have been opened up – cheaper than having them on the payroll. He watched.

The young man ran to his car. The door to the cottage closed. The Seat was driven away. Adriano eased back. He sat in his camouflage army gear in a pool of mud and water. In front of him was a scrim net with one rent in it that allowed space for his lens that was wrapped in more camouflage cloth.

A car came down the hill and would follow the disappearing vehicle, keep sight of it but not tailgate it. Adriano settled, then checked his results, and his breath came faster when he looked at her. The image of the man, *lucky bastard*, was sharp.

★　★　★

Kenny Blake drove fast, almost recklessly scattering rainwater from the puddles and the water sluiced down his windscreen and the wipers struggled.

Any other day, Kenny would have claimed that he was oblivious to the presence of the St Christopher on his chest. Could have gone through whole days and not remembered it lay there, bedded into the hair of his chest, offering up a little comfort of some sort of sanity when his fingers found it, felt the contours of the figure on the disc . . . He had broken the spell that he had hoped he had fashioned with that girl. Did not know who she was and did not know her past, but had thought he shared more than her bed: enjoyed being with her on the cliff paths with the echo of waves on rocks and seeing the wind rip her hair and flatten her clothing, and had heard often enough to worship it the crackle of her laughter, and had seen something serene settle on her face when she squatted on the three-legged stool and worked at her easel.

He took the narrower roads fast, tested his driving skills, challenged himself while holding the treacherous road.

There was a bar north of Malpica, just a shack, and a guy there whose money he held, and where only locals went on a weekend.

Kenny thought he had lost the girl and that dominated his thoughts, and alcohol – the instructors, the psychologists, preached the message that it didn't help – was cheap.

He could have snapped the chain, removed the St Christopher, lowered the window and chucked it out. But he let it lie there among the hairs of his chest.

If anything, the weather had worsened.

How long?

The skipper, Diego, shrugged.

How much longer? Matias poked his finger into Diego's back.

Four more days – the whole of Monday and Tuesday and Wednesday and all of Thursday, then landfall.

Diego clung to a rail beside the wheel at the front of the cabin. He had the wheel and the compass to study. Matias was at the rear of the cabin, close to the diesel engine, and seemed immune to the fumes that choked and spilled round them.

Matias shouted, "The boy, I don't think he can last."

"He has to fucking last."

"Look at him . . ."

The boy, Emiliano, tried hard to be sick. He had nothing to offer. As a sop to him, before it was launched, the craft was named *Maria Bernarda* and he had painted the name on the forward hull. He retched, his chest heaved, he gasped for more of the polluted air to get down into his lungs, and heaved again. Maria Bernarda was a saint much loved in Colombia. The boy had the lower part of his body on the bottom bunk, and his chest and head were hanging out over the perforated decking. Her saint's day coincided with Emiliano's first communion. His head was a few centimetres from the metal flooring that was designed to allow surplus water to run through it should the spray come in if the windows of the hatch were open. They were not. It had seemed good to call it by that name – Maria Bernarda. Running through the decking was the last of the vomit that Emiliano had managed. The diesel fumes minimised the smell of what had been lifted from the boy's stomach. He had a cut on his head from when they had lurched far down, then slammed into another wall of water, and the boy had been tipped off the bunk and had cannoned into a metallic post on to which the outer fibreglass frame was riveted. Matias had staunched the bleeding, but the head wound was not the boy's main problem.

"Can you not see? He is failing."

"I see he is on the bunk, is sick . . . What do you expect me to do?"

"I don't know."

"Then stop snivelling."

"You could show concern."

"Concern can help him when he is sick? You astonish me . . . I should hold a cup of warm milk to his lips and sing him a lullaby, tell him I am his mother? What do you want me to do?"

"I don't know . . . I don't think he will last."

"I tell you something. You keep the engine well. The engine is good. Tell you also that we have a good course . . . and we are not seen. Too low in the water for radar, camouflaged from the satellites, and there has been no aircraft over us . . . that is true. No aircraft?" He looked first at Matias and then at Emiliano. Repeated it, there had been no aircraft, and the boy, sluggishly, had shaken his head. "We are doing well, making good progress – four more days."

Diego thought the glance from Matias was one of pure malice. Did he care? Not a fuck . . . And the craft rose up, teetered at the top of a wave and the front of the structure was exposed and glistened, and under the fibreglass were the bales that held four tonnes of product. That was what Diego cared about, what the craft held, and its value.

Midway through planting out a trug of spring flowers, David Potter looked down at what he thought of as "that pesky nuisance" and had seen the weed in the paving stones on the far side of his low wall, and had noticed the blob of gum.

Throughout his working and adult life, Potter had never been regarded as a fool. Had he been one then he might have taken action. He stared at the gum. Started to feel the cold on the back of his neck. His hands shivered inside his gardening gloves and the trowel shook in his grasp.

He knew that *she*, from across the road, was out. He had seen neither the girl nor the younger boy. Too often, looking at the house across the street, residence of what the *Liverpool Echo* at the time of the owner's arrest, described as "a top-flight organised crime gang", he believed he saw the flicker of people moving behind the net curtains, though they seldom had the lights on in the rooms at the front of the house to minimise the chances of being seen. He should not have been outside in that weather, but the flowers had to be planted and the forecast was that the weather "low" was set to last. He saw the piece of gum glistening as rain dribbled over it. On his own side of the wall, emerging from between the brickwork, was a cable that ran into a cluster of herbaceous plants and then to a neatly stacked pile of plastic compost bags. Under the bags was the battery that powered the camera: each month, dead of night, "someone" came and changed the battery.

He realised the gum capped the lens – did not know what to do.

David Potter took the easy road. Went inside and called for Jenny – was chided for bringing mud into the hall. Do nothing, she told him. Leave it. As instructed, nothing was done and the gum stayed in place, and he hurried back out to shove in the remaining plants and then scurried inside ... Should never have done it, never have allowed himself to be beguiled by DCI Fanny Thomas, never have permitted himself the role of concerned and dutiful citizen. Thought what they could do to him.

The man was scum, a Covert Human Intelligence Source. Jimbo Rawe took his call.

"You could go looking for Bengal ..."

No thanks, no acknowledgement.

"... And the reason you should go looking for Bengal is in A&E, at the Royal."

The call was cut.

A bad time for Jimbo Rawe to be called. A Sunday morning. He was teetotal, except on his annual summer holiday at the bungalow he would one day live in, on the Kilmalin road out of Enniskerry, on the edge of south Dublin. In Liverpool, he was dry but every Sunday he went to Costa and had a "fix" of two *cappuccinos* and a double Danish. The girl who served him always managed a shamrock motif with the chocolate dust.

Jimbo Rawe was on borrowed time in the city that had, after a fashion, adopted him. In Liverpool he was, almost, an honorary Englishman, but his old-fashioned, even dinosaur attitudes remained in the Republic across the Irish Sea. He was a legend in the Merseyside force, and many attempts to retire him had summarily failed. His writ ran wide, or had done until recently ... He could have gone to the Royal Liverpool University Hospital and taken himself into Accident and Emergency, and found the bay where a beaten-up wreck of a man lay in a smock. Could have smiled in a friendly way, and asked the question: "Don't suppose you'd like to tell me who put you here? Don't suppose you'd like to volunteer yourself for a Crown Court session in the box? And don't suppose the only thought in your pitiful little head is giving evidence against that shit-face, Bengal?" A normal response would have been to telephone the DCI most tightly linked to the family and report what his informant had told him. In more normal times, a raid would have been mounted with a warrant authorising a property search to bring in Xavier Govier, child of Doloures Govier, whose progress up the criminal ladder had been observed by Jimbo Rawe since the wee fecker had been nine. But times were not normal ... He phoned an Assistant Chief Constable, found him hiking in the Pennines.

"Does that blanket instruction that prevents any action or overt or covert investigation into the Govier clan still exist?"

"I say this, Jimbo, with the same pleasure as if I were eating ground glass. We are forbidden to act against those persons directly, and all matters relating to them are first to be run past a certain Jonas Merrick of the Security Services. Don't rant at me, Jimbo, because the matter is above my pay grade. Am I in the loop? I am not."

His temper building, Jimbo Rawe permitted his ACC to continue his moorland walk and good feckin' luck to him.

He set himself to find a number, usually managed to unearth one with his blarney and false charm. Might take a drop of time, but if he were to miss his Sunday ration of coffee and Danish he would make certain he found it.

She searched in each room of her apartment for the small caches of money she had hidden. They were the sums she had skimmed, maybe one euro out of each ten donated. Her roof leaked and the landlord would not repair it. The walls were mouldy in the winter. She rented a living room and kitchen, one bedroom where the worst of the damp showed on a west-facing wall, a bathroom that was big enough for a pan, a basin, and a walk-in shower.

Luna Perez had once been a fine woman. Could attract a national TV crew, have a crowd of a thousand at her back when she stood with a bullhorn at her mouth and confronted the gates of a narco mansion on the outskirts of Pontevedra. She had denounced the cocaine trade as a "national disgrace", and the monies it made as a scandal, and the turning of a generation of kids into zombie teens as a toxic disaster. A celebrity in her own right. And she was a mother . . . one son now living in a Moroccan squat . . . a daughter with a brood of kids whose father beat her for amusement . . . a son, gone 18 years now with a grave in the municipal cemetery, dead at 16 from an overdose of high-grade cocaine. And she had been a wife . . . her husband abandoning her because he drove a truck for a shellfish company and her campaigning was an embarrassment. All past. Now, she cleaned hotel rooms. If she called for a public protest to condemn the drug importation through Galicia's coastline, she was fortunate to gather a dozen listeners if the sun shone, six if it rained.

She had done her best. She was no longer heard. She turned her back, that Sunday morning, on the struggle of three decades. She was known to all of the principal families: she had been threatened, she had been intimidated, she had had envelopes stuffed with money thrust in her hands from her supporters.

Now she was ignored. She searched for those sums of money that she had secreted, set aside from what her charity had officially declared. The extent of her theft from the cash raised at public demonstrations, at meetings and from donations, along with town hall grants, was 1700 euros. Her bicycle needed new tyres. Her refrigerator needed a kick to activate its motor. Two hundred euros would deal with the tyres and buy her a second-hand reconditioned refrigerator; she would save the rest.

She could make the case that she deserved some small reward for her campaigning against the evils of drug taking, and the greater evils of drug importation, and the greatest evils of the bastards and the bitches who lived high off the trade. Fifteen hundred euros in cash counted three times, and now consigned to an envelope. She had heard of this young man, that his terms were good, and that many poor people used him. That Sunday, past the hour when the bells of the church of Peregrina called the dwindling number of believers to worship, she put the envelope in her handbag, and used her phone to find out the time the bus for Corunna would leave Pontevedra the next morning. All shame gone, too old and too tired to feel it.

Vera was standing in the doorway as his phone rang. Jonas answered it.

"Is that Merrick, Jonas Merrick?"

Vera said that lunch was ready, on the table.

"Merrick, yes."

Vera said she needed him to come and carve.

"The Merrick who has hijacked the Govier show?"

"Who am I speaking to?" he asked with apparent politeness, but his forehead had tightened and a frown deepened.

"I'm Fergal Rawe. Detective Inspector Fergal Rawe, Merseyside."

Vera called again for him.

"I am just about to have my lunch, Mr Rawe. Can the matter not wait?"

"It can't, but your lunch can."

Jonas knew the name. He could imagine the frustrations swirling in the veteran detective. The man had the source in the travel agency that had identified the flights the crime family would be taking. And knew the name better because Rawe, better identified as Jimbo – not that Jonas would use a familiarity – had been the first recruiter of a Level One to go into Galicia and set up the Biscuit Tin. Rawe had believed the assignment over, had been happy to withdraw the officer, and Jonas Merrick had intervened. He heard the hiss of Vera's impatience; it was not often she let him know her displeasure.

"Your problem?"

"Quite a substantial one."

"Briefly."

"Don't feckin' tell me, sir, how to report a problem because you are about to eat your feckin' lunch. . . . In this city, which I doubt you know, we have an excellent hospital, the Royal Liverpool. It's

A and E has a reputation second to none for patching up unfortunates who have suffered gunshot wounds or the fractures that result from beatings. That reputation, sir, has been gained through frequent exposure to criminal violence. We know about it. A man is currently there, needing extensive work, and I have information that leads me to a principal suspect . . . except that my Assistant Chief Constable refuses me permission to lift the responsible shit face that is Xavier Govier – Bengal to his many friends. The permission is refused because you, sir, have demanded no action be taken that disturbs the Govier clan. I might, just *might*, if I act fast, retrieve some item that provides a decent link to him. You, sir, obstruct me. You are a block in my way. I want that instruction rescinded."

Vera again told him that the lamb needed carving. They would have it cold the next night and she'd do a cottage pie the night after, before they towed the caravan north.

"No, there will be no change."

"You show, Merrick, the attitude of a small-minded bureaucrat and . . ."

"No change."

"Obstinacy, arrogance . . . Let me remind you that it was me, feckin' Jimbo Rawe, that put the undercover in place. Me. Don't feckin' treat me on Need to Know basis."

"No change, and it is now my lunchtime."

"And another thing . . ."

"Another thing, sir, is that if you impede my work in any way you will be as dead a piece of meat – professionally – as the lamb I am about to take a knife to. Good day."

He ended the call, and switched off his phone and went into the dining room. They always took Sunday lunch in the dining room.

Vera asked, "Do you have a difficulty, Jonas, a problem?"

"Not a difficulty, not a problem, just something of nothing . . . Looks a very decent piece of meat."

6

Normally on a Sunday evening, Jonas Merrick would have enjoyed a sense of elation, his mood would have lightened, might even have managed a smile and a conversation, at the thought of returning to work in the morning. Taking the regular train to London, doing his usual walk, using the elevator, slipping into his cubicle.

His face wore a frosty frown that evening.

Sufficiently obvious for Vera to query, "You are quite wretchedly miserable tonight, Jonas. Why?"

A blink, a shake of his head.

"Is it this crime thing you're doing? Not interesting enough?"

Jonas raised a finger, almost a show of irritation.

"Is it because you promised we would get away this week? Are you having cold feet? Want to call it off?"

A deep breath taken. "I don't. Absolutely not. We are going."

"Then the least you can do, Jonas, is cheer up, and . . ."

Vera returned to her lists. What food to take, what maps, what extra items, all the paraphernalia of a holiday in a caravan. And she would have to take the car to the garage to have it fuelled up and the tyres checked. She worked methodically through the necessary paperwork.

The quiet resumed. The cat lay on the carpet and snored. Jonas attended to his own lists, needed no paper, no pencil; every item seared in his mind.

Things that needed pulling together. All governed by this damned contamination which was *corruption,* and him existing in a world where he must deceive at worst and at best be economical. The strings that he pulled into place emanated from an Amazon river tributary, from the proud city of Liverpool, from London, and there were other lengths that stretched into inlets and valleys along an Atlantic coastline, and a police force there who would have expressed outrage at the suggestion of malfeasance. And there were two middle-aged herdsmen who loved their goats, and there were criminal clans whose ancestry was based on smuggling . . . and the string most prominent was the one linked to Kenny Blake. He tutted out loud, then let slip an intake of breath, loud enough for Olaf to lift his head, for Vera to pause her pencil and look up at him.

Kenny Blake . . . just the one photograph, a druggie on a street corner, leaning against a shop's door jamb. Knew his legend, knew that it had been tested, stretched and examined, probed, yet had – to the best of his knowledge – stayed intact. It was an inexact science lining up bogus biographies that could stand close examination: a school teacher had been quizzed, with disarming carelessness, and an accountancy course looked at and a lecturer approached, parents who it was believed had emigrated to Australia, or was it New Zealand. . . . When it was over – however it worked out – the conspiracy that was paid big money to look into "legends" would be hammered, wrapped up, destroyed . . . So many strings. He coughed, as if a bad taste left a residue in his mouth, and was hard to be rid of. The cat stared at him. Vera put down her pencil.

"Is it the responsibility, Jonas?"

"It weighs a bit. Some days heavier than others. Some days more bearable than others."

"About people?"

"Yes, about people. Moving them around, hoping it's for the best."

"Shouldn't others be helping to carry it?"

"There are times when a committee is an obstruction and therefore best avoided . . . Sorry, my dear, but I don't see the point of us talking in this vein."

"Jonas, you are anxious, you are difficult. You are stretched. Is it possible to go on this trip? Have I pressured you?"

"I don't think so, I doubt it."

"You've never been ambitious, Jonas."

"Never known how to be," and managed a weak smile.

"And now you seem to carry so much and have no one to help."

"My final word, please – that's the way these things need to be done – and we should move on . . . It was an extraordinary centre of trading, all round Snowdonia and the island of Anglesey. Shipments of copper going all over the place from the mines there and I learn there are bronze pieces found in Central Europe made from copper ore from where we're going, and that would be two thousand years before the birth of Christ. And millennia later the Romans prized the area, so remote, because of the mineral wealth. It will be fascinating."

She stared at him, thought she witnessed something manic. He was peering down at the floor and his shoulders were hunched. Felt so tired, so bowed. Had not sought this lofty pedestal, just had been dumped on it. They weighed heavily, the lives.

Kenny Blake, without enthusiasm, nursed his third beer. The lunch customers, all local, had left their tables and would be spending the afternoon visiting family or watching football on TV. Only the simple quality of the food would have brought trade to the bar, not the aspect. Rain lashed the picture windows and the tide was high and the wind fierce . . . The forecast said that it would get brighter from the west, from the ocean, but that the gale would not drop. A grey beach and a grey sea and grey clouds and the uniform colour broken only by the waves cresting and breaking. He sat alone in a corner.

"Kenny, not good to drink as a solitary. You need company."

"Was hoping, Werner, that you would show up. Been waiting for you." Kenny laughed at his preposterous untruth.

"You show misery or anxiety when you drink by yourself."

"Join me, *please*, Werner."

Werner was a client. He told the same story on each visit to the Biscuit Tin. His father had been a U-boat officer and had sailed out of the submarine pens of Bordeaux, and had done a patrol off southern Spain and Gibraltar in 1944 and then had put into

Corunna for "rest and recreation" which was the least that fascist Spain could provide for the fascist axis war machine as the tide turned against them.

Werner's father had gone to sea on that mission leaving a French girl two months pregnant, and had served four weeks in the dangerous waters that were heavily patrolled by the British, then they had sailed north to Corunna for the rest (sleeping) and the recreation (shagging and drinking) and resupply (torpedoes, fresh food, water . . .). A week of it and then the whole crew was dead within hours of leaving Corunna. Hit by an RAF bomber . . . A mother who had delivered a bastard child with blue eyes and a thatch of fair hair, hounded without mercy, and she had put stones in her pockets and walked into the Garonne river. Werner had been brought up in an orphanage. At 18 he had come to live on the Coast of Death. He knew the location of his father's sea grave, had once taken a boat over the place, a boat that had been piloted by Laureano. The Munoz family used him as an interpreter when they needed German.

At 78 years of age, Werner had deposited 19,000 euros in the Biscuit Tin. He lived well enough, called himself a property consultant, had a salesman's fluency, and was fond of young Kenny Blake . . . Not many were interested in the story of his early life and the fractured hull of the submarine, his father's grave. Kenny thought him useful. Pretty much judged people by that criterion, how *useful* they might be. And well connected because the Germans were liked in this corner of Spain. Kenny would betray him but not for another five days. They hugged, more beers were ordered. Actually, he rather enjoyed his company, and that late afternoon wanted company without complications.

How was he? He was fine.

Why then did he "look so fucking miserable"? Said with the gravel accent of a German who had smoked the softness from his voice. Replied that it had been "a difficult week". A shrug, no more explanation given.

"You have a business problem? Need more clients? Want to buy a Maserati? Have the attention of the tax bastards? A lifestyle problem? You want advice, Kenny?"

"I *always* want and welcome your advice, Werner."

A gesture to the barman, more beers. The last time he had been drunk, seriously losing control, had been the night he had left his family. Another row, more shouting, then stumbling up the stairs and throwing clothes into a bag, and filling his rucksack, and the kids whimpering and Hannah howling and not knowing how to repair the damage done. And, not prepared to put his warrant card in the post, an envelope addressed to SC&O10, and he had quit. Had taken a train to London, had sat morose in the carriage, and then had gone to the Pimlico pub which they used when they stayed in the hostel provided for them when in transit. Had staggered out into the night and groped towards the door. A room had been reserved for him . . . In what name? Could not remember. What name was he using then? No recall. Had sunk down on the hostel steps, had wet himself.

Werner was hunched forward, conspiratorial. "Go where the money is. What the Galicians do, chase the money. The best advice – forget women and fancy cars and fine wine, concentrate on the money. You have a fine reputation here, Kenny, are trusted. A reputation that came quickly for you, faster than for me. You have to be trusted here, Kenny, always must be. What I say, it is hard to gain trust, is easy to lose trust . . . What was it we were talking about?"

"This and that, Werner." He laughed and the beer was slipping down easily. "That and this."

"Afternoon, ma'am – no, sorry, evening – apologies for calling you. Before you ask, ma'am, we didn't think it should hold till the morning."

She was in the kitchen when the mobile had rung. The sink was full. She had cooked the lunch, had then tried to catch up on her paperwork. Had suggested that the kids clear the table, wash up the pots, might even have surpassed themselves and put some powder in the effing dishwasher and pressed the effing button. Her husband was asleep, the TV bawling at him. The kids were upstairs and music played out of their rooms and she doubted schoolwork was being finished.

"Give it me."

"It's not good news, ma'am, sort of has golden bollocks hanging off it."

"Just give it."

She knew how to wedge the phone against her ear, reach for the powder from under the sink, to open the front of the dishwasher and fill the slot, slam it shut, press the button. It was Sandy, one of her best. Older than her, devoted, always passed over for promotion because he'd refused to go up the ladder, preferred to stay as a bag carrier on her team.

"The surveillance on the Goviers."

"What of it?"

"The camera in the wall."

"I know what it is, Sandy, give me that modicum of intelligence . . ." She immediately regretted sounding cruel but the sink was full and the fat had congealed on the roasting tin, and the sound from upstairs was raucous, and her bloody husband was snoring, and she had only managed to complete half the work she'd intended and had meetings in the morning. "Yes, the camera?"

"The feed's down."

"Meaning?"

"The camera's not working. Well, it *is* working but not showing anything."

"Which is telling us?"

"Telling us, ma'am, that the battery is still functioning and the transmission is good, but the lens inserted in the wall has somehow been blocked off. The picture is obstructed. Seems the feed has been off for a while, but the people monitoring it thought it was broken, and that it would wait until Monday morning for notification to the customer – us, ma'am. What to do?"

She kicked the kitchen unit in front of her, hard enough to take some paint off and to hurt her toe. She reflected . . . had promised that the family were going on holiday – together, another effing miracle – at the end of the week. She had agreed weeks before and it had gone into the household diary, and the two previous times she had cried off. A big promise, a "cross my heart and hope to die" level promise. She reckoned that half her team were either living in bachelor pads, or contemplated it. Thought the divorce lawyers were coining it from the serious Crime Unit personnel. It had attractions, a one-bedroom flat . . . She started running the hot tap.

"Have the householders been telephoned, been asked to check it?"

The rain beat hard on the window, ran rivers down the glass, and it was hardly likely that Potter could be persuaded to put on his coat, get a torch and go out to peer at the brick wall and find the obstruction.

"They've been telephoned, yes. Either not there or declining to pick up the phone. I did not think, ma'am, we could send a uniform round in a marked car."

"Of course – thank you, Sandy. Another for Monday morning."

"And more . . ."

"Can't wait – make my day."

"A guy in a bed in A&E at the Royal. Rumour mill says he had issues with our friendly family. God knows why, but it was fielded by Jimbo. Nothing further on the allotment. Jimbo says he had a right barney with some wee blighter down in London and is refused permission at ACC level to pull in Bengal. It's getting, ma'am, to be my definition of a mess."

"Be in at seven-thirty. Thank you, Sandy."

Fanny ran the hot tap until it scalded her hands and squirted in the washing-up liquid and bubbles swarmed over her cardigan and skirt, and she set to work and clattered the pans and splashed water on the floor, did it noisily but insufficiently to raise a helping hand – not one, not a single effing hand . . . The system had to change. Clear as a pikestaff. Disparate units failing to knit together and losing out, and Organised Crime Groups walking all over them. And the answer? No idea. Only knew they were losing, which hurt. Only knew that in her neck of the woods they were forgetting how to win.

★　　★　　★

The photographer waited in an underground car park. Times were different from when he was a youth and being given his first photographic assignments by the Munoz clan. On the second floor of the apartment building above the parking area, lived a prominent local politician who was frequently seen on the region's private TV channels. Thirty years before, Sergio would have been entertaining him, interested in his responsibility for development contracts, on a yacht or a launch moored to a pontoon in the sheltered marina. Not now. Sergio would have slipped into the building via the parking garage and would have taken a lift to the second floor, and it was predictable that the interior cameras throughout the complex would have been switched off, and would stay "off" until he left. Extravagant days were gone. Not that Adriano complained. If they were discreet, cautious, suspicious, then he thought his chances of staying out of gaol were improved. Before, they would have met in the harbour haven and the women would have been at a party, dressed to kill, and the power of the families would have been on display. No longer . . . nothing ostentatious, Adriano reflected, but still with the same level of authority. He saw the light signalling the descending lift. He had a cardboard envelope in his gloved hand. Not leather gloves, nor suede, but thin, strong kitchen gloves. The envelope would carry neither his DNA or his fingerprints, nor would its contents. The lift door opened, Sergio emerged, looked around – then saw the photographer and gestured to him. Also a sign of the new times . . . in the days when the great clans had strutted on the streets of Galicia's towns, the cars would have been a top-of-the-range Mercedes, a Ferrari or a Rolls-Royce. Sergio's key turned on the lights of a SEAT family car. The envelope was handed over, opened. Sergio eased into his seat and spilled the photographs into his lap. Saw the Dutch woman passing the floor-to-ceiling windows and punched Adriano's arm, then lingered on the other images. Sergio's breath sang in his teeth and a frown furrowed his forehead. He checked his phone then dictated an address, said it slowly so that the photographer would remember it, not to be written down, and was told where he should be and why. Not for Adriano to expect confidences from Sergio Munoz, but the shock displayed was enough. He ducked his head in respect. Sergio looked again at the photograph of the Dutch woman and her guest, and the kiss that represented both intimacy and annoyance, then he powered up and drove out of the car park. Adriano had not been praised, did not need to be . . . He allowed the merest of smiles to flicker at his mouth and seemed to see the rolling passage across a floor of a live hand grenade.

A navy blue skirt and jacket were Luna Perez's choice. She lifted them out of her wardrobe.

She had worn that suit when meeting a junior senator from the US east coast and the American had congratulated her on her courage in fighting the massed forces of evil, cocaine smugglers, and there had been film crews there because he was considered a rising star and might, the election after the next, be a Presidential candidate. He had thought Luna Perez a woman worth being photographed alongside. She had worn the same suit when she had been a guest in the office of the Interior Minister in Madrid and a delegation from Strasbourg had asked to meet her in person. But when she was demonstrating with the Mothers Against Drugs at the gates of the Baion estate owned by the Oubina family, armed men glowering at the women, she wore jeans and a T-shirt, sweat-stained from the heat. As she did at the demonstration of triumph outside the gaol at Pontevedra when Luis Falcon was arrested. She had not worn this suit since her boy was buried. It had fitted her well and some photographers had been present at the burial, not as many as when he had overdosed two years earlier, but respectable.

She held the suit against her body and thought age was doing a good job of ravaging her. A weekly magazine from Barcelona had once called her *La Pasionaria* of her day. The smugglers had beaten her as convincingly as the Francoists had broken through Madrid's defences. She was yesterday. Her present was an envelope in her handbag, and her future was a bus journey to Corunna in the morning and a visit – no appointment made – to an investment manager. She could no longer make a difference, accepted it. Would bank the money she had stolen, was past a sense of shame . . . thought herself irrelevant but would want to look good in the morning and so would wear that suit.

The gates were opened. The men who oversaw the security of the home of Isabella Munoz saw the approach of the car's headlights, would have noted the registration, then moved smartly so that Sergio did not have to slow on entering the grounds in which the villa sat. Not an elaborate building, not one that dripped luxury. More important was that it could not be seen from the road, and was surrounded by fencing topped with discreet strands of razor wire, and the trees beyond the fence had been felled and cattle now grazed meadows where once there had been woodland. The men who operated the gates, with their colleagues, also had responsibility for the security of the perimeter, and had access to firearms should the compound be attacked . . . Sergio drove to the door of the house, snatched the photographs from the seat beside him and hurried inside.

Laureano was sprawled on a settee, watching sport on a satellite channel from Germany, with a can in his giant hand. He found Concepcion who would make him coffee. Found his mother in her retreat, what served as an office. No greeting, just a nod and a flick of her head towards a chair and he laid the pictures in front of her, and studied her reaction.

His coffee was brought.

Isabella raised an eyebrow, nibbled at her lower lip, gave a quick shake of her head as if something needed clarification . . . and looked amused as she studied the images of the naked Anna Jensen, and glanced at her son who she knew slept with women in the village and shop girls and prominent men's wives, and sometimes even with his wife . . . then the mask settled. She studied the photographs that showed Kenny Blake, investment manager and founder of the Biscuit Tin laundering and tax evasion business.

A soft voice, one that was seldom raised in mirth or anger. "The woman? Remind me."

"Dutch national. Been here nearly four years. A Person of Interest to the GRECO crowd. Spends too much time on the cliffs and spends too much time on third-grade daubing. She would not gain entry to any art college here. She was presumed to be a rich kid, and apparently in love with the Coast of Death. I think GRECO wonder who she is, what she is . . . and Customs, and the Finance people. That was the information given. Just a warning. Just the suggestion that more should be learned of her when the boats go out . . . and now we are bringing in the submersible, and . . ."

"Nothing that is clear?"

"Nothing that seems to threaten. She takes a lover. Kenny Blake. We are involved with him . . . not at my suggestion, nor Laureano's. At your suggestion, Mama. Tonight, what I hear, the lover is drinking himself insensible in Mikel's bar and already he can barely stand and we have not seen evidence of such behaviour from him before. I hazard it, Mama, perhaps in bed she is as lacking in talent as in her art, and so he drinks away the memory. But . . ."

"*But?*"

"He matters to us. You have invested in him, Mama. You did not choose to listen to me, or to Laureano. Perhaps he is a security risk, perhaps he is not. Perhaps you are in error, Mama, perhaps you are not. You have given him your trust, Mama. Wise? I think very soon we will discover whether your trust is well placed, or was a poor decision. My father would not have so freely given trust."

She would have thought it a big card that he played. To invoke Tomas, who had not been capable of decision making since his fall, was in effect to challenge her. "You offer me nothing beyond your prejudice . . . What action have you taken?"

"Tomorrow is a working day. Perhaps he will be sober. He will go to his office. Will not transact business by phone but in person. He will be followed if he leaves his office, all his visitors will be identified. It is a difficult week ahead, Mama, and again it was your decision to bring in this foreign family, and your decision to make a major contribution to the building of the submersible, and your decision to guarantee a considerable part of the cargo's purchase price. You have made many decisions, Mama, and made them alone."

Still quiet, but angered, she attacked her son. "We had him checked. Everything about him in England was looked at. You, *you*, found those people to do that work. Parasites, but recommended. They speak to a schoolmaster who taught him. They go to the college and find a tutor who lectured him in accountancy. His income tax is confirmed, and his driving papers, and his bank details. All confirmed. I paid ten thousand euros for the guarantee that he was clean. His business was tested: would have failed the examination if not genuine investments – we asked for seven fifty to be sent for that Monaco apartment, seven hundred and fifty thousand euros, and it went through, with complete efficiency. What is there not to like?"

"We will see who he meets and who he entertains. He can be a pleasant boy who amuses you, and he can be a risk. He can be a shit and universally disliked but reliable . . . I leave you with a thought, Mama. Why now – at this time – does he go out and drink himself near to the floor? Why? Do you know, Mama?"

He left his mother, turned his back on her, but paused at the door.

"Everybody *likes* him. Why he has made a success of his business. He wins affection . . . We will watch him. Goodnight, Mama."

Climbing the stairs, holding the banister rail, Jonas felt a great tiredness. Hoped to God that by the morning he would have kicked off this malaise of exhaustion. He had not, really, before, been frightened of responsibility. Moving men and women round, deciding on the priorities, as any conscientious clerk would do. Paused halfway up and steadied himself, then resumed his climb.

He rather yearned for excitement. God forbid that Vera should realise it. Had not known much of it in those decades of toil at his desk. Had deceived all of them, except for the AssDepDG, most of the time. Had felt excitement when he had buried his hand under Winston Gunn's anorak and vest and clutched a fistful of wires and yanked . . . Could have blown them both to any God waiting to receive them, then could have smashed half of Westminster's windows, knocked over Rodin's statue of the Burghers of Calais. But nothing had happened; he had just held the cables in his hand and could feel Winston's quivering chest. Excitement at quite an extraordinary level . . . and when the handcuff had snapped on to the wrist of Cameron Jilkes, terrorist or freedom fighter, and the man had gone into shock that boring old fart had so easily conned him and the pain of an almost dislocated shoulder socket was more than mitigated by the excitement of knowing that he, Jonas Merrick, had achieved the capture . . . And that same excitement, overladen by fear, when Frank, so pretty and so clever and so sweet at cleaning his spectacles and bringing him cake as he worked beside her, had dragged him over the parapet into the Thames. What Jonas thought each morning when he came off the bridge and crossed the road, and after his Danish and coffee and arguing at work, so few of them had ever known such acute excitement. Maybe not even Kevin and Leroy who stood guard duty. All swarming around him each morning at the gates, filtering the IDs, sweaty in running vests or cycling kit, and none of them – his opinion – had owned his experiences. And didn't have what was secreted in Vera's knicker drawer. Managed the last few steps and Olaf passed him.

On his list of contacts, those with whom he spoke by phone, never face to face, was an arthritic old Special Forces trooper, a veteran of much of the posturing of empire, who had described the pursuit of danger as "an addiction, same as having a malarial dose in your blood, never rid of it". That was excitement.

By the top of the stairs that jauntiness, hidden from observers, had returned. The cat watched him with suspicion. He crossed the landing, felt confident again. Did not consider that in north Wales he would fail to find, among the copper mines of prehistory and Roman garrison camps and amphitheatres and hut circles from the Iron Age, what he craved. Not in doubt that he would conjure some excitement . . . but on his terms. Briefly had lost sight of the responsibilities and the figures on the board.

★   ★   ★

Kenny's thoughts slurred and wobbled in his head.

Drunk? Of course. Comatose? Nearly.

He asked for a last beer, "one for the road". Another client had joined him. A friendly enough guy, harmless, whining about his history, a refugee on the coast.

Would have been the ninth beer or the tenth. Werner had gone home in a taxi, leaving his car parked next to Kenny's. The taxi had returned, its meter ticking, its driver sitting by the door. All the other tables had been wiped down, and the chairs stacked, and the music had been switched off. He could not remember when he had last been drunk, incapable, *and* on duty of a sort. Most certainly the first time that he had been slumped over a table, head on his arms, listening to the meandering story of a man with killing, murder, in his genes . . . and the St Christopher hung on the chain from his neck and rested against his watch.

He listened, hardly heard.

The guy was one of the *nostálgicos*, and might, alone in his bathroom, have sung the *Cara al Sol,* the anthem of the Spanish Falange, and done the straight-arm salute. His favourite quote, to Kenny, was, "In these parts you notice in the eyes if a man hates you or does not. The same with the Basque people as here." The owner shouted that it was time, and the driver stood up, and Kenny and his client drained their bottles. The last time he'd been this drunk, he'd been woken on the hostel steps by the guy on reception, had been heaved up and the remark in his ear – *Not to worry, sir. Happens to all of us when things sort of pile up. It'll seem better in the morning, always does* – and dawn had come and had penetrated the thin curtains and his phone had been beside the bed and he could have picked it up and rung the number. Hannah would have been dressing Joanne and Eddie and then rushing to get them fed, and he could have said that the job no longer mattered to him, that his work no longer consumed him – only *they* mattered. He had turned over, faced the wall.

The guy said to Kenny, "It is a good place for me, perhaps for you. The most secretive in Spain. There is a loathing of those who threaten them . . . if protection is offered they will defend you with their lives. A good place for us . . . Keep my money safe . . . There is only one crime here, the crime of betrayal."

David Potter had locked the front door and the back door and checked then both. He paused for a moment in the hall, his finger poised to switch off the last of the lights, and the phone rang. Jenny was already upstairs.

Would be a wrong number, had to be at that time of night.

She called to him, "Pick it up, dear."

He did. "Hello, yes?"

A woman's voice, exhausted. "Mr Potter? David Potter? Wretched time to be calling you. It's Mrs Thomas, Fanny Thomas. DCI Thomas. You all right, Mr Potter?"

"I am, I think, yes. Why might I not be?"

"I suppose it could have waited till the morning, but it has nagged all evening. Your feed is down."

"What's down?"

His wife was in her nightdress at the top of the stairs. The heating had been off for more than two hours and the cold seemed to have spread fast that night, and the rain hammered at the front door. "Who is it? Who wants us?"

"It's the police . . . they say our 'feed is down'. I think they mean that bloody camera. Am I going out to examine it? I am not. Go back to bed."

He heard her moving away on the landing.

"Now, Mrs Thomas, why are you calling me?"

"The feed from your wall is blocked. We're not getting any pictures of the house opposite you. We'll sort it in the morning . . . Because of who lives there I just wanted to satisfy myself that you were both all right, know what I mean?"

"Both all right, both going to bed, both happily ignored by our neighbours."

"Be sorted in the morning. Discreetly. We're grateful for your cooperation, Mr Potter, you should know that. Just wanted to be sure that all was well with you and your wife. Good night, Mr Potter."

He put the phone back on its cradle, switched off the hall light. Through the window beside the front door he could see the house across the road and a dull light burned and he could not gauge the menace that lurked there, all quiet and seeming peaceful . . . except that was a damned lie; if it had not been, then a Detective Chief Inspector would not have phoned him at that time on a Sunday evening to report a failure of a covert camera.

Mikey Govier was in his cell, had had his dinner and watched TV, had a CD to watch which was a bit of a love story and in costumes from a couple of centuries back. He liked that sort of film, romance and period and settings that showed mountains and forests and old country houses, and liked best that – after a few hiccups – it would all end well. His door was closed, shutting out much of the noise on the landing. Had had years of this sort of Sunday evening and had more to come. One drawback to a Sunday evening was that it would be followed by Monday morning. He might have done a "sickie" and told the staff to turn away his start of the week visitor. A few weeks back he had confided to a lifer, done 12 years and a few to come, that it was a pain in the arse to have her come and look down her nose at him, and treat him like he was a fucking idiot . . . There were some on the landing who talked about nothing other than what job they'd pull when they were out, or who counted the days till they could blag or deal or use a hammer or drive a car fast or run a scam. Not Mikey Govier. He was content where he was.

Doloures Govier was already asleep. Always went to bed early on a Sunday night, wanting to be fresh for the next day and the next week. Had done her duty and seen her mother, and the dog was fine. Had been to the lawyers, crooked bastards she reckoned, and expensive, and had been out in the bleeding rain up beyond Crosby where there were miles of beach and no chance of bugs and had talked with them of further investments, property – both commercial and residential – and had talked of a potential bonanza something like a lottery win with add-ons, but had not told them of the details of a shipment coming into north-west Spain. She met them every Sunday afternoon, didn't matter about the weather, and they advised on where money should go, how it should be washed and rinsed. Then home, a salad for supper, what Xavier called a "a fucking rabbit's tea", then a meeting of the family round the kitchen table. Regular as setting a clock, every week, Jazzer came to the house and swept it. There had been others who had thought themselves special years back who had been lifted because the Merseyside force had actually managed to plant bugs in their home, or had got the spooks to do it for them. The family would go through the week ahead, nothing barred, and she demanded that everything was on the table, nothing kept back. Doloures had been satisfied and was now in her severe pyjamas fast asleep. Nine years since the front door had caved in to blows of a battering ram and the cops had swarmed up the stairs and Mikey had been bollock naked when the cuffs had gone on, and then sat on the bed and helped to dress and her sitting up and holding the sheet across her chest. No other guy had been in that bed with her since, or any other bed. She thought the week ahead would be a landmark for the family, move them on.

As was usual for him, after the Sunday night family session, Xavier had done two clubs and was going into a third. Security knew him well. Most of them worked for him or distributed for him. Never called by his first name, certainly not addressed as Bengal. Greeted with respect and courtesy, and escorted to the front of any queue and then into the VIP area. Might be foot-ballers there, and music people, and they'd all smile and reckon to look friendly and he'd ignore them because they were outside his interests . . . On a Sunday night he did the rounds and heard from his guys how business was. In the clubs he drank Coca-Cola, never alcohol. Never smoked weed there, never snorted, never went to the toilets to get a fix of anything. Stayed clean and sharp on a Sunday night. He'd be doing the clubs till three in the morning, Monday, and it was pretty much a given that cameras would have been killed when he was on the premises. A hell of a strain every Sunday night because business was booming and his interests were spreading, and there were more guys to see and more to pay, and more who needed to be reminded of the result if

they played daft fuckers with him. That night he met guys from
Manchester, from Southport, also from Rotherham and Sheffield.
So much work, and so little time, and his arms still ached from
belting the bastard outside the snooker hall, and his head blasting
from what he'd drunk on Saturday night. Never got to spend the
cash. But kept on, no other way – and stayed free which was more
than his useless father had managed.

In her room, music playing, Theresa worked. Always studied on
a Sunday evening. Should have done that on weekday nights too
but watched TV instead. Tried to get up to speed for the classes
she'd have at the business school, but her mind was fouled up,
distracted. In a couple of years she might get to work as a paid
intern at Jean-Luc's company . . . Now, she sat at her desk, wearing
a nightdress and robe, and thought of Cocky. Did that most
evenings, not just Sundays. If she had to have a hero in her life then
it would have been Cocky Warren – Curtis Warren to the police
and the prison service and the courts. They said he was the biggest
personality, celebrity, to come out of Liverpool, said he was bigger
than the Beatles, bigger than any of the footballers. Public Enemy
Number One. Top of the Ten Most Wanted. Sat in her chair and
gazed at the screen, the information floated past her. She had a
picture of him, from the *Liverpool Echo*, taken by a police surveillance camera, and he was grinning, in control. They said that
Cocky ran the whole of his empire, the biggest the UK had ever
seen, from his mobile; had some enforcers, and some lawyers on
call, and a few cops, but did the deals on his mobile and was known
in Amsterdam and in the Colombia markets . . . Theresa had once
met a girl whose mother's cousin had seen Cocky, actually locked
eyes on him. At a fuel station in Crosby, and the girl's mother's
cousin had been filling up at the next pump, and he'd smiled at her
and she had followed him inside and to the counter, and he'd filled
an SUV and had dug a wad of notes from his hip pocket. Dreamed
of Cocky, the big man of the city and a legend – and now stuck in
a shit-hole gaol, and years more in front of him. Theresa liked to
look at Cocky's picture and to imagine, did that late at night . . .
and was bitching to herself that she was being left behind, that

Patrick was going with Ma to Spain. Sunday night drifting by and the list of investment opportunities for the family that she had been told to produce was not yet written, let alone researched.

There was a party across the city and Patrick had been asked. Ma had told him to accept. Music, food, booze, and probably something else at the bottom of the garden. Patrick did not do drugs – none of the family did. Xavier would have beaten the lights out of him if he had been into coke or smack, had even smoked a spliff. And Patrick did not drink, which was clever. He would dance a bit at the party but he was tone deaf. He was there because another family had a girl who needed marrying off. Happened most months and he was supposed to take a look at the girl and report back to his mother. He always went with minders and they'd be waiting outside in the car and there were other kids at the party who were supposed to keep an eye open for him. Could have been a target, could have been taunted, could have been used as a punch bag because no one loved the Goviers. A pretty normal Sunday evening for Patrick. His future looked good which was why parents paraded their daughters, skirts high on their thighs and necklines low on their chests. Life seemed easy and the prospect of the future was fine and he backed the trip to Spain and progress up the ladder, had the confidence that Ma was smart enough to keep them at liberty . . . Patrick would not be visiting his father the following morning, never went. Would have sent a message about mistakes, fuck-ups, lives falling apart, did not want to be reminded of the downside of life. Those who schemed against them, the police agencies, were rubbish: he knew that because his mother had told him. Before going to the party he had hung his suit on the door of the wardrobe, and laid out some new shirts . . . seemed confident, did not know of any reason he should not be.

"What do I do? What should my action be?"

"Jak, for Christ's sake, it's Sunday evening."

"Tomorrow morning I have to authorise three months more of resources – and I have no idea what's happening. On top of it I have some Neanderthal DI from scouseland pleading to me to give him a briefing. He's the guy who bid at auction to get KB and drop him into that bloody corner of Spain. Getting anxious for his boy. Thinks I can open the door and salve his worries."

The kids were asleep, his wife had gone to bed. The household would be alive again in six hours. Jak Peters of SC&O10, a handler of Level One undercovers, sat in his kitchen and in front of him was another black coffee, too many already sloshing in his gut. He waited for an answer from his superior.

"The command from the celestial heavens is that we are outside any relevant loop." Then a yawn, and a voice in the background demanding to know when he'd finish. "I know as little as you, likely less."

"I have to sign off a bucketload of cash. He doesn't come cheap. Everything about it drinks money. Is it going on for three days, three weeks, three months – God, what about three years?"

"Then ring him."

"I am expressly forbidden to ring Kenny's mobile . . ."

"No, ring the new kid on the block. Disturb his beauty sleep. Tip the spook out of his pit . . . I can't help you. We handed over responsibility for our boy. You think I sleep easily with that dereliction of normal practice? I'm told he has a degree of protection, but nothing has been explained to me. Ring him."

"Met him once, walked him across a bridge, tottered a bit. Gave me a bit less than nothing. Know his name, precious little beyond."

"This Merrick. His address, not that it matters, is 3/S/12, and . . ."

"Don't have his contact number. Their Duty Officer tonight told me to send any communication through to their General Clearing Centre – insulting."

"Wait a minute."

He held the phone against his ear. Had the business section of a Sunday broadsheet and a biro in his hand, and waited. And waited, and . . . Was given a mobile number, wrote it in the margin of a page dealing with holiday home investment certainties.

"What's his rank? I learned sod all, just had the walk. Took myself over to the Lambeth Palace wall, saw him coming or rather he saw me. Did my speech, was acknowledged, and then dumped."

"I was told he was junior grade. Past retirement, kept on. Down there they call crime a backwater – enough for you? Not a high flier, old, and in a stagnant pond. Try and be moderately polite, Jak. I've not met him. Bounced the name at a God Almighty here and was given a shrug, told nothing."

"I have to have answers."

"Wish you luck. Remember, Jak, we are all supposed to be singing from the same hymn sheet . . . that sort of crap. Good night."

Light out, Vera asleep, and the cat, and the street was quiet. Jonas stared at the ceiling.

The phone trilled.

"Yes?"

"Jak Peters, Mr Merrick."

"Yes?"

"I'm SC&O10."

"Yes?"

"Many months ago you walked with me across Lambeth Bridge and we talked about the undercover that I was control for."

"Yes?"

"And you took him off my hands."

"I did . . . Mr Peters, where are you calling from?"

"My home, south London."

"I, too, Mr Peters, am in south London. I doubt we have a time difference between our different parts of south London. My bedside clock says 11.48 p.m."

"I am not apologising. I have to know how much longer I have to authorise the ongoing budget for my man. When I allocate the budget, it's locked down and that affects other operations. I am sure you are aware, Mr Merrick, that your agency does not make a contribution to the basic budget. And another thing, I am concerned for his welfare and whether he's getting the back-up and support to which he is entitled."

"Now, 11.49 p.m. . . . I do not discuss the use of the undercover you refer to. I will not give any guidance as to how long the operation will run. You can play it two ways, Mr Peters. You either fight me and waste your time and make yourself tedious and a loser. Or, Mr Peters, you concede gently that you are not going inside the loop, accept it – and go to bed. Good night, Mr Peters."

He rang off, chuckled.

Vera murmured, "That was a bit full frontal, Jonas."

"All coming to a bit of a climax – which raises stress levels."

"And you are able, at such a time, to go off towing the caravan towards a bit of history. Right?"

"Interesting history. Goodnight, Vera. Yes, well able to."

7

"When are you coming back to us, Jonas? When can we expect some proper work from you?" The AssDepDG shared the lift to the third floor, south facing.

Jonas had been greeted with the brief nods of recognition from Leroy and Kev, hands on their H&Ks but also a little tap of the index finger against the nose which he assumed was intended to reassure him: he still owned that degree of protection. Had acknowledged them but sparely. Had decided that when the time came for his next leaving party in the atrium they would receive embossed invitations – not that the party date loomed, God forbid. Had enjoyed his coffee and Danish in the café. Had sat briefly in the gardens just down Horseferry Road. Had smiled to the gardener, conversation not required, but a man whose advice Jonas tapped into when facing a crisis . . . Would probably get him to the party too. Into the lift. Too early for the main stampede, but the AssDepDG had squeezed in.

"I'm rather enjoying it," Jonas breezed an answer.

"How much longer, simple question?"

They came out of the lift together. Bad sign, indicated that the AssDepDG, who worked from a higher floor, wished to pursue. Jonas went briskly along the corridor towards Room 12. He paused at the door.

"Just a little bit longer until this one winds down, then might look for what else is currently over the horizon."

He went inside, was followed. Assumed the matter had festered over the weekend.

"Too much to ask, Jonas, that you don't treat me as 'need to know' – that's the rest of the law enforcement family. You are leaving angst in your wake. I cannot always provide a secure fire-wall. When we dumped you in crime we expected you to be far from sight and far from mind. Instead you have cobbled together an empire, are hooked into American agencies, have ridden rough-shod over domestic police elements, are running up bills with the fervour of a casino addict . . . So, Jonas, I am irritated if you regard me as outside 'need to know'. Got me?"

They arrived at Jonas's cubicle. He had been presented with many opportunities in the last two years to move into a proper work area of his own, not lurk behind a temporary frosted glass frame, and had curtly refused. He went in, unfastened the chain holding his briefcase to his wrist and began another of the Merrick routines. Computer switched on. Briefcase on the floor. Coat on the door hanger, trilby on the hook above. Sandwiches in their plastic box on the left corner of his work surface. Thermos on the other corner and the cap that served as a mug unscrewed. Files removed from the briefcase; expressly forbidden that confidential documents be removed from the building and taken home. Safe unlocked, files returned. He sat in his chair. Then he cleaned his glasses, the replacement pair for those still bumping around upstream or downstream or on the riverbed – and remembered how the Sixer girl was so attentive at cleaning them. His screen image was a photo of Olaf, scowling.

Jonas said, "Vera is rather fond of the old slogan *Make Do and Mend*. Hard to get a worn shirt off her before she's turned the collar. On that theme, I find *Careless Talk Costs Lives* appropriate. That good enough for you?"

"You push luck a long distance . . . My question warrants an answer. Is it near the end game?"

"Probably."

"Like getting blood from granite . . . I have calls, queries, protests, mounting in my tray, quite a pile, and they are copied upstairs. The Administration are 'interested' on who it is at our place that is on the most sensitive feed of information out of Bogotá. Their air force apparently scrambled from the Azores when a satellite feed went down: for who? For a Mister Jonas

Merrick, whoever he is. An Assistant Chief Constable, Merseyside, is reporting that experienced officers are now blindsided on a particular Organised Crime Group investigation, and are starting to chuck crockery around. Maritime agencies are working for you . . . The head of the Yard's SC&O10, undercovers, has issued a formal protest to us saying that the safeguarding of one of their people has been removed from their hands, negating their duty of care obligations, and they additionally complain that no risk assessment on current operations in Corunna, wherever the hell that is, has been lodged. I have to field that, others may not be so patient . . . Jonas, are you fucking listening to me?"

"Not long, tell them not long and then they can get back into their muddy ponds again."

"And the budget is busted. Ours and others. This banking system is . . ."

"Expensive, but not out of control."

"Jonas – what is 'not long'? I have stood your corner too many times to be screwed around by you and your excessive demand for confidentiality."

True. Could not be denied. Had been given enough rope to hang himself or to see through an operation when pressures mounted. Allowed to follow his own nose. Entitled him to display raw initiative. Fizz had been popped on the upper floors when the bomb carried by Winston Gunn had been defused, more fizz poured when Cameron Jilkes went into the cage, and plenty of fizz called for when they had "helped out" their Sixer chums and identified an activated sleeper in their midst . . . But those had involved twin gold medal disciplines: terror and espionage; this was only crime, the backwater.

"I'd prefer it's not shared . . . 'not long' is a 'few days'. Good enough?"

"And the action will be where?"

"Most of it in Spain."

"And you have the full cooperation of their people? Is that Intelligence or police? We have excellent relations there, good cooperation and protocol. Who are you dealing with?"

"They are in the dark and will stay there until I wish to enrol their help. When they can be useful they'll be informed."

"You are comfortable with that, Jonas?"

"Very comfortable."

"And what level of danger do your principals face? Am I allowed to know that?"

"Considerable danger, predictable danger. I have to believe my way of handling the matter mitigates the danger."

"You had better be right."

"I think I know that – yes, I think I do."

"A last question. Jonas, what you are doing in this fiefdom of yours, will it make a difference? It's just *crime*. Isn't up there with the headline snatchers. Will anyone notice? Is it important? The same question but I'm coming from different angles. Assuming too much blood is not slopping around your feet, and it is a success, will anything have changed?"

"Not a lot, but that's the game."

"Bluntly, Jonas, will you have created a shortage? Will the price rocket?"

"Shouldn't think so."

"Then what, for fuck's sake, Jonas, is it for?"

"It's the job. One that I find worthwhile. The job is what all those people in Administration, in Merseyside's Serious Crime Unit and the people at the Yard do all day, every day . . . Anyway, most pieces are in place and I'm planning a little break with the caravan. Don't think I'll be missed."

He was tapping at his keyboard and peering at his screen. He heard the door close. Had to be worthwhile or he could not justify the hazard in which people were placed as he moved them across the board.

He pushed the swing door. Same time and same place every workday morning for the founder of the Biscuit Tin, and its principal fraudster. Kenny Blake felt fine, had no right to. The café was crowded, despite the early hour – Corunna men liked to get themselves a sharp fix before heading to work, and they jostled for the attention of the owner and his staff.

He thought he appeared the same as he did any other Monday morning and acknowledged that he did not deserve to. Had showered long and dressed carefully and brushed his hair. Did not want any of the locals, who invested in him, thinking he looked bladdered. Caught the eye of the owner, nodded and smiled, the sort of exchange between a regular punter and a rail-side bookie. Except that Fredo had the look on his face, haggard and drawn, that ought to have been on Kenny's. A gesture, a slight flick of the eyes at a far corner of the café, where there was a coat stand and a couple of framed pictures of the football team. The barest indication, properly Galician, of where Kenny should go park himself.

Kenny was regarded as the honest man who could be relied upon to harbour secrets. Could also be a shoulder. It had been a crap team last year and there were no signs of improvement for the season ahead. Fredo came with his coffee, and wiped an adjacent table. He had not rung Anna that morning. Would not have described himself as an expert on reconciliation, noted for awkwardness, stubbornness. Had not telephoned, nor had he shed the St Christopher. Fredo sat opposite him. Heavy talk expected if the owner chose to absent himself from the busiest time in the day, heavier trade than at lunchtime. The man looked grim. Had not shaved, wore a clean shirt but with buttons off kilter. Had a shake in his hands, and leaned forward.

"My friend, my good friend, my friend Kenny. I have to talk to someone. You are my friend but are separate from Corunna. I can talk to you, like I talk to no other, not even at home. You know where my Gabriel is? Of course, you know. You know also, Kenny, where is my cousin and you saw him leave to get the flight to Madrid, and from Madrid to Bogotá which is a place of savages, of barbarians. Once, Kenny, it seemed easy to run with the pack who could plaster us all with money. Where did the money come from? Unimportant. How was the money acquired? Of no interest. My cousin took money and as a result he provided services, and from those services came sufficient money to begin his business – and next they ask for my cousin's son, and he may enjoy a holiday in an exotic place. Of course, my cousin cannot refuse the request."

He was not expected to speak but leaned forward and listened and managed a decently sympathetic look. The words tumbled at him, and he thought that soon tears would come.

"Myself, I provided services. I cannot tell you what they were, and was rewarded. Hide this and transport that. And I am thanked and I am praised and it becomes easier to work for such people – and the alternatives are few. From their money I have the cash that enables me to rent this property and then to equip it as a café, and there is *help* with the licence because this is a restricted area and such a licence is very hard to get. For me it was made easy. All my life, since I was a boy, I wanted to own a café, and it has done well – as you know, Kenny."

He nodded, had nothing to contribute but the appearance of sympathy.

"It would have been difficult not to oblige, no, impossible, but I was asked to send my Gabriel to Colombia, as you know. Not the easiest boy, but I thought a new environment and the need to behave would improve him. He goes. He does not answer his phone, no letter, no email . . . nothing. Then, a vessel is intercepted off the islands of the Azores, and it contains cargo. You under-stand, Kenny, what I speak of?"

Kenny understood. Had provided early intelligence that might have helped with the seizure of a mother ship before it unloaded its consignment, not significant intelligence, but some. He managed to appear innocent and yet concerned.

"There is a price to be paid. Money has been transferred but the cargo is lost – the life of my cousin's son is therefore taken. We know it can happen but we never believe it will happen. My cousin flew out to collect the body. Is in Bogotá . . . I grieve for that, Kenny. I am also desperate with fear for my boy, for Gabriel. Last night, my cousin telephoned to me. On a Sunday, in Bogotá, they open the mortuaries in the main hospitals if there is a necessity, too great a number of homicides for only the weekdays to handle. May I tell you, Kenny, what my cousin told me, please?"

Could not refuse, could only continue to seem earnest and sincere.

"He had been to the mortuary. His son was there. He had no clothes but they had taped his passport in a bag to his chest, and beside his passport was a DVD disc. My cousin was shown what they had done to his son. They had cut off most of his fingers, not all. They had cut off also his private parts and they were in his mouth. They had taken off his ears and his nose. My cousin does not think his son would still have been conscious but they had broken the bones in his legs. Perhaps the mercy of death came from loss of blood. They killed him to demonstrate their annoyance that a shipment had failed, and their certainty that it was a failure in Galicia that caused it, and they take no blame and do not accept 'bad luck' for the interception. With how they have killed him they send a message. They use those methods of torture to refine the message . . . But for more emphasis they also film what they have done and there are close-up images of the agony on the face of my cousin's son. He rang me, he told me."

Kenny looked across the table, over his untouched coffee and into the depth of Fredo's eyes. He knew what would be said next.

"They have my boy. They have Gabriel. I tell you very frankly, Kenny, that another cargo is coming here. If the cargo fails, if it does not reach the land then again the people there will blame the people here. I am told money has already been paid. I am terrified, Kenny . . . Should the cargo not reach here then Gabriel's death will be certain. When I was a boy, and when the courts gave a sentence of death to a Basque fighter there was the same certainty that the Generalissimo would authorise the executions. I should not tell you that a cargo is coming. But . . . here, everyone knows, not how and not where and not when, but they know it's coming, and if it is intercepted it will kill my son. Often I have been angry with him, and him rude to me and disrespectful, but he is my son, of my blood, and I know what will be done to him . . . Thank you, my friend, thank you, my good friend, for listening."

The table was wiped, the unused cup was taken. Another would be brought him. The confession was over.

He sat still, and noise played around him and an early game show was loud on the TV, and Fredo's face was now impassive. Kenny reflected: he had put his own safety, perhaps his life, on the line in order to prevent that shipment being brought ashore. It would come at the end of the week and was bankrolled by the clan dominated by Isabelle Munoz – who seemed to like him. He knew the boy, Gabriel, who was to die, probably badly, in distant Colombia at the hands of an annoyed cartel – not a pleasant boy. And reflected some more on *consequences* and his role in triggering them.

Another *Americano* was brought him by a pretty girl who smiled sweetly at him because he was a regular, a friend.

She had noticed the change in her ranking over the last two years. Doloures Govier was eyed. She was a person of interest all the way from the car park to the start of the check process for visitors.

The women who came to see their men watched her, stared at her, knew her identity. She joined a line to be passed through. The staff recognised her and would pass side-of-mouth comments. She wore trousers, a blouse, a fleece, hair roughly brushed and a smear of lipstick, and her usual pearl stud earrings. She would have thought it degrading if she had tarted herself up. In the queue were a few of the arm-candy that would have been living off the young boys who had thought themselves king of a street, and had the tattoos and the wristwatches to prove it, but had shown themselves to be fallible, made mistakes, were banged up, and the women would hang around only as long as the gravy kept seeping into their purses. Kids bawled round her. She was watched, not because she was the wife of a celebrated inmate but because of who *she* was, what she had made of herself. It would be noted in the logbook that she had attended that extra visiting opportunity. Thrown into the schedule – Mondays was usually a closed day. Suited her, that Monday morning, as the following day she would be too busy, have too much to concern her.

The smell was revolting: the stink of disinfectant and old sweat and filthy clothes, the stench that came – she believed – from hopelessness. She showed her ID. A metal detector was run over her, and a spaniel sniffed at her feet and legs and then paused at her handbag, and then showed interest in a trouser pocket where she always put treats: did that to wreck the attention of the trained dog. Usually worked, fucked them up, disrupted the system. She was expressionless when she opened out the pocket and allowed the treats to fall on the floor and the dog would be yanked away, and then she'd kick them aside. They'd make sure that the cameras had good cover on her. She ignored everyone around her, and was passed through.

She sat at the back of the visitor hall. A screwed-down table would be between them. They usually rowed. She could have told Mikey that she was better off without him, was way ahead now, with him stuck in HMP Walton. And happier, and in better health without him crawling all over her . . . but went to see him because a diminishing but important part of her authority – and the family's good name – depended on the Govier connection. He was brought in, showed no pleasure at the sight of her, carried on talking to another prisoner until they had to go to their different tables. He would have heard by now that Xavier had handed out the punishment to the brother of the prisoner who'd bad-mouthed him on the landing. A message sent, but perhaps Mikey was now more vulnerable than he'd been before, could work that way . . . Doloures wouldn't lose sleep over it. He settled opposite her. Silence at first, as if it showed weakness to take the lead.

He broke, predictable. "How are you doing?"

Doloures reckoned her husband pasty-faced, overweight by several kilos, was a coronary candidate. "Doing fine. You look shit, Mikey. Don't they have a gym in here?"

They had a code of sorts. "You doing that thing?"

"I am."

"Holding your hand?"

"Patrick is. Be good, always useful to keep moving, which you'd know if you went to the gym."

"Not necessary, that thing."

"You weren't asked. Weren't around to be asked. Screwed up, didn't you, Mikey? You happy living in here with all these losers? Must be fun round a game of cards to be doing group therapy on how many mistakes you made."

"Don't get my ear bent – how long?"

"Out Tuesday, back Saturday or Sunday." Could not be bothered with the code so had hunched forward, her mouth an inch from his ear. "A deal that's going to set us up."

"Bankrupt us."

"Wouldn't matter to you, would it? In here, heating and TV, three meals a day."

"Just telling you, Dol, those people you are getting into bed with are vicious bastards. You know that? We had one in last month while he was waiting for a Crown Court slot. From Medellín. No one messed with him. Evil beggar. You shouldn't be in bed with . . ."

"I am in bed with no one, thank fuck."

"Just wondering why you bother to come."

"Does me good, Mikey, reminds me what a loser looks like. I'll see you." She stood.

He pushed himself up with difficulty. Grunted, "You'll not clean us out, just don't."

"Might increase your pocket money, so's you don't go hungry . . . Last thing, don't be expecting Xavier to keep on wrapping up your difficulties for you. Stand on your own bloody feet. What I'm doing is going to change the family's lives. Pity for you is that you won't be home to enjoy it. Cheerie bye, Mikey."

"And you, Dol, and stay safe."

She looked hard at him, thought he had weakened. Gone soft, like the fight was kicked out of him. She anticipated that within a month, certainly within a year, he'd end up on his arse in a corner with lips bloodied and eyes closed from the bruising, and a tooth or two loose in his gums. Not her problem, because Doloures Govier was off the next day with her son, flying round Europe, ending up where the biggest deal the family had kicked into was waiting for her. A massive deal that would see the north-west flooded with the stuff. Would put her at the top of the tree, where she belonged.

He wouldn't have understood, Mikey wouldn't, because he was a loser and showing it. Duty done, she went out into the fresh air and breathed deep. Imagined it churning through the water and getting closer, and walked steadily to her car.

"Have you looked at him?"

"I look at him every fucking five minutes."

"You should look at him."

Diego had his back to both Matias and the prone Emiliano, concentrating on the instrument panel that was set into a board precariously bolted down below the narrow reinforced glass slits in the cockpit area. Had to hold course, a useless journey if the craft lost direction. About as big a disaster as was possible, to lose course for the landfall.

"He did not seem to me to have changed. Just a useless kid, needs to front up."

Matias shouted, "If you don't look at him then you don't know."

"I know enough. I know the boy is fucking useless."

Perhaps a bigger disaster was that they sink. Next to that, in the order of catastrophe, would be getting the navigation screwed and not going towards that corner of the Coast of Death, perhaps going in a great circle, or heading into the Biscay and then running out of fuel, losing power, drifting – a nightmare. And losing the cargo was another nightmare, have the hold punctured and the bales floating away. And the wind was still foul but the squally rain less frequent and there had been glimpses of the sky, which was an opportunity for aircraft surveillance . . . So many disasters, catastrophes, nightmares, squabbled for prominence in his mind. He kept his eyes on the gauges, did not look round.

Matias persisted, "He is in your care. He should matter to you."

"Should have stayed at home, stayed in his hut, stayed screwing his girl."

"He will not survive."

"Then we do without him."

Matias gripped Diego's shoulder and dragged it back. His hand was gnarled, flecked with skin cancer lesions, and the nails were bitten down but still held engine oil and grease.

"You treat us like shit in the street, like we are rubbish. I know that boy."

"Didn't know him well enough, or should have chosen better."

"He is slipping."

"And fuck all I can do about it."

Diego had lost sight of the forward superstructure. There, under the fibreglass hull, were four tonnes of pure processed cargo, securely wrapped against contamination from a leak. Also there were the bladders holding the diesel fuel. He faced Matias, had no option because of the strength of the engineer's arm. By Matias's feet, his flip-flops, and swilled by the kid's vomit, was Emiliano's head, and every few moments it scraped against the perforated decking. The kid was pale, and his breathing was erratic and dribble came from his mouth, and his arms hung loose.

Matias held a wrench in his other hand. "You can care."

"Caring doesn't help him."

"You can show you care, to help him."

"You want it, you get it. I don't care."

Which was a truth. Diego did not *care* that Emiliano was sick, losing strength. Cared about a quarter of a million American dollars, inclusive of the bonus and cared about the women the payment would secure, and the restaurants – and cared about holding the pitching and bucking craft on course. Nothing else. He shook himself free.

"You could show you care."

"And do what? Transmit a mayday message, ask for a coast-guard cutter, or a military helicopter, to rescue him? Are you an idiot as well as an asshole?"

"We do not matter to you?"

Perhaps he should have been mopping the kid's forehead and cleaning the kid's mouth and maybe wiping the kid's backside where the muscles had weakened. Perhaps he should have been talking the language of the kid's mother . . . Not the way of Diego who had a chance to gain prestige and wealth, and concentrated on that.

Matias raised the wrench. The swell was against the port side of the craft and instead of going up on its ends, bow out of the water, and then plunging back down, it rolled on its side. Diego would have had no vision through the glass, and Matias hit him with the wrench.

A glancing blow was the best that Matias managed. In Diego's mind, the engineer hit him out of a sense of frustration, a sort of madness. He felt pain on his collarbone. He cursed and spat, was about to denounce Matias, challenge him, then realised that the wrench was up again, held high enough to cannon against the cabin roof. He saw Matias's protruding eyes, saw the veins prominent on the hand gripping the wrench, saw the dirtied metal shape, gleaming grease. Was this where his life ended? Where he was cheated out of a quarter of a million American dollars?

He swivelled. And was struck again. Looked into Matias's demented face and the pain set in after the moment of numbness and Diego thought he was about to collapse, and the engineer was towering over him. There was a shallow drawer alongside the bank of dials, to the right of the wheel. He snatched at it, groped inside, covering his head with his other hand.

His fingers found the pistol, hard and cold, and fastened on it.

A skipper always carried the ultimate sanction for maintaining discipline on a vessel. This was a loaded Luger pistol, thirty-five years old, a weapon that had done the ownership rounds and was now – like an old whore – in the hands of Diego. Managed to cock it. The wrench came down again. The pistol was fired. Diego's trigger finger contracted by instinct. The bullet glanced into a portside window, froze it, and the angle was good enough for it to ricochet off and then bury itself in the side wall.

The boy had not moved. The wrench was lowered. The Luger was made safe.

Matias shouted, "You know what he did last night, while you slept? You want to know? He was at the hatch, trying to open it, but not strong enough. He was trying to open the hatch and wanted to climb out and was going to dive off the top and he was going to swim home . . . Except that he cannot swim, except that there were four thousand metres of water below him. Then he collapsed, then he was sick again . . . Do you not care?"

Diego put the pistol back in the drawer. The discharge of the shot had left thunder swarming in his ears. The waves lifted them and dropped them.

Diego yelled, "I care only about staying on course."

Four tonnes of pure and uncut cocaine powder would not be the biggest ever cargo to be landed, but up there in the medal stakes. Needed planning, needed handling with care. Those initial hours when the semi-submersible was unloaded would be supervised by Laureano . . . What happened later, the movement and onward sale, would be handled by Sergio. Every item of their concept, however well tested on previous landings, would be run by the matriarch of the family, Isabella Munoz. The time of greatest vulnerability was when the cargo was brought ashore.

Laureano had organised the procedure many times. So much better if he had been able to get the bales from the craft to his own pair of speedboats in the waters off the archipelago of the Azores. Whether or not the concept of "global warming" was shit, or whether the weather patterns had changed, he accepted that it would have been dangerous for the cargo and potentially lethal for him to have tried to shift the cargo when he was close to it. Had seen them, white-faced, clinging to stanchions in their squat cockpit, had heard them screaming abuse at each other – and had noted the algae and muck clinging to the hull as it rose and pivoted and then collapsed, and had seen the rust colouring the rivets on the metal frame to which the fibreglass was attached. Laureano knew Diego, had thought him competent and little more, but he had been chosen by the Colombians and was advised to deliver or face months, or years, looking over his shoulder and flinching in the shadows, certain that they would find him. He had seen the faces of the two men from the New World, and thought them petrified.

It was the correct decision to tell them to travel the greater distance, a week's sailing, to the Coast of Death. They were allowed one mobile phone connection. One only. They would be guided to a point a kilometre from the shore, north of Finisterre and south of the village of Muxía, and which particular beach they used would be dictated by time and tide levels. Laureano worked at what his mother called "the logistics". He had a dozen men on stand-by, picked for their strength, experience and agility. To ferry the men he had four pickups already fuelled, engines checked, and they would be moved into a barn along the coast on the Thursday evening. He would need at least ten *zulos* in the area of landing: hiding places that had been used for a century, holes dug out of hillsides above a beach or river. The bales would be rushed from the shore and away up the lanes and then buried in dense undergrowth or in wild heather . . . And more men needed there and on the tracks and the upper ground, equipped with torches to flash signals of warning rather than mobiles which risked interception. The cargo would lie in the *zulos* for up to a week and then be moved on.

And that was the responsibility of Sergio. A fleet of lorries from the seafood canning businesses would drive it away across Spain, east and into France, and on to the Netherlands . . . And the Munoz family had agreed through their broker that they would be paid handsomely because the people in the UK were *estupido* or *cretino* or *imbecile*, what the guy in Amsterdam had said, and new to this level of trade. They had said, the people from the UK, through the broker, an Albanian, that they wished to see the cargo they paid for in advance *before* it was put in the lorries; seemed to say that they did not trust the Munoz family, did not believe their word. Imbeciles, cretins, stupid people, not to believe the good faith of the Munoz clan . . . and more advance money would be delivered the following day.

Laureano, as he had done many times before, supervised the preparations, as Sergio had other plans to fulfil, and Isabella Munoz had started the process of negotiation for a two-tonne delivery that would come by another ship in two months and be offloaded on to a trawler owned by the family, and another delivery of two tonnes would cross the Atlantic by rust-bucket freighter in the late summer, or into the autumn. Business for the family was brisk – demand in northern Europe, specifically in the UK, had not slackened. Laureano thought his planning better than adequate, and there would be an additional bonus payment if the emptied submersible was refuelled and able to cross the ocean again and reach a particular creek on the Amazon delta. Sergio thought all was going well but regretted that the British people were arriving, thought the sales should have been restricted to the Albanian-born broker in Amsterdam, but . . . and nagging at him, annoying Laureano because of what Sergio had told him, was the Dutch girl who could not paint and her liaison with the English investment manager that his mother used for laundering.

The start of the working week, and early enough for both shoppers and workers to be on the move, and Luna Perez had needed to be at the bus station early to guarantee herself a seat.

The express bus took the main highway. Out of the coastal port of Pontevedra, where once Luna Perez had been a celebrity, or an interfering bitch, or an heroic scourge of the narco traffickers, the route cut inland, travelled at the maximum speed permitted. Through fields where cattle grazed, past small industrial estates, villages by-passed and the inland mountain range ever-present.

Luna Perez had attempted to alter the world in which she lived – had failed. Nothing had changed because of her intervention, no one's life course had been deflected. The bus powered on towards the city of Corunna where she would not be recognised. She had the address, no appointment, but was free for the day and would wait until she was seen by the investment manager in *La Lata de Galletas*. She had heard that he was reliable and discreet and, most important, she had been told that his performance in handling peoples' money was exemplary.

Nothing falling from the clear blue sky that Jonas knew of.

He dialled the number of an old fountain of advice, a man he valued. No "events" trampled on his reasonable humour. The man whom Jonas was calling was always there to answer him. Now confined to his conservatory, he had been a detective sergeant in Special Branch in the "Troubles" days in Northern Ireland, crippled with arthritis but still dripped experience and sense.

"But you're in crime now, Jonas. What do I know about that bucket of shit? We tried hard enough to dump our boys, the opposition, into the crime bracket. Why we had the excreta protests in the Kesh prison, they thought that crime was below their dignity – wanted to be POWs, and have a senior officer and a command structure, and Red Cross parcels and free association and the right to wear their own clothes. Stood up for it with hunger strikes, and what the cynics in our crowd called 'dieting for Ireland', except that it was serious enough to send half a dozen of them to their graves. Trouble with going on a hunger strike is that you look a wimp if you come off early . . . one of them was forever cleaning his teeth which was a way of slurping water. No status in crime, Jonas. No one gets pissed on Saturday night in a pub and sings a syrupy ballad about a bank robber or a heroin importer. You could say, Jonas, that a criminal is actually preferable as company than a terror narcissist. Don't have the airs and graces of a political activist. Not constantly squealing that conviction was a stitch-up. Take it on the chin, do time, get back to work. Kill a guy because he showed disrespect, not spin out the crap about death being in the cause of a free Connemara, or slaughtering kids at a concert to right the wrongs Israelis do to Palestinians in Jericho. But – always *but*, Jonas – big 'but', the political guy will not want to hurt you. The criminal will have no feckin' hesitation in rearranging your face, or shooting you, or kicking the daylights out of you . . . You rang for advice. Get this – do not go close to a proper OCG boy. Leave it to the people with the kit and the training. Hearing me?"

"Loud and clear."

"Next thing, Jonas. You can isolate an activist. Spin a few yarns about him, feed them into his system and you negate him. Deport him, or slap a restraint order on him, and his shelf life, never long, ends. The criminal needs evidence to put him away. Proper evidence that will stand up in court. I am not talking about the crap from a senior at Thames House from behind a curtain, and all done on a nod and a wink. I'm talking about the evidence that will withstand a ferocious attack from the guy's brief. The brief will be paid five times the take-home pay of your prosecutor, will be ruthless and without conscience and will seek to rubbish your witnesses and your forensics, and to scatter doubt in the minds of a Crown Court jury. And the funds will be readily available for the dozen in the jury box to be bought, or compromised or intimidated. Evidence, Jonas, is fundamental to locking them up. Did I gather from you, Jonas, that you have a source close to the action?"

"Something like that."

"One of their people, or what you have inserted?"

"My boy, on the ground."

"Who matters?"

"You could say so. Will be in a position to influence how it plays out, and to provide subsequent evidence."

"And are you sharing, Jonas? Daft of me to ask. You don't share. Keep it close . . . Right, Jonas?"

"Correct."

"More you share, the more you leak. If you have a source, milk it. Don't go gentle with a source, drain its udders. I have pleasant fields I look out on, Jonas, and the cows beyond my fence carry a load through every day till they get called in, and then each last drop is sucked out of them. The very last drop . . . It is a once in a lifetime chance, Jonas, to have a major investigation coming to a climax, and you don't back off. You don't go soft. I had both informants and – once in a while – a guy on the inside that we had put there. Telling it you straight, I never differentiated between the two. If the guy can get you evidence, what stands up in a court of law, what gets the verdict you want, then you take it. They are volunteers, Jonas, not press-ganged. They want the adrenaline pumping, it's their narcotic. I tell you a supreme moment, let me . . . In court, make sure you are there and see that look from the dock when a convicted felon looks back and beads straight into the eyes of the brief who has lied and twisted and prostituted himself with the sole aim of freeing the scumbag. Always a great sight. I leave you a last one."

"Thank you."

"Don't go interfering with the source. Let him run riot. Best chance is that he will know how to look after himself in the count-down when the evidence starts piling up. Yes, that is the big risk time, but . . . He'll know how to look after himself. Enough of me. When, Jonas, are you intending to retire?"

He heard his friend start to chortle, and with it a hacking cough, and he'd soon be lifting another out of the packet and lighting up again. Jonas dreaded the day when he would ring that number and be told that his friend was no longer able to take the phone – dreaded that day almost as much as the one after his own retirement.

It came up on his screen, forwarded by the AssDepDG. An "invitation" to the fifth floor after lunch. He cursed. No good ever came from climbing that high in Thames House.

And Aggie Burns was at his door, would have the stuff he'd asked for in the late afternoon, promise.

Patrick watched. Had called Theresa, then his mother.

Theresa said, "What am I looking at?"

His mother said, "Where am I looking?"

They stood at the back of the front living room, against the wall, beneath a watercolour that none of them thought special – sheep in a field and a river – but it had cost them a hundred at auction and Jean-Luc had advised the purchase was a useful investment. It had dust on it . . . Theresa and Patrick were supposed to clean the houses since Ma had refused to sanction entry into their property of anyone working with a vacuum cleaner and a duster and furniture polish. Only one allowed in was the geek who came with the scanning kit and swept the place. Ma was paranoid about bugs but neither of them would have laughed at that to her face.

Mid-morning. The road was empty except for the pick-up, cruising at snail speed and now a hundred yards short of them.

A man was trying to scrape up dirt from the gutter below the far kerb. Ma snorted, in a poor humour anyway after where she'd been. Ma was always foul tempered after going to Walton. She made a derisive noise, was best avoided when she'd come from bitching with their dad. The man had a shovel and was attempting to clean the gutter and chuck the debris into the back of the pick up – except that where he was scraping there was nothing to scrape – no leaves, no mud, no crisp packet. The pickup came towards them. No logo. Would have done if it had been part of the Merseyside Council's fleet.

Ma said, "He's never used a shovel before. First time and making a bollocks of it. Betting he's from Fanny Thomas's crowd."

"Do they think we're dumb, Ma?" said Theresa.

"Just keep watching," said Patrick.

The pick-up edged down the road, appeared to be only interested in the side opposite their own house. It crawled forward until its cab was in a line that reached from the Goviers' windows to meet the Potters' wall, just where that dandelion grew in the grouting. Patrick could not see the point in the brickwork where Theresa had stuck the chewing gum. He hissed at her to get upstairs, get a different view.

The man chucked his shovel into the back of the pick up, and drove off.

Theresa called down, "You can see it now. Shows in the light."

Patrick identified it, pointed it out to his mother. The rain had eased enough and there was probably a rainbow somewhere up by the Allerton Manor golf club because a bit of sun came through and lit up where his sister had planted her chewing gum.

Theresa was at the door. "What I said, Ma, they think we're dumb."

Patrick said, "Over there, the Potters, they'd have known."

Ma said, "Be one for Xavier to sort out."

"I think they did it," Jenny Potter said.

"For God's sake, don't show yourself." David Potter pulled her back from their bedroom window.

"It would have been that workman's cart."

"Couldn't be, looked phoney. Not the Corporation and not a private company. Fanny Thomas would have done better than that."

"I'm not liking it, David."

"Not liking it at all."

They went downstairs and she was filling the kettle and neither dared to go anywhere near to the front of their house, and the phone rang. Seemed loud enough to wake the dead.

He said, "What's done is done."

She said, "And cannot be undone, more's the pity."

Fanny Thomas on the line. Sounded anxious. Wanted him to know that a piece of gum had been removed from the lens, all done with no fanfare and would have seemed like any other road-cleaning team. All smooth and all taken care of. Sounded to David Potter that she was reading from a script.

"So, that's it, Mr Potter. Again I want to express our gratitude to you for your very positive attitude to helping us. Might be best just to maintain a low profile for a day or so. Though there is absolutely nothing for you and your wife to worry about. Have a nice day."

He was about to explode, but was beaten to the punch, and the phone purred in his ear.

A busy morning for Kenny.

Two clients, both hesitantly dipping a toe in the water. Small sums and not sure how safe they would be with him, but greed getting the better of their caution, and he had done his supremely successful sales pitch. Two letters awaiting a response – one from the body in Madrid that oversaw independent investment managers requesting further details of his UK qualifications, which he would bin, and one from the local tax office informing him that a list of clients and their monies lodged with him was overdue and requiring an answer within a calendar month, which he would also push through the shredder. And a call from the lads up the coast, needing to know times and locations for the end of the week.

A busy morning and the last Monday that, if all slotted into the frame as predicted, he would spend in his office on the second floor where the scent of fresh coffee drifted up from the café. The outer doorbell rang. He glanced at his screen, saw a woman nervously clutching her handbag. He opened the door. A woman said, full of apology, that she had no appointment but wished to make use of his services. He ushered her into the waiting area, three hard chairs, a low table with a heap of tired financial magazines, and bare walls but for a British Council poster of Stratford-upon-Avon, and requested that she wait for just a few minutes. He went into his office to tidy his desk.

When the Munoz family had first come it, too, had been without prior notice. Alone, trade slack, best part of a year earlier and Fredo had rung. "Mister Kenny, you have an important visitor on the way up, so important." It had been a woman of middle age, of understated style, a scarf covering her hair and wearing dark glasses. Isabella Munoz had come to look him over. He had heard of her from Fredo, quiet gossip, and something of her sons. He had done a good sales pitch, quiet and without bombast. Had talked through his own background, stuck close to the legend, had smiled a bit, been self-deprecating, and had described a banking system on the island of Guernsey. She had heard good things of him. He suggested a small deposit for a portfolio, and perhaps she would be satisfied with the results. His suggestion was for a sum she would not miss if . . . only then, with that word *if*, had her face hardened and her lips narrowed . . . a shrug, *if* the markets turned down, but good, reliable people would be looking after her money. He had given no indication of knowing anything of her. How much would she not miss? Four days later, and after word that the Guernsey end of the business had been looked at, evaluated, and no doubt questions asked, her idea of loose change had been carried up the stairs and into his office by a small wizened man who limped and wheezed. Fredo told him the next morning that the guy would slit a throat if told to – a million euros. He had sensed, from the start, that she was amused by him, that he fitted none of the stereotypes that surrounded her, sensed also that she reckoned she was cheated, defrauded by the banks in Panama and Cayman. About once a month she took him for lunch, a restaurant up in the hills, way off the beaten track, and they'd talk about his early life more than opportunities for better rates of interest, and he had never drank the wine she offered, scared witless that he would fluff his lines, forget the legend. Sometimes she laughed with him, always she listened ... and he noted that when either Sergio or Laureano were with her they gave him cold glances, almost threatening. The last time they'd met, the last lunch she had given him, she had touched his hand as she might have done to a nephew she was fond of. The money had kept rolling in and the portfolio had expanded, and the team in the bank in St Peter Port had done the account proud, and her part of the Biscuit Tin bulged. Each time that he had met her, after she had dropped him off at his office door, he had gone inside and flopped in his chair and clutched his head, and had shivered.

A deep breath, his desk tidier, he opened his inner door, invited the woman in and apologised for keeping her waiting.

"I am Luna Perez." Said it as if he should have known the name.

"Pleased to meet you, how may I be of help?"

"Eccentricity, Jonas, has a place, but can be overcooked."

"Can it?"

"Please call me George. There's a place for eccentricity – thinking outside the rail tracks, of bringing in a dash of unusual thought. Sometimes it has uses, but only 'sometimes'. Refusing to share is an eccentricity, in my view."

Jonas Merrick was on the fifth floor. The Deputy Director was new, addressed staff by email, had been brought in from the Ministry of Defence, and would have little influence over counter-terror, counter-espionage and the little backwaters over which the Security Service owed some responsibility. Was said to be an "organisation man". There to "smooth the sharp angles and achieve greater cooperation with other vital agencies in the UK", was his first message to the Thames House staffers. His room, across the corridor from the Director General's suite, still smelled

of fresh paint. The new look went as far as furniture and pictures
– the monarch banished, replaced by George looking sheepish in
a flak jacket scurrying through a dust cloud from a helicopter
hatch in Iraq – and the usual shots of peevish-looking children.

He explained, as if it pained him to do so, that he was fielding
an increasing number of complaints concerning the behaviour of
the man from 3/S/12, and had read them out. Jonas Merrick was
the target of criticism from the National Crime Agency, Merseyside
police, and a secretive section of Scotland Yard. And the supposed
sister service, MI6, was bleating that their traditional role in liaison
with the Administration had been hijacked by this individual.
Beside George, standing also, was the AssDepDG, as yet no
contribution made.

"I had not realised I had caused offence."

"Leaves the taste, Jonas, that very worthy people are distrusted
by us, and we are thought to be unreliable."

"I take operational security very seriously, always have, but
have never discounted the importance of friends and colleagues in
our work."

"It's the sort of business that seeps into Whitehall meetings.
Gets raised in the presence of Permanent Secretaries, even in the
hearing of Ministers, which drops me into the front line. I don't
want that, not on my watch."

He had been invited to sit, but had smiled in his limp way,
preferred to stand like a scolded schoolboy. What hair he had was
ruffled untidily, and his tie was off centre, and a shirt tail hung
over his trouser belt. He blinked as the blows and criticisms landed.
Little that Jonas did was accidental, most shows of spontaneity
were rehearsed. He had a counter-attack prepared and it would be
delivered with humility, which he thought more effective. The
AssDepDG was Jonas's most valued ally. Without him he would
have been out on his ear. He had been given room to breathe,
space to scheme, and wheelbarrows of resources on demand, but
in return he was expected to deliver. George would not have seen
the AssDepDG's facial expressions – mild amusement – and Jonas
took a cue from it.

"Sorry that life has been made difficult for you . . . Sometimes I feel it gets harder to see the wood from the trees. And my people skills may be wanting. Perhaps I need a course on enhancing such expertise. Can I make a suggestion?"

"Please, something that shuts down any animosity between us and varying agencies. And done snappily."

"Terror fatalities, other than a catastrophe such as Manchester, run at about three or four a year. I suppose I have been submerged in the statistics of organised crime and the deaths from narcotics that run in excess of four thousand a year, and increasing. Formidable . . . my mistake. I'd like to get back down to my office and issue an invitation to all of those agencies that have taken offence. Get them down here for later in the week and let them know where we hope to go and how they can aid and abet the process. Would that suit?"

"Excellent, Jonas. Very helpful." George seemed to wear puzzlement on his features, would have been told that old Merrick was difficult, cantankerous, obstructive. Yet he had heard all he might have hoped for, and delivered with a suitable acknowledgement of the wide gap in rank and grades between them. And to the side, the right eyebrow of the AssDepDG, independent of its twin, was raised and quizzical. "First class. I like to sit firmly on inter-departmental angst, whack it before it becomes toxic."

"Thank you, it will be done. I'll have them, those who should be included, down here for a meeting on Wednesday and will explain where we're going. And, I'd like you to know that if, when, this matter is concluded you will enjoy some entertaining media coverage. It'll be a good one, if, *when* – I hope. Meeting on Wednesday should resolve the issues."

And Jonas had told the AssDepDG that he would be off towing his caravan when the meeting was scheduled. Both eyebrows darted up. Jonas bowed out. Closed the door after him and was relieved that the paint odour had not reached the lobby. Had taken a chance on his future . . . straightened his tie, tidied his hair, tucked in his shirt tail, and called the lift.

8

Inside his cubicle, Jonas rummaged to find three envelopes.

Some might have described the operation as being "on a cusp" but that was not the language that Jonas favoured; he would have said it was teetering on the sharp edge of a knife blade. Some might have described his own position as "precarious" but Jonas would have said that he risked – through his own actions, demands, or pig-headedness – the possibility of swinging in the wind on the end of a rope.

On the envelopes he wrote *By Hand* and then the names of DCI Fergal Rawe, DCI Fanny Thomas, and Jak Peters Esq, SC&O10. Then he turned to the contents.

Quite short for each. Used up in his angled and spidery handwriting, half of an A4 sheet of paper. To the point, without embroidery. Thought it best to be concise and give minimal room for either confusion or argument: where each of them should be, what they should have done, when they should be in position, why they were given the role. That took him a few minutes and the afternoon pushed on and the wind seemed to rattle at the outer casing of his window and the tide of the Thames was higher than usual. It was another of those crises in his life that it had become habit for him to inflict on himself . . . Had had no need to disarm Winston Gunn, could have called for the Met's finest and their guns; could have washed his hands of Cameron Jilkes and relied on the supposed perimeter lines of armed men to intercept him; could have allowed the Sixer girl to go into the Thames or to walk meekly into captivity without his intervention with the handcuffs . . . Could have stepped aside and handed matters over to the Merseyside Police and the relevant Spanish agency. Had not, would not. His handwriting would not have been the easiest to read because excitement ran through him, seemed to speed up his heartbeat. Might have flushed his face.

A head around his door, no prior knock. The murmur of the AssDepDG. "You pissing on me, Jonas?"

Did not turn, finished the instruction for delivery to the control of Kenny Blake. "Nothing could be further from my intention."

"You told him that you were sharing and were calling them for a meeting. Not entirely frank, Jonas – or do I misunderstand what seemed remarkably clear as a guarantee of your future behaviour?"

"A meeting and sharing, it will happen."

"While you are towing a caravan?"

"It is my intention to deliver a result – I am quite busy."

"If it fucks up, Jonas, you will not be the only casualty. You as a certainty, and me as a probability and . . ."

"And others. Believe me, others."

The door closed. Jonas had not turned his head. The AssDepDG would not have noticed the mirth that played at Jonas Merrick's lips. Jonas had never enjoyed sport, nor any form of athleticism, had never watched a match or competition, but the image in his mind was of a baton being passed in a relay race. A hand reaching back and a hand stretching forward, and a damned awkward baton being slid from the grip of one into the palm of the other. Batons seemed, too often, to evade groping fingers, to hit the track, bounce crazily away and leave athletes in a state of despair, fury, collapse. What made it so damned exciting. What made fear chill on his neck. And four days for it to run, and a process that now could not be halted, and danger spiralling . . . seemed to see a baton falling.

Then the emails. To Fergal Rawe and to Fanny Thomas and to Jak Peters.

Would be most grateful if you could travel to London for a meeting this coming Wednesday. Suggest 11.00am. Because of difficulties on entry to Thames House and the requirement for excessive screening, you should come to a hospitable and warm café between our building and the St John's Gardens. *Looking forward to sharing with you the stage to which the operation has reached and how you can help it over the line.*

My most sincere apologies if any offence has been caused by my communications, or lack of them, in the past.

Warm regards, Jonas Merrick.

It had been explained to Jonas by his friend across the Irish Sea that a big untruth was always a better bet than a minor one. Also, in areas of deceit, what appeared as a fulsome apology usually deflected resentment further down the road.

Letters written and sealed in their respective envelopes, and emails sent, Jonas tilted back his chair. Sometimes he'd sleep easily, notwithstanding the noise and chatter from beyond his screen wall . . . not that afternoon. He dozed irritably, did not rest. Was worried and could not staunch the anxiety, saw the young man, could not escape him.

Because it was the last week, Kenny Blake found it hard to concentrate on his client. Which was rude, and dangerous.

She had talked about an investment with him of a few hundred euros, and the message he had was that a shipment was coming to him that was valued at a "few" hundred thousand of sterling and dollar bills. By the start of the next week, and another Monday, the sign on the door would say *Oficina Cerrada* and the noise on the stairs would be ferocious and he would be cursed the length and breadth of Galicia, and by lunchtime there would already be a price on his head.

He could have, perhaps ought to have, declined to take the woman's money. Had thought of it, offering up a poor excuse about the volatility of rates and a reminder that investments had a chance of going "down as well as up", sent her away.

"You know who I am?"

"I'm sorry but I don't."

"Perhaps you have not lived in Spain for very long."

"Been resident for three years, but have not, Miss Perez, heard your name before."

"I was a celebrity, but no longer. I raised money for anti-drug campaigners. I am sure in three years you have learned that this region is the most afflicted with narcotics abuse in all of Spain, perhaps all of Europe – no, the Scotland city of Glasgow would be worse, I correct myself – and I worked hard to have dealers and importers challenged by our police. It is what I used to do, who I used to be. To little effect. I began to take a little from what I collected. Just a little ... but over several years the sum became more substantial. You understand me? What I propose to invest in your company is stolen monies. That is who I am today. I guarantee that a hundred per cent of your clients are sending money to you that is either illegally obtained or is illegally hidden from the tax authority. Am I correct in that assessment?"

"You would not expect me to deny such a statement's relevance, nor to confirm it." He had become wary of her.

"Will you accept what I lodge with you?"

"You should understand, Miss Perez, that I do not investigate the sources of the deposits I handle. Also, you should understand that it is your decision as to what information you place with the national and regional authorities. Your responsibility. I have a document that you will sign that stipulates this."

She had handed him the envelope from her handbag. He counted a grubby wad of banknotes. He named the sum. He suggested an investment rating of "medium risk". In the next 24 hours he would be receiving the second tranche sent from Liverpool to the Munoz family, delivered by the usual formidable and suspicious couriers, and it would be transferred to the Samsonite case he retained for that purpose. What the woman who had once been a crusader would leave with him would equate to loose change for Isabella Munoz. He passed the documentation across his desk. She signed. He copied the papers on to the file on his computer. He had stood, formally shook her hand – decided he was well rid of her. Had shown her off the premises of the Biscuit Tin and had heard her footfall descend the staircase and then the slam of the door on to the street. Had not liked her, which mattered not a damn. What she had left with him might go in the shipment that Hugo and Wilf would collect that week, or might just be abandoned, left in the locked safe, along with paper files and memory sticks, and he would have wiped down his chair and his desk, and removed the desktop's hard drive, and the door handles and the kettle and the crockery. Would be well out of it, well gone. Just as he had done when previous legends had been exhausted.

He had not rung Anna. Had not called to say that a "misunderstanding" should be put behind them. Could feel the medallion on his chest and the chain on his neck. Should have called her. Recalled the cool and aloof way in which he had been seen out of her cottage, walked to his car. Should have rung.

Had nothing and no one on home territory . . . this day in a week, this morning, he would be at the first-floor offices rented by SC&O10 and Jak Peters, pompous and sidelined, would be vying for his time, or he might have got to meet the old guy who was just a soft voice on the end of a call. There would be a debrief but the arrests would already have taken place and the pictures published in the Galicia papers. And after the debrief he would draft the letter of resignation – no farewell party, no piss-up, so few people knowing who he was. And the chance of her ditching her art, so called, and her life along the Coast of Death, he rated as small – but would try for it. Would ring her, but not at the cost of the St Christopher which was pretty much all that was left of his identity.

He sat at his desk. Three years of hard work. A hell of a good scam and down to the foul-tempered and foul-tongued Jimbo Rawe who had recruited him. Made better than "a hell of a good scam" by the spook who had deluged it with resources so that the big fish had bitten, people of interest who were targets . . . but had no home.

Kenny Blake had lost his dealer's long hair, had scrubbed the pallor off his cheeks, had dumped the clothing of a street addict and was decently dressed and looked the image of a sharp manager of people's investments. Had gone back just the one time – usually disciplined but had bent the rules. A bit over a year since he had packed and left them. Stood far back, among the trees and down the road from the entrance to the school gate where parents and au pairs gathered to collect their children at the end of a day. The boy came out first, stood waiting in the play area and looking around him, and then his sister sprinted from the building and the two kids, his kids, running together and through the gate and seeing his own father there. Seeing another guy, ordinary and casually dressed, and his dad shaking the guy's hand and slapping him on the back, and the kids hanging on to the legs of the guy and him stroking their hair. Had watched from the shadows of the trees. Saw his dad walk alone to the same old car as before, saw the guy hitch the two kids up, one on each arm, and walk them to a fleet vehicle, what a fucking rep would have driven, a salesman.

He sat at his desk . . . it would be chaos when he left. Would be worse than chaos for Fredo . . . But it was Kenny Blake's job, what he was paid for and what he was trained to do.

Doloures Govier packed a lightweight suitcase. A good one for airports because it had wheels. Important, there would be miles of walkways to be covered to get her and Patrick on and off their flights.

A cryptic message appeared on her phone. It would have originated in Spain, then been sent to Amsterdam, then been routed on to her.

It was the biggest financial commitment that the Govier family had entered into, would be one of the biggest ever originating from the city of Liverpool, and it would done on trust. No alternative.

Your present arrived and well received. Sufficient. Two million euros and with a first option to buy at least a further 1000 kilos, and the money would cascade in – and would bring that most frequent of nightmares – where to put the fucking cash. Not all of it could go under the floorboards, and not all of it could be spent on apartments in southern France or on the Costa del Sol. The second shipment had been taken to Spain by what appeared to be a normal family going on holiday via a budget airline flight to Bilbao, a destination for more than five million visitors a year.

That family, two adults and three children – two of them "borrowed" – all carried rucksacks crammed with food, books, magazines, all the necessities of vacation and allowed into the cabin, and in the five rucksacks was the money they would carry on board past overworked security. They would have been met at the destination, escorted to a hotel, and then waited in the lobby while, behind a closed door, the rucksacks were opened and the packages of money removed. Each of them was sealed, and carried a waxed stamp with Jean-Luc's initials. Would they have considered disappearing over a faraway horizon? Unlikely they would have been that stupid, inconceivable they would have run the risk of the Govier family's reprisals on those they left behind.

Not much to go into her case. One good frock assuming they were taken to a restaurant – and that would be a challenge as she doubted any of them could speak English other than a few words from a tourist guide vocabulary.

There was a patio in the back garden with a bird bath. Its pedestal was easily shifted and the slab underneath could be lifted. It was close to their solid boundary fence and hidden from the neighbours' windows. She hated birds, thought them disease-ridden, and they crapped all over the garden furniture. She had sent Patrick, stopped him moaning about the problem of selecting what he might wear, to hoist the slab and bring her a phone from the store kept there – pay-as-you-go and loaded only with Bengal's and Jean-Luc's numbers and bought off the shelf in Manchester. Should have been relaxed and on top of her game, a big operator and closing on a big deal, but had problems that evening.

An important woman, one with status in her city, and on the verge of completing a big purchase of cargo being brought closer, each hour, each day, by a semi-submersible – travelling unseen just below the water level – but she had two problems, each of them major.

There was a camera on the house, confirmed. The work of Fanny Thomas, obsessional bitch. A big problem, one she had chucked into the lap of Bengal, and she might have to urge him to go careful, not to let the red mist win, but it was the work that

Bengal did. Another problem, one that was fast developing. A call from a dealer, one of their regulars. A dealer from the Garston part of the city had been beaten up the night before for refusing to give up territory to younger rivals: "Where was the fucking protection I'm supposed to have, where?" Good to expand but also to hold new ground. Something else for Bengal to deal with, needed doing fast and clinically violent so that a message was sent . . . She could not have done without Xavier, could not have survived without the fear that the boy bred. Neither matter could wait for her return. His phone was switched off so she would not reach Bengal – actually rather liked the name and the sense of mystery and something wild that it carried – until he came to the houses.

She zipped the case, attached a little padlock to it. Never trusted airports, thought them places where thieves nested. Might try for an early night, except that Patrick was still whining that his bag was too full and he did not know what to take out. Tomorrow would be a long day, but a rewarding one.

It was a mark of Matias's skill that the engine still worked, kept up a throbbing power when the propeller blades were underwater, but screamed when the craft seemed to dive in a trough or when it sliced into the height of a wave and the blades were exposed and spinning against froth and air. Diego kept his attention on the swirling waters ahead of him. He had given up trying to avoid the most extreme waves and allowed them to beat hard the hull or to lift up the forward end, where the diesel was stored and the wrapped parcels of cocaine. He thought Matias a genius for keeping the engine in near perfect order but had not remarked on it.

Diego estimated that the time of coming close to the European shoreline was still midway through the night of the coming Thursday and Friday and after that – while the craft was unloaded and the cargo taken clear – he would decide whether to attempt a return journey with an empty hold, and take further payment or let the Colombians sort it for themselves while he pleaded illness and exhaustion. Good to dream of that.

He could hear Emiliano's breathing, steady and regular, which meant to Diego that the boy had nothing left in his guts to vomit up. Matias had been humming lullabies which might have helped the boy to sleep – it was of no importance to Diego. Of importance was the prospect of the landfall and the cargo's delivery. Then he could choose between taking the craft back across the Atlantic and receive a bonus that was good but not that generous, or slip away and go south. He was pleased that the boy no longer retched, and thought that the worst for him was over and that he might have recovered sufficiently by the time they landed to help with the unloading.

The rain was less constant but heavy showers still came over them and then the skies would darken. More important to Diego was that the winds had not eased so not only was the swell of the waves just as fierce but their direction was erratic. He was pleased to have the wheel to cling to. They pitched and bucked, and sometimes his feet slid crazily on the decking because the remnants of the boy's vomit made it like a skating rink. But, Diego was pleased that the engine performed well and their progress was steady.

Matias's hummering ceased. His back was poked. "Diego, can you turn, can you look?"

Diego's mind was away. He would cross the border east of the port city of Vigo, would have a driver take him into Portugal, to the little resort town of Viana do Castelo. Would use one of his three passports and book into a hotel there, minimum four stars, and binge on sleep and alcohol and perhaps enjoy the services of some of the Romanian girls. Would check each morning for the money to be lodged in his account – usually the families were correct with payments, prided themselves on maintaining time schedules – and he would work the foulness of the diesel fumes out of his system.

Fingers caught at the material of his jacket. He tried to flick them away.

"I ask you to look. Look."

Diego hung on the wheel, and turned. He saw the stained cockpit windows, the rusting metal rivets that held the fibreglass sections in place, the peeling paint, two bunk beds where they slept in turn.

"What do I look for?"

"The boy. You look at Emiliano."

"I see him. He is sleeping. That is good."

"He is not sleeping." A grating hostility in the engineer's voice.

"Looks to be sleeping."

"He is not sleeping. He is unconscious. He has lost consciousness. If he does not get help he will die. If he does not regain consciousness, he will die, but sooner."

Diego hissed an answer. "No helicopter is coming, no cutter. No help is coming. Not before we reach land, and your job is to keep the engine running."

"He will die."

Diego did not reply. He heard the boy's breathing, and heard the metal door click as its clasp was opened, and the roar of the engine was louder as it struggled with the waves.

The day drew to its close in the port city of Corunna. Shutters were going down on the shop fronts and the cafés. Hideous scraping sounds, metal grating on metal.

An unmarked van edged out of a space it had occupied all day, a 20 euro note having exchanged hands with a parking attendant. Across the street, a sales board had been taken inside the premises closed until the morning. A man had come out of the next door building, had pocketed his key and then had used his handkerchief to wipe at a sign on which was engraved *La Lata de Galletas*. Adriano had spent all day in the van with his camera, photographing everyone who went in and out of next door. He took great pride in his work, was careful with focus. He drove away. He would go to his studio and would print the images . . . one face had caught his attention.

Many years before, as a camera assistant, working in the darkroom of the Pontevedra weekly paper, he had developed a roll of film for the senior photographer. A demonstration outside the mansion of a clan leader. Women howling abuse at the locked gates of ornate ironwork. The leader was a woman, part of her face hidden by the bullhorn she used. Adriano knew that the Munoz family dealt with the investment manager who worked on the second floor of the building beside the café. He had a good memory for faces and had recognised the woman who had gone to visit him, been there for 39 minutes: Luna Perez, one time cheerleader of the movement against drug abuse. It added to his conclusion that the investment manager kept unlikely company . . . he would deliver the prints that evening to Sergio Munoz.

"Come." Jonas answered the knock on his cubicle door.

His computer had been switched off, his safe locked. His lunch box and his Thermos were in his briefcase which was already chained to his wrist, along with the letters that he had written. He was wearing his coat and hat. He needed to see Kev and Leroy about a meeting and a delivery and both were off duty the next day. He was irritated at being delayed. Aggie Burns entered, eyed him up and down as if he were the dame in a pantomime.

"Not wanting to hold you up," she said with a twinkle.

"You have done."

"What you wanted."

A gruff response. He had always been nervous of Aggie Burns. She gave not a damn who she offended, and he was on her list of those needing a prick to their pomposity. She carried a sagging plastic bag.

"I do not intend to miss my train."

"What would happen, Jonas, if you did?" she teased.

"I catch the train my season ticket dictates. I am home when I am expected home, and . . ."

"Bullshit, Jonas. Do many in your fan club know what you asked me to get for you?"

"None, and I'd rather . . ."

"Not my fashion to gossip." She handed him the bag.

He snatched it. "Have to be on my way."

"You'll fit the part for it, what you wanted. Always do look a proper jobsworth."

"Excuse me – and thank you."

He went past her and she followed him out of his cubicle but not before her eyes had raked over his walls. Would have seen the matriarch and the family home, the addict who sagged in a doorway. All eyes in the work area were on him and Aggie, interest high because she had brazenly entered forbidden territory. He disappointed them, intended to, locked his door and headed for the corridor. She followed.

"Mind if I say something, Jonas?" There seemed to be a softness in her voice, a tone seldom associated with her, like she might care. He grinned. The world was collapsing around him if Aggie Burns had ditched her menace.

"I've said that I'm grateful, and have said I am not missing my train."

She headed for the stairs, and he had to hurry to keep up.

"Heaven forbid that anyone should get the mistaken idea that I care a damn for your health and wellbeing, Jonas. Nothing concerns me less. What you have asked for and what I have given you are pretty commonplace tools of our trade. Everyday stuff for us . . . But there's a difference, Jonas. My people are trained in their work, are on the end of communications, can get backup fast. You, I doubt it. We would rate you as virginally innocent of self-preservation. You should not go close to the sort of people you are supposed to be investigating. They don't do *It's a fair cop, guv*. Moved beyond that. If someone has to pick you up off a pavement, Jonas, don't say you weren't warned . . . Go and get your bloody train. I'm not in tomorrow but I'll wish you well now."

Nothing affectionate, not a kiss on the cheek, not a smile or a wink. A rather solid punch to the arm and Jonas winced. She broke away as they reached the foot of the stairs, nothing else to be said, and he heard her go back up, taking the steps two at a time.

He was on schedule, but only just. He went through security and, outside, almost barged into Kev and Leroy.

He begged their time, just a minute of it.

★   ★   ★

Felt like a teenager . . . Could have been the sixth-form boy in school uniform, an average academic record and pimples on his face, and longing to hear from the girl who took the same bus home as he did but was too grand to talk with him . . .

His phone rang. He gazed at the screen, saw her number come up.

Had not eaten anything hot that day, had snatched at snacks, had drunk too much coffee, had started packing. One bag would be sufficient, and his laptop in its pouch. His documentation would be coming from the goat boys.

His phone shrieked at him. Happened to have turned it loud when he had gone to shower after returning from Corunna, after closing down the Biscuit Tin. Had hoped it would ring but it had not. Could have been Kenny's fault. More than half a dozen times he had steadied himself, taken a deep breath and reached out for his phone, but he had not called her. Could not have said why he had not, why he hadn't muttered some sort of an excuse and smoothed over the sharp remarks about a St Christopher medallion. Not much time to put it right. Had got himself into believing that there was no life afterwards unless it was shared, and no one to share it with other than her . . .

Easy enough to feel like a teenager, except that he was a few days short of his 30th birthday. His image of a future was him and her and a cottage out in the Hebrides or on an island off the Dutch coast, and fires burning in the winter and hammocks on frames for sleeping in during the summer, and always blown by soft winds, and food that was simple and drink that was cheap. Her painting and him learning DIY and being in each other's arms, and trusting each other and being honest . . . and, one day, telling her who he was.

Almost obligatory, like a rite of passage, was the night with the assistant administrator in the field office of SC&O10, her place, and expected to be gone before she needed to dress for the morning shift. And one girl who was a junkie in Sheffield – which should not have happened. But, most times, Kenny made his excuses. Was smitten, and knew it. Wondering how long she would let it ring. He answered.

"You okay?"

"Good, nice of you to ask – why would I not be?"

Heard the sea, and the wind, and heard what might have been her nervousness.

"Because you went fast."

"Did I?"

"Silly boy."

"Agreed . . . If I caused offence it was not intended. Where are you?"

"Just out, just about . . . don't tell me there is nothing for an artist because the sea is fierce and the wind is brutal and it is too dark to see my hand in front of my face."

"I won't tell you, Anna, that there is nothing for an artist when they cannot see their hand in front of their nose."

"I thought you would call me."

"I thought I would."

"See you tomorrow, tell you about the thoughts of an artist. Tomorrow. I miss you, Kenny."

The call was cut. He no longer heard the waves and the wind, no longer saw the darkness. And he started again to think about what he would take in the one bag, and what he would abandon, and later – before he slept – he would start to wipe down the inside of the cottage. Thought too much about her but did not acknowledge that as weakness. Felt good because Anna Jensen had said she missed him, better than good.

A long bus ride home to complete a journey that Luna Perez now regretted.

Had confided in him and she could not now think why she had. Had recognised the sum she had left with him was minimal and the rewards she would obtain would be insignificant.

She felt she was now branded as a criminal, though one protected by secrecy. The investment adviser was not interested in her. She had made herself as guilty of going to a money launderer as any of those she had denounced all those years ago.

There was a gang of kids at the back of the bus who were noisy and stretched her tolerance. Difficult to remember that she had once been the kids' champion and had sought to free them from addiction. It had been a wasted day for her. Instead of leaving her envelope with the smooth-talking Englishman, who seemed to speak from a script, she should have gone into the Basilica de Santa Maria de Mayor and stuffed the money into the collection box.

Wilf was up the hill from their cottage, keeping guard over the beehives. They were proud of the quality of their honey, kept some for themselves and sold the rest in a street market in the local village. Its quality was also recognised by a male brown bear, *ursus arctos arctos*, which they estimated, from fleeting sightings, to be six feet, nose to tip of a short tail, and weighing some three hundredweight. If the bear came near, Wilf would clatter two tins they used to scare it. The bear, ventured out from the Somiedo Natural Park and had been into neighbours' hives but as yet had left theirs undisturbed. Much of their time was spent discussing the bear, even more was spent forecasting when two of the does in their herd would start the kidding process, and some was devoted to considering the situation of the guy down the road. They worried about Kenny, and about their goats and about their honey.

Hugo turned the radio down. Recognised the voice on the phone which was quiet, spoke quickly, to the point. They had often, the two of them, tried to build a photo fit picture of the man, a bit of a game, doubted they would succeed. What was most hard to understand was how this individual – they knew him only as Jonas – exercised such power. They realised he was his own man; if they raised a point of order an answer was given, immediate and clear. The transfer of the firearms would have been in clear breach of international law. The movement of the contents of the weighty Samsonite cases from Corunna to Guernsey was in contravention of pretty much every financial regulation agreed among sovereign states. Their pay came on the same day every month, never late. Hugo generally opted for an aristocrat, independent means, the job as a hobby, an amusement. Wilf had him as a Permanent Under Secretary, top of the pecking order, running down time before retirement and a sinecure in the City. Would they ever meet him? Wilf said, "As night follows day, I guarantee that the answer is no." Hugo's latest contribution was more nuanced. "Depends how it works out, the rest of this week. We lose Kenny, and we will not. We get him safely home, job done, he might be in the centre of a gang of penpushers and putting a glass of fizz in our fists." How would they know him? A shrug – he might not care to show them his voice.

Hugo was told what was wanted of them.

Was there a question that he wished to ask? Hugo pondered. He was allowed a moment to consider what more they would need to know, and thought about what Wilf would have asked.

"Just one thing, on behalf of both of us . . . Should it come down to 'difficulties', then we'd like the Rules of Engagement made clear."

He was told.

Hugo had the kit out – rifles and ammunition, handguns and magazines, gas and flash-and-bang canisters – when Wilf quietly let himself back inside.

Not much that needed to be said. Hugo would go down their rough and rutted lane at dawn and would beg Maria and Joaquin to mind the does when they started kidding, and be so good as to feed the herd for the next three or four days, no more. And when they had finished checking the firepower they would have a coffee and a small tumbler of brandy.

Wilf said, "I think it's going down to the line."

Hugo said, "It usually does, this sort of business."

If he had been closer, he would have heard Nanette say, "I came because I always come this time on a Monday, but I've nothing to tell you."

If he had been nearer, he would have heard Jimbo say, gravel-voiced and with a smoker's rasp, "Always best to have a routine, whatever you have to tell me, whatever the feckin' weather."

He had noted that the young woman wore an anorak with the name of her travel agency printed on the back. He recognised Jimbo Rawe, Detective Chief Inspector Fergal Rawe, from when he, a dealer in white stuff, had been waiting to be interviewed for possession and trading. He, the dealer, noted what he saw. He was far down the list of those who bought from the Govier family, but believed that what he had seen would offer him an opportunity for ingratiation.

Did not hear her say, "Anyway, she's off tomorrow – taking her boy, that Patrick, with her, and you've had from me the names on the tickets, what they're using. I've nothing more for you – and the same dates for them coming back as I told you. That's it."

Did not hear him answer, "Well, that's a good kid, and that's appreciated . . . and always remember that each time we meet it pushes back the day that I need to drop a little paperwork round to those VAT bastards."

"When'll you let me free, Mister Rawe, when?"

"Could be you'll be free one day, because then I'll be in my box and the daisies pushing up above me. Goodnight, Nansie – look after yourself."

They parted and the dealer watched them go their separate ways. She went into an underpass and he heard her heels clatter away on the concrete, and she'd be running by the time she was at the far end and had cause to if she were using that route out of the car park. He watched Jimbo Rawe saunter away and saw lights flash on his car when he used his key fob. Typical of Jimbo Rawe: it was a foul night and he'd not offered the woman shelter in his car. In the interview suite, he had noted who was the person of interest and had looked him over as if he were merely a slurp of dog shit. Not a face that the dealer would have forgotten and he knew his reputation. Lucky that Jimbo Rawe had not taken an interest in him then and added him to a prosecution case which would have tripled his sentence; he had come up, instead, in front of a kindly woman, new to the bench, and had looked pleadingly at her, and been rewarded . . . only six months inside, then out and back dealing.

Was at the bottom of the food chain. Had no status . . . except that, now, a door might have opened. Had something that a big man might want. What they all feared most was an informer. The dealer had something to trade: Jimbo Rawe was meeting the woman from Nanette's Travel on the edge of an underpass, late at night, after the buses had stopped, and the rain pissing on them. He took a last look at Jimbo Rawe across the car park, before he went to look for a big man. Bengal Govier was the biggest he knew of.

Remembering what he had said.

"The Rules of Engagement? A fair question, and one with a simple answer . . ."

Jonas stood at the bottom of the garden, by the dripping fir tree, holding an umbrella to shelter him from the driving rain.

". . . you have the kit and you would use it. Those are your Rules of Engagement. If the life, or the liberty, of KB is threatened then you use whatever level of force you reckon is necessary. Clear?"

Could barely believe he had spoken those words.

"At the end of this week, as he probes for evidence – a new world for me but not for him – he will be vulnerable and I want you as near as you can be without hampering his efforts. I have no idea how you might proceed, but believe enough in your talents for your own initiatives to win through."

And, in a West Midlands accent, the query as to what Hugo and Wilf might expect should the shit indeed hit the fan, and they felt the need to blast a bit, what then?

"Very sensible point. If, to safeguard life or liberty, you open fire and do not feel able to use warning shots but use aimed shots at those who endanger the life and the liberty of KB, then I will stand by you. I would use every breath in my body to prevent an inquest and to minimise your involvement. That is a promise. I take responsibility. I'm a bit older than you but not much. We seldom have the chance, at our age, to have a good crack at something which might just be fun, exciting, and hopefully rewarding. I have given you my promise, can't do more than that. My best effort. We will speak each day, and I have the greatest confidence in you both."

Jonas had cut the call. Stood with his umbrella straining against the wind. What he had done by accepting the possible need for violence to protect an undercover, on his own and without a vestige of authority, was to expose himself to the equivalent of a hanging, a drawing and a quartering. Difficult to believe he had said it. The volume of rain had overwhelmed the guttering of his house and the Derbyshires' and water cascaded down on to their separate patios. He was a long time out there and wished that he had brought his pipe with him. The kitchen door opened and light flooded out on to the grass.

"You should come in, Jonas, or you'll catch your death."

"Just coming, dear."

"We'll really have to get that gutter seen to. Jonas, are you sure about us going away? The forecast is awful. Is it worth us going?"

"It'll be good enough, the weather, certain of it."

9

"I don't know quite how to describe him."

Jonas Merrick never suffered from burning ears. It did not matter to him whether colleagues discussed him.

"Flattering him wouldn't be appropriate, not in terms of likeability."

He would have been indifferent to a meeting in the atrium, accidental, while both waited for a visitor. The AssDepDG was expecting a Commander from the Yard – "terrorism", always top of the priority heap. Aggie Burns's guest was delayed by a signals failure outside Paddington, travelling from the south-west out-station and hoping to get an injection of resources for a surveillance: more boots on the ground as an extremist group's phone traffic soared and the suspicion of imminent activity was reasonable.

"Playing his cards close to his chest. Any ideas what's in his mind? He's a devious sod."

"Nothing particular that I know of," she lied.

Time to kill. The AssDepDG told Reception, that nice girl and that boot-faced security beggar who sat beside her, that they would be outside having a cigarette. Went through the security barriers, down the steps and across the road, and together they paused on the bridge's approach. The rain was light, the wind was a bastard, and it took an effort with his Zippo to get a flame to hold long enough for both of them. Smoke wreathed their faces, then was whisked aside.

"Anyway," she said, "I gather he's taking leave. Going off this afternoon."

"Unusual, but so I understand."

"Seems perky. Can't say I like him, but I do have a pinch of respect."

Together they dragged on their cigarettes.

"Aggie, Jonas is odd, peculiar, different. And you are not a bag of normality, and I hope I manage a streak of non-convention. Can you imagine the purgatory of sitting on a train journey in the same carriage, opposite him and expecting conversation? He would talk about his cat, his caravan. Would not mention Vera who I sometimes feel deserves canonisation. He is the perfect intelligence officer. No sense of being a crusader, no wish to right the world's great faults. Utterly boring. If we were surrounded in this building by more stunningly boring folk then the country would sleep a great deal better at night, be in much safer hands. He has determination which I admire. Bit like one of those tracking hounds, give it a scent – a handkerchief or an old sock – point it in the general direction and off it will happily go and don't expect meal breaks to get in the way. What he's doing now, crime – I mean who gives a flying fuck about crime? – no one cares about crime. The most interesting thing about Jonas is that he has always been the same, plodded along for thirty-odd years, and no one ever recognised his innate ability to sort out problems, do it with rather devastating simplicity. He's contemptuous of anyone with a formal academic education. I have a Third in Philosophy at a redbrick, so I am just about acceptable. He looks at a problem, tries to find the basics, dumps charts and graphs in the bin, reads court reports and interview transcripts, and comes up with the goods. It was always there, his talent, but people looked at his quaint idea of dress, his stubborn adherence to that train home, and wrote him off. They did not look at the quality of the advice he was presenting. Only when he'd bagged that suicide boy did I look closely at what he was saying. He really is very dull, and with little ambition that I've detected . . . but stubborn as a pack-mule, a big virtue."

"I think you're wrong."

"I may be. Enlighten me."

"You call him 'dull', 'boring', say he has 'little ambition'. I say 'wrong' because you short-change him. He *does* want to win. Has the hunger for it – just like the rest of us, but excessive. It's not just counter-terror and counter-espionage that has winners. Even down in the prestige gutter, I expect crime has those on top and those who flunk. He cannot abide coasting, being second best."

"God help us."

He looked past her and recognised his visitor, a tall angular woman who looked annoyed because the traffic did not immediately brake to let her cross the road: the Commander from the Yard. He doubted she'd admit to hunger. He stamped on his cigarette. They crossed easily because Aggie Burns just marched into the sea of cars and vans and lorries and coaches, and they parted for her.

On the steps of their building, he paused. "Are you offering me any advice?"

"Keep your eyes open, ears open, wits about you."

"You got them?"

"I got them."

Hugo murmured, "The one with the red windcheater."

Wilf said quietly, "And the one in the blue anorak."

"They have an eyeball on him."

"That's the way it looks."

The grenades, gas and flash-bang, were in the rucksack on Wilf's back. At both their waists, snug against a belt, was a handgun, loaded. Between them, on the ground, was an empty Samsonite suitcase. They'd talked it through on the journey west along the coast, and agreed the message given them was confused. They were now supposed to offer a level of protection to Kenny Blake, an instruction from London. Were supposed to collect the latest load of cash and do the case swap. They never marched straight up to Kenny but would hang about, kill a few minutes, enjoy the view even if the mist was down over the old harbour, would hang back and check the plot and then go forward. Might exchange a few words with him, but not enter into a conversation. They expected that the case tucked between Kenny's trainers held at least a million sterling.

"He's watched."

"He is. Perhaps he is every day."

"What shall we do?"

"Get up close," Wilf whispered.

And they went forward, Hugo carrying the empty Samsonite. Kenny was near the tomb of that general . . . Neither Hugo nor Wilf thought that death could be good, noble, heroic, but believed in "looking after a mucker" . . . Had no feeling for the general who had a poem about his death on his tombstone, but had thought hard about their obligations to the undercover, Kenny, who they hardly knew and who knew nothing about their goats . . . They walked close to each other and seemed to be in conversation, and came up to Kenny, and Wilf fished a map out of his hip pocket and was bold enough to ask a "stranger" to help them, which gave them the opportunity.

"Not supposed to be doing a pick-up and an exit," Wilf said.

"Told to keep close to you, be there for the duration," Hugo said, putting down the case.

"What we're told."

"Have you in sight."

Peering at the map, playing the part, Kenny frowned and his chin jutted.

"Thank you and no thank you," he said, as if that were a sufficient response.

Kenny Blake had a mindset. Common to most of the Level Ones. Were told there was backup round the corner, were told it was all poised, ready to go, and had the kit armed up. When they were away, three or four, or half a dozen of them, they'd clear out of the building that was being used and get out into the grounds or down the street and light up. The guys who didn't smoke, would light up too and just hold the cigarette, and they'd talk. No instructors listening to them and no psychologists to interpret their thoughts. None of them would ever rely on the backup, that was the mindset. Chance was that the overtime rates for the armed guys had become prohibitive. Equal chance that it was change-over and the new shift was not fully briefed on the undercover's exact location. Could have been that it was a meal break, or a comfort break, or any break that screwed their efficiency.

"Just do the swap and be on your way. We are being watched so act it out."

So, the result of the mindset was that each man relied on his own wit and cunning for self-preservation . . . Kenny knew the pair of them, knew that each time he met them that Wilf and Hugo stank of goats . . . knew them as polite and careful, and they had come on the scene when the guy in London, the spook, had taken charge. He had had no protection before the London guy, and also had had no link with any family as prominent as the Munoz clan. He saw their hesitation.

"Guys, do it, and back off."

There was a system built into his phone. A clever system. If he hit a combination of keys then an alert was triggered. The guys from the goat farm would receive that signal and the location of the phone. Would be active for about six hours, what he'd been told . . . the system, too, had come from the spook. Everything had been cheapskate before the man with the soft, persuasive voice had taken over. All done on a shoestring. Now the system was deluged with cash: protection, light aircraft, a Channel Island bank cover, cost underwritten when the share market dipped. Seemed it was what they wanted: a Liverpool family going into the cage, a Galicia family trapped in the net, and how that fitted with spooks' work was beyond the compass of Kenny Blake. And a craft that was almost a submarine, but in reality only a semi-submersible, going into the trap was a bonus. Could not understand the interest of the spooks in the business of coke traffic. Was not paid to understand. And could remember how it had been when he had walked off the ferry at Santander three years before with a rucksack and a canvas grip and a laptop in it and a bucket of investment jargon memorised and the idea of the Biscuit Tin. Had started with an innocence and a need to dislodge the image of his dad and his wife's new man sharing time with *his* kids at the schoolgate. Coming to an end now and the hours ticking by.

Kenny said, "Do the cases, get going. I need you, I'll call you."

With his toe he edged his suitcase closer to them, and Wilf dropped his map and bent to pick it up and slid the case towards Kenny. He had seen the red top and the blue top for all of the ten minutes that he had been waiting in the Garden. The rain was light but the wind was still fierce, and waves and spray came over the Garden outer wall and, even in the shelter of the old harbour, the pleasure boats rocked and swayed and their masts rattled against the cables. The last complication that Kenny Blake needed in the remaining hours was to have two men following him, and without the necessary tradecraft. He picked up the empty Samsonite suitcase.

"I hope you find where you're looking for. Have a great day," he told them loud and purposefully, and walked away.

Had reason to be cheerful. Had had a text telling him where she'd be. The morning slipping away and the time edging closer when she'd be expecting him. Almost jaunty now, and with the handle of the empty case loose in his hand, he went out of the Garden. *Not a drum was heard, not a funeral note, As his corse to the rampart we hurried* and where *Slowly and sadly we laid him down, From the field of his fame fresh and gory.* The last time he would be there. The men in the red and the blue watched him. Was not sure if he had seen them before. Would have been routine for him to be checked over when he was shifting a million in sterling and they might have realised the cases were switched or might not.

Was thinking of Anna and where she'd meet him. The wind would be against them and he'd have to put his mouth to her ear to be heard, and she'd be hanging on to her easel.

Hugo and Wilf did not run, but they hurried out of the Garden and veered off to where the vehicle was parked. An attendant, old and shabby, advanced towards them, but Wilf opened the boot and Hugo dumped the case inside and covered it with the old rug, a faded tartan, on which hay or straw was carried, and in the boot was heavier firepower. Wilf slammed the lid down and Hugo had a fifty out of his wallet – 50 euros was usually enough to guarantee the goodwill of a parking attendant in Corunna.

Hugo said, "They followed him, not close but keeping him in sight."

Wilf said, "Going back to his office?"

"Am thinking so. And so are we."

"Not arguing."

They knew the route. They split. Wilf, faster on his feet, went the long way. Wilf was wise enough, and concerned enough, to push himself: had the twin contradictions of the principal, in the jargon they had been taught, telling them to piss off, and had the orders from the Customer, who paid the bills, ordering a close-up – able to intervene – watch on their man.

The street they came to, from opposite ends, was long and narrow, no bends. They arrived around the same time and each had a clear view down the street. Would have seen the café sign on the pavement and would have seen the car parked half on the pavement, half on the street, and would also have noticed that pedestrians were crossing to the far pavement, quickening their step as if word had passed round that it was better to know nothing, see nothing.

He came out of the door beside the café. The red windcheater and the blue anorak flanked him. A hand went inside Kenny Blake's jacket and took his mobile from a pocket and Kenny seemed not to blink. There was a hand on Kenny's arm and both the guys were smiling, like it was fun and Kenny was smiling back – all rubbish, all going bad. Only the blue anorak in the front. It went away from Hugo and towards Wilf, came fast down the rest of the street, turned with a tyre scream and was lost.

The people in the café all had their backs to the football on the TV, and were peering into the street, would have seen Kenny Blake being led out.

Wilf joined Hugo. "I don't know what we could have done, but he was lifted."

"Doesn't matter what we might have done, we didn't do it."

★   ★   ★

Not done with grace, but Doloures Govier reckoned it effective.

Was careful that her gloved hands were clear of the glass pieces embedded in the top of the wall. She teetered for a moment on the ladder, then lifted a leg and swung it wide so that it cleared the back fence, and her shoe caught the ladder on the far side. Her weight went on to it and the legs of the ladder slid a bit and then locked, and she cursed the useless little cow, Theresa, who had been given the job of resting a ladder against a wall, and had almost bollocksed it. Doloures climbed down. Once she was standing, breathing hard and regaining her balance, her case was dropped down to her. She looked around her warily but there was no one watching.

"Well, come on then, don't hang about."

He might have been her favourite son but she still, and always had, barked instructions at Patrick. He appeared over the wall. His foot came off the second ladder and he'd sagged and then seemed to panic but regained his control. His bag was bigger than hers and bulging. She wondered briefly if it had been a good choice to bring him, whether it should have been Theresa. Certainly not Xavier with his short-fuse temper and his lack of support for the enterprise. Long before the camera had been identified on the Potters' wall this had been their exit route. Out of the kitchen door, hug the high fence, down to the bottom of the garden and into the shelter of bushes and trees where the shed was. The first ladder was stacked there. Up against the back wall, the pivot at the top and then on to the second ladder that was kept on the far side. At the back of their garden was a track that gave access to the rear gardens of the next road of houses. It was overgrown, strewn with litter, and was hardly used. Theresa had already bitched about the mess on her trousers when she had been sent to get the second ladder and leave it against the wall, beneath the narrow space where the glass shards had been removed. Patrick now had the job of removing this ladder and tucking it away from sight with old planking to cover it. A little hiss of annoyance and that would have been Theresa taking the first ladder down and hauling it into the shed.

They waited, might have been a minute or two early going over the wall. She thought Patrick looked longingly at the wall, and she could see he was shivering. The rain fell lightly on them and they waited for the car. He was annoying her.

"Can you not stop that fidget?"

"Just that this is big time, Ma."

"Big and where we belong. And we're the customers, right?"

"Yes, Ma."

"And the customer is always right. And don't go asking them how much coal they can fit in their bath."

She was laughing and he joined in, and the car arrived at the top of the track and flashed its headlights. Dead on time, as she'd expect it to be. The wheels of their cases squealed and bounced behind them and the driver was out and opening the back door for her.

She had known where to look, had seen the camera lens, had tried not to draw attention to it. And Xavier had said he would deal with it, that night or the next, and she expected his reaction to be spectacular.

She sat in the lecture hall, attention wandering. Had no interest in what the guy said about the "collapse of the Weimar and hyper-inflation". Was interested in property acquisition, laundering and, tax evasion ... And what she would have said if she had met Cocky. And would there ever be a moment when the treadmill stopped and she could gracefully step off? She sat alone. Usually did. If there was a spare seat in a row where other students sat and she went to take it then she would be told that it was already taken. She was not invited to parties, saw none of her fellow students, other than from a distance in a lecture. And the tutors were wary of her, guarded in what they said, never openly criticising her work. She tried to get good grades, but it was as if they were reluctant to praise her for fear of seeming ingratiating. Had heard a student, his back to her in a corridor and holding forth to a group – his father a businessman but also a lay preacher – say, "It's all about greed. No matter how much tainted money they have, it's never enough. They keep on making more of it, and there's only one end, that's maximum security and massive sentences. You want to be lonely, then deal drugs . . . Ask her, she'll tell you . . ."

The lecture droned on and she took nominal notes and would feed occasional quotes into her next essay. Next week sounded more interesting: a French architect was due to talk to them about the property boom on the Mediterranean coast: 50,000 euros a square metre in Monaco, 20,000 euros a square metre in Cannes, a development of eight villas on a hillside back from the coast, with an annual bill of 200,000 euros to maintain the gardens . . . If you could find the property. Ma said the Italians and Spanish were buying it up and the British were late into the market.

Some days she wished she was like her mother. Other days she wished she were like her fellow students. Every day she dreaded being like her dad and banged up. She had read that Curtis Warren, Cocky, had once been Interpol's Target One: not just Merseyside and not just the National Crime Agency and not just Europol, but *Interpol*, top of the tree – amazing. Had lost the thread of what the man was talking about. Theresa was supposed to be the future. Theresa was going to be the financial guru for the family. Patrick would do the investing and she would do the big-time deals and Xavier would do the enforcing . . .

Her shoulder was tapped. She turned abruptly, and a folded tab of paper was passed to her.

The girl who delivered it jerked her head to indicate it came from behind her. Another girl, further back, made a similar gesture. Behind them were the back rows of the lecture hall. They must all be bored, and they were looking at her.

She put down her pen and unfolded the scrap of paper. She did not look behind her but assumed each face was still gazing at her, and the lecturer looked up and realised that he had lost a good proportion of his audience and he paused in mid-sentence, and she saw that he stared at her.

Am being offered 3 wraps of crack cocaine at £22.50. Wondering, Theresa, if you can better that price.

She was a Govier. She stood and ripped the paper into small pieces and let them flake to the floor around her rucksack. The laughter in the hall beat at her ears. The business school had a zero tolerance to narcotics: students were told they risked blighting their careers if identified as users, even occasional and recreational. Her Ma was on her way to catch a plane, Patrick with her, and her dad was in Walton and likely doing his stint in laundry or peeling potatoes, and Xavier was on the charge. She was on her own.

She bent. Grabbed the straps of her rucksack, shoved her notebook inside, and took out her phone.

"Fuck you," Theresa Govier shouted, loud enough for everyone to hear. "And I don't forget, and I know who you are."

She swivelled, took a picture of the rows of faces, chortling, behind her. Silence fell as she pocketed her phone, left the hall and clattered off down the corridor.

Xavier was hurrying between meetings, on his way from giving instructions, heading for gatherings where the movement of cargo would be decided. The system did not run by itself. If he were not there, signing off each detail, then the whole business would collapse. His Ma had told him a year back that he might bring the family down, and he had snapped back that the rest of them would already be on the floor without him.

Drove past the offices where the accountants were, the architects and the lawyers. Several floors in tower blocks or smartened Georgian buildings . . . all with Chief Executive Officers and Financial Directors, and Legal Officers and Human Resources and Communications Directors. A company with the turnover of the Govier family would have needed maybe three floors in a tower or maybe two of the old buildings knocked together to house their staff – and the car for him would have been a top-of-the-range Mercedes, or a Ferrari or a Maserati, or the best Range Rover, and his suit would have cost £1,500 and . . . He delegated less than any of them with the fancy titles would have done. What Ma said, "Want it done properly then you do it yourself." Could not do everything but could do most of it. Would lead the charge against the fuckers who were trying to muscle in on his territory and would have worked over a dealer who required protection . . . would handle the camera in the wall opposite Ma's front door. If he backed off, left it to others, then word would soon travel and loyalty would shrink. Two days of stubble on his face. A T-shirt that had no logo, and faded jeans, and probably his armpits smelled – and he sat awkwardly in his car because there was a CZ999 Scorpion tucked into the back of his belt and the barrel tip gouged at his backside and it carried a 15-round, parabellum, magazine.

His Ma was off on her travels – from which no good would come – and Patrick with her, and his sister was at her classes – waste of her time and all the rest of the family's time – and his dad was too long away and just wanted to sit with the other old inmates and talk about the "good old days" and bank jobs and wages vans and running cannabis through the docks. It was left to him to hold it together. Would be a shooting job to protect the territory in Garston, and he'd need the fast exit, his clothes burned and a shower and his car cleaned, and the route there and the route back all monitored for overhead cameras . . . Had it a fucking sight harder than the guys with the titles in the office suites.

There was an overspill car park behind a petrol station, gone bust, that was used as an open-air street market. He went there each day, usually around the same time. It was a security risk, going there, and carrying a weapon made it more of a risk, but it was necessary for him to be seen. A dealer wanted to come over to the family as a prime supplier, had to be able to find him. A customer had complained that a dealer using the family's merchandise had cut it again and left only crap in the wrap, and he had to stifle that before word spread. He drove into the disused car park. His people would have sanitised it, and filtered anyone who wanted to talk to him . . . Enjoyed the shooting in his workload, had films of squaddies blasting in Afghan with machine guns, would not hang about there. He flashed his lights, kept the engine running.

Saw his own people. Saw the guy they had with them. Saw them push him towards his car. A shit sort of guy, jabbering and looking frightened which was how Bengal liked punters to be. Was told where and when and what, the last evening, he had seen and heard.

"It's Jimbo Rawe. It's raining, it's late, it's not a chance meeting. It's him and a woman and she's an anorak on with Nanette's Travel on the back. What you're telling me?"

"What I saw . . . That's worth something?"

He made a gesture to his own people which meant they were to give the guy some stuff . . . not much, but something. Knew Nanette, knew the business she ran, knew that Ma reckoned the sun shone from her bum . . . And what he had learned in the car park was added to the Garston bit and the camera thing – more piling up of his workload.

He drove away, would get the shooting done first. What constantly encouraged Bengal was his certainty that the Serious Crime Unit in Merseyside were rubbish and that he walked over them – always had. Had no doubt he would continue to.

"Did you hate them?"

"Not particularly, didn't seem necessary."

The gardener had fielded Jonas's question and given his answer but had not slowed his raking of the few leaves on the path around the bench where he sat.

"And the men you fought with, did you love them?"

"Wouldn't say so, was just alongside them."

The garden at the back of Thames House, a little further down Horseferry Road from the café where he took his morning coffee and his Danish, was a favourite place for Jonas to come to. He could park his backside on a bench and allow the travails of his life to leak away. It had been a cemetery three centuries before, a renowned location for filching the recently interred, washing the corpses down and flogging them to anatomy classes, had had to employ guards with blunderbusses to offer the graves a spot of protection. Had high trees and was quiet now. It was a spot where

Fivers came to enjoy a cigarette and it was now maintained with an immaculate dedication.

"But you pushed yourself to the limits? Perhaps beyond them?"

"Had to, no option."

The gardener was an army veteran. Not clear to Jonas what horrid corner of evacuation from empire and "punching above our weight" the gardener had been involved in while taking the shilling. Knew that he had been recruited by a former star of the Service. Had been pulled away from the therapy of gardening while suffering from the hideous black dog days of PTSD and sent as a sniper to take down a Russian crime baron. The Russian had ordered the killing of a Fiver in Budapest and had taken some tracking, had been located in a villa high above Marbella on the Costa del Sol. The Russian was dead, the gardener had returned to his wheelbarrow. A light rain did not deter him. Jonas valued his opinion.

"Did you consider the importance of what was asked of you by the army?"

"Was given a job. That's what it was, a job."

"Toss it round in your head? Did it matter, did it not?"

"Never. Was given it, was told what to do. Did it as best I could."

"And made a difference?"

"Couldn't say. Not what I was there for."

The gardener raked around Jonas's brogues. There were no leaves, no dried mud, no fag ends, but the man still raked. Would have done that side of St John's old cemetery, where the headstones still stood and were well lathered in lichen, on a Monday and Tuesday, and on a Wednesday and Thursday would be over the other side, and on a Friday anywhere that he had missed. Did not matter that there was nothing to rake and nothing to brush clear with his broom and nothing to scoop up on his shovel. It impressed Jonas that however many questions he put to the gardener, and had done now for several years, the man never snapped back that it was "none of your business" nor said "Why are you asking?" Jonas had one more question.

"Did you make judgements? My side is right and their side is wrong?"

"Did not. This is my job today, that was my job then. Do the best you can and can't do more. Excuse me, sir. Could you, please, shift your feet?"

Jonas nodded his thanks that the inquisition had been treated with punctilious courtesy. He thought that Vera would have liked the gardener and have enjoyed talking about her herbaceous border with him. Felt his mind, that had been fogged, was clearer. Better not to have to make judgements. Could understand why Winston Gunn had agreed to wear the vest, and why Cameron Jilkes had accepted a suicide mission against an RAF station from which the drones had been flown that had bombarded him and his brothers in the Iraqi wastelands, and why Frank the Sixer had taken a lover when life and excitement and motherhood had passed her by and was prepared to betray a room full of snotty, snobby superiors . . . Could understand a little of the lives of the Govier family, but would work to topple them because that was the job he had. Good enough? Good and enough. He rose from the bench, felt the damp in the seat of his trousers, went back to clear his desk.

"I'm telling you this, Fanny, I laid into them. Let them know that no junior spook in London screwed around with Jimbo Rawe. This started with me. What I'm saying, Fanny, is that they have – late in the day – agreed to see some sense. I am invited to London. Meeting at eleven tomorrow morning. I don't expect this to be just a briefing. I'm thinking that my help is going to be asked for. I'm catching the 7.47, change at Crewe, in at 10.19. For sure he'll regret his treatment of Jimbo Rawe . . . What? And you? I see . . . Well, we'll go together, hit him from two sides. It's good that they've seen sense. I laid it on thick."

It took the gilt off, having DCI Fanny Thomas on the same mission, but he could live with it. Saw himself as a legend in the city where he served. Could walk into any felon's home and sit at their kitchen table and ask the missus for tea and a biscuit. Had been there through the cannabis explosion, the ecstasy volcano and the cocaine epidemic, and through the turf wars. Had seen

the families come and go, but regretted that he had failed – so far
– to cauterise the Govier family. Fanny's territory . . . He had been
at the talent-spotting session where they had been allowed to meet
a young man, wearing a wig and dark glasses, and had bid for him
as if at auction, and they had talked resources and he had put him
on the ground in Corunna. Had expected him home after an
uneventful but quite valuable two years, then had the ground cut
from under him and been told that responsibility for Kenny Blake
now lay with the Security Service, arrogant shites.

"Is that Jak Peters? It is? This is Jimbo Rawe. Got me, yes? Just
wanted you to know that I have landed some heavy blows on those
Box people and they have finally seen reason. I am invited, as is
my colleague – junior colleague – DCI Fanny Thomas, to London
tomorrow morning. This Jonas Merrick is going to share with us
what he has on matters that affect a target family here and another
in the neck of the woods where your man, the Level One, is operating. Just wanted you to know that Fanny and I will be on a train
into Euston tomorrow morning and . . . You had one as well? You
did? So, it's the three of us. I'm going to bend the rod across his
arse, Mister Jonas Merrick's arse, and he'll feel it. You'll meet
us . . .? Good man. See you tomorrow."

Was well satisfied. Would go out on a high and have people say
in police headquarters that it was the final throw of Jimbo Rawe
that clinched an investigation. Was a big man, 16 stones and no
drink taken except when at home in Ireland, a bull neck and a
shaven pink head, and he loved to shout, "Get out of my hair" at
anyone who offended him, and get a laugh. Had never taken a
backhander, never taken a free meal, woman, or holiday. He'd set
his alarm that night, rise early, would look his best when he went
down to London with Fanny Thomas . . . Liked that movie line,
Tell them we're coming and Hell's coming with us. Felt good, saw no
reason not to.

Progress was slow and the *Maria Bernarda* rolled and bucked.
Harder for Matias was the stench from the diesel engine. The
engine belched out dark fumes and too few of them were carried

away in the vent pipe and too many of them came into the cockpit. Hard to get any ventilation. If the windows were forced open, or the hatch leading out on to the deck, then they would be swamped by the swell and the spray.

The problem was easy for Matias to understand, hard for him to explain, and he cowered under the anger and impatience of Diego. And, to deal with the engine he had to abandon his vigil with the boy, Emiliano, whose colour was drained and whose breathing was fainter.

Matias shouted, "It is overheating. It is overheating because we work it too hard. Sometimes the propeller is in the water and sometimes out. It goes from needing to work hard to racing without any drag on it. You understand? It is overheating because the bearings are damaged, and the crankshaft. Maybe the pistons are expanding and are scraping the cylinder sides which would crush the head gasket. Another possibility is that the cylinder heads are swollen and may break. I have to shut it down. It will roll and will be bad."

It did roll and it was bad.

Matias worked in the cramped space with a handkerchief knotted over his nose, and his eyes stung from the trapped fumes. The heat off the metal parts burned his hands but he could not have operated in the small space, with his wrench and his spanners, in heavy gloves.

Too often, he believed the craft would turn over.

If it went over they would be flooded, would sink. The weight of the cargo, accursed powder without which the Americans and the Europeans seemed incapable of living, would drag them down and quickly. Not even a chance for a prayer. Never to be found, never recovered, and nothing for his wife and his children. He had a pitiful supply of spare parts. The people who had built the semi-submersible, bankrolled its construction, had made no allowance for spare parts. Twice the water came in over him, and twice Diego swore and made foul remarks about the Saviour and about the Virgin. Emiliano, unable to respond, had fallen from the bunk and rolled on the decking. Matias tried to reach out and push him back in, and he yelled for Diego to come and help, but Diego did not turn, and shouted that he was holding the wheel.

It was the piston rings. They had worn down.

He had spares in a plastic bag, and two extra pistons. He had bought them with his own money. If it had been the gasket or the cylinder heads, then very soon they would have been sinking.

A huge wave splattered over him and it sizzled on those parts of the engine that were too hot for Matias to touch, and there were places on his arms where the skin was burnt, but he worked on.

Fitted a piston, fitted the rings. Gave no cheer, and provided no explanation of what damage had been done and how he had repaired the fault. Threw the switch. Heard the engine cough, splutter, fail, cough again, and catch. He crawled back through the hatch and closed it. Spray saturated the windows.

Diego still did not turn, shouted for him to activate the pumps.

He sat on the decking and the engine pounded behind him and they battered forward over the swell, under it and through it. Matias saw a gull flying with them and thought it laughed at them, because it flew so effortlessly and had such grace. He had Emiliano's head on his lap and caressed it and thought the boy's breathing was fainter.

And sometimes a bow wave was thrown aside as they made up lost time, strained to go faster, and the gull stayed with them.

Perched on her three-legged stool, Anna Jensen had a fine view of the cliffs and the sea's impact on them, and the reefs and isolated rocks over which the swell broke, and she had her easel fastened by a strap that held it close to her knees. She had seen no whales breaching, no dolphins leaping, no gannets plummeting down from on high. Had not seen Kenny Blake, which perplexed her. Also annoyed her. She had told him where she would be, had expected him to come running. At home, when she was a child living in a Rotterdam suburb they had owned a short-haired German pointer bitch, and when she came into season that was an invitation to the neighbourhood dogs, the males, to come round to their house to scratch the doors and barge against the fences and howl and yelp to get inside.

He would bring a couple of beers and some sandwiches, and usually when they met on a remote coastal path, anywhere north of Finisterre, they would eat an apple each and then chuck the cores high and let gulls or fulmars do acrobatics on the wind to catch them. No beer, no sandwich, and no apples. There was a freighter going north and, in the opposite direction, an empty tanker that was high out of the water. Waves broke around them and each was too large to show the force of the wind coming at them off the sea. She watched their progress distractedly. Had no interest that day in trying to resurrect the view in front of her: rocks, wild flowers, spray, the strength of the cliffs and the mystery of caves, and the haunting cries of sea birds that seemed a good enough imitation of what generations of seamen would have yelled, flailing in the water, in the moments before they went under. She was within sight of the treacherous hidden rock forma-tions that had destroyed the second Armada of Spain, sent to conquer England in 1597, 5000 drowned and almost 40 ships sunk. Heard the howling of the doomed . . . near to a place where drowning was still commonplace but was barely affected. She was said to be tough, without fear, reckoned by some not to need love. She was irritated because, after knowing him for many months, she had finally stripped off and climbed into his bed, and four days later he had turned sour on her, and she had made peace of a sort with him . . .

"You fight them," was what the instructors said.

Kenny sat on the back seat. One of them was beside him, the other drove. They had his phone. The doors had been locked from the control panel by the driver's seat.

"If they are serious people then you won't charm them – can only fight."

The car had driven out of Corunna and was on the Carballo road. As a break from the interminable cliffs she painted, Anna had done a watercolour of the bridge there that had been built by

Roman engineers, could have been two millennia before. Who cared? A small town, good agricultural land around it. And who cared about that? There was no conversation in the car.

"If it comes down to it, our opinion is that smooth talking and being everybody's pal doesn't do the business. You have been picked up because they think you have made a mistake, or because you have been denounced. But it is unlikely they will be sure, copper-bottomed certain – so you fight."

Maybe Kenny had missed the Roman bridge, maybe he had not looked for it. They turned off the main road and into a network of lanes with high-sided hedgerows, and climbed. He did not know where they were. The two men smoked and did not offer a cigarette to Kenny which told him more than conversation would have.

"We are counselling that you fight. Not throwing fists, not that kind of fight. They will be better than you at close-quarters stuff. Will have learned what they know from street-level stuff. *Fight* means that you are confrontational when they start to question you. And remember to ask yourself what is the way to convince them of your guilt."

They had encountered no traffic but they had met a herd of cattle being taken from one pasture and being led to another. The animals had pushed past the car, either side of it, and would have smeared the sides and doors with their saliva and the dung on their coats, and a few times their tails whipped the car. No response from the two men with him. No hooting, no complaints. A farmer passed. An old boy with big pebble glasses and a ragged coat, bow-legged in rubber boots.

"Try to leg it, attempt a break out, makes the job easy for them if they get their hands on you again. You have given confirmation . . . That is not what we mean by how to fight."

The driver had slowed, was raking the side of the road. The instructors had gone over scenarios and done play-acting that verged close to realism. Had brought in Hereford boys who had done a rough-up, then Kenny and the other Level Ones on the course would do "fight back". There was no point in making small talk with the driver or the guy sitting beside him, they were just muscle and would have no role in how it played out. The wheel was swung hard, the tyres skidded, and they started up a muddied and rutted track.

"Go back over your recent days. Who you have been with. What you might have said. Use the time. Before, they will have trusted you. Now, they are not certain. Know your legend better than they do, have your story concrete solid. If you admit your involvement with police or whatever agency, they will kill you, may be unpleasant first. Your best hope is to fight."

They arrived at a barn. One of them pulled at a half of a double door, and Kenny was ushered in. A light was switched on. No cattle here, no fodder. Bare walls, except for two sets of rings higher than his head. Thin straw scattered over a hard floor. A chair was brought from the shadows and Kenny was gestured to sit on it.

He thought it was a place where questioning was done and where, if answers did not satisfy, it would become a killing zone.

Hugo steadied the office chair and Wilf stood on it, and stretched up to reach the smoke alarm.

The one with the knowledge of locks was Hugo. Could not have opened the safe but the street door was no difficulty, and the door at the top of the stairs, leading into the waiting area, were simple for him. A length of wire, a debit card, and the two doors were open. Kenny's desk was tidy. No scribbled notes on his pad and Wilf had pointed out that no indentations remained on the top sheet. There was a shredder and the box was nearly full. The poster of Stratford-upon-Avon in the waiting area simpered down at them, was from a life that neither had known. On the desk was a neat pile of brochures for the Biscuit Tin.

Wilf disconnected the smoke alarm, took out the batteries and dumped them in the rubbish bin, and with them went the laminated sign on the desk, forbidding smoking. Wilf sat behind the desk and Hugo took the client chair. They'd opened the one window. Below was a yard – be a good enough dumping ground for their fag ends. In a cupboard was a kettle and two mugs and coffee sachets, but no fridge and no milk. They smoked and they drank, and the enormity of what they had seen – and what they had failed to interrupt – devastated them. Two guys who had been press-ganged into a job they didn't need, seduced by the soft voice calling them from London, and failing when it had mattered. They drank their coffee, smoked their fags, settled down to wait, their pistols on their laps and their grenades close. Did not know where else to be or what they waited for.

The phone rang. They stiffened.

A voice on the answerphone, a woman's. "Where the hell are you?" A woman's voice, annoyed.

Two more calls on the phone, both about the Biscuit Tin, and messages left.

Hugo said, "I have a bad feeling. A call needs making."

Wilf said, "I'll not argue."

He'd had time for a burst of spring cleaning.

At home, he was banned from the task. Told he was clumsy and did not know what to remove, what to dust, what to replace.

First to be cleared was the picture of the addict, also a dealer – and also a police officer – leaning against the door of a shop. A gaunt and haggard young man, dressed for the trade he imitated. Hair cut short, eyes deep, and his gaze wary. He took down the picture, gazed at it, then slid it into the shredder. Wondered how the lad was, and supposed he was ticking off the last hours, what was left of his assignment. From his floor safe came the file on a semi-submersible, the messages relayed to him from Nikko of the Administration, and what he had prepared for a paper file on two detectives, Fergal Rawe and Fanny Thomas, and the Yard man, Jak Peters. All three of them had passed muster in the eyes of Jonas: all were class acts, his opinion, and had deserved better than to be tainted with suspicion of corruption. Their files went into the shredder. He anticipated that when he returned to London at the start of the following week the configuration of a jungle-built nearly-submarine, and the contact with a wild man from Bogotá who liked wearing fancy dress and playing with weapons, and

Merseyside detectives and an individual from SC&O10 – damn silly title – would be irrelevant to him. There was a file on a family living in Galicia, a mother and two sons, that also went into the shredder. Behind the screensaver image of Olaf were more details for deletion, and he went through them fast, and when he was back the next Monday he would have one of the geeks from the first floor come and satisfy him that they were indeed irretrievably gone. What was left was a file on a second family, one with lofty ambitions. A matriarch had her own section, and that was eaten up, and the pages referring to a younger son – no more need for it. A girl who he thought was unimportant followed them into the machine ... He was left with one file containing a photo of a house, and a picture of a man aged 29 years, and the photographs were not custody snaps but those taken from long-lens surveillance cameras – they went into his briefcase.

He fussed a little, as was his habit. He used a cleaning cloth from his cupboard to wipe down surfaces. He emptied the shredder's basket into his wastepaper bin, and switched off his computer. He put on his raincoat and hat, straightened his tie, fastened the chain on his briefcase to the clasp on his wrist. His Thermos and lunch box were in the briefcase, snug against the one file. Left his cubicle, locked its door. Dumped the shredded paper into the communal bin that Aggie Burns's team used, and headed for the lift.

Would have caused some mild astonishment, him leaving so early in the afternoon. It was remarked on at Reception. The woman there, faint mischief in her eyes, asked him if he were well.

"Very well, thank you," his cheerful reply. "Feeling fortunate. Managed to snaffle a few days' leave. Am off with the caravan."

"Lucky you, Mr Merrick."

"Very lucky me . . ."

He went down the steps. Walked briskly. Would be in at the kill. Best place to be. Had a jauntiness in his stride. It was an in-between hour for the showers but the wind blew hard and he had to brace himself against it as he climbed the slope on the bridge's pavement. His phone rang. He answered it.

And the world seemed to collapse on him, like night came early.

10

"Did you see that old blighter? Looked well pissed."

"Been on the sauce in his lunch break. Pathetic. So undignified at his age."

Jonas had heard the men exchange their views on his lurching gait over Lambeth Bridge. The wind hitting him did not help but, as he had put his phone back into his pocket, the enormity had belted him. Hard to stay upright and his legs seemed to weaken. Not, of course, that the veterans with commando history would have gilded it. Given the news straight, said what they had witnessed, not messed with words.

They had been on foot, had seen Kenny Blake led from the doorway below the Biscuit Tin office, had seen his phone taken off him, and seen him go without a struggle, had seen him driven away. Easy enough to interpret that the boy would not have cared at that moment to make a break and try to run, and might not have realised – in those first moments – how high the odds were stacked. He had not needed to ask: How did Kenny Blake seem as he was led away? "Seemed calm, but maybe the shock was settling in." Was told that they'd call him if there was a development they knew of . . . and rung off. No bedside manner, no sweetening the pill.

Jonas had struggled to reach the crown of the bridge and once his fingers had lost hold of his briefcase and it had drooped and a woman had anticipated its bounce on the pavement and had bent to retrieve it, except that it was held to Jonas's wrist by the chain and she had groped the air by his feet. He had rested there, been within a yard or two of where the Sixer girl, Frank, had put her weight on the parapet of the balustrade, and had tugged him after her, wrists joined by those damned handcuffs. Was breathing hard and pedestrians looked at him and might have wondered whether they should stop, intervene, offer help – but hadn't.

He had come off the bridge, walked beside the wall of the Archbishop's Palace, heading for Waterloo station, had felt the buoyancy sucked from him.

Could remember the first conversation with the undercover, Kenny Blake, over the phone a year before. Always was good at getting his way, achieving what he wanted. Had spelled it out in simple terms, as if talking to a child who needed only minimal information. "My name's Jonas. I'm from a different crowd to your usual control apparatus. I'm from Box. We do crime as well as the better publicised stuff. Your time at an end and no doubt you were looking forward to repatriation. There was that trial and conviction last month that you helped with – but crucially without your role being identified – and I have some rather interesting ideas that would ramp up the Biscuit Tin concept and would, hopefully, lead to something on a grander scale. The handling of investments would be subject to more talent, more resources, would attract bigger and greedier fish. I'm asking you, Kenny, to hang about there for an additional year. You will continue to be under the radar of local law enforcement. It might be quite interesting, Kenny, and I'd be very grateful if you agree to the proposition. You do? That's excellent. You'll report to me now, and the former control, Mr Peters, will look after administration costs, the housekeeping. One last thing, Kenny, you can depend on me. Thank you." Could recall each word of what he had said. Had been in his cubicle, had spoken with a lowered voice, had thought he might actually have received Kenny Blake's gratitude that his present legend still had legs, had more time to run.

He had gone into the station, through the passenger barriers, had caught his train. Would have been months, even years, since he had – almost – forgotten to get off at Raynes Park. Unless he had scampered up the aisle and barged through the carriage door as it was about to close he would have been rolling on his way to Ewell West. In his pocket, his phone stayed silent.

Others in Thames House, if they had run the show, would have been calling the number used by Hugo and Wilf, bombarding them. Not Jonas. They'd have told him if there was anything they thought he should know. He could also have gone through, word perfect, a subsequent conversation that had been held on the most secure link that Jonas's phone and Kenny's could manage. "It is getting very interesting, Kenny, because intelligence reports tell me that a semi-submersible craft has gone into an Amazon tributary and we think it will carry four tonnes of pure cocaine, and the launch and the projected route out of the river's delta and into the Atlantic would indicate a European landfall, which is almost certain to be close to you. You told me your major clients were asking you about Liverpool, seemingly casual enquiries but of course in that business nothing is casual." And feeding him titbits on the Govier family, then money movements, then flight details . . . Had not felt the need to tell Kenny Blake to look after himself, be aware, and be prepared for the fast bolt. Remembered all of the conversations, had sensed that the boy thought the care, the concern, of the man on the phone was too loaded with worry.

Their car was in the road and Vera, who had taken the day off work, would have taken it to the garage for the tank to be filled, and an oil and tyre check. She was in the caravan, would have seen him coming up their road and pass the Derbyshires' gate. Would have noticed that he hung his head, and that his shoulders were rounded, and his complexion pale, and . . .

"You all right, Jonas?"

"Thank you, yes, quite all right."

"Not looking well."

"No, not ill."

"Are you up to going?"

"Yes, I am."

"Jonas – what has happened?"

"Just something that was unexpected."

* * *

Kenny had been sitting on the chair for an hour. Had stood up once and seen that both men flexed their fists and perhaps rolled a little on to the balls of their feet, poised to intervene. He had given them no cause to come closer, had walked three times round the chair, had ditched the threat of cramp in his thighs, had sat again. Their fists had loosened and both had eased back on to their heels.

By each of them now was a small heap of fag ends. Smoked down to the filter, then stamped on. Had not seen them before but it was fair to presume a small army worked regularly or occasionally for the Munoz family. He had only been once to the Munoz villa and there had been men at the gate and others loitering in the gardens between the main building and the high walls topped with razor wire. He thought he heard movements outside the barn but neither of his minders had reacted and their eyes never left him, except when they had ducked their heads to light their cigarettes.

Not how he had known it on previous assignments. What had happened in the past would not help him now. He used the silence to go over the legend he had made for himself, tested it and could not find the fault.

He had been told, if it happened, that he must fight. It *had* happened. Out of earshot. Out of the range of Neighbourhood bloody Watch. Out of the reach of his backup. No phone.

There was power in the building. He had heard that the clans sometimes used a power drill or a small chainsaw as an interrogation tool. They would not need power for either. He had noticed an old basin, cracked china. He thought it more likely that a captive could be held here: for days or weeks. If he were missed by anyone, they would not go to the police, or the customs investigators, or the GRECO team and spill a story about their illegal investments that were beyond the taxman's reach . . . They said that everyone had a breaking point, and no one knew when the point would be. Might be the start of a chainsaw and that rasping clatter coming closer, and a head already hooded. So, they said, go to fight mode.

He heard a vehicle straining up the track, then stopping. He heard voices, men's. The men who watched him lifted their heads, listened.

A detective called Jimbo had recruited him last time round. Had been like a talent contest at a Pontins camp. Did he want to work for them? Were they good enough, plausible enough? Did he trust them? Had been under the control of Jak Peters, and after the session in Merseyside, where he had met a gang of men and women who had sought to impress him, and to minimise areas of risk and to maximise the importance of what was asked of him, he and Peters had talked it over. Were they worth the effort? It was a two-year slot in a Spanish city, with decent history and decent food and he had a decent legend, and he had ended up feeding intelligence that had put down two families who had thought their prospects were on the rise. He should then have been on his way home, except that the soft voice had poured syrup in his ear and now he reckoned he had outstayed his Corunna welcome, been around too long, used up a cat's supply of lives.

Soon, there would be more men in the building and he would be surrounded and they'd have adhesive tape for his wrists and ankles, perhaps a hood for his head, and when that was close to him then the moment to attempt a break out would have gone . . .

Which was not what the instructors meant when they talked of the need to *fight*. What they said was that it took a supreme moment of courage to go for breakout.

Kenny sat upright, tried not to show fear. Knew that the *fight* time had not yet come. The door opened. Recognised Sergio Munoz, Laureano behind him. Stared at them. Kept the fear bottled. Thought that they would be used to any man in his situation cringing, or yabbering protestations of loyalty, innocence. He was eyed briefly, then they turned their backs on him and went outside. He assumed they awaited their mother.

Fanny Thomas had her ironing board out, pressed a prim white blouse. Not often in her career had she been summoned to travel to London, never in her career had her presence been demanded for a meeting with Box, with the Security Service. She would wear a quiet suit, the white blouse, a minimum of jewellery and hardly any make-up. In her laptop would be the details of current investigations aimed at the Govier OCG: her principal target and therefore assumed to be the reason she was called for. After the ironing she would be off upstairs to wash her hair. It would be a long day and she wanted to be at her best and aimed to get early to bed. The supper plates were still on the table and neither the kids nor her husband had managed to find time to clear them away – buggered if she would. They were in the front room: a talent show played loud on the TV and they were noisy in their laughter and applause. Fanny was depressed. Came often enough, and nothing to do with the family, the freeloaders. More about her assessment of the opposition ... more intelligent, more committed than she and her crowd, and all the other teams that plodded in pursuit of target families. The commercials had provided an opportunity for the older kid to skip off into the utility room and gather up the contents of the washing machine and come up close to her and drawl that, "Since you've started, Mum, could you just do this lot?", and a grin and the clothing dumped on the floor by her feet. Likely that the other kid would be wanting help with her homework later on – when the talent show was over ... and that her husband would be on about the weekend and he'd want to go to the Lakes in her big car, not his wreck-on-wheels. It would be a big moment for her, ushered into Thames House with its facade facing the river ... She left the iron plugged in and the board up and she took what was hers and stepped over the pile of crumpled clothing and skirted the table that had not been cleared, and went upstairs, and would get in the bathroom and wash her hair, do it slowly. Later there would be shouts up the stairs.

"Mum, what about my ironing?"

"Mum, I'm ready for you to do my homework."

"Darling, did you get the confirmation from the guesthouse. You said you were going to ...?"

Fanny Thomas locked the bathroom door and offered a little prayer that she was edging closer to bringing down that fucking woman, Douloures Govier.

The impact stopped them dead.

Diego, at the wheel, was thrown forward and cracked his forehead against the stanchion between two sections of glass.

Matias crouched on his knees and with the hatch to the engine open and reasonably watching the engine throbbing and turning over better than he'd dared hope, and working by torchlight, was pitched clear and careered into the back of Diego's legs. Both were felled. Emiliano had been pitched out of the lower bunk, and had slithered over the flooring, over the smears of his own vomit, and had cannoned into the captain and the engineer.

They were in darkness. Night around them, no moon, no stars.

Diego heaved himself upright and had only the dulled illumination from the instrument panel. Matias tripped on the prone Emiliano, cursed the boy without thinking.

Who had the torch? Each accused the other of having it. The engine had cut, then reignited. Diego found the torch in the drawer beside the wheel, the same drawer where he kept his pistol. The torch, he had reckoned, was as important for his safety as the pistol.

The engine ran well. Then a scraping sound. A bitter, ruthless noise. Diego switched on the torch. Great barnacle shapes seemed to cover the glass on the starboard side. And they bobbed away and would have been moved by the wind.

He said, "We hit a cargo container."

Matias said, "You should have seen it."

"I could not have seen it, idiot."

"Because you did not see it, we hit it. Because we hit it, we may now have a leak."

"There is no sign of a leak."

Matias said, bitterly, "Perhaps you do not know that a leak begins as a dribble, then becomes a flow, and finishes as a flood."

Diego said, "Even for an engineer, you are a cheerful bastard. We are in a storm, it is pitch dark outside, we are rolling and unstable. Perhaps we last through the night and perhaps we do not. In daylight we look."

Matias turned away and for a moment the torch beam followed him and Diego would have seen the engineer's oil-stained hands reach out and lift the boy, manoeuvring Emiliano away from the residue of the vomit and back on to the lower bunk. Diego turned off the torch, put it back beside his pistol in the drawer. Perhaps there was a leak. Perhaps the rough barnacles had weakened the fibreglass hull or damaged it where the sections were fastened together. Perhaps the water was already in amongst the cargo bales, four tonnes of them, and perhaps they had not been well enough wrapped when the craft was loaded by those fucking peasants far up the river. Perhaps . . . they would not know till it was light.

They pitched and rocked and climbed and fell, and would know nothing until the morning unless – before that – they sank. Behind him, Matias had given up on the engine and was holding the boy and was crooning to him. Diego lit another cigarette. He needed to be afloat, and the engine running for 48 hours more.

Kenny met her glance.

Not at ease, the body language said. Seemed to hesitate as she came into the barn, but they could just have been the dark shadows playing inside the building. The light outside was drifting away, and the rain was back, heavy and dripping, and the wind catching the roof, whining in it, and leaves scattering. She stood, her feet a little apart, and then turned to Sergio and nodded to him, like a performance could begin because she was now present.

"You know a woman, Anna Jensen."

"I know her."

"Her nationality?"

"Dutch."

"Your relationship with her?"

"Not your business."

"Anything I wish is my business."

"A friend."

"What level of friend?"

"A good friend."

If they had been in an interview suite at any police station the pair of "detectives" would have done their homework and would have had files in front of them and phone records and images from CCTV. Would have worked through the previous night to be up to speed. But Sergio and Laureano stood and had no notes ... Laureano cracked his fingers and looked as if the business bored him. They would, as Jak Peters might have said, very soon "cut to the quick".

"Just a friend?"

"A girlfriend – and she is not a whore and is not the daughter of anyone I employ."

The start of the "fight". Sergio's mouth narrowed, and his mother's head flicked upwards, and Laureano grinned.

"What does she do?"

"You know what she does."

"Do not fuck with me – what does she do?"

"She is an artist, as you know."

"A poor artist, without talent?"

Kenny managed a false smile, "Did she turn you down? Wouldn't she let you in her bed?"

Sergio Munoz was a grand man, the heir apparent to a crime family in Galicia, a man who dealt with the cream, or the scum, of the Colombian entrepreneurs. He was not familiar with anything other than humility from locals, from those who worked for him. A slight flush showed on his face and a bead of angry sweat built on his forehead. Laureano would have been waiting for different methods to be used, and the men who had brought Kenny were outside, and Kenny could not read Isabella Munoz.

"Who employs her?"

"Perhaps nobody employs her."

"She lives here, lives in style, is a rubbish painter, is out on the cliffs, is a watcher, and she is with you. Who does she work for?"

"Works for herself."

"No pillow talk? Which agency? Police, her government? And you . . . who do you work for?"

"Perhaps I work for you."

"We have put faith in you."

"Yes, and I in you."

"And, and, you are visited by Luna Perez."

Confused, wrong-footed. "Who, who is Luna Perez?"

Sergio coming close to him, his questions now laced with spittle, as he tried to frighten Kenny. Was intended to provoke a reaction. The light went out and a torch was switched on. Had to stay calm and knew the line he would follow . . .

"She visited your office."

From a pocket inside his suit jacket, Sergio took out a folded photograph, straightened it to flick at Kenny's face, then dropped it on Kenny's lap. Remembered her, remembered the face. Remembered the confessional, remembered what she said she had been.

"Yes, she came."

"Hates us, hates what we do."

"She came as a customer."

"Is entertained by you, a woman who detests us. And earlier you have been in bed with a woman who has no visible means of financial support, and we are warned of her."

"You let your imagination make a fool of you."

He kept his eyeline on the mother. Never on the accuser. Not on Laureano who had the big fists and the muscles. The mother had touched his arm, had lingered in conversation with him . . . Ridiculous to consider that Anna Jensen, with whom – in the fantasy future of Kenny Blake, or who he might become when that snakeskin was shed – he would spend time far into the future . . . Ridiculous to think she was anything other than a spoiled rich girl with a smile and little talent.

Sergio said, "I believe not a word of you."

"Believed it when you dumped money on me for washing, and weren't conned, weren't cheated, weren't left short."

Sergio's face was now close enough for Kenny to feel his breath. He could not see beyond the torch. Could make out the heavy shadow of Laureano's shoulders and the sleeker, narrower frame of their mother, and could stare at her but was no longer able to read her reaction. He thought the time of articulation had run its course. Like Sergio was now bored with word play. Would hand over to his brother. Thought he lived on borrowed time, and the hands would move fast. Past the opportunity, though he had not recognised one, when he might have pushed up from the chair, and run for the door, having only the chair as a weapon but that would have slowed him. Still had the chance to *fight* but needed the ground – did not know where to find it.

Sergio said, loud enough to be heard by his mother and by his brother. "You have a chance, one chance, to be honest with me. We think you infiltrate us, abuse our trust. The woman, Anna Jensen, her life is an untruth. The woman, Luna Perez, detests us. You are the friend of both . . . Tell us who you are, Kenny. Be honest with us. One chance only, Kenny . . . There is no back up squad. There is no protection. One chance I am willing to give you."

Kenny, quietly said, "You seem to me to be a frightened little man. You have tried to poison your mother's mind, and you have lied to your brother . . ."

He was hit. A stinging blow across his cheek and the wedding ring on Sergio's finger caught the side of Kenny's mouth and his head was jolted and it took a moment before his blood flowed.

Sergio hissed in his face. "One chance, almost gone. With an informer, a betrayer, we make a bad death. Never quick. We would record the death on a phone, with sound. Pictures and the noise that comes with going slow to death. That is what faces you, Kenny . . . and no back up, no rescue coming, and . . ."

Her voice. "It is definite? He has no wire? He was searched?"

Had Kenny Blake been frisked for a wire? Not just tapped down but properly done? By whom? He recognised it, the back-sliding, the excuses. Men were coming in from outside and closing ranks around him, and the two who had brought him were taken away and Kenny heard shouts, accusations, slaps and yelps. Her voice was icy with complaint.

One chance. How to fight? The instructors didn't tell them. They said, "Up to you, lad. If you have to, you'll know how to. But fight, because you've fuck all to lose."

The dark seemed to come early that night, but the street lights in Raynes Park were not yet lit, and Jonas had retreated to the end of the garden. He would not be overheard by either the Derbyshires or the people whose property backed on to his. No one other than in a pit of despair would have been outside as the rain spat and the wind rustled the shrubs. He had claimed that Olaf needed the borders for his "business". The cat was beside him, as stubborn as Jonas.

Made a call, needed advice . . . His bag was already packed. He would wear the same jacket of Harris tweed but needed spare flannel trousers, a couple of spare Tattersall shirts, some under-wear and some socks . . . At the bottom of the bag, wrapped in plastic, were the items that Aggie Burns had procured for him. He had made other calls satisfactorily, but needed this one for guid-ance and had little hope of sympathy: there would be words like "backbone" and "stiffening".

It was answered. Always economical, he described his position.

A distant voice, "A pleasure as always, Jonas, to hear you, and too long. Good to speak, and you still working. Extraordinary. Not me. Future employment prospects for a one-time agent handler with experience of East Tyrone Brigade, and an office address in Dungannon's barracks, are not plentiful, so I do bed and breakfast up here on the Norfolk coast. You've lost a jo. Makes a bit of difference whether he's one of theirs who you've turned or your own boy . . . Your own? Harder to swallow, but needs must. So, your own . . . You don't hang about and wring your hands. Not much you can do except change the locks, know what I mean? You said this was crime, Jonas. What the fuck are you doing on crime? Crime is about violence. It is about enforcement, about inflicting pain, and stabilising authority. In my day, the locals would call in a guy from Belfast who could do nasty things to a prisoner, before killing him. But on the scale of nasty, I'd say that crime is a mile ahead, no contest. Your boy has a bad time booked ahead for him unless he is God Almighty lucky – and luck seldom rears its head in the real world. He'll spill . . . That's why I say you should get on and change the locks – top priority. Phone numbers, contacts, addresses, they all need to be binned and reinvented. Won't be nice what happens to your boy, Jonas, but you should not be sentimental. I assume this is a bigger operation and you say it is about at climax. You write him off and get on with the main picture . . . What I always used to say when we were out in the lanes and picking up the stiffs who had a bullet in the back of the neck was that – after a fashion – they were volunteers, knew what it was about. You win some and you lose some. He probably made a mistake and you can't protect a jo from that – got pissed, got laid, that's usually the mistake. What I'm saying, Jonas, is that you change the locks and you carry on. Got that? Now, are you still pulling that caravan around? Come and see us. You can nearly see the North Sea from our place and I'll do you a decent rate . . . Hope I've been of help, Jonas."

He bent, stroked the cat's head.

Wanted a moment of quiet, to himself.

Would call the AssDepDG, would talk to him about "changing the locks" . . . and thought of Doloures Govier who was on the final stage of her journey.

And thought of Kenny Blake, and Jonas bit at his lower lip, did it hard enough to draw a fleck of blood, and felt shame.

He made the call, then picked up Olaf and carried him inside. They'd leave soon, when Vera was ready, and he'd drive through the night but he doubted it would help him get the image out of his head. A man leaning against a doorway, a man without a name and probably without a life.

Kenny sat, waited.

Not long, two minutes or three. The time used up in the argument, and hard men watched over him. They did not speak or offer him water or give him a cigarette. And a secondary argument had been spat between Sergio and his brother, and a sneer from Laureano that his smart brother had not first ensured that a wire was not worn.

"Stand," he was told. "Stand up."

Sergio's voice first, then Laureano's.

"Stand up."

The torch beam was full in his face. He stood. To Kenny it seemed that neither of the brothers had yet taken primacy . . . It was time to fight because he doubted another and a better time would offer itself. He stood, straight-backed. He peered into the beam, and then a little to the right where he could see the outline of the shoulders and head of Isabella Munoz. His focus point.

Hollow laughter from Sergio, and annoyance at being caught out – might even feel humiliated. "We see if you wear a wire – then we use other methods to know if you lie to us."

Kenny said to her, "And whether you lie to me."

"Don't give me shit, little man."

"Not so little that your greed did not send you to me, wanting a better return after washing and rinsing. Just greed."

Holding the shadow in his gaze and attempting to suffocate a quaver in his voice and sound like a man who was angry, was wronged, and did not cower.

"Take your coat off."

No switch of his eyeline, but took his time and unbuttoned it and loosened the Velcro. Shrugged his arms out of it. Did not drop it or throw it aside, but folded it and then crouched and put it down on the ground, beside his feet.

"And you?" Kenny challenged. "Your coat?"

"Fuck yourself . . ." And anger flaring in Sergio, which was good because calm was the key. "And your shirt."

Again, care with the buttons and then easing the arms clear of the sleeves, and the cold and damp of the evening on his skin, and folded it and bent to place it on his anorak.

"And you? Because I do not trust you."

"When you are naked, when we have seen if there is a wire, or not a wire, then you will regret . . . I promise you . . . fucking regret."

"Take your own shirt off. Show me how you do it, when you have paid the whore and want value for money. Or do you keep your shirt on?"

Kenny did not look at Sergio. He had set down his chips, like there was the one chance, laid them on a square and a colour and would let the wheel spin. He could not see her face nor any movement from the shadow.

"And the next."

Lifted his vest, ducked his head and lost his view of her and smelled the sweat on his body, and drew it up and over his head. He folded it and placed it on the pile. He attacked.

Spoke softly. "People like you, Sergio Munoz, have no morality, no loyalty, are just crap. You would betray Laureano who is your brother if that were to your advantage, and your mother. Perhaps you inform. Perhaps you are the Confidential Human Intelligence Source at the GRECO. Perhaps you wear the wire – and it will be me in court and with me will be your brother and your mother."

"You will suffer," on the edge and rage rampant, as Kenny intended.

"Where is your shirt, fuck you? Where?"

"And your belt, and your trousers."

Could see her, and could focus on her, and the aim of the torch moved from his face and was no longer full on his chest and settled on the buckle of his belt of frayed and faded leather. The beam caught in its perimeter of light a little part of her. Saw her face, interested, might have been amused, and might have enjoyed the assault on her son, but gave no evidence of her mood and stared hard at him.

"Because I believe, Sergio, that you lie. I took the chance with you. The reward I get, look at it. Make money for you, feed your greed, and how am I treated? Where is your goddamn shirt?"

"Your trousers."

"I drop them, same as you do with a whore, or do you let them dangle at your ankles because you can't hold it in? For what I have done for your family, I will get twenty years. Twenty years to think of you, and your lies."

Thought it went well. There was no alternative to his plan.

"Your belt, your trousers."

"Not even a shirt off, Sergio. You know, I trust Laureano because he has balls. I trust your mother because she has intelligence. I do not trust you. I think you hide behind others, and I think you a coward. What is under your shirt?"

Kenny was hit again. Had seen the blow coming from the right side of the torch beam, and rode it, but the glancing blow was sufficient, with the aid of the wedding ring, to slash a gouge in the softness of his cheek, above where the earlier blood was now drying.

"Your belt. Your trousers. Show me."

"You'll see plenty there, but not a wire."

His hands were on the buckle of his belt. Thought it went as well as it might have, but the game would not have long to play. The buckle was awkward, hard to prise open, and harder because he did not look down but had found the shadow shape again. His eyes were not locked at the centre of the beam but she would have seen that he stared at her. Kenny could not have described how he accomplished it, what exercise in his willpower, might have been only the drowning man's survival reflex. Managed the slightest of grins and she would have read it, but not Sergio, who had a hand ready to strike him again, and probably a foot poised to kick him where he had no protection.

"Do it."

"Don't I get to see your shirt off, your trousers dropped. Don't I? Do you only undress in the dark? Don't you like the whores to see your body, don't . . .?"

Two punches, but neither landing hard, little more than slaps. Kenny laughed but held the line of his eyes, had the shadow and never left it, and saw a movement. Delicate and shimmering, and a little gasp from Sergio and a grunt from Laureano, and the torch beam wobbled as if the guy holding it did not know where he should aim it. He had the belt free. He threaded it clear. It was put on the pile.

Kenny remembered when he had made a similar pile. All folded and neat and nothing thrown down. His clothes had been like that when she had wafted across the room in bright daylight, not a stitch on her. A movement where the shadow was but he could not see the detail of it. His belt was off, and his trousers sagged. He stepped from them, then lifted them, matched the seams and they too were folded and laid to rest on the coiled belt. He eased his underpants down, freed them from his feet. Took them over his shoes. Shoes next, and last were his socks. He straightened. Then turned and swivelled and showed them his back and his cheeks, and turned some more and let the beam fall bright on him, and the movement in the shadow was matched by her laughter. She had removed her coat, and a cardigan that would have been cashmere. Not folded but dumped. A blouse that was likely silk. And more . . . Sergio's coat was off and was held out wide in front of his mother, as if he were a matador and his coat was the cloak – and Laureano was hissing his embarrassment at her. A slip was lifted high over her head and he doubted that a hair would have been disturbed. And her laughter was louder.

Kenny waited. He could not see what else she wore, did not know whether she would strip further.

None of the men laughed, only Isabella Munoz – who might have been worth a hundred million euros, who might have been among the premier league, a *matriarca* of note, in all of Europe – but not loudly, as if her amusement was shared only by herself and by Kenny Blake, her personally appointed money launderer. Then she bent and the torch was aimed high so that it would not light her and its beam was among the rafters of the building, old timbers and huge spiders' webs. She gathered up her clothing and started to dress.

Kenny waited.

He stood, was cold, shrivelled up, and with a feeling of great tiredness as if the *fight* was now drained from him.

She told him, in a measured and calm voice, that he should dress himself. She said the matter was finished. He would be taken back to Corunna.

A car started up outside. Brilliance pierced the doorway as headlights came on. As he had thought, not a hair out of place, and as she walked she flicked her fingers, and both Sergio and Laureano followed her.

He started to dress. The men hung back. He had expected a session with pliers or with a drill or a chainsaw. Instead he would be driven to Corunna.

Kenny dressed, took his time.

One choke, a sort of cough. Matias stopped crooning, ended the lullaby.

"That's it, the end."

Diego did not turn, hung to the wheel and studied the dials, and called back, "Not the end. The engine's good. Incredible how it works in this weather. Going well, and we are still on schedule. It is incredible what we have achieved – if there is no fucking leak."

"The end is the life of the boy, of Emiliano. He is dead. Or do you not care?"

"Do I care if a kid from out of *los barrios bajos* in some shit town up a river that is full of shit, has died? No. I am tired and my head aches and I am steering this bastard boat towards land and towards my payday. I have nothing to say."

"Fuck you."

Diego imagined that the engineer would have closed the boy's eyelids and tucked him up on the bunk, and then found a towel to put over his face. Imagined also that Matias had his hands free to grope towards the wrench. Diego had the drawer open, could have reached fast for either the torch or the pistol. He did not know if he would be able to sleep for anything more than a few minutes . . . And there would be no payday, and no girl to ride, if the hull was damaged and the hold was leaking.

Cold enough to freeze his privates. Standing in the water up to his stomach, Xavier had not a stitch on him, except for flip flops – would not have wanted to cut his feet on a fractured shell.

The sea, off the old gun positions of the fort, halfway between Crosby and Hightown, was where he usually went after he had fired a weapon, leaving residue on his clothing and his body. He had taken strong soap – not fragrant but powerful – with him. He scrubbed himself, then let the bitter chill of the water wash over him. Satisfied, he began to wade back. It was about protecting one small parish in his supply area, but worth doing thoroughly, which he supposed was a lesson his Ma had drilled into him, because if the message had not been sent about their parish then another would have been lost, and another . . . Xavier had heard of stags who wanted, needed, sex, called the "rutting time", and the big bastard with the big antlers was run half to death not just by the effort of shagging but also by keeping the young bastards away. He felt the same.

He came out of the water and walked the few hundred yards across the sand, and into the dunes, and finally up to the old concrete outlines of the gun positions. They'd have protected the approaches to Birkenhead, and the superstructures had long been dismantled but the fortifications were too solid to destroy. A good place, and useful. A towel was handed him. Using a firearm, one brought in from the far side of Manchester, was work he kept for himself, to be certain it was done right. The car he had used to leave the site of the attack was in the parking area and its interior had already been doused with petrol. The clothes he had worn were piled on the car's back seat. A hell of a performance because

he had to drive himself: would not allow anyone else in a contami-
nated car.

Now he was clean and dry. He could dress in fresh clothes. The
flame was lit, tossed, and caught inside. No houses within hundreds
of yards. Did not take many minutes for a car to burn sufficiently
for DNA to be destroyed. The weapon, the CZ999 Scorpion,
would by now have been well on its way back to an address in a
housing estate east of Manchester, and the magazine was eight
rounds light. Had not shot the guy who had muscled in, tried to
win trade in Garston, but had gone instead to the home of the
guy's mother, where she lived with his stepfather and his two
young brothers. Just an ordinary semi-detached house, in an ordinary street, and ordinary curtains loosely drawn and TV belting
out crap. What had not been ordinary was him leaning out of the
open window of the car, stolen to order, and firing four bullets
through the downstairs bay window, then another four through
the matching bay upstairs. And all fucking hell left behind him.
The guy might have believed himself at risk and taken precautions
for his own safety, but now his mother was screaming hysterically
and his stepfather moaning about his heart condition and the boys
blubbering.

Bengal was on his way back into Liverpool, going home.
Tomorrow he had the travel agent to deal with, and the camera . . .
It was unlikely that the fire brigade would bother to turn out for a
burning car on a dark night nowhere near a residential area . . .
and he always had so bloody much to deal with. Ma said they were
going to be rich – beyond their dreams – because of the deal she
was off to clinch. Always running, didn't often see the evidence of
their wealth, drove fast.

The plane put down. The wheels hit the runway, the aircraft
bounced, then they hit again, and the taxi run started. Doloures
Govier winced in relief and beside her Patrick clung to the arm
rests with white knuckles.

The pilot would have been confronted with heavy rain and a
fierce crosswind as he had lined up the final descent. The last

flight of the evening had reached Santiago. A spontaneous burst of clapping congratulated the cockpit crew, and many of the pilgrims on board fervently crossed themselves.

They did not hurry off the aircraft. Were among the last to stand and move down the aisle and on to the walkway. She thought she had a trained eye and was looking for surveillance, something more than the inevitable cameras, but saw nothing that alerted her. Approaching Customs and the green exits she joined a group of fellow travellers, and made a remark about not the easiest of landings and not the most hospitable of weather, and they had a priest with them and their faith might have been tried in the last minutes before hitting the runway, and they were pleased to talk, the sort of idle conversation that seemed appropriate among strangers. Would have seemed to any onlookers that they were all part of one group, one with a religious bond.

It had not been confirmed whether she and Patrick would be met, was unsure whether a driver would take them to their hotel. They stood in the rain in a taxi queue, and paid for the ride into the city. She reckoned they were ripped off because the meter was not switched on and it was like a stone in her shoe that she might have paid over the odds. The hotel was booked for them, in the name of Sergio Munoz. Needing paint, and a new carpet in the lobby would have helped. Four nuns, off their plane, followed them inside. Patrick carried their bags . . . She had to check their passports for their name when she filled out the forms. They went up in a slow and creaking lift, and left behind the ground floor already darkened and the dining room closed.

She paused at her door. "What I said before, remember who we are, and remember what we're here for – and remember most of all what we will be when this lot comes through the system. Top of the tree, that's where we'll be. Get some sleep, and be sharp tomorrow, because I'll not trust these people, not a bloody inch."

And rare for her, she kissed the boy on the cheek, and he blushed bright, and she went into her room. There were no flowers.

★ ★ ★

"Thanks, guys. Thanks for doing the chauffeur job."

Wilf was awake but Hugo was gently snoring. The street was commercial and at that time of night there was little traffic. Wilf was alert and held a pistol loosely on his lap. He heard the car coming down the street, slowing, then stopping. Had heard doors opening and some muttered remarks that sounded humble. Then had heard Kenny's voice, quite loud and in English, and the ironies would not have been understood. Heard a key in the outer door, and more voices and doors closing, and the car pulling away.

He gave Hugo a shake, and his friend jerked upright and clutched his handgun. Wilf said to Hugo that it might be like Christmas morning had come early . . . the boy was back. They heard weary steps coming up the stairs and Wilf opened the door wide, showed himself, saw that Kenny flinched, then recognised him.

Both of them helped him into the room and the tiredness looked to be coming in waves across him, and he sagged. Blood had dried on his face. Carrying his phone. They lowered him down into the chair just vacated by Hugo, and his eyes closed.

"Don't talk about it. What happened will keep," Hugo said gently.

"Maybe a coffee, then sleep."

Made him a mug and Wilf obliged with a slug from his flask. Used another mug from the cupboard for hot water – Hugo's handkerchief was the cleaner and he used it to wipe Kenny's face. Kenny gave no sign of feeling anything, and before Hugo had finished he was asleep. Well asleep, deep and breathing like a child.

Wilf said, tears on his cheeks, "And pigs can fly, and I believe it. God, and I never thought I'd see him again. But he's come through – God alone knows how – and that is incredible but there's no end game yet, all still to play for, and ratcheting risk . . . Never thought I'd see him."

They had come off the ring road, had joined the M40 and were trundling steadily towards the north-west. His phone rang.

Late at night and there should have been little traffic, three lanes for lorries and vans to spread themselves over. But it was one of those awkward little moments when he seemed to be fenced in by HGVs, some with trailers. The phone was in the inside pocket of his jacket.

And his car seemed to have lost acceleration – and he was wedged in, and needed to concentrate. An insistent ring filled the inside of the car, and there was no conversation as he concentrated on the road.

It had been an example of the stubborn streak that Jonas recognised as part of his mental make-up, that he had set out from home at night. There had been curtains edging aside in the neighbours' windows as Vera had stood in the road and requested that two motorists wait while he towed the caravan clear and did the sharp turn necessary. An extraordinary time to be going on holiday, they'd have thought. Olaf was loaded in his crate on the floor of the caravan. No talk because he had nothing to say about Neolithic remains, Stone Age artisans, Roman road-building talents. Was, frankly, devastated by the earlier news. He did not feel able to take a hand off the wheel and fish into his pocket to get his phone out and now they were going fast and his view was not much more than a Dutch-registered trailer's back end, and an Irish lorry was at his side, and a Cumbrian one on Vera's, and huge engines competed with the phone's impatient ring.

And the obstinacy, that familiar stubbornness, had been reinforced by the AssDepDG. "Know what time of night it is, Jonas? Calling me about a backwater problem? Do I care? Do you comprehend the importance of crime in the pecking order of what matters, Jonas? Do you? If we are talking about Islamist fundamentalists, we would say that crime comes about six paces behind the donkey. Understand? The bloke walks up the high street in Jalalabad and his most precious item is his donkey, and six paces behind trail his women. That's *crime*. For fuck's sake, Jonas, you need a sense of humour in this trade. So you've lost an intelligence source. That's the way life goes. Those people don't get a hearse ride through Wootton Bassett, as you well know. They are unsung, have a shelf life but not a long one. They are exploited and you know that well. The idea of pulling down the shutters because one individual is having a hard time is quite lunatic. How much has this fucking caper cost us, Jonas? Bleeding us dry on your say so. We go on to the end, got me? Never thought I'd get to hear that our dearly beloved Jonas was losing the streak we value, and going soft. Don't like the heat, then fuck off out of the kitchen . . . I don't want a running commentary. Enjoy your holiday, and – of course – my best wishes to Vera."

So, in poor humour, Jonas had finished packing the car and stowing supplies in the caravan's cupboards, and his planning was set in motion, and the deceit maintained, and they had set off, and he had not known at what level was the chaos in the world for which he took a degree of responsibility. He had not eaten supper, had sulked and given Vera no explanation, had been a casualty of self-pity, but the AssDepDG had lanced that boil. The phone kept ringing and – if honesty ruled – he dreaded its message.

He could not take a hand off the wheel and his wipers were going hard and spray deluged the windscreen. Vera reached across and rummaged in his jacket pocket, tugged out the phone. He murmured the code to her and was rewarded with a snort because she knew it, and her finger tapped the keys. She peered at the screen. Jonas waited.

"What it says, 'Recalled to Life'. That's all."

"What? Say it again?"

"It says, *Recalled to Life*. Signed, *H&W*. Then three 'x's – that's kisses, Jonas."

"What does it mean?"

"Heavens, Jonas. Anyone who is half-literate understands. It is the code message to announce the freeing of Doctor Alexandre Manette, his release from the Bastille gaol. It is from *A Tale of Two Cities*, Jonas. God, what an education you have missed. Someone has been freed and . . ."

His face lit, and his hands shook and the wheel swayed and his eyes misted, and he almost took the caravan into the side of the Cumbrian lorry, and he could barely see through the windscreen and hit the brake and lights flashed behind him. If Vera had wanted to give him a Dickens lecture, she would have had to bellow. The car was deluged with the noise of the big klaxon horns around them.

He steadied himself, and they were again at cruising speed, but he noticed that the lorries around him had eased away, as if wary of him. He chortled.

Vera put the phone back in his pocket, and asked, "Are we now in a holiday mood?"

"I think so, right in the mood . . . Pity about the weather, but we must always stay positive and hope for a good outcome."

11

Still needing the headlights, Jonas negotiated a narrow winding lane that ran alongside the Conwy river. It was too early to gauge the attraction of the area he had chosen to bring himself, Vera and Olaf to, because dawn was still teetering.

He felt tired and old, and had driven more than 200 miles in the dark. They had left the motorway at Chester, and he had noted the road signs to Runcorn and Widnes, and to Liverpool, and it was fortunate that Vera had been asleep and so had not noticed that his jaw had clamped and his lips narrowed, and he had made a little whistle of breath. He had kept his speed constant and when she woke, she smiled, and seemed happy.

His phone was clamped on the dashboard and vibrated as a message arrived.

The position of the semi-submersible was logged, estimated as some 36 hours from the completion of its voyage. He acknowledged the courage and skills of the crew that had brought it those several thousand nautical miles; he thought four tonnes of the stuff would encourage both bravery and talents. Another text was confirmation from Leroy that he and Kev had arrived for duty at Thames House and had the prepared envelopes to hand. He had seen the camera feed from the Govier home, and the arrival of Xavier. And there were local news reports of shots having been fired in Garston, where the trade in Class A had erupted into near warfare and the Govier territory was threatened. Entertaining enough to keep him awake as he had driven through the night. A catch-up from Wilf and Hugo, and he thought them likely to be delightful company if he'd had an interest in goats, and both thankfully spare with words. Their charge still slept and they had cleaned two wounds on his face, superficial. He had answered their query as to future actions and responsibilities.

He imagined Detective Chief Inspector Fergal Rawe thrashing around to get himself hosed and dressed for an early departure, and Detective Chief Inspector Fanny Thomas, and that in south London the low-ranked Jak Peters would be getting ready for the start of his day . . . All grand people, thorough and conscientious and wronged because they were outside the loop, as he believed they ought to be. Lastly, and he had only their photographs by which to know them, he considered the personalities in the Munoz clan, and assumed they had started to doubt the truths spouted by Kenny Blake, had taken him in for questioning, denunciation, and he had successfully defended himself . . . His skill or their stupidity?

Jonas expected a flow of evidence would start to gather. His new world, in the backwater, involved *evidence*. Boring to the AssDepDG, and tedious to Aggie Burns, and irrelevant to Jonas Merrick before his duties with crime. Would he go to the Crown Court trials – if they happened – and sit in the public gallery? Not likely.

A decent morning. A shaft of sunlight. Still the wind, but a reflection coming up off the lane. He had to brake, as a herd of fine cattle trudged along the lane towards him.

He had been about to consider "responsibility". Nikko in Bogotá had been responsible for a CHIS and had lost him, but not lost sleep – his usefulness had expired. Rawe had responsibility for a travel agent, a source. Mrs Thomas had responsibility for a couple in whose wall a camera was secreted. And he had responsibility for Kenny Blake, a Level One . . . He supposed that all of them, and would have included himself, would have dismissed the responsibility as inconsequential, maintained they handled it with ease: they would be liars.

He could not reverse. He assumed the cattle were on their way to a milking parlour and were not to be delayed. There was room, just, for the beasts to get by him. Huge creatures, black and white markings and low-slung udders. They pushed, and their bodies filled the windows, and shook the car. The smell of the animals filled the interior. Ahead of them, past the drover and his dog, was a hanging sign for the farm, on whose site they were booked. Excreta, delivered from under a lifted tail, covered the front right wheel hub.

She said, "It's a bit of a stink, Jonas, but I'd call it a holiday stink."

"Yes, something like that. A holiday . . ."

He laughed, but hollow. Jonas reckoned that the farmer would also have known about responsibility, and how to care for his beasts.

A lilt in the voice. "Are you Mr and Mrs Merrick, come to stay with us?"

"We are."

"You're early in the season for visitors. Just a few of the newly-weds and the nearly deads around here." He laughed at his joke, seemed well rehearsed.

"It suited us."

"Hope you have a good time. Weather is set fair."

Jonas answered, "I anticipate we'll have a most enjoyable time."

He turned up a drive of broken stone and into a field, bumped across it aiming for a far corner where there was a concrete hard. He reversed the caravan on to it and was satisfied that he had done it well . . . So tired and would not have had it otherwise.

Trade in the café was building, before the shops and offices opened.

Kenny went inside.

Heads turned, conversations were killed. His scars were vivid, like they were battle honours. Fredo would have seen him taken the previous day. The radio played, and its shriek bounced off the walls, hit Kenny's ears. He smiled, like his world was at rest, and asked for his usual coffee, and went to sit at a table. His eye was not caught and he was not spoken to.

The guys had left the Biscuit Tin, an hour before the first peep of the dawn light out over the ocean. They had explained that they still had charge of a Samsonite case, and that an aircraft was waiting at the airstrip up to the east, off the Santander road, and likely the cost of it was bumping up. They would offload the money, see the flight off over the Biscay, then would be back. One of them had seemed to quibble over leaving their goats for any longer, and there were worries about the hives but the other had calmed him. He had given them spare keys for the outer and inner doors; there was a storeroom on a floor above and they'd liked the idea of creating a bivouac there. About what had happened the previous evening? Kenny had persuaded them that a misunderstanding had occurred, and probably gave them that winning smile and neither of them had laughed with him. A "misunderstanding" was a useful description of his proximity to a chainsaw or a cordless drill or pliers on his fingernails, or a shot in the back of the head, or a grave in a deep ditch – and the cold and the wet air on his skin as he had stripped and showed that he wore no wire, and had challenged Sergio to do the same and show he was not a snout, and the shadowed movements beyond the torch beam as the *matriarca* had almost matched him, garment for garment.

Not said, but he sensed that he would be in their care and had not yet squared how he would produce precious evidence and stay cosseted.

His coffee was carried to the table by Fredo.

The café owner, who had a comfortable little account in the Biscuit Tin, looked anxious. Had reason to. Kenny Blake was the banker, the investment adviser, the keeper of secrets, and had been led out of the building by enforcers. Men such as those who had taken him into the street and had put him in the car were known here; they had done time in the Pontevedra gaol and they were on permanent payrolls. Fredo would have recognised them, had enough contact with the Munoz clan to be fearful of them.

He thanked Fredo. Produced his card to pay and it was waved away. Kenny thought it important to smile again. Still had that ache deep in his gut that came from acute fear but he could act well. A good word, worth repeating. Just a misunderstanding. Used the word *malentendido*, thought it stronger than *equivocación*, and Fredo and all his customers would have seen the marks on his face. Fredo was not the only one in the bar who had money stashed in the Biscuit Tin. He, and they, had stood to lose . . . Fredo fussed over him and wiped the table as Kenny drank his coffee. Then sank on the chair opposite and leaned forward.

"I do not hear anything from my boy."

"Cannot help you, Fredo, and am sorry I cannot."

"If a shipment does not come through . . . You understand, Kenny?"

"I do."

"Then they will kill Gabriel."

"Yes."

"For them, the barbarians in Colombia, there is no mercy, no argument, no pleading . . . They kill. It is known. Also, it is known, Kenny, that very few shipments fail because the Customs or the GRECO have good luck, or the skills to intercept. It is because of a *traidor* in the clan, an *informador*. Forgive me, Kenny."

"I have nothing to forgive you for, Fredo."

Kenny pushed his cup away and wiped his mouth with the paper napkin, and smiled sincerely one more time.

"If there is an informer, if the shipment is blocked, then I lose my son. I saw you taken and I thought they believed you were an informer, a traitor, that you would kill Gabriel. I cursed you, Kenny . . . That is why I ask your forgiveness. I would have killed you with my own hands, and willingly . . . I tell you very frankly, Kenny, the shipment is late. If it fails then I will need money for an airfare, for . . ."

"Let us hope, Fredo, that you do not need money. Should you – of course – you can take money from your account."

"My cousin, he comes back tomorrow, travels with the body of his son. We, the family, have already made a down payment on the funeral cost. It is reality."

"Let us hope for the best, Fredo. The best."

The café owner leaned further over and his arms were across the table and looped over Kenny Blake's shoulders and Kenny was kissed on both cheeks. The table was cleared. Kenny pushed back his chair and nodded to those either side of the counter, and he went out – and reeled.

Waiting for the train, standing at the top of the ramp at Euston, was Jak Peters. Well dressed, and smart, he would have appeared a man aware of his status, an individual for whom personal prestige was important. If status and prestige were absent then he would wear a sour expression. As he did that morning, as he waited for the train from Crewe.

He had no friends in the family that was the Metropolitan Police. And no friends outside. Made an aloof figure at the school gate when he dropped off Benjamin and Augustus, rarely attended parents' evenings, worked through most of them as did his banker wife, Sophie. At Sunday morning football for the boys, one parent would watch and the other would be on a laptop in the car, and they'd alternate at half-time ... Most people in the office of SC&O10 thought him "haughty at best and arrogant at worst" and a usual evaluation of him was a "dedicated and professional officer and not to be underestimated".

Both Fergal Rawe and Fanny Thomas were known to him. The Irishman he reckoned as a joke who should have been put out to pasture a decade back. The woman he rated as a female jobsworth. Himself, he rated highly ... and the Security Service man who had wrenched control of Kenny Blake from him, he had regarded as nondescript, frightened of crossing a bridge and had needed his hand held. Had gone to the top man in his unit with his complaint and had been bluntly informed that the matter was beyond the level for altering. If he wanted to quit, then he should and his resignation would be, reluctantly, approved. If he wanted to stay then he should swallow the pill and ... and the pill was made sweeter because he was given simultaneous control of three more Level Ones: one did drugs and OCGs in the West Midlands; another had drugs and OCGs in the Bristol area; and the third did drugs and OCGs and links to right-wing loonies. Was not short of work, but was short of a prize, and resented the loss. Had he forced through his resignation he would have had to settle into the torpor of being house-husband to Sophie and allow her added freedom to travel further and more frequently. He had stayed, but the frustration twisted in him and he would cherish this opportunity to burn the ears of the little man, speak his mind.

He saw them trudge up the incline, a joke and a jobsworth. Had never had to describe himself, Jak Peters, and never intended to.

A brusque greeting. He led them to the cab rank. The email had stipulated where they would meet, then he assumed they would be taken inside Thames House to a conference room.

He asked the driver, brusquely, to take them to the river end of Horseferry Road to a café there. A bad morning in London, rain on the streets, and traffic slow, and none of them spoke – a relief to him. He knew what he would say to the nondescript, had assured himself he would enjoy it. Would take persuading that a year in his professional life had not been wasted, nor in Kenny Blake's life – no arrests, no swoops, no hauls, no hero-gram headlines – since his man had been stolen . . . and doubted he would be wrong in his judgement.

She had slept as well as a daytime bat. Doloures Govier was woken by the sounds of the street outside, then by the closeness of Patrick's coughing. Should not have a throat that raw, not at his age. She crawled from the bed and went to the window, found the right cord and heaved up the blind. Beside her, at his own window was her son, leaning out of it and smoking. Not often did she see his naked upper body; it was white and scrawny, no flesh on it, just bones showing through, and his hair was wet from the rain. God help the Govier family if this was the future. Patrick's brains, Bengal's strength and Theresa's business sense. A day would dawn when Mikey was out, when she was knackered, when the two of them were long gone and out of sight.

She opened her window, put her head out. "Get back inside, making a bloody exhibition of yourself."

Her son looked at her. "Sorry, Ma, but you're flopping around a bit yourself."

Not often that the kid gave her cheek. He flicked his fag down into the street. She looked down. Hadn't thought about what she might look like in a in nightdress, and the wind drifting the material across her body, and her leaning out. She ducked back inside.

"Flopping around" . . . Cheeky sod.

She closed the window, lowered the blind, went to fight with the shower – and none of them had the same controls.

The future was the Costa del Sol with Mikey. Lying low, going for a weekly shop by different routes and using different stores, and keeping clear of the bars where the local filth came trawling for the "Most Wanted", and being cautious about who had moved in down the street . . . Some fucking life. Better than the alternative: keys and slamming doors, and the smell, and always looking over your shoulder.

Not yet. Doloures was not yet ready for the future.

Footsteps in the corridor. They stopped at her door. She just had a towel wrapped around her. No knock, but a scrape and then an envelope on the carpet, and the footsteps fading. A note inside the envelope, in clear handwriting. What time they would be collected from the hotel . . . and a day to kill but an opportunity to check over in her mind the details of the transaction and the transshipment, and the plan for getting the merchandise out of Spain and across Europe, then overland in England, into a warehouse near home. Plenty of detail to hold her while time was killed. Only fucking peasants.

Any morning, weekday or weekend, Isabella Munoz was dressed and took her breakfast early. She valued that time . . . much to think of, and planning to be nailed in place. A smile lingered, and the evening had brought her pleasure and amusement.

Sergio would lead with his English language skills. He had been briefed. For Sergio, a challenge was always welcomed. She could depend on Sergio. Sergio would, if she had not been present, have attempted to beat the Biscuit Tin man to a pulp, might have required two of the men to hold Kenny while he did so. And Sergio, afterwards, had kissed her. They were a volatile family, she recognised it, all of them did. Voices raised and shouts and curses thrown were part of a daily and successful life. Sergio would enjoy himself tonight.

And the presence of Laureano would unsettle the visitors, threaten their confidence.

Laureano would drive them from their hotel to her house, would not introduce himself, would seem to be a driver and nothing more. Would not give any indication that he understood and spoke English, as did his brother. A minor problem for Isabella Munoz was that Laureano distrusted – as much as Sergio – the investment adviser, Kenny, who was – she admitted – her favourite. She had thought it magnificent when the young man, the handsome young man, had kicked back at them, and the diversion as he had fought the issue of the wire – the wire he did not wear – was brilliant. It had been a cool night, wind in the air, and enough rain spitting down for her to feel it on her skin. She had surprised herself, could still laugh at it.

And that night she might laugh some more.

Little enough to make her laugh, amuse her, in the life she led. She did not believe that Kenny Blake in any way threatened her and could see a situation when – in time – perhaps . . . She clicked the keys on a calculator, and had a busy day ahead . . . It was about judgement, and in that field she thought herself expert, and in her assessment of those with whom she would do business that evening.

"No shit, Bengal. I thought I could be different."

"Have a smart girl accent, been to convent school, on to business college."

"Thought I could get clear of what you do, what Ma does, what Patrick will become, what Dad was."

"But you learned different."

He had come round in the morning and had a swagger about him. Would have been because Ma was away, like he owned the house though he did not live there. She was pleased, so pleased, to see him. Had not slept till near dawn. But in a bad night some clarity had shown through. Had climbed out of bed, had had a shower, had dressed without a care for how she would look, ate a piece of bread, had written the draft of a college essay . . . had said it out loud, "Fuck them", and Bengal had come. Her decision made, who he was – and who she was.

"Used to reckon I might break away, just head off. Get in a car and go for the motorway, reach the Six, turn south and disappear. Be my own person. What I thought."

"Can't do it."

"Can't. Learned it yesterday."

"It would follow you. We have history. No friends . . . Allies but they'd cut us adrift as soon as we looked weak. Can't run from it. Place isn't big enough, can't hide."

"Used to want to. Not any more."

"What happened?"

"People at college pissed on me. Made a joke of me. Thought I'd cringe, lie down."

"You didn't?"

"I did not."

"Don't back off. You are a Govier. Like it or not, that's who you are. You go back to that college place and you learn all they can teach you. Go back in there and show them they are just shit and they don't frighten you. You want to be with our family, then I will need petrol and a glass bottle, and some rag. Go get them for me. Petrol, about a litre. A litre bottle. Rag, dry and about a duster size . . ."

And Xavier tossed his sister a cheap lighter and she caught it and flicked its roller and the flame leapt and she let it burn steadily for a moment, then killed it. She went close to her brother and his arms came out, strong and muscled enough to swing a baseball bat or a pickaxe handle, and powerful enough to hold a CZ999 Scorpion so that it did not waver. He told her, a murmur in her ear, where she would throw the bomb and why and when. She thought that she would not have countenanced doing it, if the note had not been passed her in the lecture hall. She had her arms round her brother's neck, smelled a tang of the sea.

"Does Ma know?"

"She'll know what she needs to know, when she's back."

They kept wigs in the house, and tinted glasses and scarves and reversible coats. And there was a small plastic box that held smooth pebbles that had been washed up on a beach across the Mersey, by Bebington. A stone in a shoe did not hurt if it were already worn smooth but it altered the step and the gait and made her or Patrick or Bengal near unrecognisable when the rest of the gear was used.

He left first.

Theresa chose a dark wig that came down to her shoulders, and a scarf that would be over her face and a pair of tinted glasses, and a sweet smooth stone, smaller than a fingernail, and put them all in a shopping bag and went out through the front door after setting the alarms. Just used a small car, cheap and mass made and swung out into the road. Saw them flick the curtains, across the street. Noted the face that ducked away.

"Not mincing my words, David, but I'm pretty near the end of living here, with them across the road."

David did not answer her. He could call one of the estate agents in Allerton Road. Their suburb of Liverpool was usually described as "beautiful". If anyone was interested in buying, but too stupid to check out their road and find who they would be sharing territory with, then the price would be good. Could go for a bungalow up in Lytham on the coast . . . But then they would be far removed from the bowls club and the crowd they played bridge with, and from the church where they were more than occasional worshippers. Would have to start again which was not welcome at their age. They seemed to be trapped in their own home, might have been self-inflicted, but that state of mind festered. As if they had barricaded themselves in behind locked doors and windows, alarm permanently set. He had just watched the elder son leave, a hideous thug, and then the girl. Didn't know about her but she sometimes had a pile of folders under her arm which meant education, and some hope: never talked to them. Had not seen the mother yesterday, nor the other boy. Part of their day, his and Jenny's, was now spent logging the family, in and out. It was compulsive. Could have lived with it if the policewoman had not soft-soaped them. With the camera in place he felt personally vulnerable, felt that he endangered his wife of 42 years . . . He knew the camera was working again, that an obstruction had been cleared . . . Might do it, ring an agent, get a valuation, no obligation. He thought that, if provoked, the family's violence could be brutal. Provocation would be that lens in the wall.

"Yes, dear. Perhaps you're right, dear."

She'd cooked breakfast and he'd taken Olaf off to a hedgerow. He had no idea of the names of the flowers, Latin or English, but the cat sniffed around and found a potential food source. Jonas had eaten his breakfast, then had dozed, and they had studied the map. She had not realised that guilt dictated his suggestion that they set off by mid-morning, the cat left in the caravan.

The Romans had built a fort at Canovium. Down the lane from the campsite was a track leading towards the steep hillsides, taking them away from the river. He could see the shapes of where the defensive walls had been built, and the beach where there would have been a quayside and the marks on the high ground where the legions' military road had been laid . . . His phone was on vibrate so merely shook in his pocket and he only glanced at the screen when Vera was turned away from him. There would have been a local commander, perhaps a veteran of warfare in Germany or in North Africa, and perhaps from the Middle East, for whom this would have been, 2000 years before, a temporary home. And on his staff would have been an intelligence clerk, not a fighting man, but a coordinator of rumour and gossip. Might have been described in Roman vernacular as "a good old boy", or might have been known as "a miserable old sod". But he would have been listened to.

A tractor passed them. Vera spoke to the farmer who had come with his dogs to drive his sheep to another field. Vera stayed apart, preferred to imagine the stamp of the heavy sandals on the stone-faced road leading to the fort's gate: now there was a rusted iron replacement and beds of nettles. He reflected that the Roman way of imposing authority, the forts with the barrack blocks, watchtowers and parade grounds, was brutally enforced. Not how it was for Fanny Thomas or Fergal Rawe or Jak Peters – or himself. Vera had wandered towards a low small church and he followed her.

Strands of wool hung on the wire, crows pecked in the dung and the sun threw long, low shadows over the walls and gates. He walked around the church, observed a huge yew tree and its massive canopy, then found a solitary headstone, marking an RAF grave and the flowers were multi-coloured round it. Vera must have seen him studying them and called out that they were mainly the yellow Coltsfoot and the orange Fox and Cubs, pretty and gentle and a pleasant place to rest . . . Had a thought that in the past he had worked alongside, hardly respected them, men and women from the armed forces. They, too, were on the front line of the so-called "War on Terror". The service veterans were photographed and lionised . . . What he liked about the backwater was that no one would ever hear of Fergal or Fanny or Jak, and God forbid they would ever hear of Kenny, and none of them would have a special stone in a graveyard. He considered whether Romans and, after them, the Normans, had been happy here, regarded it as a good posting. He supposed what he did mattered, would be a pity if it did not.

They were so low in the water that the horizon was short, seemed just a few metres ahead, but when they rose on a wave and were held at the top, Diego could see further, might be a kilometre.

The wind was constant and strong, and the swell as it had been hour after hour and day after day, but the rain had eased. The gull still escorted them. From the moment Diego had woken he was removed from the little comfort that sleep gave, and knew what he must do. He had not slept easily, had resisted it, fought to stay awake. He had lain with his weight on the wheel, had not turned, and had only drifted, dozed and finally slept, when he'd been certain that – behind him – the engineer's breath was regular.

Dawn had come and a matter that could not be delayed.

He fortified himself first on thick black coffee, then with a swig from the neck of the brandy bottle. Diego had to be the one to do it because Matias could not swim. The fucking engineer of a semi-submersible that was traversing the Atlantic could not swim. He would tie a length of nylon rope, half a centimetre thick and hope-fully strong, around his waist, and knot it securely, and Matias would pay it out and he would go into the ocean to look for a leak. Had a good reason to: a quarter of a million American dollars. There was a wetsuit in the storage cupboard. It would have fitted a fucking dwarf, or an Indian from upriver, where the craft had been assembled. He would have to strip to his underpants, and pray that the work would be fast. The cockpit area was heated by the engine, but the more they turned up the volume, there was greater toxicity from the diesel fumes. They had three towels, one each. He thought the engineer detested him but could hardly go into the water at the end of a nylon rope, the sort that was used for hanging washing from, clutching a Luger pistol.

So he stripped, and tied the rope around his waist. He knew Matias was watching. The engineer was sitting on the edge of the bunk with the boy's corpse.

Talk? None. Wishes for "good luck"? None. He unfastened the hatch. Matias pushed himself up from the bunk and followed him across the width of the cockpit, three paces. The rope was paid out as Diego scrambled through the opening, and the spray from a wave caught him, and he shivered from the impact, and the next one came. There was a rail beside the hatch that he had been holding tightly but the wave's force ripped his hand away. He went down into the water, hit the hull, and the rope was tight, and he swallowed water, and realised that the fucking engineer had not paid out enough for him to get clear. Diego surfaced. The hatch was only slightly open and he could see Matias behind it, holding it, would have been to prevent the flood, and them losing stability. He was given more rope.

Everything was about the money. Diego was in the water, coughing and spluttering, for the money. He clawed himself up on to the superstructure, crawled forward. He moved over the cargo area where the bales were stored, then over the fuel tank bladders. He had a good grip on the hand rails now. So far, so good, and his speed was constant in spite of the roll and shake of the craft, and there were moments when he was clear out of the water and others when he had to suck down air and fill his lungs, and came to the bow point where there should have been a pointed tip for a better dynamic in the water. Further forward than the name of the vessel, *Maria Bernarda*, he could see a scrape where the paint had been cleaned away and the fibreglass had crumpled. He ran his fingers over the area, could not find a split.

All along the side of the hull were the lines along which the container and its barnacled coating had run leaving scratches and dents. His body was numb and he doubted he would survive much more than another half-minute. They said in the bars where the fishermen gathered, in Corunna or Muxía or Cambados, that survival in the ocean was three, maybe four minutes in spring temperatures, and that the shock of the cold quickly destroyed a man's will to live. He realised the rope was slack, that the engineer did not take in the spare length . . . Once a fisherman had told him of being overboard, no life vest, flailing and seeing the stern of the trawler going away and seeing the wake from the propeller and shouting and not being heard – and being picked up by a sister ship. What Diego remembered was how the man had spoken, no emotion, of being adrift. He wondered what was his value to Matias, who came from the other side of the world, did not want to screw big women, did not want to drink fine wine, did not want much more than a chance to have a market stall for car spare parts and renew the roof on his bungalow, and perhaps send a kid to a good school.

He could see the rope in the water losing its slack and there was nothing on the side of the hull that Diego could cling to – he was dependent on the engineer. At that moment, as the rope went tight and he was close to the churn of the propeller and had to push himself away from its thrash, he wondered whether Matias would let go of the rope . . . Wondered if hatred would overcome the need for the money, or would concoct a tale. Gone overboard, a hero, a volunteer, to check for damage, a man of extraordinary courage, could not be saved.

He pulled himself up the rope back to a place where he was level with the cockpit hatch. He reached up, was battered against the hull, and went down, saw nothing and held his breath and his lungs ached, and came back up, and reached again and caught the bottom edge of the hatch.

His effort was sufficient to lever himself up and open the hatch wider and to pitch himself, head first, down on to the cockpit floor. Water dripped from him and on to the floor and into the old vomit. He saw that the end of the rope was tied to the hand rail beside the hatch. He shivered, had hurt himself on the decking, and his numbed fingers made it hard to unfasten the knot at his waist, but he managed it. He took his own towel and Matias's towel, and dragged the boy's towel from under the corpse, did it with force, and Emiliano's head lolled. And he dried himself and pounded his body to win back warmth, and reached for the dial that controlled the heat in the cockpit, and flooded the interior with warmth and the stench of diesel.

Diego said that he had not found a leak. Matias said that he did not think there was a leak because the craft was stable.

"Then why did you not fucking tell me? Why did you let me go into the water?"

There was no answer.

He needed another slug from the bottle. It might last until evening but he thought it unlikely. Sunlight filled the cabin and reflected up off the hull over which the water washed, and caught the wings of the gull. It pierced the narrow cockpit windows and fell on the sheet that covered the boy.

Diego said, "He's going in the water. That is right and proper."

There was a moment of hesitation inside the café, when each of them wondered who was going to pick up the tab, who could charge it to expenses. Fanny Thomas had taken charge of the order: three *cappuccinos* and three pastries.

They sat at a table and Jak Peters had taken a seat with a view of the street. Had already let them know that he had actually met Jonas Merrick, and had voiced his opinion of the man. Needed to compete with Jimbo Rawe on the denunciation. Both at full volume and louder than was wise, Fanny Thomas thought. She had no opinion, had not dealt with the man other than to receive a curt email to stress that action was not to be taken against the Govier family *and you will be advised when the situation changes.* Their coffees were brought, and their pastries, and they waited, and the first salvoes of full-on criticism were exhausted. And they waited . . . and the men chorused disapproval at being left at the table with no sign of their host. Fanny Thomas did not join them but studied her own reflection in the window. She had made a big effort to look her best, project an image of authority – so rarely recognised in her own home – and was irritated that she, and they, were wallflowers . . . and waited some more.

More coffees? More pastries? Negative. The mugs and plates were removed . . . and two policemen arrived at the café door. A greeting from behind the counter for them. Kitted up as if Putin's tanks were coming over the bridge and they were the last line of defence. Hard to get inside the door with all that gear on their belts, and big vests swelling their upper bodies, and heavy stuff draped round their necks. She heard their names, one was Kev, the other Leroy, and it was Leroy who was digging into his hip pocket while Kev fastened his glance on the three of them. They threaded between the tables and stood, tall and heavy, over them. Leroy had three envelopes in his gloved hand and they had been crumpled, creased, in his pocket.

Without any respect for their rank, each one of them senior to either Kev or Leroy, they were asked to identify themselves. Almost impertinent. She gave her name, and added *Detective Chief Inspector* for good measure. Leroy checked the three envelopes he held, chose one, passed it to Kev who checked it again then handed

it to her. She made out her name, written in a spider scrawl . . .
and Fergal Rawe and Jak Peters, who gave their ranks and it
amused her that *Detective Sergeant* Peters, for all his grandeur, had
hardly climbed the seniority ladder. A notebook was produced
and a pencil and they were asked to sign, each of them, to confirm
receipt. A cheery exchange with the counter staff and Kev and
Leroy on their way.

Three envelopes were opened. From each a single folded sheet
of paper was taken. Three faces peered at the writing, attempted
to decipher the scrawl.

"It's the feckin' limit . . ."

"He's got a bloody nerve, our minor nondescript."

Fanny Thomas spluttered the question. "Is that it? Is that our
meeting? Have I traipsed down here for this?"

From Jimbo Rawe came the detail of his instructions, four lines
of handwriting. Reluctantly given up, because Jak Peters was not
a team player and disliked sharing, was what was expected from
him. And from Fanny Thomas, disappointed at her lot, was a trip
back up north and no sunshine beckoning. Enough? Not for Rawe
or Peters. They were out of the door and she paid up and hurried
to catch them at the Thames House side door.

Both, were ranting – Rawe was loud and Peters was attempting
cold anger. The armed police were watching over the security of
the pavement, as if their job were done and dusted. Fanny Thomas
saw a receptionist behind a glass screen lift a phone: imagined a
report being passed to a higher floor.

Fanny felt cheated. Had thought she would value the experience of travelling to Box, had been sold short. Jimbo Rawe smoking
and dragging in the fumes, extraordinary the old beggar was still
alive. Jak Peters pacing, muttering curses. Fanny Thomas reckoned she had wasted enough of the day and was checking her
phone screen for the trains back north. A man came, wearing an
ill-fitting suit and a shirt that was yesterday's and a tie that was
poorly knotted and scuffed shoes, and said in a sharp voice that
the street was hardly the place for detailed discussions but it would
have to do.

"I am an Assistant Deputy Director. You have a complaint, you make it to me and do not attempt to bully our door staff. Please explain yourselves."

The men thrust their letters at him, and Fanny Thomas passed him hers.

"Seems simple enough. What's the problem?"

Another chorus about rudeness, about the flouting of courtesies, about the quality of the individual at the cusp of the dispute, and language loose and flying. She saw the man's jaw harden and his eyes narrow. She let Rawe and Peters field it, eased back and found herself close to the armed police, always liked the company of that crowd.

"Seems clear to me. You should carry out what is requested to the best of your ability, without bellyaching and without shouting. If you do not, be assured, your careers will be dead in the water, which is my promise. I know your records. Mr Rawe, I have not come across any recognition of courage that you have been in receipt of. Mr Peters, other than demonstrating the behaviour of a barrack-room lawyer with success, I have not read of you being awarded any gong for exceptional bravery in the face of danger. The man you speak of has a QGM and it has been augmented with a Bar. Understood? The Queen's Gallantry Medal times two. So, if that is all clear and you know what is required, do it to the best of your ability. And in the more immediate time frame, just fuck off and don't waste any more of my time. And don't think you are going to see Jonas in person. You are not. He has gone on holiday, with his caravan."

And the AssDepDG disappeared inside.

Fanny Thomas would have sworn that the two guns, known to her now as Kev and Leroy, had to fight to keep the laughter off their faces.

She went to look for a taxi. Rather wished she had met Jonas Merrick, but doubted she ever would. Had the feeling of a bigger game being played out and greater danger threatening.

"You stood me up," Anna Jensen accused.

Kenny said, soft, into his phone, "Had a better offer, you know how it is."

"Your phone was off. I waited. Messages on the office phone not answered."

"It is a bit of a story."

"And you want to tell me the story?"

"Could tell you the story tonight."

"Which supposes I wish to hear your story."

"I think you would find it interesting."

A pause, as if she needed the moment to reflect. He had already decided not to go direct to the spook in London who controlled him, had instead sent a message to the boys who would now be at an airfield or back at their goat farm. The text to them was blunt, simple: "Tell him, I'm fine and can cope, know what is required and will try to deliver. That'll do." He thought that his next few hours in Corunna, with or without the company of Anna, would be chaperoned by them, barely out of their sight. Had much to say, too much, and did not know yet how he would present his proposal of a future. Might do it on the cliffs, and might do it on a rug in front of a fire, and might do it as they sagged back, sweat streaming – and might have Hugo and Wilf for company.

About a future. Worth thinking on, how he would do it.

But a future came after the present. The "present" paid his wage that was accruing in a bank account that was paid into on the last day of each month. Had lived in Corunna pretty much on expenses and Jak Peters, who did the housekeeping, had never queried what it cost to run him – rent for the cottage, heating and petrol, and more rent for the office and utilities there, and money for his wallet, and the cash cards were covered . . . Not his business, nor his concern, about the backup, and nothing to do with him where the money from the Biscuit Tin ended up. Kenny was not sure where his future went, and who would be paying for it. Would take "dexterity", apposite word, or fast feet to explain to the artist from the Netherlands, that the investment management side of his life was behind him, that he was quitting, that he wanted to share a future with her that he'd rather not at this moment talk about too much. Thought it sounded a poor offer.

Did he want to tell her why he had failed to be at the rendezvous arranged for last night? Did not think he did, said it would
keep.

She rang off. He sat in his chair, behind his desk. The wind
smacked the windows. When he had met other guys who had
reached Level One status, when they were off in the grounds of
the place where the instructors ruled, and clear of microphones
and free from being watched and listened to, and away from the
psychologists who demanded opportunities to monitor them,
there was a common refrain. Difficult to get on to the team run by
SC&O10, hellishly difficult, but a "piece of piss" compared with
getting off it. Walking away raised the alarms. And if he said that
he had met a girl and that there was a chance of building a relationship, they would tell him, in a whisper, to keep screwing her
and head on into the sunset until she tired of him, and he of her,
and then after a few months, might even be a year, to come back
in. Return to where he was safe, was respected, they'd say. Didn't
want loose cannons rolling on deck and potentially out of control.
Would make it difficult.

He slumped. Took the desk phone off the hook, switched the
mobile to mute. Put his feet up on the desk and thought he might
grab some sleep – and thought himself lucky, very lucky, bloody
lucky, to be alive – and was not sure who cared. And time was
shortening until he tried to bring the roof down on his targets, and
the hour of maximum danger was approaching fast . . . but he was
alive and thankful for that.

They had made a long hill climb, to Tomen y Mur. Vera revelled
in the site, and Jonas smiled.

In his pocket, the phone jumped and wriggled enough for him
to learn of incoming calls. The last had reported tersely, the
AssDepDG's way, an altercation on the steps of Thames House.
He would have liked more from the men minding Kenny Blake,
but would have to accept the absence of detail. Their cryptic sign-
off – "Small mercies, he's still in one piece". By now Fanny
Thomas would be heading back to Liverpool with her shopping

list, and Fergal Rawe would be on the train with her and needing to collect a grip bag and his passport and book a flight from Manchester to Madrid. And Jak Peters would be in SC&O10, getting his gear ready for an early flight out of LHR. And he had been on a Welsh hillside and had imagined the tramp of men with strong sandals as they moved towards another fort. Vera had learned the history of the place, fairly bubbled with excitement, and seemed grateful that he had taken time from that "accursed building that sees more of you than I do" to bring her here, to a wind-scorched hillside, had been a garrison that could accommodate 600 fighting men, in place for over a century, with all the modern conveniences of bath facilities and a quality cookhouse and an amphitheatre . . . Why Jonas thought such a place important to visit, apart from bringing colour to Vera's cheeks, was that sense of the pettiness of what men thought they achieved then, or now, or hoped to change in the future. Valuable, sobering, even for a clerk. They had been alone there, apart from the sheep, and walked as far up the slope as where the Roman-built strongpoint had been, and the views were beautiful and the wind cut at his face. One day, quite suddenly, they were gone, and the work deemed necessary by Gnaeus Julius Agricola to have an armed presence to protect the road from Celtic tribes was abandoned. An emperor, visiting from faraway Rome, wanted to build a wall to the north, needed manpower. All for nothing, and men's best efforts ditched – heavy thoughts. Felt he was put in his place but was not offended.

He would sleep well that night, but doubted it would be the sleep of the good.

A visit to the toilets, and a look at a tourist board while waiting for Vera. He read, realised he needed to be there. They walked together to The Grave, where a dog was supposedly buried. He stared at the stone, then gazed at the bronze statue, life size, of a huge hunting animal. Gelert, belonging to Prince Llywelyn the Great, was his best hunting dog. The Prince went out one day, leaving his dog beside his newborn son. Came back, was greeted by the dog who had blood around its jaws, hurried to the nursery and could not find his son, his heir. And with his sword and in an uncontrolled rage he slaughtered the dog. And as the dog screamed, Prince Llewelyn heard the cry of the baby. He found his son and beside him was the corpse of a huge wolf that Gelert had killed to protect the Prince's son. Inconsolable, he buried his dog. It was said that Llewelyn never smiled again.

Vera said, "That is a horrible story, Jonas. An awful story."

Jonas said, face turned away from her, "I suppose he didn't keep a clear head. Sometimes, I imagine, that it is difficult, but important to try."

12

Jonas had started to fret that the cat had been shut too long in the caravan, but Vera had insisted on one last line. The detour on the map had seemed short, but the drive had taken longer than anticipated.

A hill fort attracted her. South of the mediaeval Plantagenet garrison city of Caernarfon, on the coast of the Irish Sea, and a steep climb beyond a military gun position of the WW2 era, was a windswept summit. A miracle to Jonas that he had managed the ascent. Too many sandwiches at lunch and too many potatoes with his supper, and the excesses not cancelled by the walk to and from Raynes Park station, and to and from Thames House – plus the Danish every morning.

Vera had chattered in his ear as he heaved for breath and leaned on her arm. The fort was built on top of the cliff, had been dug in the Bronze Age – she told him that was at least 1000 years before the arrival of the Roman legions – then had been occupied in the Stone Age when iron could be heated and shaped, then the Roman troops had been here ... All useless information, and she had grinned and would have known that would please him.

"It was just a folly. An enormous, expensive, worthless piece of nonsense."

"I understand."

And he was tested. "What do you understand?"

"Irrelevant in military terms. Just for show. A display of strength, of self-importance."

"I have the advantage, Jonas. I read it up."

"So obvious. An enemy would have had to turn up. Sit on the track below, tick off a few days and the defence would collapse.

No water, Vera. Cannot defend a strongpoint without water. An illusion . . . what a wasted effort. Think of the poor blighters who had to wield shovels and baskets and shape the place."

The exchange pleased him. Vera wandered away. He sat. The rain was light and the wind powerful, and the tide far below was in and the sea came up over beaches that stretched far to the south. A few dog walkers were on the sands and an ice cream van had arrived, pre-season, and had sounded a jingle but would attract no takers. He supposed that his dislike of the pomp and ceremony, of monarchs and politicians and the titled autocracy, helped him to bond with life in the backwater, in crime. The patriarchs and the matriarchs of the OCGs had little interest in dynasties, of leaving behind them monuments to their success in extortion, murder, narcotics trafficking, Town Hall corruption, the sex trade. Just hoped it would last long enough to see them safely put down into the ground with a good binge to send them off. Hoped to avoid a stretch in Maximum Security or in a hospital wing, and the financial gains not all swallowed up by ACE, the dreaded Asset Confiscation Enforcement. Limited horizons, manageable aspirations . . . Much enjoyed by Jonas Merrick, and targeting them was easier, simpler, and gave more satisfaction. Was dreaming of the dawn coming up – not tomorrow's but Friday's. Felt good again.

His wife's face was lit. She would not, of course, have plucked any of the flowers growing on these old irrelevant ramparts, but she had her hand gently under the petals of a flower of an almost translucent pale blue – a "harebell". He saw her happiness.

Time to be on their way. Down the hill, somewhat unsteadily, and into the car. Jonas always dealt with problems regarding the performance of the car . . . On the way back to the farm and the caravan, he pursed his lips, wrinkled his forehead, and muttered something about the pulse of the engine, seemed anxious concerning the clutch . . . and could feel his phone writhing in his pocket as texts came through. And the following day would be of critical importance, the culmination of a year's work, not the conclusion, but the setting of the stones in place.

★   ★   ★

"Should I put money with you, Kenny?"

"Do you want, Anna, the professional talk?"

"You do the Biscuit Tin, for savers. Should I have money there?"

He thought her mischievous, amusing herself. "Depends how much, depends whether it matters to you."

"What sort of return?"

"I advise that clients can go 'high risk' or 'low risk', or an in-between risk. I emphasise that markets can appreciate and can slip . . . And you would have to decide on your relationship with your friendly tax officer – all of that."

"Not much of an answer."

"All you'll get."

His arm was round her. The light faded.

Anna's easel was folded away, and the three-legged stool. They were perched uncomfortably on a rock. There had been no sunlight and out to sea were ever darker shades of grey for the clouds, the horizon and the water . . . Kenny thought, if the schedules fed to him were good, that the craft was a day and not much more away from the shore.

He had thought her distant, and his presence might have meant little to her. He had come along the path from a parking spot used by the long-distance walkers who traversed the Coast of Death, and checked off the lighthouses on the headlands, and seen her car. It was where she had said she would be. It was a hard climb and the path was set with protruding stones, but he wore trekking boots. The rain, Kenny thought, was a bastard, and it came in with the gusts of wind. It had soaked her jeans and her anorak, and the easel and the stool had water flushing off them. He supposed that tucked at the bottom of her bag was a tightly rolled sheet of art paper of what she had managed to create. Far out to sea were distant lights and he assumed them to be those of a freighter or a small tanker, heading north towards the Biscay. He also noticed a series of pinpricks, far down and to the south, where the beach was. Saw them briefly, then lost them . . .

He held her tight, and put it off, what he would say to her, ask of her. What to say and when to say it . . . and he thought his reaction to her asking about investment had been feeble. He kept his arm across her back and gripped her shoulder . . . thought it was love. She would barely have been able now to see the marks on his face, but had looked then at them, curiously when he had arrived, had touched them with a wet finger. They had eaten the sandwiches he'd brought, and the cake, and drunk cool coffee – and talked of the weather, then the investment possibility. But her fingers went back to his face.

"These are why you did not come last evening?"

"You could say that."

"So you don't claim to have walked into a door, or fallen from a ladder, or bumped into a street lamp?"

"I do not."

"I make a guess, Kenny – you were hit with a fist, hit twice. On one of the fingers was a ring."

"I'd rather not confirm that explanation."

"Hit hard, and I looked at your own hands and saw no scrapes on the knuckles so you did not defend yourself."

"No comment."

"But you are here, Kenny. You are not in a ditch. So, you must have satisfied those who hit – and, I suppose, questioned you?"

"I'm not denying it . . ." Kenny laughed. He kissed her ear and pushed himself up. Murmured something about the weather being revolting, the time to move was right, and they needed a fire and food and whatever . . . and then he would talk about a future . . . But she shrugged clear of him.

"Why was an investment adviser attacked and then questioned, and somehow satisfied them, these people? Why?"

"Complicated."

"Don't confirm and don't deny, of course . . ."

"Time to go."

"Tell me."

Her finger was tracing the two lines cut by Sergio's wedding ring. She pressed, and in a moment he felt the scars break and bleed. The blood would be carried down his face by the rain and would settle on his collar or would dribble down onto his anorak. After the blood came little stabs of pain as the wounds widened.

"I am an investment adviser. It is what I do. I have a little business that is nearly within the legal limits, almost legitimate. I provide a service. The Biscuit Tin. My investors make a profit. Most are small-time people and they look for decent rewards and discretion. One or two of the investors have larger funds and they require confidentiality. Both the big people and the little people require a service that brings rewards – I give that. There can be misunderstandings."

"For a misunderstanding a face is cut?"

The moment when the game seemed to have reached a point. She was looking over his shoulder towards the cliffs and the rumble of waves far below. And the rain was dense on them. He held her close against him and her finger was still in his wounds and he thought the blood came faster.

"There were people who were interested that I had been seen with you, Anna. To those people you are confusing. They do not understand. To people who do not understand, who are ignorant, it is permissible to question and to kill. I satisfied them."

"What is confusing about me?"

He could be economical, or could tell it like it was. "They were suspicious because they do not understand why an artist is so in love with something as mundane to them as cliffs and beaches, and the sea and the rocks, and the lighthouses and the trails between them. I explained to them that you are an artist, that your talent is for others to judge, and that you can afford to live here, on their beautiful coast, and work . . . It was accepted. Took some persuasion, but it was accepted."

"And if it had not been accepted?"

"I would be in a shallow grave. Maybe soon afterwards you would have joined me."

"Thank you, Kenny."

"Time to go."

The wind hurried them on their way. Beckoning was warmth, a hot shower, a fire, food, and whatever. He thought his life as a Level One was trickling away from him and he held her close and steadied her. He took a torch from his pocket and was about to illuminate the track, but she took it from his hand and put it back in his pocket. It was as if, in thickening darkness, she wanted them to grope their way to the car park.

"I describe her as *una palurda*. What is that in English?" Isabella asked Sergio.

They stood at a window and looked out on to the area in front of her house and noted that Laureano had caught the mood and had not pulled up as near as he could to the main door. Nor had he opened the doors for the Englishwoman and her boy, let them do that for themselves and had pointed at the door.

Sergio used his phone to check. "Many words in English and they are *hick* or *boor* or *yokel* or *peasant*. I think the best is 'peasant' . . . From the country, without education, perhaps a farm worker."

She said, "In Sicily it was said that Toto Riina was a 'peasant', and also Bernardo Provenzano. And both were successful in business."

"Quite successful but peasants – and Provenzano – Most Wanted in all of Italy, perhaps in all of Europe – was arrested in his hideaway because he liked his family to send him freshly laundered clothing regularly. The police chased the laundry, a change from 'following the money'." And he laughed.

Doloures and Patrick were shown into the main salon. The housekeeper, Concepcion, ducked her head. Laureano came after them. Isabella thought *la palurda* appropriate for her. The woman had hard eyes . . . Beside her, and with cause, Sergio eyed her, stripped her. The boy was irrelevant. Ducked his head when he was introduced, then remembered himself and tried to stand tall, then crumpled again, as if he were meeting royalty. She did not back off.

They sat at a table.

There was a routine . . . Isabella placed her phone on the table, and Sergio's was next to it, and then Laureano's, and gestured across the table. The boy looked to his mother for guidance and she nodded. Her phone was laid down, and the boy's. A little bell was rung, and Concepcion, trim in a black high-necked dress and black stockings and shoes, her grey hair gathered at the back of her head, came with a tray of cups and a jug of coffee and put them on the table, and then put the phones on her tray and carried them out.

Isabella anticipated a big argument, the noise and fire of an opera, and Sergio would denounce Kenny – a sweet boy who could make her laugh and smile – and level the charges against him. Perhaps she would weaken and perhaps she would not. It would be a bad death for Kenny if she sided with Sergio.

But for now there was business to be settled. She evaluated the woman sitting opposite Sergio: strong, tough, ambitious, living without love.

Laureano, choosing to speak in his own language, said, "It would be unwise for you to bring a wire into our home. We would take that as a serious offence against us."

Sergio translated. She shook her head, and the boy did. To Sergio, they seemed ill at ease. She had good cheekbones, he thought, but there was little colour in the skin stretched over them. Attractive enough if she had taken care of herself, and likely to be wild . . . old but unbroken.

He would return again to his mother with the matter of the investment man, and the Dutch girl whose art had no merit, and the woman from the past who had once made herself a nuisance to the clans. Would return to it . . . and would accept that the investment manager had played supreme theatre, had provoked his temper, had captivated his mother. He would not let the matter rest because he did not believe in his mother's judgement . . . Laureano had just shrugged and would be busy that evening, and the next day, with the arrangements to bring the cargo ashore . . . He would take down the Englishman, but only when their money was safe.

His mother said nothing, poured coffee and passed the cups. Laureano glowered at them. Sergio spoke.

He talked of the imminent arrival of the semi-submersible and how the crew were permitted to make one call when they had sight of land and would then lie offshore until darkness, then lights would guide them to a bay, and a creek beside it for the unloading of the cargo. Said that now, and knew that through the rest of the evening, a rehearsal was being enacted, lights, pickup transport, short-term concealment of the cargo.

A calculator in front of him, his eyes locked on hers, Sergio spoke of the stages of onward trans-shipment, and planning for the movement of £2 million worth of quality cocaine, the value of what Doloures Govier bought, towards Amsterdam. It was what they wanted?

Her eyes on his, lips barely moving, and a question of alternatives.

Options were to have the bales, what they had bought, stored indefinitely in Galicia, hidden but making no money ... To move the bales five kilometres inland and take responsibility for their onward shipment ... to have them shipped by the family's agents from the Corunna area and driven across France and Belgium and delivered to a broker in Amsterdam – and pay at the Dutch end for the bales to be brought into the UK.

What did she want?

Sergio thought she steeled herself. He thought that, in the past, she would have purchased from the Amsterdam brokers, allowed them to import to the UK, and arranged for collection to her home city – and paid top price for the privilege. She had quite a pretty nose.

He tapped on his calculator, summoned up figures, passed the calculator across the table, let their fingers brush, and she would bob her head in agreement. He thought her probably twenty years older than himself. Wondered whether the Munoz hospitality should include a village girl thrown in for the kid. Thought the boy too scared to fart. Thought his mother blossomed as detail was given her, like she had been promoted to an upper league.

The business was dealt with, and drinks were brought by Concepcion . . . Laureano declined. His mother would apparently drink a small glass of sherry, but in reality it would be coloured water. Himself, it would be a glass of gassy water with ice and lemon, no gin. For the two guests there was a stiff gin, and a fierce whisky and water, and neither refused.

Dinner next, and conversation, and Laureano could be guaranteed to talk about the Colombians and their punishments – which would send a useful message . . . And after dinner he would go upstairs and show the "peasant" woman what Concepcion had collected for her that morning from the boutique in Pontevedra. Twice his mother caught his eye, and twice seemed to smile as if amused. He thought that by the next evening they would be down on the coast, not eating, not drinking and watching for the craft to breach the surface swell.

Matias said they should sing a hymn. He thought of the hymns that the Father led, and which a choir sang in the big church in his home town, now 5000 kilometres away, maybe more.

Diego told him that he did not know the words of any hymns.

Diego said that hymns were wasting their time . . . He was outside the cockpit hatch again, a rope lassoed around his waist and knotted on a rail along the top roof of the cockpit. Matias was at the hatch. Emiliano's body was wrapped in the three towels and his trouser belt held them in place along with lengths of rope, and his head was covered with a bin bag, black plastic.

Matias said they should at least say prayers, but Diego claimed he knew no prayers, claimed also that they were losing time and were getting behind schedule.

"We owe it him, to have prayers and hymns."

"We owe him nothing – and his family will be lucky if they are paid."

The gull was not frightened by the movements at the hatch and on the superstructure, had adjusted to a slower progress. Diego and Matias had agreed that Emiliano should have a seaman's funeral, be buried in the ocean. But they had nothing with which to weight the body. No pieces of lead, no rocks, no bags of stones, no heavy pieces of metal. He might sink, or he might float.

They had slowed to around half their normal cruise speed and, in the swell, the craft rocked, bucked, swayed. Diego and Matias were already soaked and the three towels had been allocated to Emiliano's corpse.

"Get a fucking move on, shift him."

The body had stiffened, and it was difficult for Matias to heave it into the open hatch. He had been close to a month on the submersible, and his legs and arms were weakened, and he had eaten little because to shit in the bucket in full view of Diego upset him. He struggled with the body, and murmured a prayer and the sound of the engine and the battering of the waves made a nonsense of his efforts.

Diego reached out, caught the boy's shoulders, heaved, grunted, and swore, and had lifted the body out of the hatch. The bin liner ripped in his hands and Matias saw the boy's face, white, shrunken. The body of Emiliano, 22 years old, Colombian national, his identity documents zipped in his hip pocket, had slid off the hull and had gone into the sea. The water was clean and clear, and Matias could see Emiliano's face ... Diego was back inside, shivering, cursing the loss of their towels, and the hatch was closed.

Matias saw the body, which had come to the surface, and the gull flew over it, evaluated it. He went to the engine again, and Diego checked the instruments. Nothing said, nothing left to say.

They were well into their dinner, when the screaming started.

A sound that was terrifying, one of those screams that "would wake the dead". Vera had a fork raised and was about to eat the half potato skewered on it. Pain and terror in equal measure. Jonas was cutting a slice of cold pork. The caravan's door was ajar, for Olaf, and the cold of the evening came through it and their heater was inadequate ...

Jonas knew where the submarine was, had an idea where Doloures Govier and her son would be eating their own dinner, and knew that their house in Liverpool was empty, and knew that

Fergal Rawe and Fanny Thomas and Jak Peters were primed for what was required of them, and knew where they were going in the morning, and where Kenny Blake was, and what he was doing. So little else that he could contribute . . . Only one man existed in whom Jonas could have confided as they entered the last hours of the operation. Only the AssDepDG . . . except that his protector, guardian, stanchion of support, regarded crime as third-rate.

The screaming outside the caravan was that of a crime in progress, of murder. Nothing that Jonas could do to save the victim. That sort of noise pierced imagination, transmitting both pain and fear. He saw that Vera was shaking . . . nothing much that he could do but he knew he must do something.

The torch was easy to find. They had "facilities" on board, but it was easier to visit the site toilets than fill up the chemical system. He left his pork and Vera lowered her fork. Jonas had read that hands tightening on a throat, shutting down a windpipe, until breathing ceased and death followed, could take a Sicilian, masters in that particular art, a full five minutes of exhausting effort.

He went to the door, switched on the torch and let the beam play out, swept it along the hedgerow. He caught sight of sheep gathered in a defensive laager: they too would have been unsettled by the sound of death coming close to them. He saw the cat. Olaf, Jonas's pride and his joy and who could do no wrong, was crouched at the edge of the hedge. A rabbit's back legs kicked weakly. He watched . . . Olaf had a hold on the rabbit's throat and would be using every muscle in his jaw to suffocate his prey. This was the way that killing was done, and there was little Jonas could do to block such instincts. Assumed that the Govier family and the Munoz family, and their parasites and affiliates and all those who lived off them, had – to lesser or greater extent – the same urges. Were motivated by the exhilaration of inflicting pain, creating terror, having the power. The kicking of the rabbit's grey back legs was losing impetus, but not the voice. The cat looked up at Jonas. It was the same animal that spent evenings on his lap or on Vera's knees while he studied his phone, while she read or sewed. No thought of violence, or viciousness, when Olaf was settled. The cat stared into the beam. Jonas saw the flash of its eyes, directing pure malevolence at the interruption. It might have been that the effect of the torch, and the moment of distraction for the cat, gave the rabbit a moment of desperate hope. It kicked some more, renewed its effort, and screamed. Jonas switched off the torch, went back inside.

More to reflect on . . . the authority of the families was based on the premise of extreme violence. Without violence the families had no voice. He thought of what *he* did, his own work, debated whether he was capable of "making a difference". Jonas closed the caravan door. Left the cat to finish its killing in darkness. He returned to his cold pork and made conversation about the hill fort that was useless without a water supply, and a garrison camp that had been abandoned because an emperor wanted a wall built elsewhere. And he told Vera that he approved wholeheartedly of her refusal to pick a posy of wild flowers, from the Coltsfoot, and Fox and Cubs, and Harebells blooms, it was a shame she could not have made a little display in a glass . . . And she talked about the flowers, and he about the annoying problems of the car's engine, and they discussed where they might go the next day – after getting advice on the vehicle. By the time their plates were clean and a new course served, the sounds of pain and terror were over. There were no rabbits in Raynes Park and so, safe to assume, Olaf believed that he had walked into a true believers' Paradise.

Without the sound of pain and terror, they heard the wind and the rain beating on their windows. Jonas thought it had been useful to dwell briefly on death; it had left him aware of consequences.

His mother had long gone from the table. And the long tall dick who had been eying her, and the other one who had talked relentlessly about the tortures inflicted by the Colombians, that had quite spoiled Patrick's enjoyment of the dinner – fancy food and foreign, but it would have been nice to eat had what the Bogotá and Medellín cartels practised not been dripped into his hearing.

The smart woman, head of this clan – Isabella Munoz – had understated beauty and was dressed to kill. She had made conversation with Patrick, when the others had left. Then she had pleaded work, had told him that his mother would be back soon . . . He had no phone, nothing to read, no earphones and music system. Sat there, waiting.

He was 21 years old. He had moderate acne, not across his cheeks but on his neck, under his ears. Sometimes, he would turn up his collar to hide the red blotches. They were a humiliation to him . . . Like a sour and lingering taste in his mouth were the stories of the Colombians' techniques. Patrick was thought to be the cleverest of Doloures's children, what she said anyway, the quiet one, dedicated to the name and prestige of the Govier family. But he could not enforce their status. He had been sick, violently, when he had seen Bengal "punish" a guy who had short-changed them. Patrick, as a teenager, had exposed a small fraud – worth only a few hundred pounds – and what Bengal had done with a pick axe handle, and the thoroughness of it, had caused Patrick to throw up.

He did not understand why his Ma had gone, and both the men, one tapping twice with his little spoon, on the rim of his coffee cup. Nothing said. His Ma had carefully folded her napkin, linen and hardly used, had not acknowledged Isabella Munoz or the quality of the meal, had stood and had kept her gaze on the carpet, had never looked up. Had not spoken to Patrick, had ignored him. Had gone round the table . . . For fuck's sake, nothing had been said, how did she know, why – and why? . . . and through the door. Had heard his mother's footfall on the stairs, polished wood, and echoing. Isabella Munoz had asked him quietly about his studies, and what had been his specialities, and he had tried to answer, stammered his responses. She had excused herself, shown courtesy, had said that she had work to complete, had fluttered her shoulders as if he, so young, would already understand the pressures of work in their trade . . . He heard a car scattering the drive's gravel as it drove away.

He sat alone until the woman in black came into the room.

He heard bed springs squeal.

In halting English she asked him if he wanted anything.

No answer. He listened to the slow rhythm from the room above.

Beer, wine, Coca-Cola?

Shook his head violently. Wondered if his mother was on top or underneath, and wondered how she could do this to him – and why. What the hell had he done to deserve . . . and the speed growing and the sound louder.

She said that she needed to clear the table, and worked around him. Glasses, cups, plates, unused spoons, knives, forks, went on to a tray, stacked noisily, but the clatter of cutlery and crockery could not drown the sounds that came from upstairs faster and more intense.

What girl Patrick was with was of less importance to his Ma than who dated Theresa, or tried to. His sister mattered in terms of alliances, and who she hitched with would be a matter of debate in the family, amongst all of them, and the question travelling as far as Walton and to Mikey. But Ma liked to know who he proposed taking to a dance or to a club, and might veto it if the girl were not thought *satisfactory*. Most of the girls crawled over him as if he were the equivalent of an Anfield kid and on big money, and if he tried to make conversation – finance or current affairs or the politics of the city – then their eyes glazed. If he kept his mouth shut, then he could have had it every night – except he could not bring a girl home and screw her in his bedroom which had the same fucking pathetic wallpaper from when he was a kid, and would have to go to a hotel, and . . . had never heard from his Ma any indication that she was going short and that she cared. Going faster and harder, and the springs complaining.

He dropped his head on to his arms. The woman in black, fucking crow, was wiping the table around him. He could see her run her tongue across her lips, and back again, not looking at Patrick. He imagined his Ma with the sweat running on her and her hair wild and her clothes draped across the floor, and shuddered.

Heard his Ma cry out from deep in her throat.

The woman had finished at the table and gave him a last glance – without expression – and then ducked her head as if that were a gesture of respect to which he was entitled, and carried the loaded tray into the kitchen. He listened for any further sound from upstairs, but none came. He assumed his Ma was exhausted, perhaps on her back, perhaps on her stomach, and wondered whether she was offered a cigarette.

Footsteps on the stairs, descending.

Patrick stood.

His Ma came in. She looked at him and her hair was messed and she'd a red patch spreading on her throat. Most of the buttons of her blouse were fastened, but her skirt was askew and she carried her shoes and her jacket. She blazed defiance at him. He thought it all planned, done with tested choreography, a demonstration of supremacy, like his Ma was a tart. Outside a car engine started up.

Mother and son went out into the hall and Sergio was standing at the bottom of the stairs. Not a word said, barely a shared glance. Their phones were on a table in the hall. They walked together, Doloures and Patrick, to the car. A driver opened the rear door. She slid in first.

"Don't look at me like that . . . In this life you earn your luck. I've just had a terrific shag, and I fucking earned it."

The first decision had been whether to go back to his cottage or hers . . . resolved, Kenny's.

"Something I need to say."

"Then say it."

But the second decision was harder, when to launch the talk . . . As before, their clothes were neatly folded on chairs.

"Something to say about us."

"God, that sounds serious . . . You have some plague, Kenny?"

"Not this week, but . . ."

Had thought about it, had thought too much about it, which had downgraded what they did on the bed. She seemed to

recognise it, and trying harder hadn't helped . . . The oldest of the
instructors, with a permanent exemption from retirement and an
expert on all things at Level One and whose words they hung on,
liked to say that instinct was better than thinking: used to quote a
mythical recruit about whom all the catastrophic anecdotes were
told – probably didn't exist but had his uses. One of them was
about thinking . . . *Every time he thinks it through, he then fucks it up.*
Her fingers tracing lines on his stomach and his fingers drawing
trails on her back, and he had done too much thinking. Probably
better to have let it rip when they were undressing or starting out,
but had baulked. Then thinking about the words he would use,
how to pitch it. Their heads were close together, shared a pillow,
and their mouths were close and their eyes scrutinising each other.
If he put it off much longer, she was liable to say that she was
going home, given him a pecked kiss which meant something or
nothing, and left.

"It is one week, Anna, just a week – and we had known each
other, acquaintances, then friends, and then moved on – just a
week since you came back here . . ."

"Are we going through your diary, Kenny? Didn't seem a bad
idea a week ago. Is it a bad idea now?"

Had started. Would finish. Alarm bells were clanging. Her eyes
were on him and he thought he detected a hardness but it might
have been puzzlement. Her fingers had stopped moving, and she
stared at him.

"About a future."

"What about a future?"

"You and me, that sort of future. Because I think I know you,
and . . ."

"Are you asking me to move in here? No. Asking if you can
come and shack with me? No. Does that deal with the future?"

"Thinking of us, Anna, you and me, doing an item – something
permanent."

"Am I permitted to ask, Kenny, why we need this formality?
Do I sign something in triplicate? Why?"

"If I was not here?"

"Where are you going?" She was laughing, softly. "Where are you going? Going to make coffee, going to have a shower, going to have a quick flip with the accounts and a calculator? Kenny, don't tell me the figures don't add up – going to do a runner?"

"I wanted to say that if we were somewhere else – what I was thinking – another place. There, and you were with me. Would make me happier than any other time in my life. You and me. Other cliffs, other beaches, other coastlines ... Anywhere, anywhere else than here, somewhere that you can paint. That is what I am saying."

"And your face is cut."

"Yes, but healing."

"And cut because of me?"

"Because being seen with you created a 'misunderstanding', yes."

"And a 'confusion'?"

"Something like that."

"And you persuaded the people who were *misunderstanding* and who were *confused* that I was a suitable person for you to know?"

The questions were drilled into him. Her fingers had moved higher, and she was holding the St Christopher, and there was a sharpness in her voice.

"Yes. I believe so."

"And when might you move, Kenny? Am I permitted to ask?"

"It was just a thought. One day, someday, another place."

"And the Biscuit Tin? What happens to the Biscuit Tin? Would that move somewhere else along with you?"

"Forget it – was just a thought."

He had thought what he would say, and had fucked up. He twisted away from her and the chain at his neck tightened, and she was wriggling to get clear of the bed and the chain snapped. His anger flared. He twisted and snatched at her hand and prised open her fingers and took the St Christopher from her. Something precious taken from him as if that were a red line crossed. If he hurt her, she did not cry out. He clutched the medallion – all that he possessed of his past. Had tried to move on, had failed.

He thought she would walk over to the chair where her clothes were stacked, get dressed, and he'd hear the front door open and close, and her car engine start and . . .

She kissed him lightly on the forehead. Then cuddled close to him and stretched out her arms and welcomed him.

"Not going to give you an answer now, Kenny. Will think about it. Maybe later, maybe next week."

And Kenny Blake, Level One and star performer in the team run by SC&O10, did not know where he would be next week. Nor who he would be . . .

She raised her arm, smelled the stink, felt the warmth of the fire that ate at the rag.

Theresa had been the teenage kid who was above and beyond the family's tactics of enforcement. Had called on Bengal when a boy had violated her upper thighs and he had come to her rescue and he had shattered the boy's fingers. More important, the boy had not squealed a denunciation from A&E. A lesson sent by Bengal. Enforcement. Recognised by Theresa, his kid sister.

Threw it towards the wide window of the travel agency owned by Nanette who had been bankrolled by Ma. Who had shown enough fucking gratitude to go and meet Jimbo Rawe; and Jimbo Rawe was a burden on the family, not as big a one as DCI Fanny Thomas, but fucking big enough. Threw it with all the muscle in her body towards the window, the darkened interior, and in an office at the back she could see that a light burned.

The business studies college should have ensured she would never dirty her hands, spoil her nails. Dirtying and spoiling were to be left to Bengal. Her role would be wearing a black trouser suit and a starched white shirt, to evaluate how the family money was best preserved. Where to invest in property, what shares to buy and which to avoid, and to be confident it was safe and beyond the reach of the Revenue people.

Should have turned, should have run. Wore the wig and the head scarf and the pebble was in her shoe. Knew where the street cameras were and when to duck . . . Should not have lingered to gawp – but it was her first time.

It arced. The rag, embedded in the bottle neck, was burning brightly, and the petrol would have bounced and sloshed, and some would have dribbled further up the wedge the rag made.

Knew about petrol bombs. Knew that the Molotov cocktail was the weapon of choice against the power of the state. The building, where the travel agency was based, was controlled by a cocky woman, full of self-importance – and Jimbo Rawe's tout. Seemed the right weapon for Theresa to use for her first time.

The flame shone brightly as the bottle climbed. It shattered the plate glass and the petrol spilled. Theresa squealed in excitement. Better than anything she had known before, better than the tongue kissing with that German guy in Spain and where he had felt her. Something supreme, the keenest of elation – and knew what she had missed out on. She watched as the first flames licked.

The alarm went off.

The speed with which the flames moved astonished her. They went in every direction and the posters carried the fire up the walls and then curled where they hit the ceiling and the flames fell back and moved faster.

She knew the woman. Had been with Ma to her back office. Had not thought anyone would be in the building at that hour. Had thought it a security light. Saw her coming out of her office, arms flailing which would have been about as daft as she was able. Theresa watched. A stuck-up bitch, thinking herself part of the family: nobody was, not without blood. Her hair caught. Her clothes were already burning and the fire was above her head and below it, and she was lit by it.

Nanette cannoned through the front door of her travel agency, no fiddling with locks or bolts, and the fire made a crude silhouette of her. She spilled out into the street, the rain making the flames hiss on her. People had come running, had started to roll her on the pavement and she was screaming.

Theresa walked away. Thought she had seen enough. She did not think Bengal would have run, so she walked as he'd have done, and her hands stank of petrol.

It was a dilemma. To let the cat back into the caravan with what was left of the prey . . . To let the cat back in and then fight it to retrieve the headless carcase and chuck it out of the door while hanging on to Olaf . . . Allow him to spend half the night scratching at the door and howling in anger . . . Shut cat and partly eaten rabbit out of the caravan for the night – and then try and sleep and know whatever he decided that Vera would worry . . .

The cat decided. It came in, bringing the rabbit, took it into its cage and settled down to feed further.

Jonas and Vera lay in their narrow bed, close and warm together, and the noise of the wind and the rain competed with the steady crunching of bones. The shoulders of the rabbit and its backbone would all be minced between Olaf's jaws.

Jonas always had his phone close to him at night, usually the bedside table. When it shook, he eased it down under the bedding and scanned the screen. A view of a house in a pleasant Liverpool suburb, a far bigger and better located property than he and Vera could have afforded: a mirthless smile. Little chance that Jonas would be attempting to import a tonne of pure processed cocaine powder and let it loose on the streets. Saw the girl hurry along the pavement and turn in at her front gate, and then glance either side of her, before diving inside the house. Lights came on and he tracked her into the kitchen and watched till she had started up the stairs. He felt like a voyeur . . . not certain whether Vera was awake and feigning sleep.

The phone vibrated. He would not switch it off, not now, not when the conclusion was so near. Frozen frames appeared in the form of a slide show. There would have been an accompanying commentary but his sound was turned down. A travel agent's premises was burned out, one person injured – the burns were probably life-changing. He saw the fire brigade there with pumps and hoses, saw an ambulance flashing blue lights. Saw the glowering face, along with the uniforms, of Fergal Rawe . . . He knew the woman's name, knew that she was a CHIS, knew that she was the source of the Govier woman's itinerary, knew that a price was paid . . . And he wondered how Nikko was and how it was on the last legs of the Atlantic crossing, and thought about Kenny who was Recalled to Life, and the word that played in his mind was *feral*. It rolled on his tongue and scraped in his throat, and the strength of the cat's jaws and the crushing of bones astonished him. He killed his screen, put the phone under his pillow, and wondered if Olaf would soon be sick, vomit it up – bone and muscle and meat and brain and fur – and so make room for further feasting.

"What is it, Jonas?"

"I was thinking of those persons who could have been domesticated but have broken clear of those disciplines and know no better than to kill and destroy, flaunt their violence."

"Is that Olaf?"

"It is not. It's just work. I forgive Olaf most things. It is hard to forgive people who are feral."

"Which is work. And this, Jonas, is holiday."

"Of course, good night."

She nudged him, quite a sharp blow with her elbow, enough to make the foldaway bed creak and for Olaf to stop his noisy chewing, consider them and then return to his meal . . . More than half the rabbit, Jonas estimated, was now lodged in the cat's stomach.

She said, "And tomorrow, early, you will deal with the car?"

"That's correct. Something not quite right, but you need not fuss about it." And thought of a woman whose life was changed by fire, and the ruthless cruelty of it.

"When you're dealing with it, Jonas, you will – please – be sensible."

"Sensible? A problem, I think, with the clutch."

"Yes . . . and be sensible, I beg of you. You always have been a rotten fibber."

His voice was small, as if he were humbled. "That's a promise. To be sensible."

13

It did not occur to Jonas that he should vary his clothing for holidays. Socks, trousers and the Tattersall shirt and his tie and jacket, and the brogues were all the same style as he wore every working day. He dressed as quietly as possible and was careful not to wake Vera. He stepped on the rabbit's legs, inevitable, and went outside. In the glove compartment of the car was an electric razor, always charged up, used for emergencies and when they were away and hot water was in short supply. He ran it over his upper lip and his cheeks and chin.

A little after seven and Jonas was on his way. He saw the farmer out with his dogs, hustling sheep towards another field. Wondered how sheltered was this man's life from the plague of cocaine addiction, whether he was protected from the ravages of inner-city violence, if . . . and waved to him as he set off down the lane towards the junction for the main road, west to Anglesey and the ferries to Ireland, and east back towards England and the city of a pop group and a football team. Jonas Merrick had never owned a record by the Beatles, had never consciously watched a football game featuring Liverpool, or any other side. A simple enough run. Leaving Flint away to his left, then turning off short of Chester, and connecting with a motorway and the signs for Liverpool and the Mersey satellites.

Married for thirty something years, Jonas would still have claimed that he knew little of Vera's inner thoughts. He was not one to confide when problems stacked against him, and he believed she also preferred to keep her concerns to herself. They did not share heartfelt emotions . . . Many at work in the surveillance team that used 3/S/12 seemed to want to sob on each other's shoulders and reveal details of relationships, breakdowns, illness. The way he was, and unlikely to change, but he worried for Vera. Would have been easier if she had accepted his lies, not indicated that she read his dishonesty. He was found out . . . and she probably had already realised that the only reason he had towed the caravan across half of England and then traversed the north Wales coastline, was to be here, here and now. He had never told her why, on the night of his intended retirement from the Service, he had *dared* to reach inside the clothing of a potential suicide bomber and had ripped clear the wires, had done it himself and excluded the "experts" from the palaver and circus of intervention. Had not explained why he had *braved* the fury of a Syrian veteran intent on mayhem and had handcuffed him. Had not told her what had driven him, a pinnacle of *rashness*, to link himself to the Sixer girl and get the most serious ducking in the Thames. Had thought explanations unnecessary, and probably would have been poorly articulated. Did she worry about him? He did not ask her to be anxious for his safety . . . all best left unsaid. But she had had his promise that he would be "sensible" and he assumed that would satisfy . . . He hoped to be a witness, nothing else.

Behind him, on the back seat, was the plastic bag presented him by Aggie Burns. With the bag was his trilby hat, that he would not wear, and the flat cap in a similar tweed to his jacket. His phone would guide him to the destination. Also on the phone were the early updates of the day. The only one of them likely still to be in bed was Nikko, and Jonas smiled at the thought of an untidy mess of clothing on his floor and probably a weapon leaned against a chair or dumped on a table beside dirty dishes or a takeaway's wrapping. There was a report of the positioning of the semi-submersible and its four tonnes of cargo. Fergal Rawe and Jak Peters would be heading for Departures, and Fanny Thomas going to the briefing she'd have called . . . And there was a woman in A&E with life-changing burns . . . He had started to follow the more detailed directions.

The traffic surged around him, shop workers and office staff and white vans and loaded buses, all heading as Jonas did into the heart of a great and historic community. He had no interest in the stereotype evaluation of the psychology of these people. No wish to learn why their local society had won a reputation for the greatest violence, the greatest addiction, the greatest criminal fraternity – and the greatest humour and the greatest wit and the greatest fun. Irrelevant to him.

He had no need to be there. Would have said it was a signature to his vanity, the wish to be a witness, then had started to worry about Kenny Blake and the need for evidence to be gathered in the next several hours, and a frown was settling on his forehead and he almost missed a turn at Runcorn . . . His phone rang. The AssDepDG.

"Yes?" Irritably.

"Don't snap at me, Jonas."

"Yes?"

"Merely courteous, merely asking. How near are we to seeing reward for our sloshing of cash in your direction? Reasonable for me to enquire."

"Very near, if things work out . . . And, which I am sure will hugely interest you, a young woman helping us with information now lies in hospital grievously injured in retaliation, and an agent will have to be close to the action tonight, or at dawn tomorrow if he is to gather the evidence required. We are on the edge, have to be – and many 'ordinary' people are on the front line, at risk. That is where we are."

"Jonas, I don't apologise, but you sound excessively pompous. The effect of lurking too long in the backwater?"

"Have a good day."

"And your location, Jonas, right now?"

"Pottering about, wondering which ruin to visit, which folly to examine – and I do believe the weather is lifting. Might be quite a good day."

The smell of goat lingered in his office.

An unpleasant smell and out of place. Had he been entertaining clients that morning he would have had to make excuses, but he had only three – they had declined to accept that he was shut for business that morning and had clumped up the stairs and hammered on his door. Hugo and Wilf, the back-up, had left the storeroom and taken their hardware with them. He thought the three of them made a poor assortment of bedfellows.

They were supposed to protect him, be near enough and able to intervene if he was threatened. And now he had an invitation to lunch, would be out of sight and out of range.

Anna had not refused him. Neither had she encouraged him. They were left treading water. Promised nothing . . . The alternative was the ferry home, a debrief by SC&O10, and a request from him to quit, and a gaggle of quacks turning up to check his psychological state, and the ditching of the identity of Kenny Blake. All done in a morning, the name would be erased from the National Insurance and National Health records, and the driver's licence data, and the bank accounts closed . . . Like he had never been. Had "never been" twice before, seemed repetitive, and the suggestion that he needed a "damn good break", somewhere off any well-trodden track, and a chance to sleep and shed the load, and "let's think about it again when the old batteries have been recharged, and let's not act hastily because we value you, really rate your professionalism". They could trip that out . . . The chance was that alcohol would get to be the medication, and a few girls who'd not understand why he didn't talk about life last year, or the year before, or family or . . . and self-pity would feature. He needed Anna Jensen, rated her as the ticket out.

After checking the code sequence of buttons on his phone keypad, what he had to press to alert the guys – which might bring them in time and might not – he left the office. It was tidy, paper and brochures straightened, the three gate-crashing clients apparently satisfied.

There was a mood of subdued misery in the café which washed over the customers; not even the gallows humour talk of the fortunes of the football team could cheer them.

The face of Fredo told him much. Easy enough to comprehend, did not have to be said. The cargo was close and the need for it to be successfully landed was acute. The life of Gabriel, son of Fredo, a king-sized delinquent tosser, was at risk. He took his place and waited to be served – and thought about the lunch to come, thought some more about the reputations of Hugo and Wilf, and the encrypted part of his phone messages alerted him to the arrival in Spain of his one-time control and also of the man who had first assigned him. The pace quickened, more violent than an hourglass, like they all were on a treadmill that had started to race.

"Your behaviour, Ma. So out of order."

"And if, just once in a while I want a satisfactory bedding then that's what I'll go and get," she had not snapped back at him.

"Was ashamed of you, Ma, could not believe it of you," he had not whined at her. "What you are missing, Ma, is that they walked all over us, like we were dirt."

"You'll get no apology from me, so wrap it."

"Thought we were decent players, what we are at home. Not to them we aren't, and you confirmed it."

None of that was said. No hissed exchange back at the hotel when they were dropped late, and not in the morning, and his Ma challenging him, daring him to start up on his criticism. Nothing said at breakfast where she had dug into the ham and the fruit and the cheese, and he'd managed one roll . . . and so it was closed. Not spoken of that day and would not be, Patrick thought, any day in the future.

Would not be him who told Bengal, not him who spilled it to Theresa . . . There had been no contact with home, Ma had insisted. Ma always said that addiction to phones was what brought down the families: even a guy as big as Cocky had talked too much on a phone. They were to meet again in the early evening, to agree how the cargo would travel, and at what cost. They walked out of the hotel, pilgrims and sightseeing tours all around them. Narrow streets and massive churches and stalls for souvenirs. All an industry in Patrick's mind, and one that paid well: none of the Govier family did religion, except for his grandmother, who minded Ma's dog, who went to Mass on a Sunday morning. The crowds swam around them; it was a good place to talk.

What she said about the merits of having the clan here, the Munoz people, fucking near brought tears to Patrick's eyes. He saw the grand woman who had hosted them, the one who told the tales of atrocities against informers and failures, and the one who had taken his mother upstairs. Hurt him to see them in his mind, but they would do business. He had the calculator and his Ma tossed him figures – how many kilos and how many kilometres covered, and more for the agents who did the collections and onward movements in Amsterdam. The Goviers liked to pick up their loads from service stations on the motorways of the north-east, have their cargo brought to them on a plate. Had never dealt with anything on this scale before . . . Why his dad didn't like it, why Mikey Govier thought they reached too high, why Bengal was against it . . . but Ma called the tune. They talked figures, what they would agree to – and likely it was pretty much anything that was put to them.

Later, they would be taken, Ma said, down to the coast. Would be pitch fucking black darkness. Necessary, of course, to see it happen. It was the biggest deal of their lives, the start of them being catapulted to the top of the ladder, had to be there. The landing and the unloading, would see it done . . . Back home late on Friday night or early Saturday, what Ma said.

He walked with his head up, was angry but did not feel danger.

Wilf asked, "Do you have close protection experience?"

"I don't. No."

Hugo asked, "You have weapons and firearms tactics experience?"

"Again, I don't. No."

And both said almost synchronised, "Very pleasant to have met you, Mr Peters, but can't really see what you bring to the table."

On the crib sheet of instructions listed in the handwritten note in the envelope delivered to him by the police at the café on Horseferry Road, was their number. For Jak Peters it had been a seriously bloody morning, a cab late in London and a scramble for the flight. A touchdown in Marseilles, then a sprint to catch the connecting flight, and a load of pilgrims on board – a hymn sung, even prayers said for the pilot's welfare, and a hell of a bad landing at Santiago. Another taxi, at a rip-off price, to Corunna. Sophie had rung him about Augustus's lost homework, and Benjamin had left a football boot on the bus and . . . he did not know when he would be back. She had rung again and he had not answered: she was the banker and handling billions, and he was a police sergeant and looking after Level Ones, as many as he had fingers on a hand. He had been told where they would meet.

"You see, Mr Peters, we have responsibility for his safety, and that's authorised by Box."

"So, without what we call 'experience', there is no way we'll allow you to horn in on decision-making concerning his safety."

He smelled the tang of livestock on them. Not unpleasant but out of place in the garden that was high above the Old Harbour. It fitted with his assessment of Jonas Merrick, gathered on the occasion when he had helped him cross the bridge over the Thames. They would be honourable, polite when necessary, and getting deviation from them would be harder than taking blood from basalt rock.

"Sorry Mr Peters, but we'll not tolerate interference."

"Best to get things out in the open, Mr Peters, sure you'll agree."

Jak Peters coughed it up. "Right, so where is Kenny now?"

A simple question, and a deluge of embarrassment.

Hugo said, "We left him in the café."

Wilf said, "He told us to leave him."

"And after he's finished in the café, he's doing some shredding. No visitors today, no clients. Then he's going out to lunch . . . Mr Peters, he is not easy."

"Keeping track of him is about as simple as minding frogs in a bucket. That is our problem. Where do you fit in?"

He scratched the back of his head. Looked out over the parapet wall on the edge of the garden. The tomb and its plinth were off to his right: had learned the poem at school. Thought it made death sound romantic, not a bad option. Lines learned young and not forgotten. *Slowly and sadly we laid him down, From the field of his fame fresh and gory: We carved not a line, and we raised not a stone, But left him alone with his glory.* A good way to go, except . . . could be the author knew little about gunshot wounds.

Jak Peters said, "If it were a matter of his safety, if that were the only consideration, then we could have flown him out yesterday. Wrapped him up in cotton wool and sent him home to Mum. It is about evidence. More's the pity, but evidence matters. Not suspicions and not innuendo, but documented evidence and eyewitness evidence. Otherwise it will have been a waste of his time and our money. He knows that."

"Which puts us where?"

"Between the old rock and the old hard place?"

"Going after evidence, what will satisfy in a trial, is the same factor that most puts our boy in the cross hairs."

"Ever since it started, it was a matter of gathering cast iron, watertight evidence. What convicts, what guarantees a prison sentence. That is why there is no place for cotton wool. That's my message and it won't slacken off."

He hitched up his rucksack that carried his bare necessities and a pair of walking boots. He was led back across the main drag and into the dark and narrow street where the sun had not managed to penetrate and where the wind blew hard. It would be a big coup if it were pulled off, but only if evidence were gathered – Kenny Blake's job and he was alone with it. At the far end of the street, and beyond the café sign, was a view out over the New Harbour and the ocean, all so calm and so unlike a place of war. He saw Kenny, his Level One, hunched at a table and deep in talk with a man who wore a white apron and whose face showed exhausted fear, and Kenny's hand was on the man's clenched fist, as if that might ease a pain.

The gull kept station with them.

He thought it a horrid scavenger. Diego had seen the carcase, reckoned it a dolphin's, but hard to recognise as other than more of the flotsam that floated past them. They still made good speed and the instruments told him that they were on course, that he had navigated well.

The carcase slapped against the side of the craft. It had the dull, glazed eyes of long-ago death but the gull had hovered and then dived and had pulled an eyeball clean out, almost surgical. It had flown up and had screamed a warning that the prize belonged only to this gull – except there were no other birds to hear. Diego and Matias, and their semi-submersible – of which only a metre was fully clear of the water – and the gull and the decaying dolphin were alone. Diego scanned for freighters or tankers or cruise liners or long-distance yachts as best he could, saw nothing . . . Heard nothing except the rhythm of the waves slapping against the hull, and the shriek of the bird, and the regular throb of the diesel-powered engine. When the dolphin's body began to drift clear, the bird – big and brilliantly white – went after it and settled on its skin and used its beak to puncture it and took a gobbet of flesh. Diego thought as time went on and his efforts to stay awake, alert, became ever harder, that he should begin to form a relationship with the gull, give it a name.

The lack of sleep was his greatest difficulty. Because he could not sleep his mind was alive with nightmare images. Always worst when Matias grunted or murmured a prayer, or belched, or gasped when they went into a trough and were shaken by the impact and then carried up high and again allowed to fall. Many hours since Diego had eaten, and many more hours since he had dropped his trousers and squatted over the bucket. He had leaned across from the wheel and half-opened the hatch and urinated towards the cresting waves but only with partial success and most of it was either blown back on to the ribbed flooring, swilling with what remained of the boy's vomit, or splattered his trouser leg.

Matias was asleep on the lower bunk, where the boy had been. Close to the bunk was the door to the engine. It was ajar. Out of it came the noise and the fumes from the clanking diesel workings. The interior of the cockpit area was now coated with a film of black oil. Diego's mother, who cleaned villas in Vigo, was the only woman he knew who had the muscle and the dedication to attempt cleaning the interior. He had used his elbow and a cloth to wipe the window glass. His own hands were blackened and every wrinkle was filled with dirty oil, and his fingernails. Matias's hands were the same.

Matias had slept, would not have realised that ever more frequently, Diego clung to the wheel with one hand and twisted round to check on him. The engineer used no blanket because the heat in the cockpit was intense. Each time that Diego turned and looked at Matias – he looked for his hands. The tool most used to keep the engine firing was the big wrench, dirty and rusted. If Diego had slept, *if*, it would have been a mere four silent steps across the cockpit and the wrench raised, and coming down on him.

He forced himself to stay awake, and the nightmare images were harder to escape.

The image that stayed longest with him was that of the face of the boy once the bin bag had slipped. He saw gulls competing to sink their beaks into the boy's flesh and the disturbance on the water would attract more of them. Should he have slept then Diego believed that the engineer would wake and his hand would grope and flutter until it found the wrench. Diego estimated that the wrench would weigh more than two kilos, maybe three. He would be sleeping, and Matias would creep close and cross the ribbed floor and would raise the wrench and bring it down on his head. Would not matter if he were merely stunned. He would be helpless, incapable of self-defence, and the hatch would have been opened and he would be manoeuvred through it, heaved out, might be conscious and might try to grab at a rail, but would slide away. It was what he feared most. Would be alive in the water and watching the craft, almost submerged, move away, and the gap would grow and his tiredness become ever more acute. He would drown, a blessed relief, and then the storm of gulls would descend on him: his eyes, his throat, his flesh, would be their reward . . . He thought that by now, if the boy floated, he would be unrecognisable.

Diego had evaluated his situation . . . No skills to fix the craft if the engine failed. Matias would know what to do, would coax more out of the beast – not Diego. There were intermittent squalls of rain but the wind kept constant and between the deluges – short and sweet – the horizon was clean. Without food, without sleep, without a sit-down on the bucket, Diego steered the *Maria Bernarda* towards the horizon where his gambling instincts told him was the shoreline . . . They would tell the story. Gathered in cafés and bars, the veteran smugglers would toast Diego, the semi-submersible captain who had brought the craft from the Amazon delta, had crossed the ocean, had brought it ashore, had landed a cargo worth in the region of £300 million. Only if he stayed awake, only if the wrench was not used to crumple him. He could not shout at the bird as a way of starting a friendship. Had he shouted he would have woken the engineer and his hand might have taken hold of the wrench.

Softly spoken, and no window open to carry his voice further, Diego murmured, "You are the only friend I have, only faithful friend, are not from the clans and are not employed in the brothel on the road to Ribadavia and are not peddling coke. Will the friendship end when you have a feel of the land being close? Will you leave me then? Will there be more bodies in the water for you? Tell me, is my body there, will my eyes be the delicacy for your stomach?"

He thought madness was close, and the engineer slept and Diego did not dare to.

He had aimed for the Tesco superstore and had found it, which was a pleasant surprise for Jonas.

He parked in the huge forecourt, shunning the bays near the main entrance, choosing a corner which had spaces around him, and doubted he would attract attention.

The wretched Aggie Burns had a viperish sense of humour. He slipped the high-visibility vest over his shoulders and rearranged his flat cap. The wind played havoc with the rubbish but the edge was off the early morning cold: he watched as plastic wrapping and dead leaves careered across the open space and towards the store entrance. On the front of the vest was stamped *Key Worker* . . .

It was hard to make Aggie Burns crack a smile, but when she did it usually bit . . . and on the back was the word *Potholes*. On both front and rear were the logos of Liverpool City Council, a complicated heraldic montage, featuring a cormorant and much else, and the council's motto, *Nisi Dominus Frustra*, and Aggie had included a note that this translated as, "Without God all is in vain." And more from her treasure chest – a lanyard with his ID card as John Smith, which he slung round his neck. He glanced a last time at the map on his phone, turned it to mute. Had a main road to cross, and the traffic blasted past him.

He carried in his right hand a spray can of blue paint.

He walked the length of a pleasant enough road, on the left side, and looked at the gaps between parked cars until he found his first target . . . The note left by Aggie Burns reported that a Council inspector would only ever visit pot-holes that were more than 25 millimetres in depth. He bent and sprayed a rough circle around it.

After crossing another road and having found another pothole, Jonas realised that it was quiet. There was sunshine on his face and it threw his shadow across the road. Vera would have noticed it before he did, but Jonas could have sworn that coming into that road he met an absence of birdsong. Little beggars should have been glorying in the change of weather. He was used to the shouting of tits and chaffinches and blackbirds in the neighbours' gardens every time that Olaf went out on a safari patrol round the garden in Raynes Park: heard nothing.

He kept his head down, appearing to examine the road surface. The house was at the far end of the road, would be easy enough to identify as it was the only detached one on either side. And he had gazed at that home on his phone screen or his desktop screen every day for almost an entire year. He would be on the opposite side of the road and at the end of the road would take another left and dawdle back to the superstore. Only a reconnaissance. He already knew much of the life of the road, when the workers left home, when the kids went to school, when the Govier family showed themselves.

It was a nearly clean pavement with only one heap of dog excreta and only two places where the previous week's rubbish bags had been split open when collected. He heard a clunking noise behind him, an impact and an engine straining and a white van came alongside, its sides displaying the contact details of a plumber. A voice yelled at him.

"Heh, you lazy bastard, what about that one I just hit. Near broke my tyre. You just walked past it."

He did not back off from the accusation. Smiled in a kindly but helpless way. "New regulations. Doing the left side today and the other side tomorrow. It's not me that makes the regulations."

The van drove off. He was eyed by a passing postman, like he was a dinosaur from a long-gone age. He smiled and studied the road surface and considered how the residents of this pleasant road, with bare trees and neat gardens, enjoyed living cheek by jowl with a serious criminal family. Perhaps they were the nicest of people and supported the church roof fund, and donated to help spina bifida fundraising. He was approaching the camera. Knew where it was. Aggie Burns's people would have made a better fist of it. Jonas was a rookie. Supposed to be examining the road but allowed his eyes to drift up and across to the far side.

A bland house. A recessed front door between matching bay windows that were mirrored above. Blinds down. Built of mottled brick and a slate roof with chimneys at either end. A neat garden in the front, and a small car parked on the street but room on one side for an off-road pull-in. He wondered how she did, Doloures Govier, and whether anxiety built in her mind. A defining moment was fast approaching . . . An interesting woman, he thought, and not displaying the bling and baubles that were supposed to go hand in hand with her trade. Lived quietly, what they called "under the radar", and the house fitted that image. The attraction of travelling to Galicia, liaising with the Munoz clan, was that the family would have money coming out of their ears. Except that Jonas Merrick, a clerk, a little man, a witness and a voyeur had noted her. His concentration had drifted, and a car came fast and braked behind him.

He recognised Xavier Govier.

A glance was thrown at him as the car door slammed. Jonas thought he looked haggard. Tired, drawn, unshaven and yesterday's clothes that might have been slept in. The glance interrogated him. Then indifference, would have seen the signs on the vest. He thought Xavier showed no more polish than a working scaffolder might have displayed, or a brickie. Would like to have made eye contact but did not, stayed within the disciplines. Xavier went up the path and was taking a key from his pocket as the front door opened. Jonas could not stare, just flicked his head and scratched his ear as if it itched and badly: a little lesson in surveillance practice. Saw Theresa Govier. Had expected rather a good-looking girl, something a cut above the rest of the family, with her academic ambition, perhaps the one who could be weaned off the family influences, might even be a Crown witness – would fight tooth and nail to stay out of gaol. Untidy hair, jeans sagging on her hips, a T-shirt with a latticework of creases, and big eyes that caught Jonas. She clung to her brother, and they went, arm in arm, into the house, squeezed through the door. The matriarch was away and they were home alone . . . and it would be worse for them, Jonas hoped, and saw in his mind the young woman whose life was altered, and . . . a shout was directed at him.

"About damn time. You know how long it is since I rang the council? God, what do you people do all day? Look at it. Damn great hole. Could turn your ankle in it. Could wreck your tyre. At last you deign to show up . . . when are you going to fix it?"

A woman stood beside the man. He knew them. Elderly, his own age, crushed and angry. Knew them well from when they walked out onto the pavement and past the lens and never looked down at it. She clung to his arm.

"It's not the man's fault, David. Leave him be. It's the cutbacks. I'm sure he's doing his best."

Jonas nodded to them, and touched his cap. David Potter strode into the road, took his arm and led him to the hole. Jonas had not the heart to tell him that the dip in the road surface was probably not deep enough to qualify for repair but thanked him for identifying it and circled it with the bright blue paint and ambled on, and noticed the glint of light that was the camera.

Back inside, David Potter said, "I was going to give him a piece of my mind. Did you see him? What sort of people do they employ? Doubt he's ever seen a day's work in his life. He hadn't even noticed the hole I rang about. So frustrating . . . Don't know how many times I've rung about that hole. Jenny, I don't know what we're going to do. I'm going to speak to that Fanny Thomas. Have it taken out. Getting chest pains, all about them over there . . . That man, have you ever seen a council worker dressed like that?"

"I didn't know she'd be there."

He stroked her hair, like he was a girl child, and she was a doll, did it softly.

"You did well. Fast and clean," Bengal said, little more than a whisper.

"Never seen anything like it, when it burst – the fire. Just fantastic." A giggle from Theresa.

She sat at the kitchen table. He was behind her and her head was against his stomach.

"Did better than well, and tonight we go again."

"Can I say, Bengal, that . . .?"

"Say what you like, girl, exactly what you like. Deserve to say what you want."

"Bengal, we are worth millions, real millions, and there's going to be more. Too much to count. We are going to be the biggest people in all of this shit-heap city. It's what I think it is, a shit heap. This place cuts nothing with me. But it's where we are and we are going to be the biggest. We don't have limos and rollers, don't have parties in the big hotels and fizz splashing. We'll not show it off here, not make it easy for them. But, it's our time."

She faced her audience in their ready-room.

"And here, guys, is the DCI from the Serious Crime Unit, Fanny Thomas . . ."

She was introduced by a sergeant, a veteran of the Armed Response Teams whose face and its almost bored look was designed to say "seen it all, done it all". Except he hadn't.

". . . over to you, ma'am."

There were five of them sitting at a long table in front of her. Water bottles on it, and notepads and pencils, and behind them and filling a wall, was a map of the Merseyside area for which they had responsibility. In policing terms, they were the nuclear option, firearms. Their cars were in the parking lot, and in the secure boxes were the H&Ks and the gas and the flash-bangs, and the ammunition, and the vests that were proof against low-velocity incoming fire, all the paraphernalia that marked out their different status. She knew most of them, but there was one young lad who was new. In her line of work she was their most frequent client. They took their mood from their sergeant, seemed only marginally interested but that would have been for show. They sat, she stood, and behind her was Joe, and he'd be scowling at them. There were four men and a lone female; she had a love bite on her throat, and her efforts at covering it with her shirt collar were unsuccessful. Fanny thought her lucky, long time since she'd owned one.

"I don't want to start a revolution. Don't wish to cause offence. I can't tell you the target for an operation that will hopefully get going tomorrow morning, early. Nor can I tell you the location. Why am I keeping you in ignorance? Because I am instructed not to divulge. Why? Because those from higher echelons do not fully trust me with such information, nor do they trust you. I do not gild it – that is how it is. To me, this lack of trust is insulting but it is handed down to me by those, and I've confirmed it, who sit high above my pay grade. The rest of the day is your own, but the team, and my crowd, will be operational from midnight. Events will happen which will cause us to deploy. I want you all to know this is a first for me . . . I have never before been required to give such an asinine and humiliating briefing. But I have to live with it."

None of them, their sergeant included, could be said to have "seen it all, done it all". Fanny knew the soft underbelly of the firearms gang. They carried the weapons, had the high-powered performance cars, liked to think of themselves as an elite. None of those sitting in front of her had ever done it. None of them had ever squeezed the trigger sufficiently to discharge a bullet, or do a "double tap", and drop a man. Had never shot to kill, seen the target collapse and then the blood start spilling . . . and none of them would know how they would be in the first few seconds after the discharge and while the recoil of the weapon was still numbing their shoulder muscles.

Joe told them where they should be at midnight, when the shift started.

One of them asked, quiet and innocent, "Will this be, ma'am, a rural or an urban location? Quite different engagement procedures if . . ."

"Don't go trawling. You'll be told when you need to be. Why this procedure is adopted is simple. It's about corruption. That is the world we live in, and don't go bleating to the Federation about it. Corruption exists . . . and this is how we beat it. Thank you."

Fanny left, and Joe with her. Likely she had pissed them off and she would have accepted that is a price worth paying, well worth it.

"It's not my feckin' fault I can't tell you. Don't go blaming me."

"And what the hell am I supposed to do?" was the DLO's response.

Met in Arrivals at Madrid-Barajas, Jimbo Rawe was not yet out into the fresh air before the scrap had started.

"You are supposed to do what I ask you. Supposed to be able to get favours done and fast, have contacts that facilitate. In other words to do your feckin' job."

"This is not, didn't you know, some hick place in the third world where the colonial power snaps its fingers and it's action time."

Not in a best humour, Jimbo Rawe had been up before dawn, had endured a fast ride to Manchester, then caught the first flight to the Spanish capital, and the leg room had been wanting, and breakfast off, "staff shortages", and Freddy Ashe had been at the barrier with that look on his face of a little bastard that's gone native. Most of the Drugs Liaison Officers, in Jimbo's opinion, were settled comfortably in their billets around Europe or the Americas or in south-east Asia and guarded their friendships jealously and represented their host nation's interests – or as Jimbo would have put it *know where their arse is covered and won't rock any boat, and have a little villa tucked away on the Spanish coast, or south of Naples or in Florida or on an island away from Bangkok . . . need shaking up, which is fun to do.* A good argument was always enjoyed by Jimbo, a dispute and raised voices always calmed him.

"Are you seriously suggesting that I use my contacts with Finance or Customs or the GRECO? In case you are unfamiliar with that unit, it's the *Grupos de Respuesta Especialpara el Crimen organizdo . . .*"

"Don't give a flying feck what they're called."

"And tell them that we have knowledge of a major drugs run into their country but we don't trust them sufficiently to say where, when, what weight, who's doing it. Is that your idea of cooperation?"

"It is what you will do."

"Perhaps you would consider turning around, walking back inside and taking the next flight out."

"And perhaps, Mister Ashe, you might consider going back to your apartment and starting to pack while telling the little woman that your recall will be with immediate effect and should be on your phone within an hour . . . and most of the cash salted away while on generous expenses will go in your tribunal fees. You will not get your dismissal overturned, I promise it."

They had reached the DLO's car . . . Freddy Ashe was from Revenue and Customs and despised by the UK police, common to all forces. Police were disliked for being overpaid and ineffective by the Customs investigators. A trait of Jimbo was that his voice dropped as he became more threatening, went almost to a whisper, and no one who flogged the same route to the parking area would have overheard a word that Jimbo uttered. The DLO had much to lose, and acknowledged it, predictably.

"You have to understand that the Spanish loathe us. They loathe our tourists getting pissed in Benidorm, loathe our clinging to the Rock, loathe our constant reminders of their recent fascist history, loathe the criminality we have dumped on them. Want some more?"

"Just want you to earn your corn. It is a Box job and you'll be told more when it suits, not before. I am not saying it will be a landing in the Corunna or Cambados or Pontevedra or Vigo area – I don't know. Not saying how the cargo is coming. Not saying where our intelligence is based. Not saying which clan is involved. You will have earned your corn, Mister Ashe, when you *persuade* your chums to shelve the loathing, put some boys on standby, and wait till we think the time right. If you can't do it then start packing and boxing your stuff."

The DLO said it was 600 kilometres, would take five and a half hours, and that it were best done there. Should not mire the request in the bureaucracy of a Madrid headquarters.

Jimbo Rawe said, "Drive carefully, but fast, and steady enough for me to catch some sleep. Just so as you understand, plenty of this is down to me, and I'll not be happy to see it fecked."

He settled in the car, and wondered if he would recognise Kenny Blake, and did not know how the last hours would play out – and who would be left standing, smiling.

She stood over him and her smile was thin, almost wintry.

Isabella Munoz said, "I include you for a reason, Kenny."

"I am grateful for the invitation – and my face is healing well."

There were three tables in the restaurant that were reserved, but they were not separated from the other punters taking lunch. The owner fussed and showed due deference but did not fawn. He had already been seated at a table when she and the rest of her party arrived. He was decently dressed, nothing more. She was, to Kenny, almost unrecognisable: faded jeans, sneakers, a T-shirt, a loose leather jacket, and a headscarf.

She said, "What happened was fun, a show, and you came through well. For me it is forgotten. But not forgotten by my younger son. You did not convince him, either of guilt or innocence. So, Kenny, you are watched by him, closely, and I hope you will earn his trust. I wish to say this, Kenny . . . should I be wrong, and rarely am, should Sergio's suspicion be justified then you would be – literally – ripped apart. Every method of inflicting pain and humiliation that has been learned from our Colombian associates would be visited on you. I am being very frank, very honest."

"I aim to gain the trust of all my clients, those with large portfolios and those with small savings. I harbour no ill will, and I hope soon my face will have completely healed. I appreciated your support."

Which was the dry and coded way of saying that her stripping along with him, her in darkness and him in a flashlight's beam, had been noted. She touched his wounds, briefly, not with tenderness but perhaps with concern. There was a local official, also with a stake in the Biscuit Tin, a policeman but in rough civilian clothes and two trawler owners who had been up the stairs to his office and had brought plastic bags full of bank notes, and the chief executive of a factory for processing canned fish who lodged regular sums with him – and others that he knew vaguely, and the Liverpool pair.

Doloures Govier interested him. She seemed ill at ease, anxious to be somewhere else, anywhere else, uncomfortable, and she wore a dress that his mother would have called "frumpish". There was a boy who looked just out of his teens, young enough to have acne throbbing on his neck, and suspicious and glowering and staring hard at Kenny. He was not close to them, was at the end of a table and next to a trawler skipper and opposite the factory manager, then another table, and beyond that were Isabella and Sergio and the English couple: he was not introduced to them.

Kenny chose octopus, and would later have some cheese. He would not drink. He would make pleasant and asinine conversation, and the stress welled. Ever closer, the moments when he would provide evidence, indisputable and which could not be challenged, or all the weeks, months, years here and living the lie were wasted. How hard should he push to gain such evidence?

He recognised what he had already achieved, but it was insufficient – and recognised also the inevitable dangers, stacking up, of the next hours.

"I can't get closer," Hugo said.

"The place is crawling with their people," Wilf said.

"Which leaves him on his own," Jak Peters said.

They were parked a good quarter of a mile from the restaurant. They had no view of it. Any other time, it would have been pleasant to take a stroll into the village and walk along the esplanade, not minding the wind nor the chance of a rain squall, and see the pleasure yachts and launches at their moorings, and the trawlers tied up and the crabbers, and see the faces, good and old and interesting, of the villagers. Not that afternoon. They had seen Kenny arrive, and then a small cavalcade of cars – not special, not extravagant – and the escort for a person of importance had been obvious. They would have stood out, so they sat in the car.

"What does it mean?" Jak Peters asked.

"Pays your money . . ." Wilf said.

". . . Takes your choice," Hugo said. "My thought, the beast comes in tonight."

From Jak Peters, "And the little runt who called the shots is off on his holidays."

"In full battle gear, they were lined up across there, Vera, and led by big women – the chroniclers said they were fierce, bare-breasted, formidable, coated in body paint – and they shouted and yelled and . . ."

"There is no call, Jonas, to be vulgar."

"A matriarchal society. There were druids as well, and all the human sacrifice stuff to bolster a chance of winning. And we are where the legions were, and Suetonius Paulinus, and he had the full force of the Fourteenth and the Twentieth and the Ninth. To succeed he had to cross the Menai Strait. A day like this, Vera and just short of two thousand years ago, and this would have been a vantage point."

"Somewhere for an eyewitness?" She had humour, never over-cooked, and she had not asked him whether a mechanic had managed to fix the problem with the car's engine, or how much it had cost, whether they would have to send off for a spare part. His lie had been ditched, but he had not explained where he'd been or why: nor would that have been expected.

They were on the south side of the channel, racing because of the incoming tide, that separated the north Wales mainland from the island of Anglesey. The water patterns had a rip to them. On the far side was a steep bank, cluttered with houses, and further west were the road and rail bridges spanning the water. He did not expect Doloures Govier, the matriarch currently of interest to him, to make a final naked stand, as the druids' women had, or that Isabella Munoz would match her but thought both of them formidable. Not that Jonas Merrick had three battle-hardened legions to direct, nor did he rate himself the equal of that Roman commander who would have stood close to them and evaluated them, and who'd have had supreme confidence in victory . . . would lose men, suffer casualties, yes – would expect that, but would win. He doubted Suetonius Paulinus would have worried about poor Nanette or the Potters beleaguered in their home, or Kenny Blake who was beyond reach of protection, almost.

"Get on, Jonas. What happened?"

"It was bloody. The bare-breasted women had a bad time. The cavalry horses swam across and the boatmen from the Rhone used flat-bottomed craft to get the heavy infantry over . . ." He was pleased that he had been able to get a glimpse of Xavier Govier, and of Theresa, and of the house, and he would be back the following morning with his Council vest and his spray can of blue paint. And he would be well back and out of their reach when he gave Fanny Thomas the signal to move forward. Would all be choreographed on his phone as reports came in from the Spanish coast, and arrests were made there, and then the final swoop on the Govier's territory. ". . . I suppose that for most of those Romans

– and they were written up by Tacitus – who caused the mayhem with the women it was just another day at the office – know what I mean?"

"Let's hope they managed to stay sensible," she said.

They went back to the car and decided to cross the bridge and drive to the extremity of the island and see . . . He had not told Vera that Tacitus reported the beheading of many of the fallen, and their heads being dunked in honey as a preservative, and they were the trophies of the day and likely taken all the way home for display – and the women's were of greatest value. First stop would be the Din Lligwy farming settlement, Roman and British, which he imagined Vera would find interesting. They'd go afterwards to Ty Mawr, Iron Age, and see hut circles . . . He thought it a new addiction, to be there at the end – and a contradiction of his old name in 3/S/12, *The Eternal Flame*, who "never went out".

Jonas smiled limply and led her back to the car.

14

An excavation team was working at Din Lligwy. It was a small site, less than half an acre, but the foundations were in good order, and sheep must have recently cropped the grass around the stonework. A board explained that the place had been an Iron Age settlement, then home to Roman marauders searching for mineral wealth, then the start of an interbred community, Romano-British. He wandered, was wrapped in his own thoughts, but attentive to his phone texts. He peered into the shallow trenches where eight or nine adults were kneeling in wet mud, and used spatulas and trowels, and one couple boasted toothbrushes, and all were working busily. They seemed content, but Jonas harboured no envy. He fielded messages from Fanny Thomas, from Bogotá and Nikko, who probably by now was dressed in his jungle camouflage, and from Fergal Rawe who was en route to Galicia, and turned suddenly on uneven ground, could have been an old rabbit hole, and saw Vera.

She stood on the far side of the settlement, her back to him. A man sat on a huge-faced stone – a miracle how it could have been put in place 2000 years before, or more. A dismal looking man, hunched inside an overcoat and with a beret pulled down on his head, and his legs wet from the previous shower, and he was talking to Vera. Seemed a one-sided conversation without pause . . . and his wife looked round, seemed to need help. The archaeologists worked on, ignored him. He looked bored, like a child taken on an adult expedition and then left to amuse himself, and failing. Not that Jonas was an expert on any childhood except his own.

She came to him.

"Everything all right, dear?"

"Nearly, but unsettled. Him over there . . ." She pointed at the man on the stone. "Rather extraordinary, Jonas. He said his name was Knacker. Never heard of anyone called that. Isn't it about collapsed and old horses, no longer able to carry on, and taking them away for cat food, what Olaf eats probably? That's what he called himself, Knacker, and I was silly enough to stay and listen to him. Said he had worked for the Secret Services, time in the field, handled agents. Said that he had been with them until the life was drained out of him. Went on about 'ordinary people', whoever they are, sleeping safe in their beds at night because – I am trying to quote – *rough men stand ready to visit violence on our enemies*, and he said that he was running some of them, but he was out of it now, not wanted, of no value. He just had memories, and damn all else, he said. He went on, 'I played God – was then heaved out and dumped. No gratitude, it's what they do with Secret Service officers when it's thought they're past their time. I'd like to tell you about Murmansk, my time on the Russian border and close to the wire and running a Joe on the far side and not knowing whether he'd make it out. My responsibility for sending him – doing the God imitation. Have you got a minute or two?' I'm sorry, Jonas, but I fled."

The man sat on his stone, did not move and might already have forgotten Vera. But a woman from the dig, smeared in mud, had crawled up out of the pit and had come over to them.

"Sorry about that. Was he nattering about playing God? Being let go by one of the intelligence outfits? The pills usually shut him up, but perhaps their effect is dipping. We all have our little crosses to carry, and he is mine, bless him. He has a vivid imagination, and weaves a good tale. Again, my apologies if he bothered you."

He took Vera by the arm and led her smartly towards the gate, and back towards the parking area.

Vera said, "You don't need to drag me, Jonas . . . Was that a truth or just the rambling of a sad mind? What do you think?"

He did not answer her.

The man's words, repeated to Jonas, had struck deep. He doubted there was a false word in the speech as delivered to Vera. He could remember, with crystal clarity, the evening that he had been scheduled officially to leave Thames House, attend a gathering, one glass of warm *prosecco*, accept a gift voucher, be turfed out into the evening air with the titters behind him of those who had bothered to attend. In a remote field and eyed by ragged sheep, he felt sympathy for Knacker.

He turned, yanked at Vera's arm, and led her back towards the settlement, across the open space and between the outlines of the dressed stones, away from the digging.

He faced the man, who seemed puzzled that the two of them had returned and cringed slightly.

"No need for that, sir," Jonas said. "Just wanted to offer you my thanks for sterling service. Much appreciated. Doubt any other beggar will tell you that. All good wishes, sir . . . they're an awful crowd who have charge of us, and best ignored. I wish you well, sir."

Vera was looking for flowers and Jonas was sobered. He tried to smile, made a pig's ear of it, felt the burden of it, playing God.

He would walk behind her but not beside her.

Lunch finished, Kenny realised that he was to be part of a show, a display of power.

He did as he was told. Beside her were her sons, a half dozen steps back were the Liverpool woman and her own son. She walked in the road and the traffic melted to the far side, hugged the kerb and stopped. Motorists wound down their windows, chucked away their fags, smacked their horns. Shoppers and mothers collecting children, and men who were gathered on the corners, all ducked their heads in respect. Hands were held out and she took some, and old men tried to kiss her hand, and old women wanted to hug her. She was the power in this community.

He had seen Sergio pay in the restaurant but that was only because it would have been a loss of dignity for her to accept a

free lunch. So many people were dependent on her – on the
trawlers and the speedboats, in the canning factories. They would
be out at night to bring a cargo ashore, driving the lorries for the
short-haul journeys to the hiding places in the hills, and to the
French border and beyond. He saw the affection, the gratitude,
saw that none of these people would have considered taking a
government reward; would not have informed on her. He heard
the word "Arnela". Had heard it used at the table where the chief
executive officer and the fishermen had sat.

Word would have spread in the village that she was entertaining
guests, at a local restaurant. A thin line had formed along the
pavement and she had a word for most of them. She was the
government, the authority in the village. He had sat near to a
policeman at lunch and they had exchanged banal talk about the
football team, and about the weather, and about the price of potatoes. He had no doubt that the officer would not relay intelligence
to his superiors, let alone to the retained agencies. He would have
been valuable eyes and ears, and his wage from her would have
made a difference to his standard of living. Had heard it said
again, an older man who might have been deaf from years in the
engine room of a trawler and who she had spoken to and who had
declaimed he would be there: would be at "Arnela".

She did not hurry herself, took time to talk, and to listen. One
car came, would have been driven by an outsider, and was held
up and just the once the man hit the horn, and he was surrounded
by those from vehicles that had stopped – had not needed telling
– and he would have been lectured, and would also have seen
the hands that fingered his wipers and could have torn them off,
and seen the car keys that were held so close to the paintwork of
his doors, and had needed little persuading before switching off
his engine. He thought it a "progress". Kenny assumed that
disputes would come to her: arguments about old land sales, the
payment of debts, bad faith among neighbours. Not wanting
lawyers nor officialdom but satisfied to accept simple justice –
and perhaps to have work given to a problem child – anything;
above all the sense of being with the team that did not know

defeat. When she stopped, Kenny stopped. When she moved forward, he did.

He was recognised. Some of the men, standing patiently on the pavement waiting for their turn to catch her eye, to bob their heads, had come to his office. The connection they saw now was of importance to the future of *La Lata de Galletas*. The future . . .? It had none. They were in ignorance . . . He was seen to walk a few paces behind her, but that was acceptance. There were body-guards who went at her pace, wearing jackets that sagged under awkward weights, and she decided whom she would stand beside, or crouch if the old person was wheelchair-bound or if a woman had a handicapped child.

Kenny understood that none of this was for him. Nor to impress upon a woman and a kid that they were merely small-bit customers. Probably did this once a month . . . might have been in any village along the line of cliffs and creeks, bays and beaches, that was the Coast of Death – where she did business, where her millions were made.

Her cars were parked some 150 yards from the restaurant. She had quickened her pace, did not turn to smile and wave as if she were a "celebrity", did not need to; she was the matriarch. At the car, driver already behind the wheel and a guard in the front passenger seat, she turned and, beckoned, for Kenny to come forward.

He thought he had been tested, had not been found wanting, had deflected the idiot in paranoia about the artist, and the bitter woman who had thieved from her own charity. Reckoned himself, in their eyes, to be clean. Not hurrying, staying as his own man, he went towards her. He passed the mother and her kid. All of the family, as he would have expected, spoke good English, augmented with the guttural accent of Galicia. He had learned enough of their native language to be able to speak in short sentences and use the codes and dialects of the Atlantic coast.

"You enjoyed your meal with us?"

"Very much, thank you."

"We have business tonight."

"I wish you success."

"And business for them."

"I hope you meet with success in your business."

"Would you like, Kenny, to be with us on the beach tonight?"

"I think not. I am an investment manager. Happy with that."

"It would be entertaining, a diverting experience."

"Thank you, but no . . . And there is a girl, the artist."

She looked keenly at him, then got into the car. Her entourage loaded up. Kenny Blake noted that the English kid frowned at him.

They drove away and the traffic was moving again. He nodded absently to those men whom he knew. Kept going, wanted away. And passed two men who hugged in friendship, but would meet again, and soon, and at "Arnela".

And realised he had achieved the pinnacle for a Level One. He was inside the clan, was accepted, and knew the names and had the memory sticks. Had the records of how money had come, cash in banknotes and squashed down into suitcases before the transfer to St Peter Port. A supreme moment in Kenny Blake's professional life. He could only shrug because the pride in what he did was leaching. There were cliffs at Gavioteiro, a remote headland and far from a lighthouse, and a good road, and the Praia de Arnela was a beach hardly known except by locals who needed secrecy for their chosen trade . . . It would be the place where evidence could be gathered.

A last throw. He went in search of Anna Jensen. In his pocket, not yet mended, was the St Christopher and its broken chain. He needed to be with Anna Jensen and watch her work. Lived in hope, but fragile, and should have been punching the air and did not.

They were dropped at the hotel in Santiago.

The driver told Doloures when they would be picked up, but approximately. A call would be made to the desk to confirm: they should prepare to get wet and be cold . . . like it was a bloody school outing, Patrick thought.

They stood on the hotel steps. He tugged at his mother's arm, pointed towards the big square where the grand church was . . .

He tugged at her arm. They walked among the crowds, the believers who sought inspiration, had that look of happy adoration, and he led her where there was no chance of bugs, microphones, wires.

"So . . . what is it?"

"Where we've just been, what we've just seen."

"We saw her do a walkabout, like she was royalty. She would have reckoned that was class. Not as I read it. I think she's just pushing her fucking luck. You'll not get me doing that, and . . ."

"Not that, Ma."

"Didn't cut with me. They treat us like we are dirt, Patrick. Last night and again today. What happens, happens. What's done is done . . . I reckon Cocky could have done that, show-boated. Where is he now? Banged up, likely going to stay banged up for years more, going to stay banged up so long he'll be old when he gets to walk out, and . . ."

"Ma, can I have a chance to speak?"

"What? Speak about what?"

"About that guy."

"What guy? Spit it out. What guy?"

"The finance one."

"Didn't have a word to say for himself. Never spoke to me. Speak to you?"

"Didn't need to. Just watched me."

"What the fuck are you saying, Patrick?"

"What I thought, Ma . . ."

"For God's sake, before I wet myself, what did you think?"

"I thought he was a cop, Ma."

She was rooted. Crowds swayed round them – nuns and clergymen and pilgrims and sightseers and hustlers flogging fridge magnets and keyrings. She gazed at him. Would have been working out the chances that an English investment manager, running a little business in a back street in Corunna – what she had been told – well trusted, and with clan business in his pocket, was an undercover cop. And the sums, because she had led her family into sending the Munoz people two million in advance, two fucking million, and the space under the floorboards bloody emptying. Believing Patrick, doing a runner and cutting adrift, going home?

"Good try, Patrick . . . I don't think so."

"I think so."

"Sergio says they checked him over. That's the reason for the marks on his face. Says he gave the right answers."

"Pillow talk, Ma, was it?"

She slapped him. People stared. She was hurrying away in the direction of the hotel.

He followed her. No one ever listened to what Patrick had to say. He was sure of it. Would not have said it if he had not been sure. It was his eyes. When he was a kid, not ten, he had sat with his Dad, and Mikey had told him about undercovers, and what to look for – the guy who was too good to be true – and Mikey had said it was always in the eyes.

Kenny had gone to a backstreet jewellery shop with his medallion and the broken chain. Jak Peters was across the street, and held a tourist map and looked confused. An easy enough moment for Hugo to walk towards Kenny's car and seem to drop his fag packet and then manoeuvre it with his boot so it was further under the chassis, then bend, almost kneel and reach forward to retrieve it. Peters admired the tradecraft. The bug was deeper but with the same width and length as the fag packet, and had a heavy duty casing on it, and a magnet. The bug would have gone live, and the fag packet put back in Hugo's pocket. Wilf had stayed in the car.

Kenny had been looping the medallion on the repaired chain over his head. Across the street, holding a map . . . a year almost to the day since they had seen each other.

Evidence is what they were shouting for back in London. That was the cry of the little runt now running them, Peters had said.

Peters remembered the wry grin. He was told that "evidence" was what he hoped to pull together that night . . . and they were welcome to track him, but not to be close enough to be obvious – and they'd be better off in wet weather gear. No small talk, and nothing about "good luck" nor "How have things been?" nor

"Stay safe". Peters had seemed to thank him, and the wind had torn at the map as it was folded and put away, and the parting of strangers . . .

They followed Kenny's car. Had seen him several times on his phone, and had gone in and out of his office, and watched as he waved to an ashen-faced man who wiped down the tables in the café alongside the door with the Biscuit Tin sign.

The tracker had a range of close to a kilometre. The car travelled along the narrow lanes and the high hedges, and round rock-strewn hills and woodlands, and fields where cattle waited at gates to be escorted back to their milking parlours.

Peters said, "I hate this sort of place. From the smell of you two, I'm assuming you can handle it. I'm a concrete and small parks man. He has done an amazing job in getting his feet under the table. We know they checked his legend. Would have been expensive and done with the proverbial toothcomb. He's walking a tightrope, hellishly high and we are hardly a safety net. But it is all about evidence, as I told him. It is where we are."

They passed a cottage, and the cursor on the screen was stationary and they did not have to slow to confirm that his car was outside, and he was slamming the front door behind him, and they would go on up the hill and then turn, and look for a space to park.

Wilf asked him, "You do this sort of thing all the time? If that's not impertinent?"

"It's what I do. Try to make it easier for them. Try to keep them on the rails and not become sympathetic to the people they're nailing."

Hugo remarked, "Pretty gutsy people that you have."

"Or lunatics. That's the job description."

Jak Peters closed his eyes and wondered how his other Level Ones were managing, and was drifting off. He heard the men in front talk anxiously about the couple looking after their goats, and whether they were collecting the eggs, and if the hives were secure. The light was dipping and leaves were scurrying across the windscreen, and a squall came on, short and heavy.

★   ★   ★

Jonas said, "I think it's time to go back."

Captivated by the hut circles, of Ty Mawr, Celtic Iron Age, Vera remarked that there was no hurry and there was still much more to look at.

His response was peevish. "It's time we were back. For the cat."

Which was a cheap shot. His wife might care – apparently – little for him, but she was devoted to Olaf. After the previous evening's huge meal, meat and tissue and bone and fur, the cat would likely sleep through the whole of the day, hardly shift a whisker.

The site was high above the Irish Sea. It was open, exposed, and the wind should have been invigorating. It flushed Jonas's face. There was a group ahead of them with a guide and they seemed both knowledgeable and keen to learn more . . . Excavated here had been a stone axe, arrowheads of shaped flint, pottery ranging from Neolithic times to the Bronze Age. Did he care? Not greatly.

"I'm sorry, Jonas, but it was you who wanted to be here, and it's no longer raining, and the wind has dropped, and . . . is it because of what the poor old man said about the Service? Has that upset you?"

"Of course not. A fantasist. Plenty of them."

"How would I know? In my humble opinion, I'd say he was once what you call a 'Sixer'."

The guide had a good voice, didn't seem to mind Vera tagging herself to his group . . . Not just sleeping accommodation he was explaining, but areas for livestock, for storage of food during the winter when it would have been perishingly cold, and some were large enough to need corridors off which rooms led, and some were small and humble.

Jonas Merrick had not known Knacker, had never met him, but had heard of him. There had been leakages of a mission north of the Arctic Circle and the state-sponsored murder, damn near – by Her Majesty's Government – of an intelligence officer on the far side.

"I doubt it very much . . ."

Everything, best laid plans and the worst, seemed to leak. If the mission off the Galician coast was successful, then that would seep out through the cracks and his role would be discreetly acknowledged. If that same mission, and it was now running beyond the eleventh hour, was a failure, then he would be hung in the wind, the dishcloth on the line. It was his demand that, success or disaster, he be there at the death ... not stuck up a hillside peering down at the foundations of hut circles put together several millennia before. He flicked on his phone, and checked a feed from a lens buried in a suburban brick wall. Looked at an unremarkable villa, saw no movement, and remembered each pavement slab, each weed, each colouration in the brick. And both the faces of those to whom shock would soon be visited.

He went to the guide. He could do obsequious charm. A simple request, one that would earn gratitude, and was given tomorrow's itinerary, and where the guide and his party would be leaving from the next morning.

"So kind of you, sir. I'm not sure whether it's the carburettor or the clutch, but I've got to have it seen to. And am truly grateful my wife will not be disappointed – you know, it's an anniversary."

The final light of the day and quite soon, well before the bridge over the Straits, Jonas needed his headlights.

The wind had dropped. Dusk had come. A wall of cloud was all that Diego could see through the smeared windows of the cockpit.

The screen built into the instrument panel told him that land was within range. He called over his shoulder that the engine speed be halved.

Diego was beyond tiredness, was in a state of extreme exhaustion. He yelled again, for Matias to reduce their speed, but the engine pitch stayed steady. He twisted round and saw Matias, standing motionless at a side window of the cockpit, clutching the wrench. They travelled faster than Diego wished because the tide at that time of the year, that part of the month, had extreme power. Earlier, while still some strength was left in his voice, he had called for the thrust to be reduced and they had almost drifted, but were now back on full power and heading fast towards the cloud wall.

He saw the gull and the swell of the waves. Diego blinked again, and again, and saw nothing more. One hand held the wheel and the other hovered close to the handle of the drawer where the Luger was, armed, but with the safety catch on. The gull flew without effort, cruised and with grace, seemed to escort them toward the cloud wall. Diego did not know how long it was since he had last eaten. Rolling by his feet, lightweight and emptied, was one of the last of the plastic water bottles that they had taken on board on leaving the Delta of the Amazon river, and he did not know when he had drained the last drops of the contents from it.

"I told you to slow the engines."

He was not answered.

"Slow the fucking engine."

Silence.

"Do as I tell you."

No movement, no response.

Diego filled the cockpit with his anger. He had his hands on the engineer's shoulder, then his arm, then his throat.

Matias found his voice. Hoarse and rasping. "Where is Emiliano? I look for him. I cannot see him. I think the bird watches for him. He should be here, beside us, in the water with us . . . Must stay with us for a good burial, a Christian service, a priest. I think the bird watches over him."

Diego believed that madness had now reached them both, and the two men did a strange and clumsy dance, wrestled with each other. The wrench was now hard up under Diego's chin and he thought his skin would burst from its pressure, and he was reaching back, sliding, slipping, and lost hold of the wheel. Could not find the strength to push away the wrench as it gouged deeper into his throat. It was extraordinary to Diego that the engineer still possessed such power and he felt his breath. What there was of air in the cockpit was filled with the noxious fumes of the diesel. They would have been down now into the dregs of the bladders that held the fuel. He could not shift the wrench and was gasping, but the fingers of his other hand found the pistol, and he yanked it from the drawer.

The wrench pressed so hard on his windpipe that his lungs had emptied and could not be filled, and the Luger barrel, and its foresight, were pressed with the same intensity into the engineer's chin. Neither man was capable of speaking. Diego heard the faraway rumble of mechanical sound, a dulled blast, and could not tell the engineer what he heard and could not *plead* with him for the pressure of the wrench to be removed. His finger was at the bar of the trigger.

It was the time of the day's last light. The rain had stopped, and the wind was dropping.

They went towards the wall of cloud, and he heard the sound again. His thumb moved the lever, pushed it forward and up. He had no breath to speak, and saw a brightness in the engineer's eyes, and thought it the light of loathing. Diego pulled the trigger, not a squeeze as the manual said, but a jerk as panic dictated. Did it as the deep blast of noise was in his ears. His throat was released, his breathing returned. Matias slumped, and his blood was warm against Diego's face.

The cloud was wrapped round the cockpit.

He did what would have been done to him. Dragged the body of the engineer, and with part of the top of his head splattered on the cockpit ceiling. Opened the hatch, let in the elements, heard the roar even louder, and saw the gull as a shadow. He levered the engineer out through the hatch, like he was rubbish to be tipped from a bin, gave a last push and Matias slid head-first down the side of the hull, leaving stains that were quickly rinsed, and was in the water. The same would have happened to him, to Diego, if he had not fired.

He heard the lighthouse call, either Finisterre or Touriñán. They had not been more than two minutes in a wall of cloud. An extraordinary feat of navigation. There were blood and brain and bone chips on the ceiling of the cockpit, and in the hold were four tonnes of pure cocaine powder.

Diego yanked on a lever, slowed the engine and felt the throb slacken . . . The speed reduced and the waves were less severe as the wind dropped. He saw the twin lights, little pricks bright on the horizon ahead of him. The pistol was back in the drawer. A telephone was there, for single use, and every third day – a mark of optimism – he had checked the charge in its battery.

He did not know to whom he spoke. The call was answered, his message given. He was told what he should look for, and the call was cut.

Darkness was around him and he could no longer see the gull and did not know how much distance was now between the craft and Matias's body. And already a story rang in his mind of mutiny and of greed, and of the need to defend himself. And the boy? Would think of a story for the boy.

Diego felt more alive than he had for many hours, and did not notice his tiredness nor his thirst or hunger. He was back at the wheel, and steered the *Maria Bernarda* towards the coastline.

Telephones rang, and a codeword was given, in dialect. Car and pickup engines purred to life, and those on the larger lorries and vans that could take greater loads. Men roused their neighbours. Women, many in their nightclothes, hurried back to their family kitchens and prepared flasks of hot coffee and slapped together fresh bread and slices of local cheese. Feet slithered out on to cobbled streets and cigarettes were reluctantly abandoned because of the flash from matches or lighters. The old ones would have remembered – given the chance to bore – when the cargo was tobacco and made fortunes. The grandfathers of the oldest men, had they been there and with an audience, could have told how the *raqueiros* – the pirates on land – would light the fires on the cliffs above sunken reefs, to direct the ships onto them, with wrecked cargo to be salvaged. And the grandmothers of the old women would have remembered how they had washed the bodies of the drowned before burial, off the *Serpent* and the *Captain*, and strangers' graves littered their cemeteries. The old people would shake with laughter when talking of the massive consignment of tinned condensed milk washed ashore, thought to be paint, and applied with brushes to doors and window frames, and the biblical plague of flies that had descended on them . . . So many stories of

the wreckers and the smugglers, and of the great wealth accumulated in Galicia, all beyond the reach of the men from the Revenue.
The coast had been known, 500 years before, as the "murderers'
corner". Not a place of charity, and no chance of it when a cargo
was to be brought ashore and handguns and rifles were taken
from their hiding places.

The men on the move that night were from Finisterre and
Corcubión and Lires and Muxía, from Camarinas and Arou and
Laxe, were from as far up the Costa de Morte as Malpica. All
serious men, without banter, not teasing or laughing, concentrating hard because this work was the lifeblood on which so many
of their community depended. The men were disciplined and
knew where they should be and what was their role, all planned,
practised, proven. There was a penalty for failure, a harsher one
for betrayal: all knew it. Without headlights and guided by the
height of a frail moon, the vehicles made slow progress towards
the coast, and the designated beaching point. There was a refine-
ment that night, one used half a century earlier, and an instruction
was given to a man working the night shift in a power station. All
prepared, tested, foolproof.

The image appeared on the desktop screen on Fanny Thomas's
desk.

She had her back to it.

The screen was watched by Joe, her sergeant, faithful as a
lapdog and never seeming to need to be home early, to have to
hurry away. God, she envied Joe. The evening meal for her
husband and children was on the middle shelf of the fridge and
she gave them the privileged decision of choosing between Greek
or Neapolitan. Joe would go to the canteen for chips, her dinner,
later. The night closed round the building, and on the screen the
road was well lit. Her back was turned because she had a large-
scale street map laid out on a conference table, and the car park of
the superstore was highlighted with a chinagraph, and the route to
the relevant street, and she had also marked a back entry at the
rear, and at the far end of the street.

Word was that the Armed Response guys, and the girl, were showing predictable *angst* at being excluded. Difficult to tell them, and the uniforms who would be behind them, that they were shut out because loyalties were, to a minimal degree, not trusted. Fanny Thomas had worked in Serious Crime for long enough not to know how much cash slopped around the OCGs; what was life-changing to a cop was loose change to the Goviers. The room was quiet except for the shuffling of paper, the whisper of a couple of keyboards, the squeal of a highlighter pen. They were, the AR team, entitled to flounce, shout a bit, go to the Federation, probably walk off the job, and she hoped they would not. And she had to prepare what she would say in the final briefing, in the small hours, and get it right because arrests involving the likes of Xavier "Bengal" Govier were not routine. Plenty on her mind – and would have been pleased to have a big bear hug from Jimbo Rawe. And was beginning to itch for a trip to the car park and a fag, and . . .

"Fucking hell . . . what the fuck was that?"

Which was not the usual language of Joe, her sergeant.

She turned, looked at the screen. Saw the image was crazily angled, and saw a tyre come over it and squash the aperture, and saw a gloved hand reaching for it, and saw a screen that had a snowstorm breaking on it.

"Hit it again," she yelled.

Bengal reversed back into the middle of the road, revved, surged, and hit what was left of the wall.

It collapsed.

His turn to shout at Theresa. "Get the wires, get the workings, rip them all out. Move it, girl."

He had always regarded his kid sister as stuck-up, booky, more concerned about her fucking fingernails than the real world she was supposed to share with him. What she had done with the petrol-filled milk bottle, a rag and a cigarette lighter, had altered her beyond, almost, Bengal's recognition.

She charged forward, possessed. He saw her skip above the fallen lumps of brickwork. She wore jeans, an unmarked T-shirt, had a beanie on her head and a scarf across her mouth and cheeks, heavy gloves. He had not used the headlights on the car and she was scrambling in the darkness. The entrance to the Potters' home – miserable snobby bastards – was in darkness. One brick, thrown up by his first impact with the wall and spun clear of the mortar, had looped up and fallen on to the rear window of their motor, just above the fluffy toy sat on the back ledge. Had not broken it but had left a mosaic of fracture lines.

She crouched. A little yelp of triumph. She held it up, not enough light for Bengal to see it clearly, but saw one winking flash that would have been the lens. Clever girl, she had laid it down on a brick and had lifted another and had whacked the two of them together. She was looping up the cable and kicking aside more bricks, and a light had gone on at the first-floor window overlooking the driveway, their car, their wall and their gate – and the vehicle in which Bengal sat, revelling in the entertainment his sister gave him.

She yanked and the box came away. Would have been basic stuff. He knew, everyone knew, that the Merseyside cops operated on a shoestring. She had the box in her hand that would have been lodged in the flowerbed on the other side of the wall. He looked up . . . glimpsed a face peering down at him, a pale white face, dishevelled hair and the gaudy red collar of his pyjama top. He did not need to urge her to move faster. She knew – was a new girl, and bloody marvellous, and would be Bengal's best friend, had the spirit. She hung on to the cable and the box and unplugged it from a length of wire leading further back. She turned to face him and raised a thumb.

He swung the car – Bengal could not have said what make it was. Just a household car pinched two hours earlier in a street close to the Huyton Village shopping centre. Half an hour in a lock-up garage where a reinforced iron bar had been wired into place beyond the front bumper, and a decent spike welded on it. Delivered to where Bengal had waited, ready for use. He leaned across and opened the passenger door. They had left home over the back fence, and would come back the same way when their evening was finished.

"Put your belt on," he told her. On her lap were the cables, the wrecked lens, and the box. And he broke into shaking laughter. "Wouldn't want us getting points because you weren't belted up."

Out on the main road he slowed, and they were cruising well under the speed limit. He took a hand off the wheel and let it lie on his sister's knee and she leaned across, inside her belt's constraints, and kissed his ear.

"They don't walk over us, Theresa, they don't."

And she read him. "Dump it where it's noticed, but where they can't make a link that sticks."

"Not what Ma would have said, or allowed."

Theresa said, "Ma is what, at college, they'd have called 'risk averse'."

They stopped at the lights. Nothing coming from the other direction but he waited with patience, and let his hand stay. He headed for St Anne Street. Would be well lit there, and it had a high wall round it, blocking off the pavement from the front entrance of the four-storey building from which the Merseyside force was run. He imagined . . . and a slow and satisfied smile played on Bengal's mouth . . . her gathering together the cable and the fractured lens and the box, and opening the door as they came alongside the wall, and on his call she'd throw it all out. If she managed it, and he'd no doubt she would, then all the kit would clear the top of the wall, and the spikes on it, and would land inside their yard, right in front of the main door.

Doloures would not have sanctioned it, would have said it was provocative, would have said they needed to keep their heads down. Sometimes, Bengal thought his Ma was right in her decisions, but not always. Later he would take the car back to the lock-up, and the iron protector for the fender would be taken off and the car would then be ferried to waste ground where it would be torched, and with it his clothes and hers . . . He drove carefully through the darkened city.

"We're making a team, sister."

"Too right, Bengal."

            ★   ★   ★

"For God's sake, Mrs Thomas, we are in fear of our lives."

She had said that it was best, in the circumstances, to stay calm.

"Difficult to stay calm when our garden wall has been rammed."

Stay calm and ride out the night.

"Do you not accept responsibility? Are you not prepared to station policemen outside our property, to protect it?"

She could not explain the current strategy, nor was she able to put a presence in the road. Should stay calm, be patient . . . she felt vile.

"We have moved into the back bedroom. My wife is sobbing into her pillow. My blood pressure is off the chart. Your camera has gone, all ripped out and taken away. Are you not prepared to do anything for us, Mrs Thomas?"

She looked at the clock on the wall. If the man in London – now on holiday having washed his hands of the business – was to be believed, and his schedule in the handwritten note to be adhered to, then less than twelve hours remained for this pensioner couple to "stay calm" and be "patient". In an adjacent room, pissed off mightily by the lack of information fed to them, were her heavily armed and motivated "dogs of war". It would be her pleasure to lead them from the supermarket car park, shout "Havoc", and "let slip" those dogs: she knew the line, recalled that it gave advance warning of an act of vengeance . . . overdue.

She told David Potter that she could not share a timetable with him, urged him to be satisfied that his home was locked, bolted, whatever . . . and rang off. And felt humiliated and inadequate, and would follow to the letter what had been asked of her in the handwritten note . . . and the bloody man was on holiday.

He had not found her.

Kenny had driven almost as far south out of Corcubión as the track to the Finisterre lighthouse, then had branched off. Had passed one sign, bent by years of weather, that directed traffic towards the Praia de Arnela. Was irritated with himself for chasing after her, going to her home, going to two headlands where she sometimes set up her easel, bombarding her with phone calls. He was at work now and the sideshow, his romance, was ditched. He switched off his headlights when he left the metalled surface and came on to a gravel track. He had seen only one parked vehicle and that was almost hidden by a stock fence. There were few trees, and those by the track were misshapen from the winter gales. Figures loomed in front of him.

Kenny was hemmed in. Men crowded close, on either side of his car. A torch was shone in his face, blinding him, and the reflection of the light showed the barrel of a shotgun, sawn short. Wetting himself, almost. A cackle of laughter, decent laughter and genuine. If he had needed confirmation of a landing site in the next few hours, this was certainty. A worn hand, walnut brown, snaked into the car, took his fist and shook it, and a cigarette was passed him, and the match flashed and he saw the faces. One had been in the barn for his "interrogation", would have seen him strip. Another had been part of her escort, a couple of paces behind and away to the side but careful for her safety when she had made her promenade up the village street after lunch. They laughed and another pushed forward and took his hand and squeezed it but with respect. He understood. He was *their* man. He washed their money, invested their money, was a part of them. He had passed a test posed by the family, had eaten with the family, had walked with them. Kenny Blake was included.

It would have been assumed that he had the right, had been given clearance, to go up the track, to head for the coastal path. There was a moon: what his mother would have described as a "fitful moon", and he supposed he had thought of her because the assignment was now close to being wrapped and him returning to whatever life might be. He reflected. The culture of the men who manned the road block was to be suspicious, hostile towards outsiders, wary of establishing a friendship with anyone beyond their own blood – but he was accepted. He was told he should leave his vehicle in their care. If he were going further, on to the path above the cliffs, then he should go slowly, and should show no light.

He parked. If they had doubted him they would have slit his throat or strangled him, done it in silence . . . There were slaps on his back and he had merged into the darkness and the stones under his feet were the indicators of the path and he could hear the waves on the rocks below, could hear the amplified blast of the two distant lighthouse towers, but the *Vaca de Finisterre* was the louder.

Typed *Block ahead* and sent the text into the night.

The clouds came over low, mingled darkness with what little light the moon shared.

About evidence. Feeding the timing to Peters, his control, and the messages being passed for action, immediate, by Jimbo Rawe . . . then the final message sent to the man in London who now ran him. He doubted he would see Anna Jensen again. Did not know what else he could have done to build a relationship, give it some permanence. Tried to shut her from his mind but made a poor fist of the effort.

The noise of the sea grew stronger, was more ruthless. He would have been above those rocks where naval and cargo ships had foundered, where bloated bodies had floated. He thought it a strange and frightening place. There was enough light from the moon to see the cliff edge, where the heather stopped, and the drop would have been sheer. He could make out the beach and was heading for the point where he would be the eyewitness, the gatherer of evidence. He would appear in court, shielded by a screen, and would identify men and women, be on oath, convict them . . . All the months of work here, and the building of the Biscuit Tin business, and the training with the instructors, ending here, stumbling and sliding and alone and . . .

Kenny tripped. Fell headlong, and his foot was trapped at the ankle. He had barked his shin and scraped his hands and was winded, not hurt.

A cloud crossed the moon, light shafted, and he saw his foot hooked in the strap of a shoulder bag. He recognised the logo Popeye the Sailor . . . It was usually filled with paper and paints and brushes.

He heard a sharp voice. "What the fuck are you doing here? Or is this the right place to find a money launderer?"

★   ★   ★

There was little Jonas could now do to influence the finale.

He had been outside the caravan most of the evening since Vera had produced supper, had stood by the hedge, kept Olaf company, and had talked on his phone. The Maritime Agency reported that the semi-submersible was now close to the shore, near to the headland of Finisterre, and a buoyant Nikko had rung from his Bogotá office to confirm and to offer "God speed" and had signed off with, "And don't you fuck it up, Jonas, or all shades of hell will be visited on you . . . and call me at the end." Jak Peters had spoken to him from a clifftop where birds howled and the wind sang, and he thought he heard a faint lighthouse blast. And Fergal Rawe had linked up with Peters, and then the DLO was at work – no apologies, just bullshit – getting the Spanish agencies off their backsides but without a possibility of leakage. A call also, from Hugo, who had told him they would do their "best and double damn certain it was their very best" to keep Kenny safe, but that the patient was not an easy man to cuddle close to. The last one had been from his supposed mentor and protector, the AssDepDG.

A crisp voice in the late evening, not a great signal and its distortion competed with the rustling of the hedge's undergrowth as gusts caught it. "Just needed to say, Jonas, that I'll be happy only when the plaudits roll in, we get a basket full of credit, and we have prised you out of the backwater. I don't wish to hear that anything daft has been visited on the streets in the north west. Get on with your holiday, enjoy it. Leave any fine-tuning to the people in place. Don't interfere. Can I rely on that? Jonas? I don't hear you, Jonas – where the fuck are you?" He had rung off, wiser to. Never resort to a lie if it were not entirely necessary. His phone writhed in his pocket and he checked the incoming number, the AssDepDG three times, and let it continue to bounce.

He looked out over the fields beyond the hedge, already black, the moon not yet high enough to light them. He stayed because he had thought it necessary to allow Olaf plenty of time to prowl, learn the lie of the land. Perhaps he, with his interminable phone calls, had frightened off the possible prey. Perhaps, the gruesome death of one of their own the previous evening had scared the rabbits into spending the night deep in a burrow . . . Kenny Blake would have known about living alongside predators, and keeping clear of them.

A call came in from Fanny Thomas.

"Just hoping, Mr Merrick, that you are having a very rewarding holiday. I'm still at work. Unlikely to get home tonight, I thought you should know that the feed from over the road is down. The setting in the wall was rammed and the device removed. The people in the house are understandably traumatised and are now barricaded in. I am obeying orders, through gritted teeth, and have not deployed a guard on their house: the couple believe I have cut them adrift. I look forward to hearing from you when I can give my team a substantive briefing to prepare them for operations in the morning, and await your permission as to when to go after our Tangos. For the record, the gear for the camera has been thrown on to the site of Merseyside police headquarters, and a vehicle of the same make as that used to ram the wall is subject to a fire brigade call-out and will have been gutted of evidence . . . My call sign tomorrow, when I am authorised to let slip my boys, is 'Cry Havoc'. Goodnight, Mr Merrick."

She had cut the connection. She would have been spitting.

The cat was against his legs. They went together back into the caravan, and he'd volunteer for an early night. He thought it would be a hard day tomorrow, a high stakes day, hoped fervently it would be.

15

As he changed into his pyjamas, Jonas Merrick had doubted he had any more power than that invested in a clerk in any government department. Always a rather precarious and undignified operation, undressing and then getting into his pyjamas, but Vera seldom watched him. The cat was back in the caravan, in its cage.

Words played in his mind, merged with dreams and nightmares, had freer rein while he was asleep . . . He thought of the couple, living in a leafy road inside the boundaries of their pension, who had accepted their civic responsibilities and had allowed Fanny Thomas to have a camera lens built into their garden wall and were now near hysteria. They had no patrol car outside their home because Jonas Merrick, the coordinator and facilitator, had forbidden any show of force that might cause the two young occupants of the house opposite to bolt. David and Jenny Potter had been left to flap in the wind in the interest of a bigger coup – which was playing at God. In the narrow foldaway bed of the caravan, he remembered his own words: *It's all in the name of the greater good and we hope to have it wrapped up in the morning and that's the best I can offer. It is about priorities – I'm sure you understand.* And some of his other little speeches were knifing him.

As Jonas imagined it, there would have been a team of night nurses to change dressings on a victim's facial burns. He knew the young woman, Nanette, from photographs in his files, and was grateful to her for supplying travel details, and knew of the compromising information on her VAT and National Insurance malpractice, and regarded her as integral in the late detailed planning for the round-up. He thought, from the photographs he had seen of Nansie in her uniform that she wore to work and smiling behind her desk, would likely have been a most attractive girl – not now, was scarred, would be unrecognisable, she would be known in the future anywhere in the Merseyside conurbation as having been a "tout". More words: *Very regrettable, but we are in an unsentimental world. If we do not have Confidential Human Intelligence Sources to draw on then we are working blindfolded. The priority is to put away a dangerous and unpleasant family – and we've played God with you, and probably, for us, it will all work out well.* They clanked in his mind, while Vera slept, and the cat.

He did not hear the fox who shouted for a mate while out on patrol, nor did he hear an owl in a long dead tree . . . He was well into playing God, lofty status for a clerk, one who worked in a backwater, liked to think he had no more value than keeping the trains running to schedule. Saw Kenny, the passport photo that showed the smile and that aura of trust, and saw the blood from the wounds on his face that had come with Hugo and Wilf's report, "Recalled to Life," and another speech echoed in his skull. *It's a reasonable enough gripe, Kenny, and you're entitled to complain about the pressure put on you to keep going in your posting. Hang around too long and you either get to join the natives – do the Stockholm bit – or you get careless. Either way that will likely end in tears. The man who runs me, who I sometimes report to if I can remember, is a senior cog in the machinery here, the AssDepDG, and he wants to see some 'bang for the buck'. If we're going to do crime then we need results. You can provide that. At a cost? Of course. Our gain and your pain. One of the big bonuses of playing God is that one gets to run a slide rule over 'consequences'. What's worth it and what is not. Your problem, Kenny, your safety was worth the consequences. Perhaps we'll meet up one day, perhaps not.*

Saw them all . . . Nikko on a firing range, and Fanny Thomas hunched over her desk and crowded in with anxiety, and Fergal Rawe who should have been put out to grass years before, and Jak Peters who would have known his trade as control for a Level One and who had had it wrested from him by that clerk, from that backwater . . . and saw Doloures, the matriarch, and cunning as any rodent when danger loomed, and her tribe of kids and . . .

The fox continued its patrol, ever wary but no doubt thankful that its coat stayed dry and the rain was gone. The owl screeched in the darkness and would have had a good and steady perch because the wind had dropped.

Sleep, that night when it came, did Jonas Merrick no favours.

He said, in a dream: *You want the truth, don't you, all of you? Want it unvarnished, without a gloss put on it. Don't blame me for the truth, I'm just a messenger. And all the people out there, all the 'ordinaries', don't go clucking disapproval. And what's the alternative? Let it rip? Let the trade saturate without penalties? Don't go blaming me, I am your servant and only that.* Might have shouted it. *Just that, only that, am doing the best I can.*

Shouted it louder than the fox, than the owl – and slept on.

Never confirm and never deny, the instructors said.

Kenny had not denied that he was a cash rinser. They hammered that in the training sessions.

Kenny had not confirmed he was a police officer, a Level One graded undercover. They said the reaction to an accusation should be a shrug, a smile, and nothing said.

And more than *interesting* was why she was here. Enough light from the moon to show a harsh line where the hillside sloped abruptly away; the dead ground where the path dropped sharply; and beyond, with moonlight now playing full on it, was the gently shelved gold of the beach, where small lights seemed to dance and scurry. There was another light, brighter, and he estimated it 100 metres ahead of where he now crouched, and it would have been close to the place where the path descended – and another, also strong, on the far side of the beach, high on the cusp of the next slope. There would have been lights at night, high above the shore line, on this stretch of coastline, *Costa de Morte*, for centuries.

There was a harshness in her voice that was new to him. He had not responded to the accusation.

She said, "Don't talk, don't move, don't interfere. Just don't."

He thought himself an idiot. She was sitting on the three-legged stool, but with the height of the legs reduced so that her head and

upper body would not have made a silhouette. Reckoned now that
he was targeted. Had thought of a future – cold nights, log fires, a
cottage by the sea, and her painting and him doing the outside
jobs, repairs and wood splitting, and carrying fodder to an
outhouse for a cow or a sheep or a pig or a chicken – and was told
in a voice of authority that he should not speak, nor in any way
involve himself in her business.

He thought, was unsure, he had seen a light over the water. If it
had been a light, not a flicker of the moonlight on the white crest
of a wave, then it had flashed three times.

Not much of the future seemed important. They said, those
instructors who never deviated from the duties of the straight and
the narrow, that what was between an undercover's legs should
stay there, be subject to cold baths or be wrapped in frozen pea
packets. Might have a go again, on that business of the "future",
might try it one more time . . . She rummaged in the Popeye bag,
took out an image intensifier and held it up to her eye. Stubby,
awkward to hold, and heavy.

When the wind veered up and towards him, Kenny could
hear a murmur of voices, in the harsh accent of the region.
Another thought took him. About this time, approaching the
coast further south and on the direct haul into Madrid, would
be an Avianca flight, and Fredo's cousin would be sitting in an
economy seat and beneath the cabin floor, in cargo, would be
the son of Fredo's cousin. And soon it would be Fredo's own
kid, the sour little bastard with too much lip, who would be shivering and soiling himself and whimpering as he was prepared
for a painful killing. Perhaps Fredo was down on the beach
below because it would need manpower, muscle power, to shift
that number of bales and get them up the beach to the pickups . . . and Fredo's heart would be pounding and he would be
harbouring the desperate hope that the shipment came ashore
safely and that he would not be repeating the journey of his
cousin . . .

What pleased him, but not greatly, was that Anna had not
broken his cover, reckoned him just a washer of dirty money.

What annoyed him, a bigger irritation, was that he had not read her . . . Would he come clean with her, cough out the reality of his role?

Kenny turned away. He seemed to be spluttering, the frog in the throat game, one arm up and an elbow across his mouth to stifle the sound. With his free hand, he sent the message to Fergal Rawe and Jak Peters.

The phone was back in his pocket, the cough under control. "Sorry," Kenny said.

"Just keep quiet."

"No easel? Will it be your sketch pad for doing the dawn?"

"Fuck off."

He thought her spirited. He would try again, one last time, to raise the matter of the vague "future". Thought her brilliant.

Doloures and Patrick were collected from a side street around the corner from their hotel. Both had dressed fast, would have felt and looked wrecks, with no more than three hours' sleep. His mother had had to come and bash on Patrick's door and he had followed her down the stairs with his shirt unbuttoned, his belt unfastened, his shoes unlaced. A miracle; it wasn't raining. Another miracle; the gale had blown over.

"What do I wear, Ma?" he had asked her before they'd gone to their rooms.

"How the hell do I know?" she had snapped at him.

The car went fast. There was no conversation. Patrick thought it the start of the biggest, most significant, day in his life. Darkened houses, tight hedgerows, leaves flying from under the wheels. Ma did her make-up. Had her bag open on her knee and the foldaway mirror opened, and didn't seem to care that the car lurched and swerved to avoid ruts in the road. He thought her radiant. What had happened upstairs after dinner was forgotten, would not be told to a living soul, not even to Bengal or to Theresa. And he had shed the thought that the investment manager was a cop, squashed it.

★   ★   ★

In Theresa's room were two single beds. They had been pushed together.

She had not invited him, he had not asked if he could. Theresa slept. Alongside her, Bengal also slept. Untroubled, without care, slept well.

Brother and sister had appreciated the need each had for the other. Both were consumed by loneliness. Only had each other, no one else they might have trusted, might have grown fond of, might have enjoyed the company of . . .

The road was quiet, nothing passed that would have disturbed them. The milk would be delivered to their door a little before four o'clock, but from an electric-powered wagon which barely made a sound. But the sound of the gate unfastening and the feet on the path, and the faint clink of the bottles being set down would be enough to wake Bengal.

He held her hand, was small in his fist. She'd asked, before sneaking under the bedclothes, if he would take her with him the next day, "out and about" what he called it.

He'd queried whether she had college time to put in. She held his hand while they slept, took reassurance from it.

He'd take her. She had no college tutorials that mattered, and when she did go back she would face out the bastard who had written the note, might make him piss his trousers, might bring her brother with her . . . And he would take her, had promised, to a meeting he'd set up for the next afternoon where dealers from Sefton and Aintree and Fazakerley would be told prices, might even get news of what was coming, and when, and how much quantity. She'd not talk, would stand with her arms across her chest, her feet a little apart, no cosmetics and no jewellery, reckoned that was the image that mattered – showed she'd take no shit, and showed that she was with Bengal. She had thought how well he slept, and took the credit for it, and could feel the warmth of him . . . Something to look forward to, being with him at his meeting, seeing the deference.

Mikey lay on his back. He was far enough into his sentence to have been given – bit of a luxury – a cell of his own.

The main noise on the wing that night was a kid starting out on a fifteen-year stretch – "an exemplary sentence", the judge had called it – for armed robbery and some wounding thrown in. The kid might have thought himself a big player, and the briefs might have put some rose petals on their assessment of his chances of walking free, having a jury that was sympathetic. No bloody chance. The kid might have believed, the little shite-faced idiot he was, that he'd be going back to his mother, back to her cooking and back to her waiting hand and foot on him. Wasn't going to happen, not till plenty of Christmases had passed. The kid howled. No let-up, and the men on either side of him were yelling for him to shut his mouth . . .

Mikey Govier had been inside long enough to know the geography of Walton, and his father had been there before him. He knew where the gallows had been, used in the old days, and the condemned cell alongside it. His dad had been in Walton as a youngster and served time with old lags who had been held there when there had been a hanging. Mikey said his dad was told that there were some nights when the whole gaol was kept awake by the sounds of a guy shrieking, until the big silence at a minute past eight in the morning. There would be no rope and no trapdoor for the kid near him, and Mikey thought the howling would become a fixture. He was disturbed, could not concentrate.

He wanted to think about his wife, where she was. Wanted to think about her bossing the family and his word counting for less, and respect for him in Walton was on the slide. He thought she was growing too grand. He was not listened to. Most of the wives, when they visited the long-stay men, showed some sign of affection – noted by other prisoners, and by the staff. He lay on his bed and the night drifted past.

Fanny Thomas assumed her family had managed to cobble a supper together, and did not care if they had not. She had a chair in her cubbyhole office where she could wedge cushions and make an apology of a couch . . . Along with her family's gripes she had heard that Jimbo Rawe was travelling at speed, heard also that Jak

Peters currently had no eyeball on the undercover but hoped to get closer. Heard nothing from the low-lifer who had gone off on his holidays; did not complain because she was always happier when desk-warriors were kept away, were silenced. Joe had brought her coffee. Joe was pretty near her age, seemed to be able to cat-nap on his feet. Had brought her a sandwich with the coffee, had tiptoed in and had hoped not to wake her.

Slim chance of sleep. If the lift worked out as hoped, then she would be in for a commendation, might even get as high as a Chief Constable lunch. If the arrest plan failed, screwed up, then she would be lucky to get a desk job in Traffic, and would likely be put out on the street. Back again, Joe hovered by the door.

"Feeling good, ma'am?"

"A lie if I say 'never better'. Not good, not bad, just impatient, the way it always is."

"And we're part of something big, that right?"

"Not inside the loop. We're treated, Joe, on a Need to Know, which is insulting but we have to turn the cheek. I don't know what else counts. Except, this is something substantial compared with that vile family. . . . I've spent a decent part of my adult life focused on the Goviers. I put Mikey away because he was dumb – easy. Doloures is more intelligent, has more nous in her little finger than he in the whole of his objectionable and ugly body. Bengal is dangerous, ruthless, cunning . . . Remember when he identified that tail and came after our boy who was just terrified, thought he was going to be beaten like a punchbag, and a bus pulled up, and our boy could do a runner, Bolt wouldn't have caught him. The other son is a nonentity, and the girl may be the one who bombed the travel agent. I worry, Joe, what effect it has on you, on me – and all those guys through there with the hard-ware . . . We spend our lives chasing after scumbags. May not get enough sight of the decent folks around here . . . God, Joe, I'm spouting rubbish. Thanks for the coffee."

"Can only do, ma'am, what's asked of us. Can't do more."

"I have been left clear instructions, will carry them out. I'll be told when to move by my little friend who is currently on holiday."

"Or supposed to be, ma'am. Might put in a show," Joe said and flicked up his eyebrows.

"Don't, Joe, don't tease. The thought of a backseat driver is about as near to Hell as I can imagine. Don't even think it . . . The team in good shape?"

Joe told her that the "guns" were awake, and some were cleaning weapons, and some were reloading their magazines with the bullets that the H&Ks fired, and one was arguing about the best socks for the boots they were issued with – and one and all were complaining.

"Excellent, wouldn't want them happy. God forbid that the 'guns' are ever docile, not when we need them – and might. Codeword for their intervention is Cry Havoc. Yes, we might need them."

"You slept?"

"Not at all." The words trembled from Jenny Potter's mouth.

"Nor me."

"I've had enough, as much as I can take."

"We're going in the morning. If that woman won't put a squad car outside the house then we are not staying, and there will be a letter, the toughest I can compose, on the Chief Constable's desk by tea-time." David Potter spoke through quivering lips.

Each of them remembered every contact with the family across the road: an Organised Crime Group, a narco-clan, the city's nearest living thing to a cartel. Had tried, when they had first moved in, before knowing the calibre of the home owner across the road, to be neighbourly, friendly. Had been rewarded with foul abuse from the elder boy, gestures from the sister, and the mother had ignored them and had damn near run Jenny down when stepping into the road with a smile on her face. Had watched as Mikey Govier had been led out, half-dressed but fully handcuffed, had watched it from the downstairs window and been rewarded with a shout from the teenage boy "What's so fucking special? Want to come and tell me?" Suckers they had been when the DCI had turned up, a pushover for Fanny Thomas. Jenny asked him whether he was sure the front door was locked and bolted, and the back door, and all the windows secure, and his temper was fraying and he told her that the answer was the same as he'd given her a quarter of an hour before.

David Potter, in bed and in the darkness, said, "About the ulti- mate putdown we get is who comes visiting in our hour of need. Not a policeman in sight. No, we get a pothole chappie, a nonentity with a can of spray paint. That's all we get."

"You were talking in the night, Jonas."

"Was I?"

"And you shouted sometimes."

"Did I?"

"Indeed you did, and I was introduced to a whole gang of your friends, and those you are not fond of."

"Were you?"

"All about 'playing God', Jonas."

"Was it?" He sluiced his face, slapped it to liven the skin.

She was sitting up in bed and the cat eyed him from its cage. "You sounded burdened, Jonas . . . carrying a weight of responsi- bility. Surely that can be shared? Does it need only to be on your back?"

"Nothing for you to worry about, dear." He thought he sounded both feeble and patronising, but he was unfamiliar with discussing his work with Vera. Was not supposed to happen, was contrary to the ethics of the Service.

He thought her voice sad and anxious. "You were telling us, Jonas, about a young woman with a badly burned face, and about a retired couple barricaded in their own home, and about an agent kept too long at his post . . . I suppose they are all facing those huge difficulties so that you can chalk up a success."

He pulled on his trousers. A little crumpled but still respectable enough for an elderly pothole inspector from the Council, then buttoned up his shirt.

"I think a piece of toast will suffice for breakfast." Felt old, weary . . . might have wished that he had not led a veteran's life where he was cocooned inside his cubicle and worked all day until it was time to scamper for the train to Raynes Park. Then, the "good old days," nobody actually listening to what he said, but seemed to value reading what he wrote, acted on the advice he gave . . . Damned different now. All heaped up on him because he was the man who had foiled the suicide bomber at the doors of Westminster, had deflected mayhem and carnage from the gates of an RAF station, had cut a Kremlin-funded hit squad dead in its tracks. "Give it to, Jonas," they chorused. Did he want the accolades? No one ever asked him. What did he want? To be present at the end, the man in an old raincoat, and a witness . . . He knotted his tie.

"I'll do the toast."

"But Olaf's breakfast first," and he managed a slight grin.

"Your role, Jonas, it would probably help to explain it. I doubt that the safety of the realm would be breached if you did."

Put on his socks, and his brogues, and wiped his shoes with his handkerchief, and scooped his loose change into his pocket, all done while he spoke.

"Unlikely it would. They put me on to crime. It's a cul-de-sac in our eyes. Dead-end stuff compared to espionage and terror. Real people and real fears. I thought it rewarding. And about this hideous level of Class A drug importation and the consequences of it. Trying to make a difference. Sounds so arrogant. A previous operation had put an undercover officer into northern Spain and we were about to recall him. I stamped on that, kept him there, raised his workload and exposed him to greater danger. He runs an investment management business, dodgy and sidelining legality, and it attracted, as I hoped it would, the attention of a prominent organised crime clan. They bring cocaine into Europe. The biggest importers in our country are from the north west, specifically Liverpool. I identified a rising family, looking for greater profit, searching for a higher step on the ladder, predicted an outcome. The family are buying into the clan's trafficking arrangements. There are many casualties, Vera, in this trade. Very close to our operation are a young woman with life-changing scarring from a petrol bomb attack, a couple who see themselves as front-line victims. And there is my undercover who, two nights ago, was a hair's breadth from losing his life, and talked, bluffed, deceived – and survived . . . And there is the shipment that we aim to disrupt. Quite exciting. Something that is almost, but not quite, a submarine. Journeyed the length of the Amazon river and then the width of the Atlantic ocean, tracked all the way, and should, in a very few hours, be hitting the Spanish coast. And then we swoop."

"And you've coordinated all of this?"

"I suppose I have."

"And that could not be shared?"

"I don't think so. Too many cooks and all that. Decision-making, Vera, and it seems to have been dumped on me."

"And today it finishes?"

"It finishes . . . Can never be sure how satisfactorily. That Scots poet probably had it right. A mouse prepares a warm, snug nest but had not allowed for a farmer's plough turning it over. *The best laid schemes o 'Mice an' Men, Gang aft agley, An' lea'e us nought but grief an' pain, For promised joy.* Yes, *aft agley* . . . I think one piece of toast will be fine."

Olaf to be fed first, then his toast done, and the dawn smear not yet up.

He had seen the lights on the clifftop, had flashed an answer, and now Diego steered towards a midpoint between them.

There was a good moon that slipped down behind him and it shimmered on the water ahead. The moonlight caught the wings of the gull, not more than ten metres from the cockpit. It had a languid and unhurried motion, did not seem to want to forage for scraps that the storm of the last days might have thrown up and left to float, accessible to its savage beak. It kept pace with him . . . He thought he had dozed, might indeed have slept fully but his grip on the wheel had stayed constant. There would be very little to spare in the fuel bladders when they beached. He assumed that the procedure would be to take the semi-submersible as far on to the beach as was possible, and the timing of the tides had been checked, and it was a miracle that the schedule had been met.

He would be a hero. He had crossed the ocean, had come to a point on the shore that was little more than a kilometre wide. The gap between the two lights, and the need to work the tide pattern, had been negotiated. In the histories of the Costa da Morte, not written down but told among old people in bars in the autumn of their lives and soaking up the sunshine, would be the epic of how this man had brought the *Maria Bernarda*, blessed with a saint's name, that far and that accurately. They would be waiting for him on the beach and men would rush forward as he killed the engine. They would swarm over the hull and would heave up the hatch and the unloading would start. Few lights, minimal shouting, and pickups reversing on to the sand, then speeding away.

And questions asked . . . where are they? The crew? He might have slept but the tiredness was not lessened. He must think of the explanation. The drawer stayed ajar, the Luger pistol was there, on top of the charts along with the telephone. On the floor, kicked into a corner, was the wrench. There were two small bags hanging on hooks beside the bunk – one would have belonged to Emiliano and the other to Matias, and would have held their clothes and their rosaries, and pictures of a girl and of a wife and children. Where were they? Had they fought, struggled with each other and both gone overboard? A possibility. Had they mutinied, plotted to kill him so they could claim a greater share of the reward for bringing the *Maria Bernarda* safely across the Atlantic? And to save his own life he had had to shoot them both, but with the greatest regret. A possibility but less satisfactory. Had they fallen ill? Had he committed them to the depths, to God's mercy? Had one gone overboard and the other tried to save him, and both lost? Seasickness was the best option, the greatest probability: exhaustion, malnutrition, dehydration, excessive vomiting, and both simple peasant men from the tributary of the Amazon and without experience of the ocean and its storms. Plausible. He needed to turn it in his head and recite it.

The craft went towards a line of mist, and he had begun to see a horizon above it, the high points of the cliffs . . . He would beach and the tide would rise as they unloaded the bales, and the craft would float and other men would take it from him, and it would be refuelled and it was someone else's problem to take it back, or sink it and write off the million bucks it had cost to construct. Not his responsibility.

He liked that story . . . was pleased to have concocted it. He had not raked through their possessions, did not dare to. Diego had the story . . . and they were only fucking peasants, and no one would care. Both families, Diego reflected, might do well from the deaths . . . And repeated his story, but could not be sure if he told the same one the second time.

He edged open a side window of the cockpit, just two or three centimetres. Enough to let in the cold chill of the night air and a rewarding splatter of spray that fell on his face, and the movement of the window might have disturbed the gull. It broke its rhythm and dived down, and then splattered the surface of the water, where the bow wave lifted it, and it shrieked and fought, and came up again and flew.

Diego saw that it chewed on a scrap, saw also that its beak was red, and he knew it as blood. The body floated less than ten metres from the cockpit, on the starboard side. It was on its back, and the clothing was tight across the stomach and chest and would already have been filled with the build-up of gases. He saw it clearly. The bird had fed and was satisfied and now hovered above it. The tide would have had a run as great as the slackening engine speed. He had thought it was the diesel motor of the craft that drove it forward, and now realised that the engine had failed and the power was off, and the screw silent and the throb silenced. When had it happened? Diego could not have said. Minutes before? Hours before? He did not know.

He opened the hatch wider. They were approaching the low line of the mist that was made golden in the moon's light: the craft, the *Maria Bernarda*; the body, which was Matias who had sold engine parts from a stall in the Colombian city of Leticia; and the gull that had no name but a bloodied beak – and Diego who was cursed. Drifting and rolling and being taken towards the shore by the strength of the ocean's tide.

He opened the main hatch fully and could not reach the body, but saw it clearly when the waves lifted it. The face was the worst, the eyes and cheeks and mouth of the engineer had made good meals for the gull. And the hair on the upper part of Matias's skull showed the hole where the bullet had exited, where the bone had been carried away, and under the chin was the hole of the entry wound. But where the gull had been was the worst.

In the hold, driven by the tide, were the bales of cocaine powder which might have been worth $100 million, and might have a street value when cut of $300 million, and if there was a shortage and this plugged the hole then it could be pulling in $400 million, but the face, and the wounds from the gull's beak, were more prominent than the stacked heaps of cash, and the story of seasickness was slipping from his memory.

Diego no longer cared about the wheel. He thought they would land together, and the body would be caught on the sand, and the hull would beach and the gull would find a rock to perch on and might then begin to preen its feathers. He was on his knees, held his head. He thought he heard, far away, the rustle of breaking surf.

Kenny could have said, "I have a vision, Anna. A simple one. Does not matter who you are, or who I am. What I am seeing tells me that we get on well, and we are both at that wretched sort of time when all the charging about gets a bit wearying, and we might pack those lives in, do our own thing – and never look back."

Could have said, "We don't do the past, not even the present. Just look at the future. No one runs our lives, and we live at subsistence level. Don't have to wallow in cash. We can go somewhere where the only certainties are that *they* cannot reach us and the sun rises each morning and sets each night. And we have each other – and you'll paint and maybe I'll learn how to do frames and mount your pictures. We'll be far from here and we'll find happiness. It is possible, Anna."

The wind ruffled her hair and the moon shone on her as she crouched low.

Kenny could have said, "Where you want to go, I will follow. Be at your shoulder. If you stumble, I will catch you. If you need love, I am there. Don't want anything else, Anna. Or anyone else. I can't say where we would be but it is a place that does not tolerate all the shit that is around us now. Make a life, make babies, make art. But especially we can make love, build it and worship it, you and me. Will you make a stab at that, Anna?"

Said nothing.

Kenny was close enough to reach out and calm her hair, let his fingers play on the nape of her neck. He thought it the one time in his life that he had fallen headlong, and did not try to help himself, and shook his head as if that might lessen the hurt. She ignored him, had the image intensifier up to her eye and used both hands to hold it steady. He could not see the ocean, only the beach and the crisp moving lines where the surf ran, stalled, fell back. Beyond it, further out, was a low wall of mist. The gale was gone and there was no hint of rain and the stars were fading, but the moon stayed strong as it dipped and its light straddled the sand.

Who was Anna Jensen? Identity unimportant.

Who was Kenny Blake? A compilation of a legend and backed by fraudulent paperwork, and separated from his name and his past.

Both of them were inventions . . . and neither would confirm or deny. There was more movement on the beach. He wondered if she too were muddled with where she came from, and why she was on the cliff, and who she would be next week, month, or the next year. Enough . . .

He stared down at the beach and saw that she had tilted the device, aimed the lens towards a vehicle's sidelights, which were then doused. He thought that when the moon had dipped into the level of the mist a greater darkness would fall on the beach.

He recognised the shadow shape of Isabella Munoz. Could not have said what she wore, recognised her by posture, the throw of her shoulders and the line of her backbone. Men came to her, ducked their heads and respect was shown. At her shoulder was Sergio. Could recall every word of the challenges thrown him by the man, and congratulated himself on having outwitted him, played the game of strip search – and had recruited her, the *matriarca*. Had to squint to see better but the moon was full and it hovered above the mist ceiling. Thought it would have been Laureano who ran the length of the beach, getting vehicles in place, no lights, and marshalling the men who would carry the bales to the pickups in wheelbarrows or porters' trolleys. Another vehicle came.

He thought that she breathed harder, as if excitement had won through, and the pretence of being an artist was ditched. He had not known her because of deceit – and she had not known him because of deceit. When the dawn came up, and the conclusion, he might say something. Wrong, he *would* say it.

A second vehicle had pulled up at the top of the beach. What Kenny knew of the Praia de Arnela, remembered from one of those expeditions he had made when first happening across Anna Jensen, was that a single rough track zigzagged down to the beach.

He thought the Liverpool couple, the defiant woman and the prickly boy, were out of their depth. Good enough for where they came from but they were dealing with heavyweight players and he thought they would be struggling, mesmerised by the power of the clan, would have wanted to climb too high and too fast, were doomed.

Kenny shrugged, like it was not his business. He wondered whether Fredo were down there, assumed he would be, and would have been told that the lights were beyond the mist and would have thought the shipment secure and that the life of his boy was saved.

Her attention was on the beach. She did not use a notepad to record what she saw, nor did she speak into a microphone wired to her body, nor use her phone. He assumed she provided to her employers, immaterial who they were, a report which would be sifted and then stored in an intelligence databank.

The moon flickered a last time above the mist ceiling, then dropped, and the tide was thrusting further over the sand and the wind eddied in the gorse and the heather.

Kenny sent his own message . . . he was concerned at how far back were Jak Peters and Hugo and Wilf, whether they had stayed further down the road than the "block" or whether they came around it, using old skills of combat movement. Wondered whether the weapons were loaded, armed, and whether they would dare to shoot. He realised now that a waiting time had started. In the centre of the beach, prominent by her stature and the haughty cut of her back, was Isabella Munoz. He had seen her strip in the darkness, had been summoned to lunch with her and to observe her progress along the harbour side of a village where men earned far more from bringing ashore a catch of cocaine than one of sardines. And could assume that by the following weekend, when more cash was dumped in the Biscuit Tin fund, that he might be invited to dine with her in the back room of a restaurant – or that she would knock on his door late at night and her driver would carry the dinner, portions for two persons and wrapped in tinfoil; into his kitchen and put them down along with a bottle, and would then back out and doze in the car until she was ready to go home. Wondered if he would be the first, and the last, or whether when an itch took her then a stud was procured . . . Would never know, would not be there. Kenny would be gone that evening, would not know . . .

He waited. And she did.

A realisation came to Kenny. He was one strand in a web as woven by a master craftsman. He thought the mesh of the web was dense, proof against struggles and failed attempts to escape. He was small, even smaller were Jak Peters and Jimbo Rawe, and likely there were others who he would never hear of. He thought that – very soon – the web would strain to entrap its victims, and at the heart of the strands, where they were thickest and came to a knot, was an elderly man whose voice was soft, persuasive, and chilled if challenged.

He could have stood on the cliff edge, raised his right hand in a clenched fist, and shouted, "Well done, Jonas Merrick. Well done."

But he sat in silence, and waited, and watched the mist fall, and felt the warmth of her as she sat on her stool in front of him, and yearned to touch her and make his speech.

"I'm calling in a debt, a monumental one," the DLO had told him. "Just as long as it's called," Jimbo Rawe had answered him.

The Drugs Liaison Officer, on a decent ticket in Madrid and wanting to keep hold of it, would have been using up precious stuff from his treasure store. He had rung a "friend", an officer in a section of the Spanish police. The debt had hung over the friend for a few years and he had been roused from his bed to take the call, and needed to accept the "terms and conditions" demanded of him. The origin of the debt was the DLO's knowledge of a messy little business in the past, and the disappearance of a percentage of a haul of Class A stuff, and the value of what had gone missing would have paid, amply, for the plot on a hillside between Malaga and Marbella and for a pool and a tennis court. A good amount of the haul had gone walkabout, and the British HMRC man had evidence of it – complicated but sound. A debt had been created. Years of silence, as Jimbo was told the story.

Then the call in the night and a few spluttered protests about what was asked for, and a gentle reminder of those "terms and conditions", and agreement, and the procedures that would be followed. Probably 30 men involved and that would be the whole of a night shift operating in the Asturian coastal city of Luarca: any man or woman capable of holding a handgun and aiming it, and fit enough to head out on a night-time ramble along the cliffs – and three minibuses to ferry them. It had been done, and four Guardia Civil personnel had been added to the convoy. The use of officers from outside Galicia was prudent, and the reach of the clans embedded on the Atlantic coast did not stretch to the attractive, quiet, tourist-favoured Luarca ... A bonus for those being driven through darkness, excitement barely contained, was that a massive overtime gratuity was in the pipe-line for them. Radio silence was demanded, and the use of mobile phones forbidden.

Past four in the morning when they had gone through the
motorway toll gate, and the one sleepy attendant had failed to
focus on the convoy, and though paid to warn clan people of
police reinforcements on the move, had seen reference only to
traffic cooperation on the sides of the vehicles. Past five o'clock
when they were south and west of Corunna, after an hour and
three-quarters of spirited driving, at the outskirts of a village, and
near enough to smell the sea, and waiting for them in a cemetery
parking area were the DLO, and with him his new best friend,
Jimbo Rawe.

Beside the DLO's car, Jimbo stood and smoked. The new
arrivals hung back as their commander was briefed. They would
have been the men and women who were always sidelined when a
matter of importance was planned, always left behind in the
canteen, always having to watch the swagger of a supposedly
"elite" unit when serious business against major criminality was
launched. Would they be good enough, when push came to shove?
Not worth considering, they were what was served up on his table.
The *subteniente* sidled away, bristled importance, to tell his men
and women what would be expected of them.

Jimbo Rawe was told, "This is a league, two leagues, above what
they're used to."

"Appreciated."

The DLO said, "If it goes wrong then the shit is well and truly
stuck to the fan."

"That also is appreciated."

"And if it goes wrong then we do a fast exit and were never
here."

"Very much appreciated. And if it 'goes wrong' then there is a
little runt in London whose face will feel the force of my toecap –
except that it won't go wrong. That's not my promise but my prayer."

And they shivered in the night cold, and stayed under the trees,
away from the moon's light, and waited . . . And in the quiet was
the sound of weapons being readied . . . and waiting, in Jimbo
Rawe's experience, was seldom easy.

★   ★   ★

She put the image intensifier back into the Popeye bag, and turned.

"I don't do conversations."

"Noted." Kenny's answer was little more than a whisper.

She was now rummaging in the bag. "You should go, Kenny."

"Thank you for the suggestion."

"Not for debate . . . go. Go fast, and far."

"Perhaps, when I am ready."

She took a camera out of the bag, and a lens, and slapped them together. She was good at handling surveillance gear in darkness. The camera strap was looped over her head.

"I mean it, Kenny."

"Will probably be moving on, but thinking about a girl."

"Not the place, not the time. Go."

Her hand went into the bag again and emerged holding a pistol. She armed it, made that scrape noise that would have gone out into the light winds playing over the heather and the gorse, and the sound would have carried. She held it close to her face and would have squinted to see that the safety was in position. It would have been a PPK Walther, a police weapon used across northern Europe. He remembered how he had defended her, and had championed her art, and how his life had been on the line because of his meeting her, sleeping with her, and in his own way loving her, and he had the scars on his face, knitting well, to prove that defence. He thought it was a big deal for her, telling him to quit, and generous.

"Don't interfere."

"I won't."

"Otherwise, you'll spend the rest of your life looking at the bars on a cell window."

Could have been clever, or trite. Could have said something that was dumb, stupid. She pushed the pistol into the waist of her jeans.

Almost kind, almost fond. "Silly boy. Go, go on, get clear."

She caught his sleeve, tugged at it, then scooped up the Popeye bag and looped it over her shoulder. Did not look at him. As if neither of them had anything more to say. And she was gone, a fast athletic crawl close to the ground. He thought it generous of Anna Jensen to give him warning of a risk of arrest and advising him to lose himself: he would, and he'd have cause to. She was gone without sound, as if crawling over rough ground in the night was something she had trained for. He saw her backside slightly higher than her body, and saw the heels of her trail boots and the tiny fluorescent dots on the back of them.

He waited, and looked down on to the beach, and the activity there had died. He could see the groups that had formed. He thought that Isabella Munoz was still at the centre of the beach, and Sergio with her. Thought that the mother and son from Liverpool were sitting on a rock on the far side of the beach . . . Remembered places like this from when he was a child and taken by his mother and father to Devon or Cornwall, with his sister, family holidays with swimming and rock pool adventures. And remembered the hurt that he had done them when he walked away from their lives, and doubted they would have understood the need for their own protection by his severing all links. Worth it? Was the job worth it? Was the end game worth it? The instructors said, *Someone has to do it, pay that price, get the work done – and best that 'someone' is a stupid fucker, dim, like you.*

Had never anticipated that truth about her, had thought her an artist without talent and living out her life on the cliffs and above the beaches and creeks and river inlets of the Costa da Morte. Had not seen what was waved in front of him – which made him the "stupid fucker, dim". Kenny inhaled, then whistled. Chose not to use the phone's emergency button. Did not want them charging towards him. Made the cry of a sea bird, might have been a fulmar's or a shearwater's or a petrel's. He watched the line of the mist on the beach, the tide advancing over the sand, and the line keeping pace with it.

They were close. He smelt the goats.

The camera was with Jak Peters, and the binoculars with Hugo, and Wilf was unscrewing a Thermos and pouring and passing.

Hugo said, "They were dozy beggars at the block, so we just went round them."

Wilf said, "Get that down you, and there's a splash of *Veterano* in it, warm you up."

Jak Peters said, "Hope that bloody woman isn't going to screw it. Where is she?"

He gestured with his head, forward and towards the beach below. "Have to hope she's better at the day job than at painting."

And all of them settled, watched and waited.

Jonas waved.

Vera stood and watched him from the caravan's door, and held the cat tight against her. He had to strain to hear what she called to him.

"Bye, Jonas. Let's hope you get a clean bill of health from the mechanic."

"Let's hope so."

"And that you're sensible when you see him."

"Will be very sensible."

He drove away across the field. Might have gone too fast, and mud spewed out from his rear tyres. None of the other caravans in the field yet showed a light. He went as far as the gate, looked in his mirror and saw that Vera, with Olaf, was still at the door but she no longer waved to him. He supposed it a degree of selfishness, how she coped with the next few hours, and whether she enjoyed a visit to a passage grave from the Neolithic Age. He opened the gate, drove through it, closed it and called back across the field.

"Absolutely, most sensible."

Illegal, of course. Ignored, of course. Jonas scanned his phone screen, saw the text from Jak Peters, acknowledged it. One hand on the wheel and the one that he used to message Fanny Thomas was also required to change gear. Would be needing to do that on the approach track to the farm and the avenue of bent, distorted trees leading to the main road. Alerted her, then the gear lever, then two hands on the wheel and good scope here for a Pot Hole wallah and the car bounced furiously as he accelerated.

He hit the road that would take him down towards the coast, and east. And a first trail of light from away over the sea and the city that was his destination, and in the car boot was his vest and his spray can. But he needed still, his headlights on full power and near to the farm a fox froze, caught in the beam, and he wondered if it were the same one that had yelled in the night, or a friend of that one, then it dived from sight, was gone for cover. Jonas Merrick felt that sense of acute excitement, which – not proud of it – he craved.

But his role now was only that of witness, and being a "sensible" one.

16

His corner of the supermarket car park, most likely not covered by a camera, was empty. Jonas parked, unfastened the seat belt, leaned back, closed his eyes. Two outcomes to reflect on. A lunch party thrown by the Deputy Director, a Chief Constable down from the north-west, and a couple of Home Office mandarins, with the FBI and DEA sending their station chiefs, and even the Spanish ambassador and the AssDepDG there to act as greeter and oiler and provider of flowing alcohol. Mutual congratulation would be showered, and Jonas Merrick would be in his cubicle two floors below. The talk would be of cooperation and the value of trust, and discreet leaks to favourable media outlets, "getting on top of a difficult and dangerous problem". Or an inquest held in a conference room at the Home Office, biscuits and coffee served, and the same mandarins and the same Chief Constable, and the same people from the DEA and FBI, and an attaché from the Spanish delegation, snorting with the energy of a wounded bull. And the DG on leave and his deputy unavoidably not available, and Jonas Merrick in his cubicle and a bathtub of criticism due to be dumped on him.

Would be the celebration or the inquest, nothing in between. The celebration would be rich, and the inquest would be brutal.

And he realised that he did not particularly care whether he was alone in 3/S/12, with the noise and bustle of the A Section people beyond the flimsy wall, or whether he would be grudgingly praised or damned. He was expecting to be back on the island of Anglesey by late morning. He took off his glasses, and with the handkerchief from the breast pocket of the Harris jacket, began to polish the lenses. New ones, of course, because that rather sweet girl, the

Sixer, had caused him to lose his old pair . . . Funny thing that she
had tried to drown him, then had changed tack and had tried,
tried very hard, to save his life. He still felt a fondness for that girl,
wherever she was. Had never believed that the river had taken her.
Felt an even deeper fondness for the young man, Kenny. Was
relieved to know that Hugo and Wilf, and Jak Peters, were now
with him, and that danger to his person was minimal. Could not
imagine how the lad felt, whether the same excitement lifted him,
that Jonas was experiencing.

Another car had come alongside. A man stepped out. A big
man, heavy shoulders and a heavier belly straining behind a wide
leather belt, a crew-cut head and a night time's stubble on his face.

He extracted the brimming ashtray from his car and emptied
the contents on the ground. Noticed Jonas and grinned. Then
went to the back of he car, lifted the boot and took out three plastic
bags that bulged with rubbish, and tipped the contents on to the
fag ends and then dropped the empty bags on top. Jonas gave him
his familiar inane smile. The car was driven away. Jonas had the
registration number. The driver would be nailed. The right time
and the right place, but not now, when the dawn was coming up
and he was alone.

Jonas left his car, crouched down and refilled the bags, with
every last piece of packaging that had contained pizzas and crisps
and nuts and chocolate bars and fags, and all that he could manage
of the filter tips and even scooped some of the ash. He dropped
them in a nearby bin. The best he could do, and so much better
than being pulped except that anger was left rampant.

And sat back in his car, did not dare to close his eyes, and waited.

Kenny was focused on the line of rocks that fringed the bay below
him, and had not seen her.

His control, whose authority had been ceded, would have noted
that Kenny's attention was not on the beach and not on the mist
wall, and that he did not watch the haughty figure of Isabella
Munoz, her family and attendants and parasites around her. Nor
did he watch the Liverpool pair, the mother and her son, who had

been abandoned, and might have been thankful merely to be able to watch the arrival of what they had paid for.

The light grew, with a watery, milky pallor. He would have been entitled to feeling anxious that she would appear, wreck it all, create chaos by giving warning of the intervention that would be led by Jimbo Rawe. Remembered him at the talent show when he had gone to Merseyside, been slipped in through a rear door to the HQ block and had worn a balaclava, and only a very few of those he had met had regarded that as theatrical. Had been quizzed and challenged, and they had sought to unnerve him. He had realised that they went to the edge of the budget available and beyond. DCI Rawe, overweight and an addicted smoker, had the smell of a thief-taker – the jargon for a better than average detective – and had said: "I don't want a crusader. What I need is a nerveless little fecker who will be proactive. Who will attract local business from this little corner of the country – top of the tree for cocaine traffic. Not more, not less." But the money had run out, and Rawe had said the tank was empty, time to come home. They were ready on the beach, and the light grew and the first shadows were long and went from the sand to the surf, then were swallowed in the mist.

He saw Laureano, in a small Zodiac rib. He was standing with the engine clucking and was pointing behind him to the wall of mist. He thought the talking on the beach stopped and there was silence as the men walked into the water. The engines of the pick-ups were revving behind them . . . and he saw Fredo, splashing in the surf, like a kid.

It was always like that. In the moments before a Class A delivery was about to materialise, and the message had come to the team that all was well, on schedule, they thought themselves untouchable. He had seen it with the shipments reaching the buyers on each of his two previous legends, and then had been in the background and merging with the shadows and had done the signal on the phone or the gear he'd been given by the boffins. Had seen the euphoria and the yelling and the clenched fists and had been edging away. His eyes scanned the rocks in front of him, and he looked for her. Jak Peters, cold beggar and a reader of intentions and moods, would have noted it.

"Seen her?"

"No."

"What is she?"

"Not my business."

"What division of the Dutch cops is she? Not your business?"

"She's an artist."

"For God's sake, Kenny. Get real. Must have been crowded, two undercovers on the same beat. Did you know her well?"

"I knew her."

"You're not telling me that this girl, fronting as a painter, was your squeeze?"

"It doesn't matter, and I'm not . . ." Brutal, basic, the interrogation was off limits. ". . . not going down that road, who she was. Close it down."

"Sounds like she was more than your squeeze, Kenny. Like bed-time company."

He flailed out with his fist, and Jak Peters rode it easily. Hugo had a hold of him and then Wilf had a grip on his arm, and he thought both handled him as if he were an hysterical kid. There was sufficient light for him to see that a grin played at Jak Peters's mouth. Common talk among all the Level Ones when they met up on courses, that the controls regarded them as children, and that they all needed breaking and made to get back in line . . . It would go on Kenny Blake's report that he had enjoyed an "improper relationship" with a Netherlands-based operative: was scarred. Jak Peters had amused himself enough with Kenny, and the light enabled him to do the important work evidence gathering. He had the camera up to his eye, and the telephoto jutting out, and was clattering the shutter, and let out little tiny whoops of pleasure. Hugo first, then Wilf, loosed him.

He saw her. She was moving easily among the great granite rocks, was almost at their base, and the spray climbed close to her.

A roar came up from the bay, consumed Kenny's attention.

★ ★ ★

It shuddered.

An impact, then it freed itself, then lurched forward again.

Diego, the only survivor, was on the cockpit floor. Alongside him, the gull howled, but he did not see it. With each minute more light filtered through the haze made by the dirt and debris of the sea that had settled on the windows in front and beside him. He could see their beds, their bags, seemed to hear their voices. There was a grinding scrape and the craft tilted and seemed to be held, but another wave came and lifted it and then let it free again. He could not remember how great had been the load of fuel in the bladders when he had started out from the Amazon delta, many litres of it, and now exhausted and the craft more buoyant. He could see patches of greater light where the cloud thinned, and the day was dawning on him. At first, Diego felt a sense of gratification. At such a moment, he might have thought of a religious blessing, such as the priest passed round on Feast and Carnival days – or might have thought of the beauties of the woman that the management of the hotel would provide – or might have thought of a fine wine in his throat or the cooking of seafood in this region in his gullet, and its taste. Might have entertained any of those thoughts for seconds and savoured them.

He was jolted again and the craft rolled and water splashed over the cockpit and the window was partially open so it spewed among the ribs of the flooring, lifting the last of the blood, and shifting the white stuff that might have been bone, or might have been brain tissue. He saw the gull alongside, and the bird was the witness.

The mist closed around them, like a great sheet had been draped over the windows. Diego pulled himself up. The pangs of his hunger were desperate and the dryness of his throat, and he needed to cling to a handrail to support himself. He tried to recall what he had rehearsed, but the stories were muddled between a mutiny, sickness, an accident where the boy had slid off the hull, and the engineer – a hero – had gone in after him, and both lost before Diego could turn the wheel hard enough to go back for them. Was unsure whether he had the strength left to get on to his hands and his knees and use strips from his T-shirt to gouge out the blood stains between the ribs and find all the bone or brain. Another scrape and the hull teetered, then freed itself.

He saw the gull at its airborne station, and saw the body. Still on his back, Matias floated alongside.

They were trapped together in the mist: the body, and the hull of the *Maria Bernarda*, drifting on the incoming tide, and a light wind from the west enabled the gull to stay with them, using minimum effort. He had no view, but he could hear sharper and more recognisable sounds. Might have been the surf on a beach, might have been a small outboard motor, might have been shouts in the language and the accent of his home.

Matias's head looked the same, the wounds for the entry of the bullet and the catastrophe of its exit were unaltered. The blood was the same, the colour of a splash of *rioja* on a tablecloth, shit on the gull's beak and he thought it would have gouged deeper into Matias's eye sockets. Diego was sick, vomiting a sort of slurry from his stomach that caught in his throat and he needed to heave to get it even to dribble from his mouth . . . and could not recall the story he would tell.

It was a supreme effort but he managed to combat the weakness and stand by the wheel, cling to it, and then reach into the drawer and take out the Luger pistol. He knew what would be his target. Again the hull scraped on rocks and he remembered the tales of the wrecks on the Costa da Morte, off the lighthouse away to the south, which had brought him in and was at a place named the End of the Earth. The craft rocked and shook, and he lost his grip and fell to the ribbed floor.

He heard the cheering, as if he were an honoured man and this was his homecoming.

It broke through the mist.

Hugo murmured, "That is just incredible."

Wilf whispered, "Like a beast, a monster."

They were both trained as Royal Marine Commandos. Had been in conflict, had become used to the sea and treated it without fear, almost as a friend, and both had gasped at the sight of what was emerging. The tide brought it in, gaining clearance from the surface fog. It was painted grey, and had a stubby bow, not stream-lined like a shark, but with the profile of a whale and seemed built for sturdiness, not speed. As the seawater surged on the forward part of the hull it was easy to see a large paint scrape, and a long, angled dent, and both men would have realised they came from a collision.

"Near scuppered them."

"The bleeding obvious, that's a heavy clout they took, and a puncture the size of a fingernail would have done for them."

It had pockmarks along the hull, and clusters of living creatures had made a home there. It kept on lurching further up the beach, and plain to both Hugo and Wilf that it had no power left. Each wave brought it further in, and out of the mist wall, and then breaking the swell was the outline of a cockpit.

"Could you have been in there, Wilf, for that distance?"

"Close to five thousand miles, Jak said, and three men as crew. Hugo, Not a chance."

One more heave from the waves and it would have been the final movement, and Wilf grabbed Hugo's shoulder and pointed and they could see crude paintwork, first only identi-fiable as a jumble of letters on the hull, painted in white, and they had Jak Peters's binoculars up, and Hugo read it out loud. *Maria Bernarda.*

"What, who is Maria Bernarda?"

"Just a name – even that brute has to have a name."

Behind them, Kenny Blake identified those gathered on the beach. First was Isabella Munoz, clan leader and raw power.

Hugo gave the commentary, and had Kenny to prompt him. "Huge moment for her. Her biggest deal. Done major trafficking but this is the biggest. She'll have a massive financial investment in this, and it has landed, is waiting for her. A moment of triumph . . . Look at her, doing a sort of jig. Heh, wasn't that what

Hitler did in Paris? The dance of success? It makes her the top player in the Galicia market. Queen of all she sees."

Wilf said, "That will be her son, Sergio, beside her, clapping like they are at a bullfight. He's the one who recognised that Kenny was the danger, read the runes right, and now will have shut his mouth. Real excitement. Won't matter how many times he has taken delivery of a cargo, this is the best because it has come out of the deep, out of that bloody creature. Unique for him."

More directions from Kenny.

Hugo said, "So that is Douloures Govier, the traveller. The woman on the climb. Nothing that has happened to her in Liverpool could have come close to matching this. She will have dug deep into the family funds, stripped them damn near bare, and this is the supreme moment and she can see the doomsters laid flat. She has won. Look at her, fist up, clenched tight, that's the gesture – supreme . . . And the boy, Kenny? That is her son? Patrick. Out of his depth, a fast learning curve . . ."

More gestures from Kenny, more identifications.

Wilf said, "That's Fredo. Decent café. Perhaps he has the biggest stake. His boy a hostage and far beyond reach. And his cousin had a son in the same sort of place, and is landing with him about now, in Madrid. Except that the cousin's son is in cargo. Look at him. On his knees, on the sand, close enough to the prow to touch it, and will be offering prayers of gratitude . . . Going to be bad for him, Kenny. You can take that? Making it bad for him?"

And Kenny had more for them. There was a German and his father had piloted a U-boat to this coastline in the war, and there was a man from down south in the country who had made a new home here after his father was denounced as a killer in the history of Spain's bad times . . . and more clients to the business of the Biscuit Tin that Kenny had run.

Laureano was noted, crawling forward down the length of the hull and near to the cockpit.

Then screams, and shouting.

Hugo and Wilf exchanged the binoculars, lips pursed, and tension spreading. Always was, to both of them – veterans – a cause of tension when "death" showed up.

Hugo said, "Watch that gull. Look where it lands."

Wilf said, "Watch what the gull lands on."

Barely recognisable as a human head, and the body more like a half-emptied sack and the legs like stray lengths of wood that had been tacked loosely to the sack. It was on the beach, at the water's edge and the surf came up and shook it and then receded. The gull held court.

"It is a male body."

"Not been long in the water."

"A slap-up dinner for that bird."

"Has come up on the tide. The body, the bird and the boat."

More interesting to Wilf were the efforts of Laureano, powerful and muscled and dripping, to open the hatch from the outside. He called out, and men hurried to obey him. A sledgehammer was brought and passed up. Laureano swung it and the noise of the impact was heard by the watchers. Wilf watched intently. The windows of the cockpit caved. Laureano felt inside and freed a catch. The sledgehammer was tossed aside. The hatch was opened, and Laureano seemed to recoil, as if a stench eddied round him, then he took a deep breath and dropped down inside. Minutes later he reappeared, carrying a man on his shoulder, the way firemen did. Lifted him clear, and both were retching, and dropped him, allowing him to slide down the side of the hull and into the water. It was cold enough to jolt the man. First he sat, then started to crawl. No one helped him, everyone gazed at him. In his path was the body, and the bird flapped away, its beak full. The man howled, like a wolf, and was reaching into his belt and . . .

Hugo said, anxious, "The woman, the Dutch woman, she is going too close."

Wilf said, "I can't see her. She does not need to be that near. She should hunker down, stay back . . . Look at him, that guy."

★   ★   ★

The monocular hard on his eye, Jak Peters watched from the cliff.

Men were swarming forward, wading into the water, and some brought wheelbarrows as far as they could be pushed. The light was spreading fast, and there was an urgency. Isabella Munoz held her place on the beach, arms folded across her chest; Doloures Govier was standing in the surf, the water above her ankles and pushing Patrick forward so that he'd be of use . . . The first shot was fired. The man from the cockpit, who had come from the far side of the world, had aimed haphazardly at the gull that shrieked above him.

Jak Peters saw it, was the witness. A second shot was fired, from close range and into the body which absorbed a bullet and barely trembled. More shots were wildly aimed at the gull, and more at the corpse, and there was screaming and shouting, and bullets flew high into the first light of the morning, clean and clear, or striking the chest of the man. Jak Peters heard the click that told him a final round had been fired, that a magazine was spent . . . and the man who had crossed an ocean, brought with him a cargo worth millions, lay on his face in the sand, water running off him, and beat at it and splashed himself.

Jak Peters said, "'Those whom the Gods would destroy, they first make mad.' That's Euripides, Greek, fifth century, before Christ. Bit of a race on now. Get the stuff out, then all shoulders on the push, get the bloody thing refloated. Wonder what he'd done that gave the Gods the hump. But they did for him, took his sanity . . . Kenny, I'm thinking it's time the cavalry came."

He scanned the rocks, and so did Hugo and Wilf. Only Kenny ignored the stones and the pools and the weeds lit by the first low, creeping sunlight of the day. Toyed with a medallion hanging at his neck. Jak Peters could not see her. He made his call.

The first bale came out, from a hatch on the hull and two men staggered under the weight of it.

"Rawe, move your crowd, get them here. They're starting to unload. Ten minutes? Move in on them . . . it'll be a royal flush."

"I said ten minutes – was that generous or flinty?" Jimbo Rawe said to his new friend, the DLO, Freddy Ashe.

"Probably optimistic."

"Do what you can, please. Get that sense of urgency boiled up."

He went toward the car. Ashe, big gestures and machine-gun speech, was in the ear of their officer. Men started to run and load backup, and half-smoked fags were chucked down. The engines hacked into life, and they were starting to roll. Jimbo Rawe understood. Would have been the same in Liverpool, his home city, adopted, had he been to any of the outlying cop shops and rounded up the desk people and the custody people, and a few from traffic, and schools liaison, ignoring the specialised Serious Crime Unit teams and the firearms "elite". The ones who were in the three minibuses leading the way down a narrow lane with high banks and going as fast as they dared, without headlights – all of them would have had the local equivalent of relations or neighbours or friends who knew what the spread of Class A stuff was about. Would have known someone with a kid they despaired of, on a downhill canter, addicted and heading fast for court and custody and a fecked up life before, most times, it had even started. Knew what it was about, had learned in the quiet of their own company to loathe the people who spread the toxic mix of chemicals and waxed fat, feckin' fat, on profits. Nothing "elite" about Jimbo Rawe's private army but he thought they'd be fingering their never-used sidearms, would give it their best effort.

He had started to hum. Beat his fingers on the dash. His personalised, bastardised and croaked version of 'McAlpine's Fusiliers', and Ashe picked it up and the car rang with the sound of their awful rendering of the jig. And the light was behind them and growing and soon they would hit the first of the blocks set up for a tripwire warning – were going faster . . . but his estimate of ten minutes seemed fanciful.

Kenny saw her in the rocks, almost at the level of the beach, and the tide was far in and swell broke around her, and threw up spray and shifted great banks of weed. Between them was a rough track, good for a goat or an agile walker, and not to be charged at, and the stones would be loose and the mud would crumble. Not a descent to make without care.

She might have slipped on the weed, might have tripped on a rock ledge, might have cracked her camera lens and hissed a curse – whatever . . . She was seen. Her clothes were wrong. Would have been useful up on the clifftop and squatted against heather and dead gorse, and probably the colour of the Popeye bag was also wrong – pink when there was nothing else around her to match it. She had a camera and a lens, that could have photographed the width of the beach, and the principals would have been easily enough identified, and yet she had gone closer. Would have wanted a "perfect" picture, one that made targets recognisable without enhancement. Unnecessary.

Wrong clothes, wrong camera and wrong bag, wrong place.

Their hands were on him and he smelled their goats, and thought they'd have been tended with the same gentleness as they were using on him.

She was clutching at a rock for a better grip, and one of her feet went down on a floor of weed that only covered a pool, and she lurched. And was spotted by an elderly man, who watched that part of the shore line, too old to help with the unloading of the bales, was along for the ride. His arm went up, his cigarette was caught at the side of his mouth and wobbled, and he pointed, and the yell came from deep in his throat. Had called for help. And, instinctive from her, she had to stand at her full height because only then could she see around her, do the panorama, recognise what force she had unleashed and start her flight. Could not crawl away, needed to judge her ground.

Heads turned. More of them saw her. A gradual cry going up and spreading on that side of the beach. A swell in the voices on that side of the beach and attention switching from the gull and the corpse and the guy whose pistol magazine was exhausted and was lying at the water's edge. Ignored by those in the line who were starting to shift the bales.

It was one minute and a half since Jak Peters, behind Kenny, had called up the intervention from Jimbo Rawe – and eight minutes and a half from when that intervention might be effective. Too long? Kenny did not know.

She was starting to scurry back towards the cliff path, but the rocks and the weed and the pools did not make for easy flight, and she fell again. The fingers on Kenny's back tightened, held his coat.

Men were running, voices were raised, and some were faster than she, and the gap on her closed. The younger men from the coast, brought up in the bays and inlets of the Coast of Death, were surefooted. Kenny knew she had the pistol, short range . . . but to use it she had to stop, turn, find cover, have a good overview of the rocks, steady herself, and aim. If she fired high she would not slow them. If she fired straight, wounded or killed, then there was the possibility that they might stop, *might* back away, might wait for someone to reach the front of the pack with a rifle or a shotgun. Might work out for her, might not . . . Kenny saw her face.

Kenny knew that face from the pillow in his bed, her bed. Knew it from when she stood at her stove and grinned at him as she fried their supper. Knew it best when she was astride her stool and it was close to her easel, and the wind came off the sea and danced her hair across her cheeks. Knew the face . . . and he held tight to his St Christopher as if for comfort. The hands on his wristwatch seemed to have slowed. She should have ditched the Popeye bag, should have dumped the camera. Ought to have lightened her load, but the bag was everything about her and the camera was what her work involved, and she hung on to them – and she was slower than the pack.

A crowd was pursuing Anna Jensen, would reach her while she was still among the rocks at the tideline, would catch her before she gained the cliff path. The unloading, Kenny saw, had not slowed and the first of the pickups was backed up as far as the line where the tide ebbed and sharp tracks marked it. One bale already in, but more to come, and another pickup waiting to be called forward. The pack closed on her.

He looked at Isabella Munoz. Something disdainful in the way she had turned her head briefly, seen a security breach being dealt with, and had returned to watch Laureano supervise the unloading from the gaping entry to the cargo hold. Sergio was beside her, his phone at his ear. It was their moment of triumph and a fast, short, failed, intervention would not destroy it.

She had the pistol out. The camera bounced on her chest, and the strap of her bag slid on her shoulder. He did not think that Anna Jensen, four years on the coast and all that time learning the local culture, would have believed that the sight of a small handgun – good for show on a police officer's hip in Amsterdam or Rotterdam – would slow them. They closed on her. Within a minute, Kenny thought, they would engulf her.

He glanced at Doloures Govier, and thought she cringed. Would have been swept away in the belief that all was foolproof, and saw a woman being chased and hunted down. Patrick was at her side pointing, yelling in her ear . . . not hard to read. Kenny could remember the lunch in the restaurant taken over by the *matriarch*, and recalled how the boy had eyed him – hostile, suspicious – and had looked away each time that Kenny had smiled at him. Assumed the boy had denounced him, assumed the denunciation had been ignored . . . Some might have wondered why Kenny Blake was not on the beach after her endorsement of him.

She tried to stand, was aiming, but the barrel was wandering. There had been film once – shown by the instructors – of two soldiers in civvies in West Belfast and it was said the driver had driven into a crowd of Republicans and the vehicle surrounded and him trapped with his colleague, and he had waved his pistol at them but they had not backed off and had swallowed him, then had killed him, and the second soldier. The scent of a quarry had overwhelmed fear of a handgun.

He saw Fredo in the line that staggered under the weight of the bales as they were shifted from the hatch and through the surf and then heaved up and into the pickups. At that distance he could not tell whether the worry lines had started to crease the café owner's forehead, whether he saw an image of his son.

They were on her. She had not fired. He did not know why. She went down, and one of them must have pushed into her upper legs, and another had a hold of her clothing.

The hands were firmly on Kenny's shoulders. His wristwatch told him that less than three minutes had been used up of the ten that it would take Jimbo Rawe's gang to get on to the beach. Her head came up and her hair was dripping wet and weed had garlanded her neck. A hand caught her arm, the one holding the pistol, snatched at it. He heard an intake of breath from Wilf, sharp and prolonged. Heard the murmur of Hugo's advice: "Take one with you, my dear, or take two. Get it done, dear." And saw anger in her face, bright eyes flashing and a man wrestled her for the pistol . . . Kenny recognised him: in the electronic ledger of the Biscuit Tin was a little north of 25,000 euros of that man's money, and his breath always smelled of garlic.

They were body to body and another had hands round her throat, and another had ripped her clothes . . . There was something terrifying about her, what he did not know of her . . . The pistol fired. The one who wrestled with her sagged. Hands tightened on her throat, another man picked up a rock the size of a kid's football and smashed it down on her head. Kenny saw the blood in the gold of her hair, and she sank. No cry, no shout, no curse. Four or five crouched over her and water frothed. He thought they held her under, drowned her.

He could not have moved had he wished to.

Assumed that Jak Peters had orchestrated the restraint.

He lay on his stomach.

Would have been a full minute before Hugo and Wilf marginally relaxed their grip on Kenny. He turned his head and could see that Wilf had a foul crumpled apology of a handkerchief in his hand, and Kenny knew that if he had sucked in air preparatory to shouting then it would have been stuffed down his gullet to silence him.

They pulled her up out of the water. There was no movement. They left her. Their priority was their friend, the investor of 25,000 euros in the Biscuit Tin, a nice little earner and tax-free, but not of great use to a man with his chest slashed open by an entry wound, a shattered ribcage, and the detritus of broken bones. Any *triage* medic would have shaken his head, Kenny imagined, and dismissed the chances of getting to spend the nest egg as slight. They were carrying him back towards the sand, and the unloading line had gathered pace and it was safe to assume nearly a quarter of the cargo was unloaded already and stacked on the hull, waiting to be shifted. The gull hopped about and watched them; the man with Jak Peters's madness lay still, his head in the surf; and she had been laid on a rock. He could not see her face, and she did not move.

Kenny thanked Wilf and Hugo. "Nice kid, good kid, just allowed the excitement to get to her, and made mistakes. How long till Jimbo shows up?"

Four fingers and a thumb shown by Jak Peters.

Kenny said, "The way you hope things will turn out – they seldom do."

He pulled the chain over his head. Gave the medallion a squeeze, tight on the St Christopher head, and then reached out and hooked the chain over a strand of gorse, and it fell and was hidden. He did not think it important to tell any of them that he would not have moved from their vantage point, not made a grand gesture, not hazarded the work of three years, not shown his love. He thought it was a good place to leave the medallion which was about the only item of personal importance he had owned. Left it for her, with her.

"Good morning, Mrs Merrick. Come on in and join us."

The small coach had pulled up at the end of the farm lane. The tour guide, cheerful, greeted her. She had fed Olaf, had allowed him to saunter around the hedgerow, but his hunting had been unenthusiastic and he'd been happy enough to settle back in his cage in the caravan, and a litter tray was available. There was a glimpse of sunshine, and she assumed that the paying punters had been told there was an early start that morning, and that she was responsible, and breakfast might have been curtailed. Challenging stares greeted her. She boarded and found a seat.

The coach started up.

"As soon as your husband explained the situation we were only too happy to help."

"It is very kind of you."

"The least we could do. What with it being your wedding anniversary and this such a special holiday, coming back to the place of your honeymoon week. We're delighted to help, and then the problem with your car, and your husband needing to get that fixed."

"I'm sure he was very eloquent. I'm most grateful to you."

"An anniversary and a car playing up. It's the least we could do . . . I told him where we'd be, and later."

They headed for the Telford bridge, and the island of Anglesey, and a passage grave from the Neolithic era.

Where Jonas sat in his car, head down and cap peak forward, he had a view of the car park.

The police had arrived, in unmarked black vans. The windows were smoked glass and impenetrable, but the back doors were open and he imagined that those who needed to smoke were hanging clear of the vehicles . . . There were men and women in Thames House who had discovered which windows opened on to the street at the back of the building and they'd lean out, at risk to life and limb, to puff at a cigarette. Not all of them could slip away from their desks, go to St John's Gardens, find a bench and watch the gardener sweeping imaginary leaves and find relief from the craving.

He saw Fanny Thomas, an acolyte hovering close to her.

She was fidgeting, fretful, pacing . . . She was, pretty much, the final piece in the jigsaw. Most times that would have been an easy item to slot, the easiest. Nothing was easy. He knew that Kenny Blake was under the watchful eyes of Hugo and Wilf. Knew that Jak Peters had taken charge on the ground, and that they were high above a beach where that most extraordinary of beasts had emerged, was now like a marooned whale, its innards – in 50-kilo bales – being removed and taken through the surf and towards the sands. Knew also that Fergal Rawe and an army of police from outside the immediate region were now driving through a warren of lanes and unmade tracks towards the landing site. He needed one more confirmation – that arrests were in progress on the beach – and then he would call on Fanny Thomas to move forward. Not a minute before . . . The risk was that, without coordination, either the mother figure of the family or Xavier Govier, its muscle power, would have warning and would bunk out, that one or other would remain at liberty. Needed a clear sweep, needed the ends of all the lengths of string tied together. The call would come from Kenny. From a small white van, the sort a butcher's delivery boy might have used, a young woman had emerged and by the grass edge of the parking area and had set up a small drone, a rotary wingspan of not more than a metre. Below its body was a camera kit that was beyond Jonas's technical understanding, except that he knew what it would give them.

It was launched. It flew over Jonas, and climbed from his sight. Useful heat-seeking technology. Perhaps one day he would offer his congratulation to Fanny Thomas for the drone's introduction.

He would be at the top of the road, wearing his high visibility vest over his tweed jacket and holding the paint spray can, and would be able to look down the length of the road, past the cherry trees not yet flowering, and the parked cars. He would be able to see the front of the Govier home . . . felt his excitement mounting. The vans, where the firearms team now smoked, or read, or looked at their phones for predictions on the next day's football fixtures, would come sweeping past, and the guns would pile out in drills they practised each day, each week, and the ram would impact against the front door and splinter it open. Jonas had been told that both Xavier and Theresa Govier were still on the premises, were in bed together, asleep . . .

He waited. Felt an almost supreme satisfaction. Had promised to be "sensible" and had no intention of abusing his given word. By now Vera would be on her way to the island and to the historic gravesite where he would meet her. He waited for the call from

Spain that would tell him the net had been thrown and that the targets were trapped in its mesh.

A call did come. "Hello, Nikko. Yes, greetings . . . yes, all on course . . . yes, the wrong moment for speaking to you . . . yes, go away."

Bengal padded out of the bathroom.

He shook her shoulder. "Come on, girl, time to be on the move. Get yourself together."

She blinked, and swore, and gazed up at him with a child's adoration, and swung a bare leg out from under the sheets.

It did not seem strange to him that they had shared the two beds pushed together, or that he had held her hand while they slept . . . They would be gone in a few minutes because his schedule for the day was busy – always busy. Meetings, and more meetings . . . it would be good to have her with him and he liked the wild look of her when she wore no make-up and hadn't brushed her hair. She had the posture to go with it, arms loose and feet apart, and the weight on the balls of her feet the chin forward and a sneer at her mouth. They were the new team, and Ma would be told. He would not hear from her while she was in Spain unless there was a crisis. Only if there were a crisis would she call him, would he call her. He was lacing his trainers, and knotting them. She went into the bathroom.

He called after her, "I'm not hanging about – we're going pretty bloody soon."

It was Jimbo Rawe's finest hour.

Could not remember any time that matched it, even remotely.

They swept down on to the beach. They had crashed a block on the way, and the lead vehicle had dented its wing and smacked its headlights cannoning into a vehicle that was stationed across the road. Two men had fled. Down the hill, following a pair of pickups that were in blessed ignorance of what came after them, and then out on to the sand.

Only the good Lord knew how many months, hopefully years, were left to Jimbo Rawe. He saw the beast on the beach, tilting high above the army of worker ants busying round it, and others struggling to lift down the bales tightly wrapped in grey plastic. Saw the dent on the front of it, and saw creatures fastened to it, either shrivelling because they were out of water, or gleaming because the early morning light caught their shells. Saw a body in the surf line, twisted and abandoned and saw a gull that flew and shrieked at interruption of its feast. Guns out of their holsters and handcuffs held ready, his "Fusiliers" ran forward and began to corral prisoners. The surprise was total.

He yelled instructions. His foghorn voice, with its Wicklow accent, bellowed. He marched, right to left, forward and back. The volume of his shouts and his ever-moving presence did not mean that he was listened to. No notice was taken of him by the *subteniente*. The process was efficient, fast . . . and Jimbo Rawe saw himself as the principal architect . . . There might be times in the future, back in Ireland in the bar tucked away on the Kilmalin road from Enniskerry, in his retirement and with a Guinness put in front of him, that he might talk about this morning before the dawn had reached cockcrow time – talk of it to trusted friends.

He saw Doloures Govier. For a moment he was silenced and his arms dropped to his sides. All around him the police who had been press-ganged, happily, into the lift, were grabbing failed fugitives and handcuffing them, then forcing them to the ground, making them sit cross-legged. A line of bales stretched from the sand, over the tideline and on to the hull, and police were climbing up on to the hatch beside the cockpit. He stared at Doloures Govier. Could remember when he had been in her house and had needed to draw in his stomach in the hall while Fanny Thomas brought out the cuffed Mikey, and then she had been full of abuse for him, not stopped, kept shrieking it, and the kids mimicking her. Had seen her in court. Had dreamed of her. Had hated her, and now it welled.

"Good to see you, Doloures Govier. This your brat, the whey-faced shrunken brat?"

He would like to have thought that her shoulders crumpled at the sight of Detective Chief Inspector Fergal "Jimbo" Rawe

– legend on Merseyside, by his own rating – and her head dropped. So composed. Standing her ground, looking back at him like he was dirt on her shoe. Would have realised that the world was collapsing, and the boy had started to convulse out of nervous capitulation. She did not dignify him with an answer, which made his anger more acute.

"I am grateful to you, Doloures Govier. You have given my life new purpose. I aim to stay alive as long as it takes. Because of what happened to that girl, to Nansie, because of what you and your revolting family did to her, then I have to live long enough and when you croak in gaol, alone and unloved and frightened, then I want to be around to dance a reel – I've been practising the tune of it – on your grave, a pauper's one."

She spat towards him but it did not carry. She was handcuffed, pushed down on to the sand. The boy's legs were kicked from under him.

He walked away from her. He saw the *subteniente* personally arrest the matriarch of the Spanish clan. Done with deference, no cuffs on her wrists, no fists on her arms – and she was allowed to walk freely back up the beach and to the vehicles. Sergio was held but not manacled. The workforce were corralled and the police, as always on a big arrest day, strutted and enjoyed the glory moment, as did Jimbo Rawe.

Freddy Ashe tugged Jimbo's sleeve. "We get the hell out. You were never here, detail to be sorted out later. We get on the road . . . likely we'll be in the shit for not going through the channels and dump it on the Yanks, probably the Bureau. Come on, enough gawping . . . but I'll say this, Mr Rawe, you brought us a tasty one."

"Are you packed, David?"

"Yes, Jenny. Same as I told you five minutes ago. I am packed."

They were abandoning their home. When he backed the car out of the garage and stopped briefly in the drive for the bags to be thrown in, and her to get into the passenger seat, they would have locked the front door, would have quit. She was sitting at the

kitchen table, nursing a mug of tea. How long they would be gone
was undecided. Whether they would actually complain to the
Chief Constable's office was unresolved. The extent to which they
were beaten, fearful, was too obvious to talk about . . . Might go to
a hotel, might go west along the Welsh coast, or might go north
towards the Lakes. The heap of rubble that had been their front
wall was an eloquent reminder of why they were leaving. More
important, and more wounding, none of their neighbours had
called round to see them, to offer comfort, solidarity . . . and
Fanny Thomas had merely done cheap words, laced with the
usual honey, but had given no promise. Would never be the same
for them in that house, which was enough, almost, to drive them
to tears.

"I'm almost ready," he said.

"Just let me finish my tea," she said.

Jonas eased into his pothole officer vest, and put on plastic gloves.

The young woman still flew her drone and had a microphone
on a cable coming down from her earpiece. A few yards away
from her, Fanny Thomas had a headset balanced on her hair; she
looked as if she'd slept in a ditch. The team were back in the
vehicles.

His own phone wriggled. Jak Peters's message. *JM, Hope you
enjoying holiday. Dol and Pat lifted, cargo intercepted, local clan
nabbed. Finish it off . . . JP.* He sent his own message. Factual and
dull, and without a clever word, and thought that was how he
wished to be known. He'd seen Fanny look at her phone then go
to the back of the lead van. She was briefing them, and guys from
the other vehicle crowded round her, dwarfed her. Engines were
started, doors closed, and she hurried with her own guy to the car.
Time for Jonas to be on his way if the need were to be satisfied, the
addiction fed.

He got out of his car, locked it and walked briskly. Did not wish
to be late for the main event of his year in the backwater. He could
have copied Jak Peters's message to the man he answered to, the
AssDepDG, but it was a trait of Jonas Merrick that he rarely sent

a message of achievement before it was settled, the door slammed on it. Time enough when it was finished – and then he would be on his way to a passage grave, and would nod seriously and make out that his day had been blessed by being there. His breathing came faster, and he walked with a longer stride.

The police wagons and Fanny Thomas's car had not passed him, but he hurried. If the wagons came by and he was this far back then he would not see the action. Jonas kept going – had to be there, there at the finish . . . then he slowed, realised that a pot-hole officer would never scamper, and chuckled.

17

That morning, birds sang. The sun was low in his eyes. Jonas Merrick turned into the road.

A man came from his front garden, and a small terrier bounded towards Jonas's ankle, but was held back by a straining leash. The exchange was brief, but the man seemed cheerful, and finished by pointing out a hole in the road a bit further along.

Jonas had nodded attentively, was polite, and thought he covered well his total lack of concern for any potholes in their road. But where the man had pointed to, close to a tree that looked in the last stages of life and just short of a parked saloon, might well be the position he'd choose as his vantage point. He did not wish to be too far down the road and become a possible interference with the smooth running of the arrest process, but did not wish to be dawdling and therefore drawing attention to himself.

"Good to see you, chief. Very good. Trouble was that the gas didn't talk to the electricity, who didn't talk to the cable TV people. This part of the road was excavated by the gas, and filled in, then by the electricity, and filled in again, then dug up for the cable. Made an absolute rubbish job of it. Years, we've been waiting for something to be done."

Strange for Jonas Merrick to be accosted by "ordinary people". The phrase was much used, in tactical briefings: he disliked it. Disliked it because he regarded himself and Vera as ordinary people, and thought that their rights should be accepted as being as great as anyone's.

The drone, he assumed, was up but would be high enough so that its engine was silent at pavement level, might have been the sound of a distant bumblebee, and inside that property nothing would be heard.

He marked an imaginary hole by the gutter. He was left to himself before a woman came past and was pushing a buggy with a sleeping baby aboard, and she smiled at him and his response was limper, but almost a smile. He was less than a hundred yards from the position of the one that had been mentioned to him. The sun had become warm and his vest was zipped. He felt himself almost cooking inside it, and his jacket was snug, and his tie tight at his throat . . . He felt both stress, and that wonderful sense of fulfilment, of anticipation.

He was surprised that Fanny Thomas and her people had not yet swept into the road, charged past him, applied their brakes, and sprinted towards the front door. Half solid wood, half twin panels of coloured glass, a letter box. Would take a single blow from the ram if the locks and bolts were conventional, two or three if they had been enhanced.

Two school kids passed him, in uniform of a sort, and one smoked, and they regarded him as dirt, probably because he portrayed himself as a worker in a dead-end job, partly because he was old, and the cigarette was chucked down in front of him, and no attempt made to squash it, extinguish it.

He made another circle on the road surface but the crack it identified was minuscule.

Jonas was suddenly irritated that the police wagons had not come past him. He glanced at his phone but no new message showed on it. And suddenly there was movement ahead, on both sides of the road.

Jenny Potter was locking the front door. Her husband had the bags and was entering the garage. He backed the car out, then stopped in the driveway. Jonas had a good view of the rubble where the wall had been flattened. Jonas understood. They would have felt hounded, abandoned and isolated, their home had been violated. And they were "ordinary", as ordinary as Jonas and Vera, and he remembered the pent-up anger of the man the previous day. They were in flight, obvious. He could recall how it was, a

year before, after the near-drowning experience, it had been
suggested that he and Vera, and Olaf, leave their home, and he had
refused. Nobody would have, could have, told the Potters that a
police operation was scheduled to take place and would remove
the blight on their lives. He saw the tears on Jenny Potter's cheeks,
and the fury on David Potter's face, from humiliation.

The Potters noticed the movement across the road.

They came out, brother and sister. Stood in their porch, stared
in front of them. Theresa had the key to the front door, Xavier
stood beside her. Relaxed, calm, and without a vestige of panic,
which told Jonas that the first section of the arrest programme had
gone as oiled clockwork, and that a message of warning had not
been sent.

Jonas had the protection of his pothole officer high-visibility
vest, and his paint spray can. He was a hundred paces from the
two front doors. He had a view of both the Potters and the Goviers.

There was eye contact – had to be. The Potters stood by their
car. The Govier boy and the Govier girl stood in their porch space
and Theresa had the key at the lock. A High Noon moment.
Xavier, in Jonas's opinion, oozed power, authority, threat. Theresa
was a confused item of baggage . . . He could not read her, except
for an expression of aggression. The Goviers would have despised
the Potters, the Potters would have loathed and feared the Goviers.
A powerful brew, Jonas thought.

They stared at each other. Both held their ground.

Where the hell was Fanny Thomas?

The sensors slung beneath the drone had detected movement
inside the house. First moving inside, then heading for the front
door. Queries now competed in Fanny Thomas's mind.

Where to hit was the question.

At their front door, on the pavement and the wagons trundling
into sight? Ample warning for Xavier to start to run. Might go
round to the back garden, through a side gate and into a back alley.

Give him the opportunity to get in his car, turn the key, start to
move and have one wagon approaching from the front, and one

wagon from the back, and nail the bastard between the two of
them, block him there, H&Ks pointing at him through the window?
"Good shout, Ma'am," from her sergeant. "If that's what you
want, Ma'am, that's what you'll have, and do the *Cry Havoc* and
we go get them" from the gun club guys . . . and the rider of that
one wagon now had to go double damn fast up to a parallel street,
then do the right turn, then get to the top of the target road at the
same time as another wagon was reaching the bottom of the target
road. Fanny was in her car, waiting for Joe to power them into
position, waiting, cursing . . . and the sweat running on her because
of the weight of her bulletproof vest.

"You know what you are, Govier?" Jonas heard the raised voice
with its quaver of anger.

"What am I, Mister Potter? Going to tell me?" Jonas heard the
reply, the tinkle of derision.

"I *will* tell you. We are sick of bowing down to you."

"Am all ears, Mister Potter."

One had reached, Jonas saw, the limit of his self-control, and
the other saw an opportunity for sport . . . He hoped that Jenny
Potter would pull her husband back, heave him towards the car
door and get him behind the wheel. Hoped Theresa would drag
Xavier off toward the car in the driveway. Jonas stood. No car
came down the road, no dog walker, no buggy pusher, no school
kids. And no police wagons. The schedule so carefully manufactured by Jonas was already flying in the wind, tattered.

"You are scum. Hear me, scum."

"Not educated like you, Mister Potter – could you, please, spell
that."

"Bloody scum, you and all your vile family."

"I think that calls for an apology."

"You'll get no apology from me."

"Not used to that type of language, not in a nice road like ours.
You are lowering the tone of it, Mister Potter."

Jonas silently urged Jenny Potter – red-eyed, haggard, hair
haphazardly combed – to have the sense to pull him away, and

dump him into his car seat. So damned obvious that it was a spat that David Potter would not win, but could lose and be hard hurt.

But Jenny Potter's shrill voice joined in, "You are horrible and disgusting people, all of you. And the sooner you are locked up, the whole verminous tribe of you, the better."

And Theresa growled, "Don't you bad-mouth my family, you ugly cow . . . Go on, just fuck off out of it."

"I'll not take language like that, not at my wife."

"Won't you? And what are you, you long piece of piss, going to do about it?"

Jonas winced. Saw that Theresa Govier had eased a step ahead of her brother, her eyes blazing, her chin thrust forward, and her hands tea-pot fashion on her hips. Nobody came. No cars, trucks, delivery vans. No pedestrians . . . no police wagons.

Theresa Govier stepped forward, and so did David Potter. Jonas thought the couple had fallen into the trap set for them. The Govier brother and sister, smirking, had stood their ground on their doorstep as the Potters suffered, then cracked.

Jonas knew it from his friend who had been a detective sergeant in the disbanded Royal Ulster Constabulary and who used to do interviews with "bad boys" in the interrogation rooms at Castlereagh in what the retired 'tec called the "good old days". A familiar technique was to abuse a suspect about his wife, his kids, especially about his mother. Needling and annoying and that would lead to a flaring of the nostrils and the start of a shouting match and often broke through the ice when a Provo was stubbornly staring at a point on the ceiling and refusing to answer, not even giving a "no comment" . . . *ugly cow* and *long piece of piss* would have met the criteria laid down by the detective as likely to bring about a full scale shouting war, and the No Man's Land in the middle of the road would be challenged. One big difference from the interrogation suite was that the provocations did not end up in violence because Jonas's friend had always had a couple of stout men who would have slapped down a prisoner coming over the table at him, fists swinging. There was no protection for David and Jenny Potter.

It had not been intended to play out in this fashion. Should have been over, the matter dead and buried, and him back in his car and on his way to Anglesey. Jonas ducked his head, saw a crack in the road surface, and squirted at it, and covered his right toecap, too in cobalt blue.

David Potter, a man well past reason, started to walk. Jenny Potter kept up the conveyor belt of shrieked criticism, that had been building in her mind for ten years. Theresa walked down her garden path and on to the pavement and would not back off, her brother a pace behind her. Jonas watched, as the Govier daughter and the Potter husband reached the middle of the road.

Behind them, as if they were prize fighters, were their seconds, the Govier son and the Potter wife.

Jonas was not sure exactly how it started, where the first slap or scratch came from. He was shifting to hide behind a tree where he would have a more worthwhile view. David Potter could have swung an arm in front of him as a way of swatting the girl. Or she could have lashed out with a fist or with her fingernails. One moment apart, and then the mayhem of close-quarters fighting . . . Jonas thought David Potter a year or more older than himself, and that Theresa Govier was a third of that age, wiry and sinewy and, although she was wide-hipped, had no fat on her belly. Who had made the first contact was immaterial. The conclusion was clear. David Potter staggered from the impact of his hand against her, tripped over his own feet. Then she launched herself at him and he went down.

In the middle of a leafy road, a better suburb of the grand city of Liverpool – middle-class in convention and attitude, conservative in taste – where potholes were expected to be repaired by Council workmen, an old man and a girl fought for supremacy. And at stake, some sort of pride that Jonas thought warped, but he could not look away. The great plan that he had pieced together, the interception of a virtual submarine, the running of a counterfeit investment consultancy, the trapping of a matriarch, the safety of a Level One – all now fell down the pecking order as a hooligan scrap filled the road. He saw at least two front doors open, and then close, and he doubted phones would be lifted. He saw a mother coming along the pavement with a toddler in a harness, and she swept up her child and turned back. Theresa stood over the man, laughed into his face, slapped it and spat into it. David Potter raised an arm as if to deflect her, and his fingers might have gouged at Theresa Govier's eyes, and there was a scream of anger, and the fun was over.

The "seconds" came into the ring. Jenny Potter, skirt hitched, started to claw at Theresa's shoulders, and Xavier loped forward and had his hands on the woman's shoulders and was dragging her back and she might have bitten Xavier's hand. The Govier boy tugged his hand back and held it up and blood was starting to seep.

Where the hell was Fanny Thomas?

Jenny Potter was heaved clear and pitched out of the fight by her hair, and brother and sister had eyes only for David Potter, and the humiliation started. They ripped at his shirt and the buttons flew off. A vest was torn and a scrawny chest exposed. And then the trousers. Jonas knew about violence but had never seen that level of brutality on the street. The Potters fought back but to increasingly little effect, and her sobs were louder and his moans had replaced his first bitter and shouted complaint.

Jonas had given his word to Vera that he would be sensible.

He had intended – for personal gratification – to be a distant spectator of the last legs of a year-long operation. A voyeur. To experience something that might hold up as well in his memory as the medal and the bar to it that were secreted in Vera's knicker drawer.

He considered if his word mattered.

The laughter was more raucous and the crying more hysterical, and David Potter's trousers were at his knees. Jonas reckoned it a degree of outrage that would haunt the man to the end of his days. No neighbour came, and no police vehicle swung into the road, no young officers with their guns in their hands sprinted up the pavements to intervene.

Jonas took a deep breath . . . did not think he could again look himself in the eye, stare into a mirror, unless he intervened. Left his promise ditched, binned, trashed.

He took off his glasses and put them into an inside pocket of his Harris tweed jacket. He could not run but was able to manage a brisk crabbing advance towards them, and the fight was almost over. No contest at the start, and not now. He had only the can of spray paint as a weapon, and went as fast as he was able.

The police wagon, with the guns on board, was stuck behind a refuse truck. Fanny said the driver was not to announce their presence with sirens and lights. Fanny Thomas – out of sight and around the corner of the approach to the other end of the road – was assured that the refuse team were hard at it, loading their bins into the back of the truck, and in a couple of minutes, not more, they'd be out of the way and the wagon would be in place and ready to seal off the second potential escape route. And . . .

. . . and the drone operator, reported a fracas in the road but the drone lens was unsighted by the canopy of branches from a tree.

"Stop it, stop that," shouted Jonas.

Not a wise moment to announce his arrival. Too far back, and surprise lost. Xavier Govier had just lazily swung a kick into Potter's stomach, and not even been rewarded with a scream. The victim had gone pale, was now both a football and a punchbag. Theresa had scratched Jenny's face, and she was curled up and out of the game. So, brother and sister had time to prepare for Jonas's intervention.

Xavier came to meet Jonas. Theresa was pushing herself to her feet. Amusement showed on Xavier's face, but something more animal from Theresa. He left it to her – like this was part of a young bitch's training programme. She launched at Jonas, her mouth wide. The Potters were forgotten.

Jonas did not understand why there were no police vehicles clogging the road, no guys in black overalls and black vests, their black-painted weapons on the charge. He was supposed to be "sensible", had given his promise . . . He raised the can and had a finger on the button, was ready to depress it, had nothing else for his protection, and he hesitated.

She leaped at him, hands in front of her and knees raised. He squirted. Well done, Aggie Burns. She had not short-changed him with the cobalt. The paint went on to her body, coated her hands and covered her face. He saw a grin form on Xavier Govier's face. Theresa was on to Jonas, and her knee went into his groin, went hard, and he gasped and the can fell from his hands, and her other knee was under his chin and hooked back his head. He saw the sky and the treetops and then her head and her hair blotched blue, and her face that dripped, and the fury. She was raking her fingernails down his face, raining punches down on him and then she twisted sideways . . . and she seemed to poke around at her hip pocket. He tried to get a handful of her hair, but the paint made it slippery, sticky. She used her knee again, and the pain ran rivers in his old body.

He saw the blade.

She caught at his collar, found his tie, yanked it and exposed his throat. The blade shone.

If he had wanted to scream, he could not.

Jonas Merrick gazed into the eyes of Theresa Govier: he thought it an initiation for her, the moment she proved herself. Had to show she was a part of that family, worthy of inclusion . . . Some people, Jonas had read, used the last moments of their lives to babble. Might plead for mercy, might want to tell of the love of their kids, their wives, their parents, might start howling and let tears stream, might cringe . . . He tried to kick her and failed.

She was yelling at him, abusing him, mocking him.

Jonas had no doubt that his lifespan as a husband, as owner of Olaf, as clerk and analyst in 3/S/12 overlooking the river, was about done.

The knife was raised.

She screamed, "You interfering old bastard – well, fuck you . . ."

Her mouth moved but he could no longer hear her. The blade dropped and her head jerked, and the blood splattered on to the blue of his paint, and there was silence around him, and she fell forward and covered him, and he could no longer see the light, the sky, anything.

"Well done, Jocky. As good a double tap as we'll ever see."

"Too right, Jocky. Brilliant."

"Better late than never. I reckon she was about to skewer him," Jocky said, and the Glock was already back in the holster strapped to his thigh.

They had stripped Xavier Govier's clothes off him, left him only with his briefs. He was on his stomach, his wrists fastened with plastic tape and held in the small of his back.

"Bit of a mess, isn't he, the old boy from the Council?"

"If that's his blood then it's a hell of a mess. You took a risk, Jocky, her being so close."

"Had to. No option."

The body of Theresa Govier had been rolled clear. She had been patted down as routine and carried no further weapon or device. Quite dead, and the anger still on her face, but her eyes were already dulled. The pothole officer lay on his side, was out to the world, but was breathing and the medics were on their way. The Potters had been led to their garden and were sitting on a bench. A neighbour had belatedly visited and ascertained that they were "walking wounded" and mugs of tea were on the way. Xavier Govier had his mouth shut, said nothing, might have been reflecting on the actions of his sister, might not.

"You feeling good, Jocky?"

"Not bad."

The sergeant reached them, Fanny Thomas in pursuit.

"Jesus – is he all right?"

"Think so, don't know. Don't understand what a pothole chap is doing out at this time in the morning. It's not even half past seven now. And look at him. I mean, he's dressed for an old fogies' bingo session. Look at him."

The ambulance was coming, its bell clamouring.

The sergeant, Joe, eased aside Jonas's tweed jacket – seemed a shame that it was in that state, blood and paint – and the guy was out cold and didn't blink but was breathing. His dad had a jacket like that, bought in a charity shop, good quality from the Hebrides. He felt inside, and gingerly lifted clear a battered wallet, would have seen long service.

Fanny Thomas waited.

He read what was on the ID, safeguarded behind a plastic screen. "Bloody hell, Ma'am . . . big day for surprises. He's not into road mending. He's from Box. Name of Merrick, Jonas Merrick."

"All I need," she said. "Them having horned in, going to make it all untidy. A name that fucking haunts me. Leave it to the quacks to tell them at Box."

"Yes? Hello. Yes, who is this?"

On a Berkshire golf course, the AssDepDG was doing "swish fuck" with a colleague from Finance. It was A&E, he was told. A&E at the Royal Liverpool University Hospital. He and the colleague played their version of the game – swing the club and hit the ball, watch where it landed and then curse – every other Friday. He bit at a lower lip, and a bad feeling swilled in him.

A broad Irish accent on the phone. "We have a patient here, and there is identification material in his wallet. We rang a number listed on the ID to verify the name. They declined to answer but gave us your mobile phone contact."

"Did they now?"

"Merrick, is the name. A Mr Jonas Merrick: Would he be known to you, sir?"

"I think I can confirm I know that name."

The old bastard, he thought. The damned silly old bastard, and he saw a keenly competed game winding speedily down.

"We've patched him up, can discharge him in three or four hours. Severe testicular bruising which will be uncomfortable . . ." No snigger, not a hint of one, but it would play well with the people in A Section . . . "multiple abrasions, split lip, bruising on the arms. We thought he was worse because of the blood, and all the paint on him. We had to check with you because he was wearing a Merseyside Council high-visibility vest, was a pot-hole officer, and he used a paint spray can on the other party. With the blood, he looked pretty awful. The blood, good news for him, is not his. The police shot dead a woman at the scene, it was her blood. He's cleaned up now. And he's deaf. That won't last, but he's 'deaf as a post' right now. A policeman discharged a pistol beside his head, killed the woman. Not saying anything at the moment, rather subdued. I don't have all day and we are short of space so please arrange for him to be collected since you confirm he is one of yours. Thank you for your time."

The game was abandoned. Work to be done. And a strip to be ripped off Aggie Burns because she would have been the origin of a Council works' high-viz top, and that would have been the cover used to get himself on site, and been there too early, or whatever . . . He rang Harry, his driver, and requested the car with the tow bar be made available and he was to be picked up from Reading station, and Harry had murmured, "Oh, Jeez, not him again?" On the way towards the clubhouse his phone had started to spew out messages of congratulation. One from George, DepDG, encapsulated the triumph. *Very well done. You should take great pride in your efforts and our warm thanks to the team working for you. Plaudits from other agencies will cascade.* He walked briskly, had much to do and miles to travel.

He was asked by the Finance man, "Are you smelling of pig shit or rose hip?"

"Am starting to wonder whether you might find a billet with your lot for an Eternal Flame. Never goes out, doesn't go out because the bloody man is destined to be chained to a desk. I have a call to make. Yes, rose hip, baskets of them."

Standing at the entry arch into the passage grave, Vera took the call.

She said, gritted, "Where I am they used to put bodies. Four thousand years ago, north or south of that. I've seen several little corners where I could stuff him, then wall up the entrance. I suppose this is his idea of honouring his promise to be 'sensible'. Can we let him stew for a bit?"

The local police had been instructed to meet her from Bryn Celli Ddu, and drive her to the campsite. There she and Olaf would be picked up by Harry and the AssDepDG, the caravan hitched and driven into Liverpool, and two of the Thames House constables, relieved of guard duty, would be volunteered to travel north and collect the Merrick car from a supermarket car park.

"And, Vera, something you should know. A woman was shot dead by police during an arrest operation in Liverpool this morning. There were only two independent witnesses to the shooting and they have been told what they saw. Jonas was not a player there, was not in any way involved, and was on a training exercise in the wrong place at the wrong time. Best you believe that, the authorised version."

"Understood."

"A final point, Vera, a bit of a downer. You are entitled to administer a most severe *bollocking*. Yes – that is what I said – to him, and keep it going all the way back to Raynes Park, except that the proximity of a firearms discharge, twice, has left him – temporarily – stone deaf. Bollock all you like but, very sadly, he won't hear you."

She leaned against the stonework, faced and cut by a craftsman four millennia before, and tears ran on her cheeks.

In the three days he had been with them, Kenny Blake . . .

. . . wrong name. Wrong legend. Wrong passport. Wrong ID on the baggage labels on his rucksack and his bag . . .

. . . had grown fond of the goats. Had fed two kids, had carried fodder, had moved the electric fencing in the paddock, had done some of the repairs to a lean-to roof on a shelter, and had helped with the fence protection to the hive boxes, and had slept.

He had needed to sleep, and to rest, and to go missing. While the embassy in Madrid beavered at getting him a new passport, with back stamps, and an adulterated photograph duly stamped, he had been in hiding with Hugo and Wilf. By now, he had been told, a Europol international warrant would have been issued for a Kenneth Blake, financial consultant, British national, to be arrested following charges laid in the courts at Pontevedra of money laundering and conspiracy to defraud the Spanish exchequer.

He paused at the gangway.

The two military veterans were behind him. They had boarded at Santander, had escorted him to his cabin, shared with Jak Peters, and he'd assumed they had done a night of guard duty in the corridor. They would see him on to the gangway slope, then would stay on board while the cleaners worked around them and would sail back later in the day. They would go back to where, they had urged him, he would always be welcomed if he returned. He had a clean shirt, trousers and a jacket that the control had bought in Oviedo and new shoes. Would have looked like just another businessman returning to the UK. Job done, a legend finished and ready for binning, and no party for a returning hero. He would fade into the distance, and the name and times of Kenny Blake were bound for the office shredder.

He followed Peters. No backward glance at Hugo and Wilf. No promises they would stay in touch, because they would not.

He had stood a long time on the upper deck as they had come close to the Cornish and Devon coast, seen the ramparts of similar cliffs, and the indentations of similar beaches that he had known for the last three years, and had thought how it would play out. Did not know whether he had used his time well or had wasted it. He would go to the funeral. Jak Peters would learn where Anna Jensen would be buried, what cemetery, with full police honours. Probably in Utrecht. He would of course lurk in the shadows – most certainly not Kenny Blake, investment manager and lover, a fugitive. Would watch from a distance and be out of sight and beyond reach by the time the committal was over. No remote cottage, no log fire, no neat piles of clothing, no deceit. The end of a dream . . .

He would be sent to sessions with the shrinks, and more sessions with instructors, would undergo the debriefs, and would threaten to leave, walk away. They would look at him seriously, nod their heads, not try to alter his intention. Would let him go. The boredom would kick in . . . might go to see how his parents were, from a car with privacy windows, or stand back as the kids came out from school, or see how well the new guy was embedded with Hannah. And when the boredom became worse than an itch and needed serious scratching then he would pitch up again, at the little office out of which Jak Peters worked. No one would seem surprised, and they'd get to kick ideas around, and might talk of a talent contest where bids could be made for him . . . like a damn treadmill. He followed Jak Peters down the gangway. And across the Biscay the cells at Corunna and Pontevedra and Vigo would all be in use, and a café in a side street would be closed and its owner on a flight to Bogotá, and in Corunna an upstairs office had been trashed and a sign prised off the wall beside the door and dumped in a gutter . . .

They went through passport control. His travel document was looked at, copied, handed back. Through the Green channel and the only additions to his possessions was a jar of home-made honey, what the bears had not been able to eat, and a tinfoil-wrapped triangle of goat cheese, and one tightly rolled crayon picture of a lighthouse perched on a clifftop. They kept walking. Peters held a briefcase, and in it were the memory sticks from the Biscuit Tin. In time, when it was necessary, the details would be traded with the Spanish tax police.

Out of the terminal, into pleasant afternoon sunshine. There was a line of drivers ahead of them, holding signs on which names were written. Theirs just said *SCO*, had been the relevant initials in his past, and probably the future. And Peters saw the man . . . A talent of who he used to be, of Kenny Blake, was to recognise eye contact. Saw it between Peters and the man, and both had attempted to disguise it. Glances that locked, then broke, and saw a faint bob of Jak Peters's head in acknowledgement. The man had a stitched lip, one well-blackened eye, scrapes on his face and seemed to need the stick he leaned on. He wore well-polished brogues, and a pair of neat grey flannels, and a Tattersall shirt that was new on that day, still had the creases, and a neutral tie, and the jacket was Harris tweed but had dark patches on it as if stains had been removed, and a trilby hat, and the spectacles under it had sellotape strips fastening the arms to the lenses. He had looked away but did not think the man had, thought every step was watched.

They were led by their driver to the restricted parking area, and their car was behind a vehicle hitched to a caravan. The door of the caravan was open and a woman was inside drying dishes, and a supremely large cat sat in a cage on the step enjoying the rare warmth.

He knew, and nothing needed to be said. They would not meet, had no call to.

Gratitude was in the air.

Jonas Merrick walked a little slower than usual, and the stick needed getting used to.

Being grateful was the order of the day, and flew in most directions.

When he came level with the Archbishop's Palace, he turned to his right, and set off across the A3036 main route, and traffic needed to swerve to avoid him, and he churlishly waggled his stick at a driver who abused him with a horn blast, and he managed it with a degree of safety. It was his first day back. He had learned already that he would need to leave earlier, because he was handicapped and had lost the pace of his previous schedule, if he were to catch the 17.39 back to Raynes Park.

He was aware, via his phone, of who was grateful and to whom. The Federal Bureau of Investigation was grateful to everybody which meant they had received undeserved plaudits, and had done sweet nothing. The Drug Enforcement Administration were grateful to their European friends for the successful targeting of a trafficking route, and the interception of a semi-submersible craft, the *Maria Bernarda*. And everybody on this side of the "pond" – ludicrous phrase, Jonas thought – was grateful for American cooperation in differing degrees. The Spanish authorities were grateful to British colleagues, teeth clenched in minimal sincerity, for a late tip-off that had enabled a scratch force to be deployed and arrests made, and a consignment seized, and the details of the coordination of an operation at Praia de Arnela would be left vague. A Public Prosecutor in Madrid was grateful that the Munoz clan and associates were in custody along with a basement full of compromising evidence that would convict them to years in gaol, and chests swelled with undeserved credit. Jak Peters received gratitude, though few of the senders of congratulations and thanks knew of him nor his part in the matters on the Coast of Death. Fergal "Jimbo" Rawe, photographed the previous day at Liverpool's John Lennon Airport handcuffed to Doloures Govier, who had declined to fight extradition, was bowed under the weight of praise aimed at him, and Detective Chief Inspector Fanny Thomas was widely applauded for her efforts to secure a most dangerous criminal, Xavier Govier . . . and flowers came to Nanette in her hospital room, and an invitation to lunch at Merseyside Police HQ was forthcoming for the Potter pair and a small cheque from the public purse would follow.

He started off across the bridge. The tide was low and the mud showed drearily at the extremes of the channel. Two of them, Jonas reflected, were left on the far side of the loop. No grateful messages for the Level One, the undercover who would by now have merged into shadow and darkness and deceit and be lost to view . . . And no gratitude expressed towards Jonas Merrick. Nothing from the DG. Silence from the Deputy DG. From the AssDepDG something about "learning, at your age, not to play silly buggers when involved in grown-up games". And a hint, dropped heavily, that a berth might be found for him in Finance – or in Human Resources, or in Diversity, or in Training – if a vacancy occurred. His lip had almost healed but there were still severe pain pangs at what he called his "privates". Vera had embarrassed him by demanding to see the extent of the bruising on his body and he had stood naked in the bathroom while she had voiced disapproval: his hearing had returned. They had gone south, had been driven by the poker-faced Harry, and the AssDepDG had shared the front of the car with him . . . at least Olaf had seemed pleased to be home.

He reached the top of the bridge, the high point. The sun shone but the wind was slick enough to justify his tweed jacket and his raincoat, and he needed to ram the trilby down firmly, and at the weekend he would try to get his spectacles repaired in Coombe Lane, close to the Raynes Park station, because they wobbled on the bruised crown of his nose. And the wound in his lip itched. Vera had seen him off, and again a promise had been offered.

Thames House was ahead of him, and the windows of the third floor, and the one where the blind was permanently drawn and where a cubicle had been fashioned, and a desk and an easy chair, and not much else. The walls were empty but for a calendar and a leave chart, where previously photographs had been fastened, now taken down because an operation had been concluded . . . Satisfactorily? Not for him to judge.

He swung the stick, tried to lengthen his stride and stiffness trapped his leg muscles. They were waiting at the roundabout for him. Good to see them . . . He had already been carted off to the hospital when Kev and Leroy had travelled up to Liverpool to collect his car from the supermarket parking area. He believed neither in familiarity nor gushed thanks, but they had been helpful – and so had many others: some of the "others" had paid a heavy price, which weighed with him.

They stepped out together into Millbank which was heavy with traffic. They had the firepower slung on their necks and at their waists that, as Jonas liked to say, could have kicked off a small-scale war. Cars, vans, buses, stopped . . . further along there was a crossing that the majority of Fiver staff coming to work in jogging gear or on bicycles would use . . . all held so that one elderly man, with a stick and a scowl on his face, might cross the road. He reached the pavement. Brusquely expressed his appreciation for the help rendered.

Kev said, "Glad to have been useful, Mr Merrick."

Leroy said, "Something you should know about your motor."

"Which is?"

Leroy said, "I reckon it's the carburettor. Thought that was the difficulty when we were bringing it down."

Kev said, "Sounded like the carburettor, very like it."

Leroy looked at Jonas and seemed to say that a problem with the carburettor was a problem that should be faced head on. "Very much advise you get it seen to, the carburettor, Mr Merrick."

They had stern faces, both of them, and their expressions were aloof, but the light in their eyes danced. He supposed that by now, through the whole of the last week, the story would have seeped from confidentiality and spread among the police guarding the building.

"I will, most definitely."

And wondered whether it had reached the ears of Aggie Burns, and whether she was preparing to confront him and would demand recompense for the paint- and blood-soiled high-visibility vest of a pothole officer, and for £4.99 for a can of spray paint. The vest might be soon, if he knew Aggie Burns, displayed on the wall of 3/S/12 as if it were a trophy.

He was escorted to the café entrance. Plenty would have seen him sandwiched by the armed pair, and would have seen the blatant respect on their faces. Did they want a coffee? They declined. He was about to go inside, push open the door, but the question was put.

"There were plenty of folks involved in this, Mr Merrick?"

"I suppose there were."

"And the opposition were out in force?"

"They were. Big battalions." There was a protest from inside at the door being held open, but the complaint was hushed by the counter staff because Jonas was a regular punter with them, and already his *cappuccino* would be in the machine and his Danish on a plate.

"It was a good win, Mr Merrick? Makes a difference?"

"And it ended well? And you're on the mend and back with us?"

Jonas said, "I am mending and back at work but don't know where they'll dump me. I think it ended quite well, but there are good people who have suffered hugely, and stood up and were counted and were not sufficiently protected. I take that to heart . . .

and so it was 'a good win' but with limitations. Will it make a difference? Depends who you listen to. Up there on the fourth floor, or on the fifth among the angels and the cherubims, it will be hailed as a game-changer. I'll give you some names: Jimbo and Jak and Fanny you delivered letters to them. Right here. Ask them if it'll make a difference and they'll tell you that a vacancy existed in the line-up of OCGs. Probably was a void for a half-day, maybe even a whole day, and then the lesser brethren would have been clawing into the space left empty, and the supply will come from a new source, and a price hike may be seen and a few bodies left on street corners while authority is sorted out. I don't have an alternative strategy. I just do my job as best I can . . . The scale of the *difference* I leave to others . . . Actually, it was rather exciting. Apart from the ache in my 'privates', I found it quite exhilarating . . . For God's sake, don't tell anyone . . . a worthwhile experience."

He went inside the café and allowed them to return to their patrol pattern.

And was greeted, deadpan, "Hello, sir. I hope the door you walked into is equally damaged."

"Yes, splintered a bit." His smile was wintry, as he remembered the blood of a young woman and the drawn exhausted face of a young man who had once been Kenny Blake. Jonas collected his coffee and his pastry and took them to the garden and would watch the man, carrying his own combat scars, working there with his hoe and his rake, and then he would go to Thames House, to his cubicle, and discover what was thrown at him and what was wanted of him. He was a bit player, no more and no less, would not have had it otherwise.